VISITORS

Also by Orson Scott Card

PATHFINDER

RUINS

VISITORS

ORSON SCOTT CARD

Simon Pulse
NEW YORK   LONDON   TORONTO   SYDNEY   NEW DELHI

SIMON PULSE

An imprint of Simon & Schuster Children's Publishing Division

1230 Avenue of the Americas, New York, New York 10020

First Simon Pulse hardcover edition November 2014

Text copyright © 2014 by Orson Scott Card

Jacket design and illustration by Sammy Yuen Jr.

For information about special discounts for bulk purchases, please contact Simon & Schuster Special Sales at 1-866-506-1949 or business@simonandschuster.com.

The Simon & Schuster Speakers Bureau can bring authors to your live event.

For more information or to book an event contact the Simon & Schuster Speakers Bureau at 1-866-248-3049 or visit our website at www.simonspeakers.com.

Interior designed by Mike Rosamilia and Tom Daly

The text of this book was set in Cochin.

Manufactured in the United States of America

2 4 6 8 10 9 7 5 3 1

Library of Congress Cataloging-in-Publication Data

Card, Orson Scott.

Visitors / Orson Scott Card.

p. cm.

Sequel to: Ruins.

Summary: Rigg's journey comes to an epic and explosive conclusion as everything that has been building up finally comes to pass, and Rigg is forced to put his powers to the test in order to save his world and end the war once and for all.

[1. Science fiction. 2. Psychic ability—Fiction. 3. Time travel—Fiction.
4. Space colonies—Fiction.] I. Title.

PZ7.C1897Vis 2014

[Fic]—dc23

2014027524

ISBN 978-1-4169-9178-6 (hc)

ISBN 978-1-4442-1429-7 (eBook)

To Kathleen Bellamy
Part of every project,
Shepherd of so many sheep:
Thank you for the freedom and support

VISITORS

CHAPTER 1

Copies

The Place:

From the surface of the planet Garden, it looks like a plateau surrounded by a steep cliff, with a mountain in the middle. But from space, it is plain that the plateau is a huge crater, and the mountain is its center point.

Buried deep beneath that central mountain is a starship. It crashed into the planet Garden 11,203 years ago.

Yet the starship was launched from near-Earth orbit only nineteen years ago. It journeyed seven years, then made the jump that was meant to create an anomaly in spacetime and appear near Garden instantaneously.

It *was* instantaneous to Ram Odin, the pilot of the starship — the only living person awake on the starship.

But compared to the surrounding universe, the ship arrived 11,191 years before it made the jump.

In the process, it divided into nineteen ships, one for each of the onboard computers that calculated the jump. All those ships contained a duplicate of Ram Odin, along with all the other humans lying in stasis, waiting to arrive at the world they would colonize.

All nineteen ships were deliberately crashed into the surface of the planet Garden. The simultaneous impact slowed the rotation of the planet, lengthening the day. Each impact formed a crater. Protected by anti-inertial and anti-collision fields, all the starships and their colonists survived.

Nineteen colonies were created, each separated from the others by a psychoactive field called "the Wall."

This starship is in the middle of the wallfold called Vadeshfold.

The People:

In the control room of the starship, there are either four men, or three, or two, or one, depending on how you count them.

One of them is the sole surviving Ram Odin. If you say that there is only one man in the control room, he is that man. He has survived all these centuries by rising out of stasis for only one day in each fifty years, or sometimes for one week after a hundred years—whatever is needed in order to make the decisions that the ship's computers are not competent to make without him.

Another of them looks like an adult man, and speaks like one, but he is really a machine, an expendable. He is called Vadeshex. All the humans in his colony were wiped out in terrible warfare more than ten thousand years before. In the years since then, he

2

has devoted himself to creating a version of a native parasite that might be a suitable symbiotic partner for humans, if they ever came to Vadeshfold again.

The two other men were born as a single human being named Rigg Sessamekesh, fifteen years before the present day. Arguably they are not men but boys.

Both of them wear upon their heads, covering their faces, the symbiotic facemask created by Vadeshex. The facemask penetrates their brains and bodies, enhancing their senses, quickening their movements, strengthening their bodies, so that some might consider them no longer to be human at all, but rather some strange new hybrid, only half human at best.

The Situation:

A half hour ago, Ram Odin attempted to murder Rigg, but with his faster reflexes, Rigg avoided him. Then, using the time-shifting power he was born with, he went back half an hour in time and preventively killed Ram Odin. It was not just a matter of self-defense. Rigg believed that it was Ram Odin whose actions were destined to destroy the world.

Then Rigg went forward two years and saw that eliminating Ram Odin had done nothing to prevent the complete destruction of the human race on Garden. Far from being the worst menace to the humans of Garden, Ram Odin was the only source of information Rigg would need to figure out how to save Garden. So he went back in time and prevented himself from killing Ram Odin, and Ram Odin from killing the earlier version of Rigg.

The result was that now there were two copies of Rigg—the

one who had done the killing, then learned it had done no good and returned; and the one who had been *prevented* from doing the killing or being killed, who had *not* experienced the inevitable coming of the Destroyers, and who now called himself Noxon, recognizing that he could never be the same person as the other Rigg.

Thus there are four men, by stature and general shape: Ram Odin, Rigg, Noxon, and Vadeshex.

But Vadeshex is not a living organism, so there are only three men.

Rigg and Noxon are really one person, divided into two separate beings half an hour ago. So there are only two genetically and biographically distinct men.

The Riggs are only fifteen years old by calendar. Older than that by the number of days they have lived through, then repeated, but still they are only boys, not men.

And the Riggs are both deeply and permanently connected to the alien facemask, making them by some reckonings only half human, and by other reckonings not human at all.

So only Ram Odin, of all the four, is a pure man; yet he is weakest of them all.

Far away, in another wallfold, Rigg's sister Param and Rigg's friend Umbo also have power over the flow of time, and are also working to save the world of Garden from the Destroyers. But it is these four in Vadeshfold who among them have control over a starship; it is these four who know that a version of Ram Odin is still alive; and it is these four who must now decide what each of them will do in order to save the human race on Garden.

For the one thing that never changes is that, despite many

attempts to reshape history by the manipulation of time, the Visitors come from Earth, see what the human race has become in the nineteen wallfolds of Garden, and then send the Destroyers to blast all nineteen civilizations into oblivion.

The Conversation:

"The biggest problem we have is ignorance," said Rigg Noxon. "We don't know what causes the people of Earth to decide to destroy our whole world." Though in fact the biggest problem he was having at the moment was the realization that he was capable of killing someone in cold blood.

It was the other Rigg who had actually done the killing, but Rigg Noxon knew that they were the same person. If Rigg had not come back and prevented the killings, Noxon would certainly have done just what Rigg did. Only now, because he *hadn't* taken those actions, both Noxon and Rigg continued to exist as separate people with nearly identical pasts.

Am I a killer, because I know I could and would commit murder? Or am I innocent, because something prevented me from doing it? After all, the person who prevented me was myself. A version of myself.

The killer version.

"Which is why your friends have to allow the mice from Odinfold to go back to Earth with the Visitors," said Ram Odin.

"They're deciding whether to stop themselves from warning the Visitors about the stowaway mice," said Rigg-the-killer.

Ram Odin shook his head. "Why is it up to them? *You* go back and prevent *them* from giving warning."

"They had good reason for preventing the mice from getting aboard the Visitors' ship," said Rigg-the-killer. "The mice weren't going back to find out what happened. They were infected with a disease which was no doubt designed to wipe out the human race on Earth."

"When you say 'no doubt' it means that there *is* reason to doubt," said Ram Odin. "People only say 'no doubt' when they know they're making a judgment based on insufficient information."

"They don't have facemasks," said Rigg Noxon. "They can't hear the mice or talk to them. They can't ask."

"*You* can hear them," said Ram Odin. "*You* can ask."

"We don't necessarily believe the mice," said Rigg-the-killer. "They already killed Param once. Our goal is to save the human race on Garden, not provide mousekind with a depopulated Earth for them to inherit."

"There are too many players in this game," said Ram Odin.

"The mice were planning to take several billion of them out of the game entirely," said Rigg-the-killer.

"Not all the players are equal," said Ram Odin. "Make a decision and make it stick."

"You've been alone with the expendables far too long," said Rigg Noxon. "You think because you *can* play God with other people's lives, you have a right to do it."

"You think," added Rigg-the-killer, "that because you've been doing it for so long, you're *fit* to do it."

"Power is power," said Ram Odin. "If you have it, then it's yours to use."

"The sheer stupidity of that statement," said Rigg-the-killer, "makes me wonder how Garden struggled along for eleven thousand years with you in control."

"A child lectures an eleven-thousand-year-old man," said Ram Odin.

"There are thousands of examples in history," said Rigg-the-killer, "of people with power who used it in ways that ended up destroying their power and, usually, a whole lot of innocent people, too."

Rigg Noxon listened to his other self and realized: Having killed Ram Odin changed him. Rigg Noxon would not have treated Ram that way—as if his statements were worthless. Rigg Noxon would have tried to take them into account. Rigg Noxon would have spoken as youth to adult. But Rigg-the-killer must still be full of anger toward Ram Odin, who had, after all, tried to kill Rigg first.

We lived exactly the same life until a few minutes ago, for me; a few weeks or months ago, for Rigg-the-killer. But we *are* different people.

"So you leave the decision up to Umbo and Param," said Ram Odin.

"And Olivenko and Loaf," said Rigg Noxon. "We're companions, not a military force with someone giving orders and everyone else required to obey."

"Besides," said Rigg-the-killer, "I don't want to leave the future of the human race on both planets in the tiny little hands of the sentient mice of Odinfold."

"What do you plan, then?" said Ram Odin. "To sneak on board the Visitors' ship?"

"Yes," said Rigg-the-killer.

"No," said Rigg Noxon, at exactly the same moment.

They looked at each other in consternation.

"We could sneak on," said Rigg-the-killer. "We can slice time the way Param does, now that we have the facemask to let us perceive units of time that small. We'll be invisible for the whole voyage back."

"And when we get there, what will we do?" asked Rigg Noxon. "There is only a year between the coming of the Visitors and the return of the Destroyers. Most of that must have been spent voyaging. So when they return to Earth, the response, the decision, it's *immediate*. What are we going to do, give speeches? Hold meetings?"

"Your talents with time don't make you particularly persuasive," said Ram Odin. "And powerful people don't change their minds because of speeches."

"As soon as we arrive," said Rigg-the-killer, "we jump back in time and learn everything we need to know, make the connections we need to make."

"Of course," said Rigg Noxon. "We'll fit right in. Nobody will notice we're from another planet. I'm sure that in all human cultures, kids our age will be taken seriously and be able to influence world events. Especially kids wearing parasites on their faces."

"Or you could figure out who needs to be assassinated and kill them," said Ram Odin.

Both Riggs looked at him in consternation. "We know you're an assassin," said Rigg-the-killer. "We're not."

"On the contrary," said Ram Odin. "*You* came here bragging that you *are*."

"In self-defense," said Rigg-the-killer. "But you—when your ship made the jump and you realized that there were nineteen copies of the ship, of you, of all the colonists, you made the *immediate* decision to kill all the other versions of yourself."

"Precisely to avoid the kind of weak-minded, incoherent 'leadership' you exhibit," said Ram Odin. "And please remember, *I'm* the Ram Odin who didn't order the death of anybody."

"No, you're the sneaky one who hid out until the quickest killer version of yourself had died of old age and *then* you established your colony in Odinfold, violating most of the decisions your murderous self made and then living forever," said Rigg-the-killer. "Proving that you don't always think one person is fit to make all the decisions for everyone—even when that person is a version of yourself."

Ram Odin rolled his eyes and then nodded. "It's extremely annoying hearing this from a child."

"But no less true," said Rigg-the-killer.

"Once you've killed somebody," said Rigg Noxon, "can anybody honestly consider you a child anymore?"

"Then you're still a child because I stopped you from killing anybody? And I'm an adult?" asked Rigg-the-killer.

"Yes," said Rigg Noxon. "In a way. Maybe because I'm a child, or maybe because of the quirks of causality arising from the different paths we've walked recently, I have a slightly different plan."

"Either we go back with the Visitors or we don't," said Rigg-the-killer. "The difference isn't slight."

"Don't be like *him*," said Rigg Noxon, "and assume that because you didn't think of it, it must be wrong."

"Think of what?" asked Ram Odin impatiently.

"I think I should go to Earth, but not with the Visitors," said Rigg Noxon.

A couple of beats of silence, and then Ram Odin shook his head. "This ship can't fly again. The inertial field kept it from damage when it collided with Garden, but we can't raise it from the planet's surface. Even if we could get rid of the millions of tons of rock above us right now, the ship doesn't have enough power to lift us out of the gravity well of Garden."

Rigg Noxon shook his head. "You're forgetting what we *do*," he said.

"He means for one of us to go backward in time to when the ship arrived," said Rigg-the-killer. "He means for us to keep making little jumps into the past, following your path moment by moment, backward along with this ship as it slammed into Garden. I mean, as it *un*slams, backing out of this hole and up into space, backward and backward until it gets to Earth. Until we get to the point where you launched on this voyage."

"This ship was built in space," said Ram Odin. "It never was on Earth."

"We go back to when it was built," said Rigg Noxon. "Then we follow someone else's path off the ship."

"If you can even do that," said Ram Odin, "what's the point? Why not go back with the Visitors as the other Rigg suggested and then jump back in time?"

"There are some key differences," said Rigg Noxon. "First,

we don't have to spend the voyage in hiding—not the way we would by slicing time on the Visitors' ship."

Rigg-the-killer was nodding. "And we'll have the jewels," he said, holding up the bag of jewels that gave them the ability to control the ships' computers—and stored all the information the computers had gathered in the meantime.

Ram Odin looked at the jewels. "Each time you jump backward," said Ram Odin, "the ships' computers and the expendables will be sensing these things for the first time."

"And each time," said Rigg Noxon, "it will give them a complete account of everything that's been learned in the eleven millennia of history on Garden."

"So they can take preventive measures and cause us all not to exist?" asked Ram Odin.

"They wouldn't cause *us* not to exist," said Rigg-the-killer. "Preservation of causality and all that. But yes, it might cause them to prevent the terraforming of Garden in the first place. What about that?" he asked Rigg Noxon. "Do we leave the jewels behind? If we do, the ship will process us as stowaways and have the expendables put us into stasis or just kill us."

Rigg Noxon shook his head. "No. Remember what Umbo learned in his reading in the library in Odinfold? The Odinfolders—or the mice, who can tell?—worked out the math of what happened in the jump. It didn't just create nineteen copies of the ship and all the humans and machinery on it. It also made either one or nineteen other copies that moved exactly backward in time."

"So what?" asked Rigg-the-killer. "They're moving backward in time. Even when we jump around, at the end of a jump we're still moving forward in time, the same direction as the rest of the universe. And the backward movement of the ship or ships would exactly duplicate the forward voyage of the ship coming here, so we'd still be inside the ship that voyaged out. We'll never be able to *find* the backward-moving ship. Or ships."

"Not with the skill set we've had up to now," said Rigg Noxon. "But what if we could learn to go the other direction?"

"What if we could jump straight to Earth without using any starship at all?" asked Rigg-the-killer. "Because we can't. There's no reason to think we can."

"I think Param holds the key," said Rigg Noxon.

"She slices time very thin, but she still moves forward in time."

"Because all she knew was slicing," said Rigg Noxon. "She couldn't jump forward or backward, the way we can. Now, with our facemasks, we can slice time the way she does. We can see those tiny divisions and do something about them. But we can also jump backward. We can slice time backward."

"We're still moving forward," said Rigg-the-killer. "Between slices."

"So what?" asked Noxon. "If we slice time thin enough, and we jump backward two nanoseconds, stay there for one nanosecond, and then jump backward another two nanoseconds, the effect is that we move backward in time at the rate of one nanosecond per nanosecond, which is the same rate that the back-traveling ship will be moving backward through time."

"But when we're in existence, we're going forward," Rigg-the-killer insisted. "No matter how fine you chop the time."

"Maybe you're right," said Noxon. "But you're forgetting the very first thing we ever did. We saw a path, Umbo slowed it down for us, and we *latched on*. That was how we jumped, by latching on to a person. If we can at least *detect* a backward-moving person's path, we can attach and it will change our direction."

"Or maybe not," said Rigg. "Maybe forward-time and backward-time annihilate each other when they touch, like matter and anti-matter."

"So *I'll* do it alone," said Noxon. "I'm the extra copy, right? So if I get annihilated, we're back to the right number of Riggs, that's all."

"And then," said Ram, "you can take hold of the backward-moving version of *me* and pull me—him—back into the normal timestream again."

"Just what we need," said Rigg. "More Ram Odins."

"I've shepherded nineteen wallfolds for eleven thousand years," said Ram. "What have *you* done?"

"You hurt his feelings," said Noxon.

"He's too sensitive," said Rigg.

"You do realize that there was a time-jump of 11,191 years. Not to mention a leap of several lightyears through folded space. Do you think you can hang on through that much time and space *and* a change in direction?"

"It'll be interesting to see," said Rigg. "We'll find out by trying it."

"We'll find out," said Noxon, "but *I'll* do the trying."

"You get all the fun with physics?" asked Rigg.

"I'm the extra. We can afford to lose me."

"Well, *I* can," said Rigg. "But *you* can't."

"I won't be around to miss me when I'm gone," said Noxon.

"I'm not sure how your brains even function," said Ram. "Everything you say makes no sense. And it's perfectly sensible."

"We can both go back, but on different ships," said Noxon to Rigg, ignoring Ram. "I'll latch on to the backward ship and ride it to Earth, and you hide on the original ship and jump back to the beginning of the voyage."

"You both get there at exactly the same time," said Ram. "The beginning of my voyage."

"Not really," said Rigg. "When I get there, if I do it, I have to deal with the fact that I'm in the same timeflow. If I don't slice time or jump, I'm visible. But Noxon, he arrives there completely *in*visible. And in an invisible ship. I'll be there without any friends, because I can never show myself during the voyage."

"Why not?" asked Ram.

"Because I didn't," said Rigg. "It was *you* on that voyage. Did you see me? If you *had* seen me, there's a good chance it would have derailed the entire sequence of events. Leading to the non-existence of nineteen colonies on Garden." He turned to Noxon. "You see the danger? One slip, and you might undo everything."

"But I won't have to hide from the Ram on my backward voyage, because he's a *post*-voyage Ram," said Noxon. "He's not causally connected to this universe, so I won't change anything at all. *And* I'll have a ship that isn't buried under a million tons of rock."

"Moving backward in time," said Ram.

"If I can pull myself and the backward Ram Odin into the

forward-flowing timestream, I should be able to pull the ship with us. Material objects can be dragged along."

"If your venture succeeds," said Rigg, "then I won't need to go back with the Visitors. For all I know, the Visitors will never come at all."

"So while I go to Earth, you'll stay here?"

"If you succeed, then the world of Garden won't be destroyed," said Rigg. "So while you're playing God back on Earth—"

"You'll play God here," said Noxon.

"Visit all the wallfolds," said Rigg, "and decide whether to bring the Walls down."

"Or some of them, anyway. Keep the dangerous ones quarantined," said Noxon.

"Keep the technologies of Odinfold and the facemasks of Vadeshfold and the power of the expendables out of the hands of Mother and General Citizen," said Rigg.

"So you're going to make a play to be King-in-the-Tent?" asked Noxon. "They'll be eager to follow you, with your pretty face."

"I'll set up Param as Queen-in-the-Tent. Or abolish the monarchy and the People's Revolutionary Council," said Rigg. "I have no plan."

"Yet," said Ram Odin.

"I'll have a plan when I need one," said Rigg.

"In a pinch, plans kind of make themselves, mostly because you don't have a lot of choices," said Noxon.

"Aren't you going to ask the advice of someone older and wiser?" asked Ram Odin.

"When we find somebody wiser," said Noxon, "we'll ask him for advice."

CHAPTER 2

Council in Larfold

"What are we waiting for?" asked Param.

"We're not waiting at all," said Olivenko. "Go. Do whatever it is you're so eager to do."

"There's nothing *to* do," said Param.

"Then we're not *waiting*," said Olivenko. "We're merely purpose-less. Find a purpose, and go accomplish it. You don't have to wait for anything."

"What purpose *is* there? We know the world ends in a very few years. What's the point of starting anything?"

"I'm sure Umbo will take you back in time, as far as you want," said Olivenko. "You can marry and have babies. Raise an army and conquer a wallfold. Assassinate General Citizen before he meets your mother. So many exciting possibilities."

"I'm not going to marry Umbo *or* have his babies," said Param.

"I didn't suggest that you do so," said Olivenko. "I said he would take you back in time. You're the one who leapt to the conclusion that Umbo would be involved in any marriage or baby-making you might embark on."

Umbo spoke from the other side of the fire, where he had been dozing. "Thank you for finding a way to insult me in a conversation I wasn't even part of."

"I'm not having your babies *or* Olivenko's," said Param. "Or Loaf's, in case anyone wants to include him. The world is ending no matter *what* time period we go back to. So what if it's twenty years or two hundred? Knowing the whole world burns makes the whole enterprise . . ."

"The whole world always burns," said Loaf. "Or it floods. Or some insect eats the crop and you starve. Or a disease ravages the wallfold, killing nine out of ten, and the survivors eat the dead. Every baby you have dies eventually, no matter what you do. Yet we have babies and we try to go on."

"I'm not sure," said Umbo. "Is that your idea of inspiring us with new hope?"

"It's my way of telling you that only a child thinks that *anything* you build will last," said Loaf.

"What we're waiting for," said Olivenko, "and we all know it, is Rigg."

Since they all knew it, there was no point in commenting.

Umbo commented anyway. "He *could* have returned to us at any time. For instance, a half hour after he left, he could have walked back into our camp and told us what he had just spent the last week or month or five years doing. When somebody can jump from one time to another, it's just *rude* to make other people wait."

Nobody said anything.

"That was not just me being resentful of Rigg the way I used to be," said Umbo into the silence.

"Nobody said it was," said Olivenko.

"I'm just tired of waiting," said Umbo. "And it *is* rude of him."

"On the other hand, maybe he's dead," said Loaf. "In which case, our wait is truly pointless."

"Who could possibly kill Rigg?" asked Param. "He already stopped Ram Odin from assassinating him."

"And now he's gone back to stop himself from stopping Ram Odin," said Loaf. "Which means Ram Odin might still find a way to kill him."

"Even with the mask?" asked Olivenko.

"He won't try to kill me again," said Rigg.

If anyone was startled by his sudden appearance, they didn't show it. Umbo had to laugh, though. "How many times did you make a later entrance till you decided on *this* moment?"

"I came, I heard, I answered," said Rigg. "I don't have to time my entrances. You're always arguing, and there's always something to say that's smarter than anything you'd come up with."

"Good to have you back," said Param. "To remind me that Umbo isn't the only annoying boy in the world."

"So Ram Odin is alive again," said Loaf.

Rigg nodded.

"Is that a good thing or a bad?" asked Olivenko.

"Decide for yourselves," said Rigg. "Because the way I fixed it resulted in more than saving Ram Odin."

He raised a hand. Immediately two others emerged from the edge of the woods and came to stand beside him. An old man and . . . another copy of Rigg, facemask and all.

"This is so untidy," said Umbo.

"Says the one who made two copies of himself already," said Rigg.

"At least my copies are dead," said Umbo.

"And mine is alive," said Rigg. "He has chosen the name Noxon, so you'll have a way to speak of us separately. But in a way, he's a purer version of myself. He never killed anybody."

"But I would have," said Noxon.

"But you didn't," said Rigg.

"The Rigg twins even argue with each other," said Loaf.

"Rigg probably had arguments with himself all the time," said Olivenko.

"But we didn't have to overhear them," said Loaf.

"So you're the one who planned all this," said Param to Ram Odin.

"I'm the one who made decisions when they had to be made," said Ram Odin. "Sometimes good ones, sometimes bad. Most of the important decisions were made by someone else. But I accept responsibility for what I've done wrong. For things I've unleashed on the world. Like the mice. And, in a way, the three of you. Four of you now. The timeshapers."

"Look how happy he is," said Loaf. "Almost quivering with excitement. After studying you remotely all these years, he finally gets to meet you face to face."

"Quivering?" asked Ram.

Noxon answered him. "It's a subtle vibration," he said, "but the facemask makes it as obvious as breaking into a jig."

Umbo could not understand why having two Riggs made him so angry. Was it his old envy coming back? Was he so foolish as to be jealous because there was only one of him? Or frightened because now there were two timeshapers more powerful than him and Param? "I'm glad you were able to undo the killing," said Umbo. "What now?"

Rigg shrugged. But Noxon answered, "I know what *I'm* thinking of doing, but I can't decide for anyone else."

Umbo thought: The two Riggs have already diverged.

Or maybe it was just that Rigg, the one who had killed Ram Odin, was stricken silent by Umbo's reference to undoing his "killing," while it meant far less to Noxon, who had no memory of the deed.

"So . . . are you going to tell us?" asked Olivenko.

"I'm going to Earth," said Noxon. "*If* I can master the skills it will take to get there. Because I'm not going with the Visitors. I'm going back eleven thousand years and hitching a ride on the twentieth starship, backward in time."

"*If* it exists," said Umbo. "It's only a mathematical guess."

"*If* he can learn to reverse his direction in time," said Rigg. "To hook on to something moving the other way."

"I'm thinking that Param and I might be able to help each other learn some new skills," said Noxon.

"I can't help anybody," said Param. "My talent is almost worse than having none at all."

"No it isn't," said Olivenko.

"Mother made sure my enemies know how slowly I move," said Param, "and how vulnerable I am when I'm invisible. The mice know it, too. It used to be I could always get away from anyone who tormented me. But now, it only makes me weaker."

"That's how I think we can help each other," said Noxon. "I need to learn how to slice time — how to match the rhythm and duration of each increment. It's become second nature to you. I'm not as sharp as Umbo — he learned how to jump without me way faster than I learned how to jump without him."

"And what will you teach *me*?" asked Param.

"How to do it backward," said Noxon. "Because that's the direction I need to move, too."

Param shook her head. "I *skip* time, I don't change directions."

"That's my point," said Noxon. "What if, when you disappeared, you could slice your way *backward* in time? When Umbo and I . . . and Rigg . . . when we jump in time, we skip over everything in between. I . . . and Rigg . . . we can *see* the paths, and the facemask lets us see them as people in motion. Extending backward in time. But they're always *moving* forward. So when I attach to them, I attach in the direction they're going. I need to know how to go upstream. How to slide backward in small increments, and you need to learn the same. I'm hoping we can help each other."

Param shook her head again. "I can't do anything like that."

"We know you can't," said Rigg. "That's what 'learning' means. *Now* you can't; with work, maybe someday you *can*."

"And what will *you* be doing while Noxon and Param are

21

working on doing new impossible things?" Olivenko asked Rigg.

"I'm planning to go through the other wallfolds, one at a time, and see what they have. We've seen Ramfold, Vadeshfold, Odinfold, and Larfold. Fifteen to go."

"And then what?" asked Olivenko.

"Then I'll have some kind of idea about what will happen if we bring down the Wall."

Loaf chuckled. "I can imagine General Citizen and the Sessamoto army trying to make war against the mice of Odinfold."

"I can also imagine Ramfolders spreading into Vadeshfold and having an infestation of facemasks," said Olivenko. "Not the fancy versions you and the Riggs have. The original, devastating, bestial ones."

"That's an argument right there in favor of never bringing down the Wall around Vadeshfold," said Param.

"Not that we don't find the three of you lovely as wild-flowers," said Umbo.

"I'm a lot prettier than Rigg and Noxon," said Loaf. "My facemask has had time to grow to fit my original face."

"That doesn't always lead toward prettiness," said Olivenko with a smile that showed he was merely putting Loaf's own irony into open words.

"So you're appointed to judge all the wallfolds?" Umbo asked Rigg.

"I'm not judging anything," said Rigg. "I'm going to go and find out and then we can talk again."

"And by 'we' you mean you and Noxon?" asked Umbo.

"Here we go again," murmured Param.

"I mean me and you and Loaf and Olivenko and Param, with plenty of advice from the expendables and the ships' computers," said Rigg. "Though you don't have to come to the meeting."

"And what's your plan for me?" asked Umbo.

Loaf put out a hand. "Don't answer him, Rigg. If you *have* a suggestion, he'll resent you for trying to boss him around. And if you *don't*, he'll complain that you think he has nothing to contribute."

Loaf's words stung, especially because a moment's self-examination told Umbo that this was precisely how he would have reacted to anything Rigg might have said.

"*I'm* the one who has something useful for Umbo to do," said Loaf. "It's time for me to go home to Leaky and show her what's become of me. Give her a chance to decide what to make of my facemask, and whether I'm still the man she married."

"What do I have to do with that?" asked Umbo. He hated the resentful sound of his own voice.

"If I have you with me, you can swear that it's really me behind this mask," said Loaf. "You can show that you accept me as myself, and by being there at all, you'll prove I didn't wander off and abandon you and Rigg—because if I come back without you, that's what she'll accuse me of."

"It isn't just your wife," said Param. "What will all the other people in your town think of you?"

"They'll think of me the way they think of burn victims who lived and are now covered with horrible scars," said Loaf. "They'll scream and run away for a while, and then, because I'm bigger than they are, I'll beat the crap out of anybody who thinks they can drive me out of town, and then they'll get used to me."

"So you're going to stay there," said Param.

"Rigg and Umbo don't need me," said Loaf. "If they ever did."

"We did," said Rigg and Noxon at once.

"And even if we don't need you on our particular errand," said Noxon, "it doesn't mean we don't all need each other."

"Even if nobody knows what they need me *for*," said Umbo.

"I told you why I did, plus one more thing," said Loaf. "I need you to take me back to Leaky just a few days after I left. The old lady's not getting any younger. And if the reason we never had children was because some part of me malfunctioned, maybe the facemask healed me. If there's a chance of having children, I don't want to waste any time."

"Very practical," said Olivenko.

"Not to mention romantic," said Param.

"Romance is for women who aren't nearing the end of their child-bearing years," said Loaf. "Leaky pretends she doesn't care, but it kills her not to have children. I may not be pretty anymore, but *she* still is, and she can close her eyes."

Umbo realized that just because *he* had never thought of Leaky as pretty didn't mean that Loaf didn't find her attractive. And, unusually for Umbo, he realized this *before* he made a jest that Loaf might never forgive.

"What about you, Param?" asked Olivenko.

"What *about* me? You heard Rigg's plan. Noxon's plan."

"Either it will work or it won't," said Olivenko. "When Noxon goes to Earth, you'll still be here. What then?"

Param shrugged slightly. "I'm open to suggestions."

"I think you need to gather an army, destroy General Citizen, and depose your mother," said Olivenko.

"Why?" asked Param. "So I can prove myself incompetent to rule in her place?"

"Maybe you can find a better way. You've read the histories — of Earth, of all the great eras of Odinfold. The cruelties of the Sessamids and the insanities of the People's Revolutionary Council aren't the only choices."

"Mother made sure I was never trained to run a household, let alone a kingdom. I'm unskilled at every labor."

"So what? You wouldn't have wanted to learn *her* way of governing, would you? Figure out another."

Param put a hand in front of her face. "I think we've all seen how well I handle problems."

"I think we've all grown and changed," said Olivenko. "And we're not done yet. You're going to need a general to lead your troops."

"And where will she find one?" asked Loaf.

"You," suggested Umbo.

Loaf shook his head. "Nobody will follow this face into battle. And even if my original face is finally restored, I'm a sergeant at best. A commander of twenty or a hundred, not of ten thousand. And before Umbo makes some joke about my lack of ambition, it isn't just a difference in scale. Commanding great armies is a matter of planning and logistics. What I know how to do is lead a few men into combat. And drag them home from brothels between the wars." Loaf then turned to Umbo, as if he were somehow the next logical candidate for the job.

"At least you know what the job *is*," said Umbo. "I'm not even sure I could *lift* a man-sized sword. Or give great stirring speeches."

"You could learn," said Olivenko.

"I have no talent for it," said Umbo. "And no *interest* in it. I don't want to lead people."

"Well, you certainly don't want to *follow* anybody," said Loaf cheerfully.

Umbo shook his head and looked away. That's why he couldn't even imagine leading people — those who knew him best had no respect for him.

"I'll tell you what *I'm* going to do," said Olivenko. "I'm going to go somewhere with a library — Odinfold, or maybe the starship in Vadeshfold or Larfold — and I'm going to study military history and theory until a week or so before the end of the world. Then one of you time-shifters is going to come and get me, and if I'm not ready to lead an army, you'll take me back and I'll work for another couple of years in a different starship."

"Why not the same one?" asked Noxon. "Then you could have really interesting conversations with the different versions of yourself."

"Since I don't know anything," said Olivenko, "I have no interest in having discussions with myself. From Loaf I could get the common soldier's perspective. *That* would be helpful. But even if I have to pass through the same two years ten times over, there'll come a time when I might actually be useful to you, Param. If not as a general, then at least as a judge of other possible generals. As a counselor. Whatever scholarship and philosophy can make of me, I'll become, and then I'll lay my sword at your feet."

Umbo felt an irresistible thrill at his words. Olivenko had spoken simply, but Umbo could hear how much fire lay behind his offer, and he saw how Param rose within herself and straightened her back. How Olivenko's offer made her more queenly.

"I will never be worthy of such service," said Param.

"Yet there is no other possible candidate but you to displace your mother and General Citizen," said Olivenko. "If you don't try, at least, then their tyranny continues. Or Ramfold descends into chaos."

"It's a good plan," said Rigg. "I don't know what I'll find in the other wallfolds. It may be that Ramfold is the most dangerous, most aggressive civilization. If you can become mistress of that wallfold, Param, then a world without Walls might be safe. Or maybe there will be more dangerous places, and we'll need the warlike character of the Sessamoto armies to curb the ambitions of even-more-dangerous peoples."

"It's too much for me," said Param.

"If I can make a military counselor out of myself, why can't you become a queen in fact as well as title?" asked Olivenko.

"We don't know that you *can* become what you say you'll become," said Param.

"I know I can become far more than I was as a scholar serving your father in the Great Library. Far more than the city guardsman who set out on this journey. Rigg and Loaf with their facemasks, all of you with time-shifting, you aren't the only ones who can learn and change and grow into something useful." Olivenko's voice became even softer, and his gaze at Param was intense. "The very fact that you doubt yourself, my lady, is proof of how much you have learned, and how greatly you have grown."

At those words, Param burst into tears and covered her face. But she did not slice time. She did not disappear.

"Thank you for staying with us," said Loaf softly.

"We all have so much work to do," said Noxon.

Except me, thought Umbo. Nobody has any plan for me, except to be Loaf's character witness when he returns to Leaky.

Not fair, he told himself. They don't dare find jobs for you, because you're so childish and prickly they know you'll take offense.

Yet a part of him—the childish, prickly part—still insisted, inside his mind: They aren't finding a job for me, because now that Rigg has a facemask, and then another copy of himself, there's no particular need for me at all. "*I* should get a facemask," Umbo murmured.

Everyone fell silent.

"Maybe with a facemask I could see the paths like Rigg," Umbo added.

"We already have twice as many pathfinders as we need," said Noxon. "That's why I'm getting out of town."

"Off the planet, you mean," said Olivenko.

"We need all the pathfinders we can get," said Umbo. "And even if I couldn't see paths, the facemask would make me better at the things I *can* do."

"You're just assuming you have the will to master the face-mask," said Loaf.

"Umbo," said Param softly, removing her hands from her face. "How can I possibly marry you if you have a facemask? The people would never accept you as their king, if you looked like that."

CHAPTER 3

Under a Tent

Noxon and Param began their mutual training the obvious way, with Param trying to teach Noxon to develop an ability like hers by teaching him the way the Gardener had once taught *her*. It kept the two of them away from everyone else for hours at a time.

At first Umbo watched them from a distance, trying not to think of what Param had said. Did it really amount to a royal proposal of marriage? And if it did, why did she completely ignore him now? Instead of thinking about Param, Umbo wished he could be more like Rigg—like Noxon—in the way that he seemed to have endless patience when he needed it.

Rigg had learned his patience by being schooled every waking moment by his father—by the expendable called Ramex—while they tramped in solitude through the forests of Ramfold.

Rigg knew how to listen, how to concentrate on what he was hearing, how to analyze and process it.

I'm quiet too, sometimes, thought Umbo. I hold my tongue, I don't say everything that comes to mind.

And that's the difference, he realized. Rigg learned to concentrate on what Ramex was saying, and devoted himself to memory and analysis. While I, in my silences, I'm thinking of all the things I'm going to decide not to say.

No, I'm storing up things to complain about later.

Is that all I am? No wonder everyone looks to Rigg for leadership—he thinks through ideas, while I think of nothing but myself. How could anyone respect me? I don't even *have* ideas that are worthy of respect.

"I wonder if you're mooning over the princess," said Olivenko, "or resenting Noxon for having so much time with her."

Umbo was immediately filled with fury. But, trying to learn a lesson from Rigg, he curbed that first impulse. "I was wishing I had Rigg's patience."

"That was a good step, then, to answer me so mildly."

"You were trying to goad me?"

"Yes," said Olivenko. "Because it seems to be the only way to get your attention."

Umbo thought: By hurting my feelings? But he said, "You have it."

"I think she *does* like you, Umbo. She's overcome some of her snobbery and seen you for a good man trying to be better."

"You think of me as a boy," said Umbo, "so when you call me

31

a man it sounds like mockery." But he said it mildly, because it was simply true.

"I'm talking about how Param thinks of you," said Olivenko. "No matter how she *feels*, she'll marry for reasons of state."

"Thank you for telling me," said Umbo. He did not say, By no means should you let me nurse the delusion that she might have fallen in love with me.

"If you're going to marry her, you not only have to know how she thinks, you have to learn how to think the same way. The needs of the kingdom come before your personal desires."

This time Umbo couldn't keep the resentment out of his voice. "How would marrying me serve the needs of the kingdom?"

"No, I won't answer that, because you already know the answer."

"I say I don't," said Umbo.

"And I say that you already have enough information to figure it out."

"And I say I don't need a schoolmaster."

"I think you do," said Olivenko. "And since Loaf already stands in for your father, being your schoolmaster gives me a way to be useful to you. Or do you think you alone have nothing to learn?"

"On the contrary," said Umbo. "I know so little that there's no point in teaching me."

"Nobody knows more than can be learned in a single lifetime," said Olivenko, "and you already know more than you realize. Prove me wrong. *Try* to answer my question, and when you fail, I'll know you were right about what a hopelessly ignorant privick you are."

Umbo knew that Olivenko was deliberately challenging him

in order to provoke him into accepting him as schoolteacher, if only to prove him wrong. So the proper answer was to walk away from him, saying nothing at all.

Proper answer? Why would that be proper? Umbo imagined himself doing it and then realizing, after about ten steps, that the only person he injured by refusing the offered education was himself. But then pride would forbid him to return and ask for Olivenko's help after all.

Only this time, Umbo hadn't walked away the moment he realized that would be the "right" way to prove he couldn't be manipulated or controlled by anyone. This time he had stayed long enough to think of why he should stay.

He thought back to what Olivenko had challenged him to do: Think of how Param's marrying this privick boy would serve the needs of the kingdom.

"Maybe she'd marry me to prove that she wants to elevate the common people," said Umbo.

"That will be a very good thing for her to tell the common people, in order to try to cement their loyalty, but she'd better not let the great families of the Sessamoto Empire think that's why she did it," said Olivenko.

"Why not?" asked Umbo.

"No, you tell *me* why not," said Olivenko.

"An excellent method of teaching—make *me* answer all my own questions. Using that method, you don't actually have to know any of the answers yourself."

"I'm waiting for you to think about Param's political situation, instead of your own educational one."

Since Olivenko was urging him to analyze a situation outside himself, and that was exactly what Umbo had just realized Rigg could do and he could not, he swallowed his rebellious responses and forced himself to think about the new question. "The great families don't want her to have the love of the common people."

"Close," said Olivenko. "They don't mind if she has their love. They only worry about what she plans to do with it."

Now it became clear to Umbo. "They're afraid that she'd be playing for the love of the common people so she would no longer need their support." Now a further insight occurred to him. "The great families need her to need their support. So they don't have to fear the royal power."

"Now you're thinking more like a ruler's consort," said Olivenko. "Back to the original question."

Umbo had to think for a moment. Oh, yes. Why she needed to marry Umbo for reasons of state. "I'm a poor privick from as far upriver as you can get. I can't think of any other reason."

"Is that *all* you are?" asked Olivenko.

"Isn't that bad enough?" asked Umbo.

"I'm asking you to think of why she needs to marry you for the good of the kingdom. Not for reasons why she should find the idea disgusting."

That *had* been what he was doing, hadn't it? "All right," said Umbo. "What else am I, besides a person of such low standing that . . ."

No, Umbo thought. That was the kind of self-denigration that Olivenko was telling him to stop.

What am I, besides poor and ignorant and annoying?

34

"I'm the only other timeshaper besides her brother Rigg," said Umbo tentatively.

Olivenko's answer was sarcastic enough to show Umbo how obvious he thought the answer was. "You finally noticed that, did you? Why would that lead her to *need* to marry you?"

"I'm the only timeshaper who isn't in the royal family. And my abilities run rings around hers. But not around Rigg's."

"Oh, yes, her brother Rigg, the one with the facemask, so ugly and strange that she had better keep him out of the public view," said Olivenko, "because he'll make people afraid. You're the timeshaper who can show his face. And in case you didn't notice—and you obviously haven't—you're a rather good-looking young man, now that you're getting some height on you, and when you aren't pouting, you can be downright likeable. Maybe even charismatic. People might want to associate with a handsome young man who can go wherever he wants in time and space."

For the first time Umbo realized that while the people in this little traveling society of theirs might not have much respect for him, he could really dazzle strangers.

"Oh, now you see it," said Olivenko. "It's to your credit that you never even thought of it before. But it worries me that you now find the idea so attractive."

"I didn't *say* anything."

"You didn't have to. I saw your expression of resentment and impatience turn into happy contemplation. I didn't have to have a facemask to see *that* transformation."

Umbo wondered briefly if Olivenko resented the fact that Loaf now had facemask-enhanced abilities. But in the meantime, his mind was still caught up in analyzing Param's situation.

"If Param became Queen-in-the-Tent," said Umbo, "and a more-powerful timeshaper—me—was out there, I could easily become a focus for discontent in the kingdom. Her enemies might gather around me, want to follow me." And then, remembering who her enemies were likely to be, and how they were likely to regard a privick like him, he said, "Or more likely they'd try to get control of me and use me."

"Or both," said Olivenko. "There'll be as many different motives for people to gather around you as there are people doing the gathering."

"But none of those motives will make them friends of the Sessamids."

"Add to that her keen awareness of how quick you are to resent her, especially because she's treated you badly in the past, and it should be clear that in order to keep you from being a divisive force in the kingdom, she either has to marry you . . ."

"Or kill me," said Umbo. "I suppose I should be grateful that she decided on marriage."

"It doesn't mean that she doesn't *also* like you. I said you were good-looking and likeable, and she's not oblivious to that. Plus, you used to be her puppy dog, you were so in love with her."

"She got rid of *those* feelings soon enough."

"No she didn't," said Olivenko. "You're still devoted to her. Only now you know her well enough that it's not the beautiful princess that you have an adolescent crush on, it's the woman she's turning into, the woman who has stopped treating you badly—"

"Stopped treating me badly in order to neutralize me as a threat to her kingdom."

"No. Wrong lesson," said Olivenko. "Her change in feelings toward you happened during a time when nobody thought of her going back into Ramfold. When for all she knew she would go on wandering with us forever."

"It's *you* she fell in love with," said Umbo.

"Had *her* adolescent puppy-dog crush on," corrected Olivenko. "Only I knew that's what it was and guided her through that phase and out the other side."

Umbo recognized at once that yes, that was exactly what Olivenko had done. And since Olivenko had now assigned himself to think about kingdom politics, Umbo said, "You could have exploited that. You could have made her devoted to you."

"For a while, yes," said Olivenko. "Long enough to get her to marry me, perhaps, though I'm just as common as you. I do know more about the language and manners of the court, but I would have been a liability to her without any timeshaping talents to make up for it. As soon as she realized that, then she'd either be miserable, living with a bad choice of consort—or I'd be thrown away. Or killed. Not necessarily by her or by her order—there would be plenty of courtiers who would understand how embarrassing and useless I was, and would therefore help their queen by discreetly killing her husband. Or catching him in some act of infidelity."

"But you would never . . ."

"It wouldn't matter if I was actually guilty," said Olivenko. "Lack of truthfulness doesn't weaken a story if you can get enough people to believe the lie."

Umbo thought of the comparison between him and Olivenko. "But if they would try to get rid of *you*, when you know the language and manners of court—"

"You'll learn them quickly. And even if someone sees you as a problem or an obstacle, *you* won't be as easy to get rid of."

"Because I can go back and warn myself."

"Or go back and stab the assassin in the back."

"Ah, but then there'd be two of me," said Umbo. "Our old system of warning people without actually traveling back in time had the virtue of not creating copies."

Olivenko nodded. "It would be bad for the kingdom if every time somebody tried to kill you, the number of Umbos doubled."

"It might get them to stop trying."

"But what would you do with the copies?" asked Olivenko. "What Ram Odin did, when he found out he had been re-created eighteen times?"

Umbo shuddered at the thought of his own two dead copy-bodies that Odinex had killed the first time Umbo visited his buried starship. "I can see that it makes sense, but I don't know if . . ."

"All it takes is one of your copies to decide that he's the original and the others aren't necessary. But you see my point. Married to you, Param has you close, where you won't be starting a rival power center."

"Instead, my great personal charm will make people want to kill me."

"You think there won't be people trying to kill *her*?" asked Olivenko. "When it's about power, it's always a matter of life and death."

"So another reason for marrying me," said Umbo, "might be so I'd be close enough to save her from assassins and traitors."

"Yes," said Olivenko.

"Also close enough to harm her, if I chose," said Umbo. "So apparently she trusts me."

"No matter where you are," said Olivenko, "you could harm her if you chose. Yes, she trusts you. Or at least she hopes she can trust you, which is about as close to trust as powerful people ever get. There are so many incentives for betrayal. It's a lonely life. She wants you to share it with her. Partly for reasons of state. Or mostly. But I think she believes it will also be a tolerable thing."

But the way he said it made Umbo think that Olivenko thought that Param thought that it might be better than tolerable.

"I still have that adolescent crush," said Umbo. "I'm better at hiding it, that's all."

"Not so very much better. Disguising it as surly resentment fooled only two people: Param and you."

That was the first time it had ever occurred to Umbo that maybe all his feelings of resentment were not really directed at Rigg. They were really there because as long as he thought he could feel sorry for himself because Rigg was always the leader, he didn't have to feel sorry for himself because Param would never love him.

"I wish I could go back in time and explain to myself why I was so angry all the time," said Umbo.

"Would you have believed yourself? And even if you did, could you have stopped?"

"If I couldn't have stopped *then*, why can I stop now?" asked Umbo.

"Because she asked you to marry her, you fool," said Olivenko.

"It's going to be a very complicated life," said Umbo.

"What do you mean?" asked Olivenko.

"Being married to the Queen-in-the-Tent."

"Oh? *Are* you going to be married to her?" asked Olivenko.

"But . . . she asked me."

"Yesterday," said Olivenko. "And since that moment, have you even spoken to her?"

"I don't . . . I couldn't . . ."

"She asked you to marry her, and after a day you still haven't answered her."

"But she *didn't* ask me. She just announced it. As if everyone already knew it was going to happen."

"Was she supposed to kneel and beg you to cross her threshold? Give you the key to her house? Pull a symbolic tent over both your heads? Those are the traditional ways, but can you tell me which of those a princess of the Sessamids should use in asking an ignorant privick like yourself to be her consort? She was asking, and you haven't answered."

"So this whole lecture you gave me—"

"I believe I used a series of pedagogical queries—"

"Was designed to get me to tell her yes or no?"

"Absolutely not," said Olivenko. "If you had been too stupid to understand any of this, I would have gone to her and begged her to rescind the offer."

"And then what?" asked Umbo. "Would you have killed me for her, to get me out of the way?"

"Don't ever ask questions that can only be answered one

way, no matter what the truthful answer might be. It will make you doubt your friends. And *that*, in case you were wondering, *was* a lecture."

"I was joking."

"But because you asked it, no matter how fervently I said that I would never kill you and she would never ask me to anyway, you would always wonder. In fact, you'll wonder anyway. What a stupid thing to do to yourself."

Umbo saw his point. He *felt* the point, because the question was already gnawing at him. "I notice you *haven't* said you wouldn't kill me."

"And I never will say such a stupid thing," said Olivenko. "Because if you ever posed a real danger to her, I *would* kill you, if I could. So if I denied it that would be a lie. And you'd know it was a lie. But I tell you this, Umbo. You have earned my trust, and hers too. When she was at her most obnoxious, you never went back in time to harm her. Never did anything that had to be undone—only her brother did that. The whole time she's known you, you've had the power to harm her at any time, and she's given you plenty of provocation. But you have never raised a hand against her, and never abandoned her. Even when you thought she loved *me*, you didn't use your power over time to interfere."

"I can't take any credit for that. Rigg would have just gone back and stopped me."

"Before he had that facemask, did he have the power to do that? If you had wanted to go to war with Rigg, wouldn't you have defeated him easily, in the days before he learned to go back in time without your help? You *were* the most powerful, and you're still more powerful than Param or me or Loaf—have you *ever* used that power to harm any of us? To harm anyone at all? Can Rigg say as much?"

"He did what he had to do."

"But you never felt you had to do such a thing. Hurt and angry, over and over, you never once harmed anyone with your power."

"I damaged the mice," said Umbo, thinking of the way he and Param had warned the Visitors.

"You acted to save the human race on Earth from extinction, or so you thought. You really can't get away from being labeled as a person who can be trusted."

Umbo felt these words as praise. As honor. He hadn't understood how hungry he was for such open signs of respect; the emotion of relief and gratitude that filled him threatened to bring him to sudden tears. To deflect it, he turned to his old standby— resentfulness. "I'm not sure if that means I'm good or merely weak," said Umbo.

"*We* all know that you're good," said Olivenko. "Annoying, but good. That's my lesson for today. It's really the only thing you had to learn before you leave with Loaf to take him home."

"And that means there's really only one thing I have to do," said Umbo.

"Then go and do it."

"Only I should have done it yesterday," said Umbo.

"If there's anyone on Garden who never has to say such a thing, it's you," said Olivenko, "since you still *can* do it yesterday. But if I were you, I wouldn't do that."

"Why not?" asked Umbo.

Olivenko made a twirling gesture with his finger. Turn it around. Answer your own question.

"Because she'd know that I hadn't thought of it till later, and only went back in time so she wouldn't worry about it, but it would still be dishonest. I only realized I needed to answer when you told me, and I should be able to admit that to her, if we're really going to be husband and wife someday."

"Pretty soon you won't even need me to tell you to answer your own questions yourself," said Olivenko. "Though I'm always happy to provide that service."

Umbo found Param sitting in the grass by the riverbank, leaning against a sapling, with Rigg only about a meter away. They both looked despondent. Only it wasn't Rigg, Umbo remembered. It was Noxon. Though Noxon had as many memories of their friendship together as the one who was still called Rigg.

"Before you ask," said Noxon, "I'm not getting the hang of this at all. I should have her teach *you* first. Only I'd hate it when you picked it right up."

Umbo had an instant answer. Several of them, actually. But he remembered that he wasn't here to talk to his friend. He was here to talk to the woman he loved—the woman who had asked him to marry her, and had heard no response from him at all, and now wasn't even looking at him.

So Umbo ignored Rigg completely. He knelt in the grass in front of Param—and, because he was Umbo, and not the hero of a great story, he knelt on a root and yelped in pain and had to catch himself to keep from falling over and Param couldn't help but get a little smile on her face and Umbo felt a stab of embarrassment and he realized that a year ago—a week ago—yesterday—he would have resented her for it and it would have deflected him from what he came here to do.

But he refused to be that version of himself. There are two Umbos as surely as there are two Riggs, but in my case, only one of them can be visible at a time. From now on, *I* decide which one it's going to be.

So he accepted her smile because it wasn't mocking, it was honest—it really *was* funny that in trying to be serious, he had knelt on a root and wrecked it. Only it hadn't wrecked anything, if he decided not to let it.

He pulled his shirt off over his head, shook it open, and held it between them. "Param, I've loved you since I first came to know you. At first it was the princess, the *idea* of a princess, but that was long ago, and now it's you that I love, so far as I know you, and you that I want to marry, if you'll have me." He held out the shirt to her.

She took the shoulders of his shirt in her hands, and pulled the cloth over her head to make a tent. Umbo leaned closer and drew the bottom of the shirt over his own head, so it was only the two of them, face to face, under that small tent. He lightly kissed her cheek. She kissed his lips, just as lightly.

Then she pulled the shirt off her head and handed it back to him. "Next time you propose to a girl, you might bring a nice shawl or even a towel instead of a shirt you've already been wearing for hours."

"If you can't stand the way I smell," said Umbo, "this whole marriage thing isn't going to work."

"So this wasn't just a proposal," she said. "It was your first test of my love."

She had said the word "love." He wanted to dance with happiness. Instead, he pulled the shirt back on over his head. "At least *you* don't have to wear it," he said. He got to his feet. "You two still have work to do, and I'm going to go take Loaf home to Leaky."

He took a few steps away before Param said, "Hurry home."

Umbo stopped and half-turned back to her. "Oh, I'll be home before you even notice I was gone."

"I know," she said, smiling. Then she made a shooing-away gesture and slid a little closer to Noxon. Umbo could hear the two of them getting back to trying to teach each other unteachable skills as he walked away.

A royal marriage—the personal part could never be allowed to keep them from their duty.

CHAPTER 4

Homecoming

Even though Leaky had known right from the start that Loaf would go off with Umbo on a mad mission to save Rigg from the People's Collection of Twits, and had even urged him to go, it still made her angry that he had done it; and she didn't try very hard to be civil when she saw her husband and that strange time-traveling boy out the door. She threw a lettuce at them as they left, then made a point of closing the door, rather loudly, long before they were out of earshot. There'd be no backward glances to see *her* standing in the doorway gazing wistfully after her man.

She couldn't help it that Loaf was a good man—that was part of why she married him and, in her weaker moments, admitted she loved him. She only wished he could be more selectively good— good for her, then good for the inn, and maybe even good for himself. After that, other people could suck on Ram's left elbow before she thought Loaf should sacrifice anything for them.

Nice and hopelessly naive as those boys were, they were worth a bit of washing, stitching, and some food for the journey—and nothing more. Instead, Loaf had gone off with them to O, gotten himself arrested, and made his way home with Umbo. Well, wasn't that enough? But no, Umbo had to go and teach himself how to do something he had only been able to do in combination with Rigg— send messages into the past. And now, armed with this dubious "weapon," Loaf and Umbo thought they could take on the People's Revolutionary Cushion-squatters.

So after shutting the door firmly—not *slamming*, since when she slammed a door it usually needed repairs—she had a bumptious half hour, deliberately doing everything with too much force, which terrified the customers eating or drinking at such an early hour. Most of them gulped down whatever they were eating or drinking, paid without arguing the price, and hightailed it through the still-functioning front door.

Once everyone was gone, Leaky realized how foolish it was to go on handling everything so roughly. For one thing, she would have to pay for anything she broke—which included two eggs, a lettuce, and a clay pot. For another thing, there was nobody there to see, not the customers and certainly not the people she was actually annoyed at—Umbo for being so sweet and needy, Rigg for getting himself arrested as a royal, and most of all Loaf for being so abominably *fatherly*.

If he's going to be fatherly, then he should start by begetting a child on her so he could be father to their *own*.

Not a thought she allowed herself to think more than once or twice a week. She went back to bumptiousness for a moment, to punish herself for such a wicked thought. After all, *she* might be the barren one, and him not sterile at all. She had never asked him whether he had sired any children during his soldiering days—she didn't really want to know the answer anyway—and he had never volunteered the information. "You know, Leaky my love, it's obvious you're the one as can't conceive, seeing that I've fathered children in fourteen towns, and them's only the ones I know about." No, Loaf would never burden her with such information. Nor could Leaky ask, "Were you chaste as a soldier, my big old bear? Or have you by any chance noticed that you never left a bit of seed behind?"

She locked the front door of the roadhouse and went out back to chop wood for a while. Chopping wood was always useful, not least for working off some anger.

She had the ax back over her shoulder, ready to swing, when she saw someone standing right in the path of her swing. She only *just* stopped herself. "Fool! Are you trying to get—"

Then she saw that it was Umbo.

"Back already? And snuck up on me like that?"

Umbo only shook his head. "Look at me," he said softly.

She looked. He was different. Completely different clothes, for one thing. And taller. Not just a little, a lot. A man's height. Getting to be a *tall* man's height. And his face—was that a flash of fuzz on his chin and cheeks?

"Are you really here or is this just a message from the future?" she asked suspiciously.

"I'm alive, Loaf is alive, and Rigg got saved along with his sister Param. We all escaped Aressa Sessamo and left the wallfold and it's been several years."

"Years! How irresponsible! It was supposed to be only a few—"

"Hold your tongue for a moment, if that's possible," said Umbo. "This is the fifth time I've tried to have a conversation with you but you never shut up long enough to hear me out."

"Of course I don't listen when you—"

"This is the last time I'll try," said Umbo. "If you don't hear me now, I will *not* bring Loaf home to you."

"How dare you, after—"

"Still talking," said Umbo.

"You have no right to command—"

Umbo shouted now. "If you don't listen to me you will never see your husband's face again. Do you understand that? Can you control your anger long enough to realize that your entire future with Loaf is at stake?"

Leaky fell silent, but she was even more furious than before.

"I can see you're angry," said Umbo, "but believe me, this isn't the way I spoke the first time I tried this. It was—would have been—about a week from now, and I didn't come as a vision like this, I came in person."

"You can do that?" she asked.

"In the past several years, yes, I've learned a few things. I've changed. So has Loaf."

"What aren't you telling me? Spit it out—has he lost a leg?"

"Shut. Up. Now."

She thought she'd burst with rage at his domineering, disrespectful attitude.

"I've been through this confrontation and everything failed. I tried hearing you out, but when you rage, Madam Leaky, you make yourself angrier and less reasonable. So this is my final attempt. Loaf agrees with me. If you can't listen and accept what I'm going to tell you, he's going to figure it's as if he died on our journey and he'll never come home to you. So what's at stake now is this: Can you be silent, or do you want to never see your husband again?"

"Loaf *agreed* to this? What kind of—"

"If you listen I'll tell you all the whys. On my second visit to you I actually got to tell you what has changed about him, and you still behaved so badly that Loaf almost gave up then. I was the one who talked him into making another try. In fact, three more tries. Do you understand me, you thick-headed angry woman? Loaf married a woman with a temper but he thought you loved him more than you loved your own rage. Is he right or wrong?"

"Let me chop wood for a minute," she said. "Can you stand there and wait? I have to . . . I have to get this out of me."

Umbo nodded and stepped back. He did not disappear.

Leaky set up a short log, picked up the ax, and let fly. Shivers of wood flew in all directions. She set up another, pulverized it, then another, another.

"How many are you going to turn into splinters?" asked Umbo.

"Your turn to shut up! It hasn't been a minute yet!"

It was probably five minutes, but finally she was exhausted and plopped down onto the ground and leaned her forearms on her knees and covered her face with her hands. "Talk to me," she said, "while I'm not looking at that smart-mouth face of yours bossing me around."

"If you listen and then talk to me quietly and reasonably, I won't boss you around," said Umbo. "I know Loaf will never be happy if he can't come home to you, but I also know he won't come back to you until he knows you'll give him a chance."

"Give him a chance to—" But this time Leaky stopped herself. "You tell it. I'll listen. I swear I'll listen."

"The first wallfold we went to was an evil place. We didn't understand how evil. All the human beings there were dead. The only person there was Vadeshex, and he isn't human."

"A person, and not human? Sorry. Sorry. I'm sure you'll tell me."

"Vadeshex looked just like Rigg's father. He *was* just like him because they're not human. They're mechanical men designed to look like people. They're called 'expendables' but they never die. There's one in each wallfold. Rigg was raised by one."

"But his father died," said Leaky.

"His father pretended to die," said Umbo. "They're all liars, these expendables, because they think their job is to protect the human race *from* the human race. They know everything, but they understand nothing. No matter how angry you get at *me*, it's nothing to how angry I am at Vadeshex. Because he tricked Loaf into—no, wait. It won't make any sense unless I explain something first."

"By Silbom's right kneecap!" shouted Leaky.

"Loaf is alive. He's sharper and healthier than ever. But something happened to him in Vadeshfold and that's what I'm trying to tell you. But some things don't make sense unless I explain other things first. Please, please be patient with me. I don't want to fail Loaf again, the way I did the other four times."

"I thought I was the one who failed!"

"You're the one who didn't listen," said Umbo, "but it has to have been my fault because I went about it wrong. The first time I tried to tell everything gradually and make things seem better than they are. You saw that I was concealing things and so I think you were right to be angry. I thought you were going to kill me, which didn't seem fair to me, but I did a bad job. I did a bad job all the other times, too, because I failed. But please help me, Leaky. I'm going to make mistakes so you have to help me make up for my stupidity by being patient with me. Please."

Leaky was astonished to hear a sound like incipient weeping in his voice, as if he was trying not to cry. But she didn't look at him. "Tell me in whatever order you think is best."

"I'm just trying to be clear. So here it is. In Vadeshfold, there's a creature that lives in the streams. It's very tiny, but if you get it on you it burrows into your skin and grows, and it quickly crawls up your body to your face. It covers your mouth and nose and ears and eyes and reaches through them to grow into your brain. But it doesn't kill you. It just . . . takes over."

"And this is what happened to —"

"No! No, you have to *listen* and let me explain because Loaf is *fine*. Better than fine, just *ugly*. And way less ugly than he was when it first—look, this creature was the reason the people of Vadeshfold all died. Half of them got this parasite—we call them facemasks—and the other half didn't, and they fought each other until they were all dead. But when we arrived, Vadeshex warned us not to get near the water and so we *didn't* get taken by the wild facemasks."

"But you had to explain about them, so—"

"Vadeshex had nothing to do after all his humans died. He was pretty much a failure as caretaker of the colony in his wall-fold. But he thought these facemask parasites had potential. So he began to breed them and change them so that they wouldn't make the people crazy. Because when a facemask takes over a larger animal, it enhances it. It replaces the eyes with better eyes. The reflexes speed up. It hears better. So Vadeshex spent thousands of years trying to develop a breed of facemasks that would enhance human beings without taking over completely. It takes over, but if you're strong-willed enough, you can control it. You stay yourself."

"I can't pretend that I don't guess that you're only telling me this because Loaf got one of these facemasks."

"I figured you would. When I first heard what happened I wanted to kill Rigg for letting it—"

"Rigg let this happen?"

"No! That's what I thought, because they went without me into the . . . place. But Rigg couldn't stop him."

"You could have sent Rigg back in time to warn him! Like you're doing now!"

"Loaf wouldn't let him. You have to understand, Rigg was only just learning how to do this stuff on his own. He would have

53

needed me, and he didn't want me to see Loaf like that. Because it's—it's much better *now*. You won't think so, but Leaky, it was horrible at first. This thing completely covered his face so it looked like he couldn't breathe. And then it made new eyes for him and a new mouth only they weren't in the right place and—I'm sorry! I'm wrecking everything! I'm doing a terrible job of telling this."

"He looked horrible," said Leaky. "He looked monstrous."

"Yes. And I was furious and I wanted to rip it off of him but Vadeshex told us that we couldn't do it without killing him. It was part of him now, and if it died, Loaf would die. And the other way around, too. So I led Loaf around like a blind deaf-mute for a while, except that he wasn't blind, he didn't bump into anything. And already his reflexes were unbelievably quick. And I kept hoping he was still inside there. Loaf. That he hadn't been completely taken over by this *thing*."

"And you're here to assure me that even though he's uglier than before, it's really Loaf."

"It is! But I know you won't believe me and you'll scream at me that I don't know him well enough to know whether it's really him but listen to me: Of course you know him better than everybody, but this isn't going to work if you make him *prove* who he is. He's either coming home to his *wife* or not. And his wife—and these are his exact words—'My wife will not make me spend the rest of my life proving that I'm really me.' Do you understand? I'm his witness. You'll have him telling you, and you have me telling you, and if that's not good enough, he isn't going to stay. Do you understand that?"

"Understanding isn't agreeing."

"You know him!" said Umbo fervently. "He's made up his mind that if you doubt him, he's gone. He says he'll understand if you *reject* him, if you can't live with him the way he is now. The only thing he wants is to come back to you and live with you the way he did before. Except that he's stronger and quicker and smarter and prettier—he says he's prettier but that's—"

"That's his sense of humor," said Leaky.

"Yes," said Umbo.

"Go and get him," said Leaky.

"You mean it?"

"I can't believe you had to go to all this trouble. Of course I want him back, however I can get him. If you dragged him back in a sack without arms or legs, I'd take him. What do you think marriage *is*, boy?"

"Judging by my parents, it's not like the two of you. But do you promise—"

"I don't have to make *you* any promises at all," said Leaky. "You're the messenger. I want my husband back, and I believe you that the man you're going to bring me is my husband, or as close to him as I'm going to get, and that's close enough for me. Or if it turns out not to be, then Loaf and I will work it out without some fuzz-faced boy getting between us. Am I clear? Your job is done. This time you succeeded. I want him back. Bring him to me."

Umbo didn't answer.

She glanced over and saw that he hadn't gone. "What are you waiting for?"

"Do you think I'm here on my own?" asked Umbo. "I'm here following *his* instructions."

"And now you'll go back following mine," said Leaky. "Is it *me* Loaf wants to come home to? Then he doesn't dictate terms to me, and he knows it. Tell him to get his sponge-covered face back here so I can decide for myself whether to scream and run away or give him a big sloppy wet kiss on his spongy new mouth."

"It's not spongy anymore," said Umbo. "It's pretty much almost normal except not, in a creepy way."

"You're not helping now," said Leaky. "I think I've done a very good job of shutting up and listening. Now it's your turn to shut up and go bring me my husband."

"I'll tell him that's what you said," said Umbo. "I hope it's good enough."

"It will be," said Leaky. "If I said anything different, he wouldn't believe I meant it."

Umbo smiled wanly. "You're probably right. Only . . . I don't think it'll be good for you to see him with other people around."

"Everybody's out of the roadhouse, if that's what you're worried about. But why can't you bring him back right here?"

"Because to do that I'd have to get him here in the future, and I'd have a hard time sneaking him in."

"You snuck in?"

"I came in by water and where I am, it's nighttime and you're busy in the kitchen so you can't hear me."

"You got a soaking?"

"I've swum this river before," said Umbo. "When I come back with Loaf, it'll be by the road, and I'll have his face hidden so he doesn't shock the local people."

"And when will this magical event happen?"

"I'm not totally precise. But later today, probably."

"I'm supposed to keep the roadhouse closed up for hours, maybe?"

Umbo gulped. "I do it inside my head and I can't tell time all that precisely so—"

"I'm teasing you, Umbo, you sweet stupid boy. I'd keep the roadhouse closed for the rest of my life if it's the only way to get Loaf back to me."

"Then I think I'll go now because I don't want future you to come out of the kitchen and . . ."

And he disappeared.

Umbo came up from the water, dripping and smiling.

"So this time it worked?" asked Loaf.

"I pretended I was you and yelled at her to shut up and listen," said Umbo.

"That *never* works," said Loaf.

"It worked when I told her that if she didn't, she'd never see you again. She finally believes me and now she says to get you home, no matter what happened to you."

"She believed you, then? That it's really me behind this mask?"

Umbo told him what Leaky had said.

Loaf laughed. "She's right. I'm still Loaf, but she's still Leaky, and that means nobody bosses her around. Except, apparently, you."

"She chopped wood for half an hour till she was calm enough to listen."

"I bet it only took her five minutes."

"It felt very long."

"So do you think you can get me back home the same day we left?"

"Yes," said Umbo. "Take my hand."

"Yes, sir," said Loaf.

"And cover your face."

"I'll cover my face when we get out on the road," said Loaf.

"We're going to make the jump at the edge of the road so we don't accidentally materialize in a sapling."

"If we're not going to jump till we get to the road, why am I supposed to hold your hand?" demanded Loaf.

"Because it's dark," said Umbo, "and I can't see in the dark the way you can."

"A practical reason," said Loaf. "Good thinking. Only . . . now I have to wonder. Is this really you?"

Leaky heard the loud banging at the front door. "Whoever you are, go away," she muttered. "My husband and his idiot-child messenger are coming home and I don't need company here." She struggled to her feet—she really had exerted herself with the ax, swinging it too hard and moving too quickly. Now she was a little stiff and she was sure there'd be painful muscles tomorrow.

She made her way through the house and the banging at the door just kept on and on, not so loudly as to suggest damage to the door, but relentlessly, as if the person would never go away without being admitted to the house.

And when she thought of a guest that stubborn, she knew

who it was before she even got to the door. My darling Loaf, that fool boy got you here almost before he left off talking to me. I didn't even have time to get back into the house and unlock the door.

Now she did unlock it, and swung it open, and there he was, his face half-hidden in shadow by a cowl that hung low in front. But she could see at once that something was wrong with the face.

Not with anything else, though. Loaf stood at his full height. She knew those hands, knew that posture, and when he spoke, it was his true voice, only younger and stronger than he had sounded in years. "Hello, my love," said Loaf. "Nice of you to lock folks out of a roadhouse."

"I'm saving the big room for my husband and his tame time-shifter. I hear he has a head like an elephant now, and the boy has become very bossy." She reached up to pull away the hood.

His hand lashed out and caught her by the wrist—but so gently she could hardly feel the pressure of his hand. "Not yet," said Loaf.

"I can bear anything," said Leaky.

"But I can't bear the look on your face if you don't already know it's me," said Loaf.

"Come in then," she said. "But don't let go of my hand. I like the feel of you. It reminds me of a man I once slept with."

"Slept with him a whole lot more than once," said Loaf, "if it's the man I'm thinking you mean."

"What I'm trying to figure out is why that damp-headed boy thinks he's coming in with us," said Leaky. "He had his say, and now he waits outside like any other river rat. If he wants to be useful he'll keep other fools from knocking on the door."

Umbo backed away. "Don't let the fact that I'm hungry and thirsty and tired change your plans in any way."

"Me me me, that's all the boy thinks of," said Loaf. "And he ate only yesterday, which was about fifteen minutes ago, so he's just being whiny."

The door closed behind them.

Umbo leaned against it and surveyed the street. "The problem with time traveling to get here," he said aloud, "is that *nothing* has had time to change since we left." But it also meant he could go across the street to the baker, who was bound to have something edible in stock, even if it was late in the day for fresh morning bread.

Bread in hand, Umbo took his perch outside the roadhouse. When people first came to the door, he tried explaining that Loaf had come home after long absence, but they looked at him like he was crazy. "I saw the two of you set out this very afternoon," one woman said, "and if that's long absence I'm young and beautiful."

"And indeed you are," said Umbo, using his most sincere voice. Olivenko could have brought it off and won a smile from the woman, but at Umbo's clumsy effort she only sneered and left, saying, "If they don't want my business, so be it, but I don't have to be mocked by a boy who's also a stranger."

"I've lived here for months," said Umbo, because that had been true at the time they set out. "I'm strange enough, but *not* a stranger."

His wit was wasted on her—she and her husband (or whatever he was) didn't show any sign that they could hear Umbo's clever remark. But after that, Umbo didn't tell anything like the truth. "A feral cat got in there and peed all over the tables and they have to scrub everything down to get the smell out," he explained. Oddly enough, the lie was believed instantly, while the truth had been treated with such contempt.

Late at night the door opened. It was Loaf, no covering on his face now. "We're staying closed, but we can't leave you outside all night."

"Like a feral cat," said Umbo, "I think I'll pee all over everything."

"You'll go to your room and have a good night's sleep. I assume you already found something to eat."

"Why would you assume that?"

"Because you're Umbo," said Loaf. "Now come in."

Umbo wasn't quite sure how many hours he had been awake in a row, but he fell asleep before he actually got into bed, as attested by the fact that he woke up only half undressed. But it was light outside, so he put his clothes back on and headed for the privy.

He met Leaky coming back. She gave him a curt, preoccupied nod, but he didn't read anything into that because her idea of manners included the idea that a man was supposed to pretend that he didn't know that women pee and poop. So obviously they had to pretend they hadn't seen each other.

It wasn't till breakfast — with the roadhouse still closed — that Loaf said, "That worked pretty well. Whatever you said."

"He was bratty and bossy and rude," said Leaky.

"You stick with that," said Loaf to Umbo. "You have a talent for it."

"I didn't hear any yelling or anything breaking so I guess you two hit it off like newlyweds?"

"On the contrary, our wedding night was full of yelling and breaking," said Loaf.

"Your five trips to visit me were time well spent," said Leaky. "Though Loaf was acting like a man who was five years celibate, while I hadn't even had time to notice he was away."

"Meaning she hadn't even had a chance to stuff a lover in a cupboard," said Loaf.

"But we're going to leave at once. Today. Close down the roadhouse. I just need time to get some friends to look in on the place so it doesn't get taken over by squatters till we come back."

"Where are you going?" asked Umbo.

"To Vadeshfold," said Loaf. "Apparently having a facemask made me so virile and vigorous that Leaky wants one, too."

Umbo was stunned. "Are you serious?"

Leaky leaned in close. "Look at my pretty pretty face. You think I'm afraid a facemask might be too much improvement?"

"But why?" asked Umbo.

"She's afraid she can't keep up with me," said Loaf. They laughed like conspirators in a particularly fiendish crime.

Umbo realized it so suddenly that he blurted it out. "You don't want to wait to see if you can have children now just by rejuvenating Loaf."

"We don't want it to be anyone's fault that we took so long

conceiving," said Loaf. "So she wants a facemask to heal every-thing that's wrong with *both* our bodies."

"I just want to be as athletic as he is," said Leaky.

"She just wants to be able to chop wood with exquisite accu-racy," said Umbo. "But it might take more than a facemask to confer a talent like that on her."

"I need you to come with us so we can get through the Wall," said Loaf. "But you don't have to stay with us."

"Where exactly would I go?" asked Umbo. "I have no reason to come back here without you."

Hardly were the words out of his mouth than he realized that there *was* something he needed very badly to do. But it could wait until they got back. That was the nice thing about the past — it stayed right where you put it until you needed to pick it up again.

CHAPTER 5

Burning House

Rigg had planned to make his tour of the wallfolds by himself. He didn't want to make conversation with anybody, and he didn't want to have to worry about protecting someone else. Truth to tell, he would have welcomed Umbo. But not the Umbo of today—what he wished for was the Umbo he had set out with years before. Before the rivalry. Though perhaps there was never a time before rivalry—just a time before Rigg knew about it.

What Rigg certainly did not want was to travel with any of the expendables. Even if he thought they could be trusted, he couldn't get past the fact that they all looked like Father. They all *were* Father. He had spent his childhood traveling with an expendable. Learning everything from him. It. Subservient to it. Until it pretended to die and thrust him onto this path which was leading . . . somewhere.

Yet if there was anyone Rigg wanted to travel with *less* than the expendables, it was Ram Odin. And not just because he had such clear memories of Ram trying to kill him, and even clearer ones of killing Ram Odin himself. It was because Ram Odin already knew far more about the wallfolds than Rigg could possibly learn in a few weeks or even years of wandering. Rigg wanted to come up with his own information. Make up his own mind.

So of course, when the flyer arrived to take him to Yinfold, the farthest of the wallfolds, there was Ram Odin, waiting at the bottom of the ramp.

"You don't look happy to see me," said Ram Odin.

"I'm never happy to see you," said Rigg. "Though I feel safer when I can see you than when I can't."

"I'm going with you," said Ram Odin.

"I'm not sure about that."

"Are you sure the flyer will go if I don't approve it?" said Ram Odin.

"Then I won't use the flyer," said Rigg, feeling tired already. "Or I'll just go back in time and use it yesterday. Or last month."

"Rigg," said Ram Odin. "Be reasonable. Your goal is to judge all the wallfolds. I've been watching them for ten thousand years, off and on. The expendables have been watching continuously."

"So a fresh pair of eyes might be helpful."

"I agree," said Ram Odin. "But don't throw away our knowledge. We can help make your visits more efficient and effective."

"You can make sure I see only the things that will support the conclusions you've already reached."

"That's always a danger, even if I try not to. But you bring your own biases, too. You're a child of Ramfold. How long before you stop seeing everything through the lens of your experiences there?"

"I'll never stop seeing things that way. You're a child of Earth. How long before —"

"Exactly my point. I see things from the perspective of having known another world, where there was no Wall. But do you think because I grew up on Earth, I know Earth?"

"Better than I do."

"I grew up where I grew up. I knew my neighborhood, my schools. My college, but even then I only knew the other kids I hung out with, the professors I studied with. I visited a few other countries. Studied in them. Learned a foreign language — which is no joke, when you don't have the Wall to impose all languages into your brain. By the standards of Earth I was widely read and widely traveled. And I have no idea what it's like to grow up in China or India or Africa or Brazil. Even if I grew up in one of those countries, I'd only know *my* village, *my* schools, *my* friends."

"Then I'd better stop talking with you and get busy exploring," said Rigg.

"You traveled down the Stashik River. First without money, trapping animals for meat as long as open country held out. Then with Loaf to guide you and shape your experience on the river and in O. Then as a prisoner so all you saw were your invisible paths. Then closed up in Flacommo's house and in the library. You had how many hours on the loose in Aressa

Sessamo before you made your escape, and then you were in that carriage heading for the Wall. Rigg, how well do you know Ramfold?"

"I know what I know," said Rigg stubbornly. "I know the things that everybody knows, and I know some things that only I know. You may know the whole history, you may have seen it through all its history while I only know the last fifteen minutes of it, but you didn't *grow up* in Ramfold, so you don't really know it, either."

"You don't know Ramfold, Rigg. You know Fall Ford and the forests above Upsheer, and then a quick tour of the river. What do you know about the vast lands on either side? That's where most of the millions of people of Ramfold live. Village after village. Places where they've never heard the language of Aressa Sessamo. Places where even the tax collectors don't go."

Rigg sat on the edge of the ramp and put his head in his hands. "And I'll know even less about the other wallfolds. I get it. But I have to do something."

"Then do it with me. I'll try to keep my mouth shut, all right? I'll try not to shape your perceptions. Yes, I think I know what you'll learn. But I'll let you learn it."

"The best way to do that is not to go with me," said Rigg.

"I know how dangerous it is," said Ram Odin, "and you don't."

"I've dealt with danger before. I think I can get out of trouble more easily than anybody in the world, except Umbo. And Noxon."

"You won't learn much if you're always getting out of trouble.

And think of what you'll *do* by 'getting out of trouble.' Suddenly disappear. You think they won't notice? Word won't spread? You think that won't change what people believe about the world?"

"I did a lot of that in Ramfold, and I didn't change everything."

"Of course you changed everything! Just because you can't see what it would have been without all your disappearing and reappearing—that's all you and Umbo did, over and over, was change things!"

Rigg had to concede the point. "And having you with me will accomplish exactly what?"

"It will keep you from getting thrown out of every village in every wallfold. Are you forgetting that you're wearing that twitching fungus on your face?"

"I never forget it," said Rigg. "I've seen Noxon."

"So how do you propose to get past the phase where they stone you and drive you out as a freak?"

"You make it sound like all I'll find in every wallfold is terrified privicks."

"All you'll find is *humans* responding to a very strange stranger."

"At least I'll speak the language like a native."

"That will make them even crazier, Rigg! In every wallfold except Odinfold and Larfold, people are sharply aware that the only people who speak their language like a native are the people *they know*. Along comes a stranger with a misshapen face and eyes not quite back into alignment, and he speaks as if he grew up among them—obviously a sorcerer, a witch, a devil!"

"So you'll be my normal-human companion," said Rigg.

"Your grandfather," said Ram Odin.

"It's not even a lie," said Rigg, "give or take five hundred generations."

"If we go into the city, then you suffer from some weird country disease. But I don't think you want to go to the cities—in the few wallfolds that have any real cities."

"Come on," said Rigg. "People always form into cities."

"They do when they can," said Ram Odin, "but no larger than the economy and the transportation systems can support. In some places, five thousand people is a city. In other places, it doesn't feel like a city till fifty thousand. Odinfold once had cities of twenty million, but we've erased those paths through time. At the moment, with about a quarter of a million people Aressa Sessamo is one of the four largest cities on the whole planet of Garden. Most wallfolds have a largest city of no more than fifty thousand."

"And you think I don't want to go into them."

"Because you've seen O and you've seen Aressa Sessamo. When humans live together in large numbers, they make the same accommodations. They develop the same rules, because only a few rules work. But in hamlets of ten families, villages of fifty households, towns of two hundred households—there's where really interesting, peculiar customs can grow up because what evolves is exactly what suits the people in that place."

"You're already trying to shape my way of looking at other wallfolds," said Rigg.

"I'm telling you that cities converge on the same kind of system of dealing with anonymity and crowding. But villages diverge and there's where the really interesting things pop up."

"Nothing interesting ever 'popped up' in Fall Ford."

"You and Umbo popped up there."

"You know we were poked into Fall Ford, me as a baby, Umbo as a genetic alteration."

"But Nox wasn't. She just grew there. Do you think every village has a Nox?"

Rigg thought about the woman he once believed, or at least hoped, was his mother. She kept a boardinghouse that took in the rare traveler. She cooked meals that people in Fall Ford praised and envied. She was kind and protective.

And she had the ability to create a mental field around her in which she could calm people down. It didn't reach far, but it certainly was effective. You couldn't be very angry or very afraid around Nox.

"She's the mayor of Fall Ford," said Rigg, realizing it for the first time. "Nobody knows it, but everybody knows it. It wasn't just when they were coming after me. They *always* go to Nox."

"She's like a drug," said Ram Odin. "When things made them upset, they'd go to Nox and she helped them feel better. When they were calmed down, they made better decisions. They all knew it, even if they didn't know it."

"You don't know Nox."

"But Ramex did. And he told me. She's not the only one. She's the other direction that human evolution took in Ramfold. We needed timeshapers so we paid more attention to you. But I had Ramex take you to a village that had Nox. A soother. Because you and Umbo were very likely to cause some crazy things to happen. And with Nox around, things couldn't go too wrong."

"And the other wallfolds—did they develop people like Nox?"

"I thought you wanted to form your own opinions."

Rigg rolled his eyes. "So you'll be my grandfather. That doesn't explain my face."

"It puts you under an old man's protection. Instead of coming in as a lone monster, you come in as an old man's strange grandson. That solves one problem, but not the big one."

"That we'll still be strangers wherever we go." Rigg heard himself saying "we" and he knew in that moment that he had already decided to bring Ram Odin along. Because it really would be impossible to do this on his own. Oh, he could visit wallfolds alone, and observe people from a distance, but what would he really know about them without hearing them talk? Without seeing how they live? And with this mask on his head, he couldn't get close enough. He hadn't thought that through, and Ram Odin had, and so Ram Odin was going to get his way because his way was better.

"We have to have a reason for traveling," said Ram Odin. "Or they'll think we're criminals, or escapees, or wild men, or refugees, or whatever else sets people to wandering. Where did you want to go first?"

"Yinfold," said Rigg.

"Go to the farthest and work your way back. Makes sense."

"When we're traveling in Yinfold, what's our story?"

"Depends on *where* in Yinfold. It's a big place. There are only nineteen wallfolds on two very large continents. Each one is as big as—well, you don't know Earth, so the comparison—"

"I studied maps and globes of Earth when we were in Odinfold," said Rigg. "We all did."

"Each of our wallfolds here is the size of Europe from Poland on westward. The size of India. Han China. I once divided the land masses of Earth into nineteen roughly equal parts and in some of those parts, there was an amazing amount of history. Great empires rising and falling."

"But not in all."

"Well, some of them were desert wastelands. Either very cold deserts, or very hot ones. But we have no great deserts in Garden. Only little ones."

"So all the wallfolds are habitable."

"When I plotted out where each starship should make landfall, I made sure that every one of them included plenty of well-watered arable land."

"I get it. Each wallfold is huge and there's a lot of variation within them."

"More than you know. And also less. But no, I'll let you find out."

Rigg shook his head. "If you're already dropping hints . . ."

"Do you have any idea how long it's been, with no other human to talk to?"

"You have the expendables. I know from experience that they can be lively conversationalists."

"Walking, talking databanks," said Ram Odin. "Not *people*."

"So in Yinfold, what's our reason for wandering?"

"They have a lot of traveling healers and soothsayers. People who tell fortunes and then move on before anyone can tell whether their prophecies come true."

"You're not going to have me time-shift and come back with true answers, are you?"

"It wouldn't even work, because foreknowledge would change their behavior so it wouldn't come true after all, likely as not," said Ram Odin. "But I'm thinking we make up a whole new category. Something that will actually work, but something they've never seen before."

Even though Yinfold was settled everywhere, there was no trouble finding an uninhabited place to set down the flyer, even quite near to what passed for a city there. Rigg thought of Aressa Sessamo, built up out of a swamp in a river delta. Nearly empty watery land all around it, and yet what land there was, incredibly fertile with the silt of millennia of river floods. Water to carry boats and therefore cargos for trade. A huge natural moat for defense. But it still hadn't kept out the horse warriors of the Sessamoto.

"This is good land," said Rigg. "Why is it empty?"

"Good land, bad land," said Ram Odin. "People gather where other people are, so they can mate readily. That leaves lots of empty places where people can go when they can't stand the place they're in, or something goes wrong and they have to leave. A place is settled for five thousand years, and then for the next five thousand years, nobody goes near the place, and yet it's the same place."

73

"There used to be a lot of settlement above Upsheer," said Rigg. "That's why they kept building bridges over the falls. But nobody lives there now."

"They'll go there again," said Ram Odin. "Ship, where we've just parked the flyer—has this ever been settled land?"

"Three different villages," said the computer voice in the flyer. "And farmland for twenty percent of the time. Usually, though, it's lightly wooded, sharply cut terrain, because of the ravines."

"See how much you've already learned about Yinfold?" said Ram Odin.

The first morning, Ram Odin put on a nondescript robe. "I have to go alone and get clothing for you."

"Wearing that?"

"Trousers never came into fashion here. This robe is really from Untungfold, so it'll look exotic here. But mostly it looks like money, and that's the impression I need to give here in town while I buy clothes for you."

"And then I'll go with you into town?"

"Town? Why would you go into town? No, I'm getting us clothes to travel through the hamlets eight hundred kilometers from here."

"Fashions from *here* will look right that far away?"

"We're strangers," said Ram Odin. "Travelers. We *have* to be dressed exotically. But it has to be clothing that won't look *too* strange to any Yinfolder. Please trust me. I've made visits like this before. A lot more often when I was younger and still thought . . ."

"Still thought the differences between places would matter," Rigg said, completing the sentence for him.

"Still thought," Ram Odin replied sternly, "that I would learn something useful from seeing for myself. The differences *do* matter. The differences are the best and most important thing about Garden."

"Go get me my clothes," said Rigg.

Because he had given up on getting a completely unbiased view, Rigg read as much as he could about Yinfold while Ram Odin was gone. Hundreds of small kingdoms and principalities and duchies and counties and free cities, sometimes coming together into something like nations but mostly not. Some major language groups but so much change over the millennia, and so many holdovers from once-widespread languages, that the language map of Yinfold was chaotic. For interest's sake, Rigg brought up the language map of Ramfold and found that while it used to be the same there, the few centuries of Sessamid rule had already caused hundreds of languages to die out, especially near the river, to be replaced by the common speech. All very fascinating and yet also predictable. A quick scan of the other wallfolds showed similar language maps and language histories, similar political maps with small political units rising and falling, sometimes coalescing but then collapsing back into chaos again.

Like watching the seashore, thought Rigg. Like sitting on the beach at the gathering place in Larfold and watching the waves, never exactly the same, but never all that different, either. Like watching flames, dancing patterns of red and yellow heat, always shifting, never changing till the fire died.

What did the Visitors see in each of these wallfolds, with their too-brief visits? Of course, they were able to copy all the data from the ships' computers and the satellites and the expendables, so they had plenty of history—all these maps—to study on the way home to Earth, and plenty to discuss afterward.

But somehow what they saw made them send the Destroyers to wipe out all human life on Garden. Something here made us worthy of death, in their eyes.

Ram Odin came back, not with robes, but with tunics and belts and overcoats. "The weather's warm but we still wear the coats because we'll need them later in the year. It's what unwealthy travelers do, because they don't want to keep buying new coats every year."

"I'm looking for the underwear," said Rigg.

"Are you planning to undress in front of the locals?"

"Shouldn't I be authentic, just in case?"

"In that case, what's underwear? Only women wear it, and only now and then."

Rigg felt the fabric. "Ah. Not woolen. It's cotton."

"So you don't need a protective layer," said Ram Odin. "Put it on, grandson of mine."

"It's awfully clean and new."

"So maybe they'll think we must be pretty good at our work, to earn enough to buy new clothes."

"I want to see the town," said Rigg. "Just because you tell me they're all alike . . ."

"Suit yourself," said Ram Odin.

So they spent the rest of the day in town. Rigg forgot the

name almost as soon as he heard it, because it didn't matter. It was so much smaller and grubbier than O, the city he knew best, that he lost interest almost at once. He knew that was cultural chauvinism and that he had to avoid such thoughts. And it wasn't *that* small. It had three large market squares and they were bustling. But the merchandise wasn't terribly different—Rigg knew the use of every object that he saw for sale—and while the flavors of the foods on offer were spiced differently from any fashion he had tasted in his travels in Ramfold, they were based on familiar ingredients.

When he commented on this, Ram Odin chuckled. "A faulty perception, Rigg. They've had ten thousand years to breed all kinds of different fruits and vegetables and to reshape the food animals, too. About a thousand years ago they started breeding rodents to eat. They've got pig-sized rats now, about thirty varieties, and you just ate a stew blending two kinds."

"Very tender," said Rigg. "Huge rats? No wonder the Visitors blow Garden to smithereens."

"They just burn off the surface," said Ram Odin. "Hard to smither a planet."

The flyer carried them that night to the place Ram Odin had chosen to begin their experience as itinerants. They slept in the self-adjusting beds of the flyer and it occurred to Rigg that people from Ram Odin's world all slept on beds like that, not the rough places Rigg had grown up sleeping. Or maybe they didn't. Maybe such beds were only for the elite, but the elite were the ones who traveled in space so they demanded beds like this. Was this Ram Odin's whole life? In beds that shaped themselves to fit you?

Yet he came here to make a world—nineteen worlds, as it turned out—where people slept on straw, or on the ground, or on a hundred other kinds of bed. Worlds where people kept reinventing everything, but still did the same human tasks. The same animal tasks. Eating, drinking, defecating, urinating, reproducing, sleeping, finding or making food, finding or making shelter, and finally dying. Animal life, with clothing. Animal life, with better explanations for what we do.

All the animals Rigg had trapped and killed and skinned during his years with Father, Rigg had known they were his kin. That they, too, were only hungry or cold, libidinous or sleepy, seeking a way to satisfy whatever need their body made first priority. I used that against them, to lay traps for them because they weren't clever enough to foresee their danger.

That's all we are—animals who are better at telling the future, better at understanding causality in the past. We see how things got how they are, or guess at it, and use that information to make better choices for the future. Not *good* choices, just better ones than the other animals.

He thought of how he made traps of string and sticks and realized: Brains and fingers, that's what we have.

But then he felt the mattress under him, and the light sheet over him, and thought: Brains and fingers have wrought marvels in these worlds.

They woke and dressed in their tunics and strapped on their walking sandals and made small packs out of the other things Ram Odin had bought—a pot, a ladle, a spoon, two blankets, needles and thread, rope and string, some cheese, some crusty bread, a bit of dried meat—of which rodent Rigg didn't bother to ask. They hitched the packs onto their shoulders. They weren't that heavy, but Rigg could tell right away that he would hate the way the pot bounced against his back when he walked. But he also knew that in time he'd get used to it. Or find a way to repack so that the pot didn't shift so much with each step.

From the flyer it was a two-hour walk to get to a road. Ram Odin called it a road. He called it the King's Highway, in fact, but it was barely a track.

"Ah, but you can see it clearly, and it goes from the Wall in the northwest to the Wall in the southeast. We're a hundred kilometers from the northwest Wall, so it's only a track here. Farther on, it's wide enough for two coaches to pass. In two cities, it's paved and four carriages wide."

They walked along the track till, coming over a rise no different from the past few rises, they saw a cluster of houses and wide, well-cultivated fields. A few of the houses were rather substantial, with two stories; one had three. From the crest of the rise, they could see that there was another, larger village in the shimmering distance. They were in a wide valley now, and a river twisted its way through the level ground. Rigg saw no boats on it.

"No point in boats here," said Ram Odin. "There are falls not far behind us, and falls again after the lake a few dozen kilometers on. They're not much for fish."

"Humans need fish."

"They grow the substitute vegetables," said Ram Odin. "And by the way, let's start speaking this language." He switched to the one they had heard on the streets of the town the day before.

"They speak that here?" asked Rigg, in that language.

"Not at all, but they speak it somewhere in Yinfold and so if someone is hiding in the brush along the edges of the fields, they'll hear us using a language from this wallfold."

Sure enough, there were soon children darting out of cover and running down the track ahead of them. "I guess we don't look too threatening," said Ram Odin. "If the children are willing to run openly down the road ahead of us."

"But they still ran."

"To give news of our coming," said Ram Odin. "We're the most exciting thing in days, I'll wager."

Rigg remembered life in Fall Ford. The children there noticed the arrival of strangers, but didn't run to tell. That's because strangers came several times a week and always went to Nox's boardinghouse for a meal and news and perhaps a bed. Then they would go up the stair beside the falls into Upsheer Forest, or along the road—much more of a road than this King's Highway— that ran east and west below the face of Upsheer Cliff, to the other towns that lived in its shadow. He had thought Fall Ford an isolated, sleepy place, but now he saw it as a hub of traffic, compared to this.

Fall Ford was also five times as big. More houses. More tradesmen's shops. Rigg wondered if they thought of themselves as a village or a town? There was an open square in the middle that might be a weekly market. Or might not. It could simply be the place where they hanged strangers.

Ram Odin was making it a point to nod—but not smile— at the faces peering out of windows. "These aren't smiley folk,"

Ram Odin explained. "In this region, a smile means you're a liar."

Rigg noticed that people weren't peering through cracks in curtains. They were fully visible in open windows. They returned Ram Odin's solemn nod, some so slightly as to hardly be visible, some sharply, clearly, as if putting a bit of punctuation at the end of an unspoken sentence.

People must have gone out back doors and made their way to the square, because as Ram Odin and Rigg stepped into the open space, so did about twenty people, mostly adult men but some women, coming from behind houses on both sides, but only one man and one woman from the far side, where they hadn't walked.

"Good morning," said Ram Odin, glancing at the sun to be sure it wasn't yet past noon. "We're hoping to earn a bit of bread and ale in this place, if you find us worthy. And if you have enough work for us, a place to pass the night."

"That's what *you* want," said the man who had come from the far side of the square. "Why do *we* want *you*?" Rigg figured him to be the mayor or headman. He seemed to have authority. Or at least none of the locals thought it out of place that he spoke first.

"What's wrong with the young one?" asked a woman.

"Two questions deserving of fair answers. May I answer the second one first, seeing how you're all looking so curious at my grandson here?"

Ram Odin directed his question at the mayor, who gave him one of those sharp nods. It was an answer.

"The boy was a baby, not three days old, when the house caught fire. It was a thatchy roof and the whole thing was ablaze at once. Inside the house, too. My son was screaming in pain, but the mother, my daughter-in-law, she was from a strange folk. My son brought her into the village from afar, and she knew a blessing, I think, because she came to the window and she was also aflame, but the baby wasn't burning, not a lick. She dropped him out the window. Nobody was close enough to catch him, the house was so hot afire, but the baby didn't burn even though she did. My son screaming, but her making never a sound."

So Ram Odin was a storyteller. Rigg saw how the people were spellbound. He also heard how Ram Odin was speaking the local language perfectly, but he was bending the vowels to be a little like the language in the town where they spent yesterday. So he sounded a little foreign, but they could understand every word.

"When the ruin of the house cooled enough to come close, I picked up the baby. Not burnt at all, not even the blanket he was wrapped in. Whatever she was, the boy's mother was powerful. Not powerful enough to put out the fire, but powerful enough to spare his life."

"If he didn't burn, what's wrong with his face?" asked the same woman as before.

"She kept the flame off him, but not the heat. Couldn't kill him, but his face melted. I tried to push it back into place as best I could, but you can see I'm no master with clay. Did my best and the boy's used to it, an't you, boy?"

Rigg nodded.

"Can't talk?" asked the mayor.

"Now it's three questions, and me barely finished with the first," said Ram Odin. "The boy can talk all right. But he's shy and he'd rather talk to me, mostly, when meeting strange folk."

There was a general recoiling at that, some murmurs.

"Oh, now, don't take me amiss," said Ram Odin. "I know that in this place, *we're* the strange folk. But you're strange to us, don't you see, just as we're strange to you. Only we come here of our own choice, so we mean nothing wrong by it. We hope to serve you, and that brings me to the original question, the first question, Question Prime, the question of questions."

"What are you good for that we should feed you?" asked the mayor again.

"Well, I'm not good for much. Old but still strong for my age, but that says little. It's the boy, you see. A bit of the mother's blood in him. Never got no training and he don't know no spells, so you've nought to fear from him. But he's got him a way of finding lost things."

"What things?" demanded the mayor.

"Well, he don't just happen to find them and then go looking for the owner," said Ram Odin. "You have to tell him what you lost, and then he finds it, if it's to be found, or tells you what's become of it, if he can't lay hands on it. Doesn't always work, only about half the time, but here's what I offer. You give us the meal for trying, and the bed for succeeding."

"It's a way to get a meal for nothing," said the mayor dismissively.

"If you don't even want us to try, we've still got a bit of cheese and bread and meat from yesterday, and we'll leave right now. I saw another hamlet off in the distance."

"That's Stinkville Manor," said a half-grown lad, and people laughed.

"Don't like them much," said the mayor. "They do everything wrong."

"Then I suppose they're likelier to have lost things so they'll have more need of us." Ram Odin clapped his hand on Rigg's shoulder. "This is a lucky place, Rigg. They never lost anything they need to find." He started walking across the square.

But the story had made an impression and most folk seemed disappointed. Then a man, a tall man, stepped into their way. "I lost a thing," he said.

The mayor looked annoyed but didn't try to stop the man from talking.

"I went to town a few year back," he said. "Bought my wife five brass buttons with a bird etched into them, every single one. She sewed them into the back of her blouse, but now one's gone missing."

"Must be I bent over and it popped off, that's all," said his wife, who seemed reluctant to step forward.

"Cost me a bit," said the man. "I'd like that button back."

"That's not hard, is it?" Ram Odin asked Rigg.

Rigg had already marked the woman's path. Could see which buildings in town she had visited most, and most recently. He already had a good guess where the button was, and why she didn't want it looked for. But she couldn't admit that she didn't want it found.

"Where was she when they was last sure the button was on the blouse?" Rigg asked softly. He pitched his voice so only Ram Odin and the people nearest them could hear, but that meant *somebody* could hear him, so he tried to do the same thing with his vowels that Ram Odin had done. So they might seem to come from the same place.

"How can I remember?" the woman said. "I didn't even notice it was gone, till Bak noticed it."

"But you would have known when you put it on, so you know the day," said an older woman. Might it be her mother? From the way the women looked at each other, Rigg thought it was likely. And yes, sure enough their paths converged some years ago at another house. And that was where Bak's wife's path began.

"May I know your name?" asked Rigg.

"What do you need names for? No names!" said the mayor. "Ain't going to have no witchery on folk here!"

"Might help me find the button," Rigg murmured, "but it don't matter."

"Her name's Jobo," said Bak. "Everybody knows that."

The mayor glared at him, but Bak only had eyes for Rigg.

"She had it at breakfast five days ago," said Bak. "And at supper she didn't. Don't know where she went all day because we all was out haying. Second day of haying."

"I didn't feel well," said Jobo. "I stayed home to rest."

"Then he'll find the button in our house," said Bak to her gently.

To Rigg, it sounded as if he loved her. Very tender to her. But it also sounded as if he was going to find out about that button. Five days ago, and it still troubled him.

"You already looked?" asked Ram Odin.

"Turned the place upside down and shook it," said Bak. Several people laughed. The man had a way with words and people liked him. "But buttons can get themselves into places. I know how that is. Button flies off, goes into a place and won't come out."

It dawned on Rigg that the mayor might be the bossy one, and maybe the richest one. But if people had their pick, they liked Bak more than they liked the mayor, and the mayor knew it. If Bak wanted these strangers to look for that button, the mayor knew better than to try to interfere.

And sure enough, the mayor shook his head. "They won't find it cause there's no such thing as magical finding, but if you want to feed them you do it."

Since that was clearly what Bak already meant to do, all the mayor did was turn Bak's intention into the mayor's command. And everybody knew it. The mayor walked away and Bak reached out a hand to them.

"Come to my house. Sit at my table for the noonday meal. That's where I last saw the button on her blouse, if that's a help to you. And you'll see how she does in the kitchen, fixing up the food, if that helps you."

"Oh, so I have to do the work?" asked Jobo. "My button, my loss, but I have to fix up their noonses?"

"I know where the bread is," said Bak, "and I can boil eggs."

"I don't want you cooking in my kitchen!" snapped Jobo. "I married the clumsiest oaf in the village, and I'm not having you breaking eggs all over everything."

"Fixing to boil them is all," said Bak mildly.

But Rigg saw how the people didn't much like her, and liked him fine. Her snapping at him was a shame to herself, but not to Bak, because clearly none of the folk thought he deserved it. They kept their silence though. It was between woman and man, how they talked to each other.

Rigg and Ram Odin followed to a good-sized house. Not a poor family. It was a house they had passed. Rigg could see Jobo's path going in and out, as also Bak's. And children, but they must be grown because the paths went away and didn't come back.

"Children still living here?" asked Ram Odin. "Big house like this."

"My parents had seven that lived," said Bak. "We had two. The boy went off to seek his fortune, poor lad, and the girl married out. I fear they didn't like it here."

Rigg wondered if it was marital squabbling that drove them away, or simply wanderlust. Or, in the girl's case, maybe love.

"Think the boy found it?" asked Ram Odin. "His fortune?"

"If he has, he didn't come back yet to share it," said Bak.

His wife made a glottal stop to show exasperation. "He's only two years gone," she said to him.

"A year to get a fortune, a year to waste it, and then come home," said Bak. "I expect him any day."

"I'm going to see our daughter one of these days," said Jobo. "Her husband writes twice a year."

"She's afar off?" asked Rigg.

"As far as an honest girl could go," said Jobo mournfully. "Three villages yonder." She pointed toward the south. Apparently the fourth village that direction would only lure dishonest girls. Ram Odin had been right. Their world was small.

During lunch, Ram Odin kept them entertained with lies

about life on the road. Maybe some of the stories were from Ram Odin's earlier life, or maybe they were well-known tales from Earth. They were all new to Rigg, but he also didn't care, because he was tracing all Jobo's movements.

In the old days, he could only *see* paths, until Umbo slowed down time—or sped up his perceptions, they had never really decided about that. But "seeing paths" wasn't the right term, because he could do it with his eyes closed, and could examine the paths behind him, or beyond walls.

Now, with the facemask, he could speed up his own perceptions, with more precision than was possible with Umbo's help. The paths were never truly paths now, if he looked at them aright, but a continuous blurred shape of the person moving about. And if he sped himself up more, the blurs became the person clearly doing whatever it was he did at that hour, of that day, in that place.

So he knew that as soon as the hamlet was emptied out, Jobo slipped along behind the houses till she came to the mayor's house, and went in through the back door. She found the mayor waiting for her in his own upstairs bedroom—she seemed to know the way—and that was where all her buttons popped off in his eagerness. Afterward, she stayed to sew them all back on again, but there were only four. The mayor was all over that room, trying to find where the fifth button had bounced.

Rigg closed his eyes and slowed things down—or sped himself up—even more. Now they barely moved, but he could see the buttons pop off one by one. The ones they found easily. And that fifth one. It took a bounce under the wardrobe and must have lodged on some slat or in some corner because it didn't hit the floor again. Looking under the wardrobe wouldn't help. Even sliding it out, unless you tipped it or hit it to dislodge the button.

Well, Bak's worst suspicions were certainly confirmed, and if Rigg found the button in the mayor's house—well, that would only be possible if the mayor let him in.

But if I make for his house, he'll bar me from it. That won't help—Bak will only be all the more certain that his wife and the mayor were up to something.

Ram Odin must have guessed as much as Rigg now knew, because he was telling the story of a woman caught in adultery who had to wear a red letter on her clothing, always, the first letter of "adultery" in the language of the place, only when she died, the letter was also a scar on her chest, as if the letter had burned its way into her heart.

"Burning is right," said Bak. "A woman who does that sin when she's married and a mother, she's burning down her own house."

"It's a terrible thing and nobody does it anymore," said Jobo hotly.

"Only ten years since it was done."

"In Stinkville, not here," said Jobo.

"Well, that's why they burned her up in her own house in Stinkville, and not here."

"Is Stinkville really the name of the place?" asked Rigg. Thinking, meanwhile, *That's* your punishment for adultery? To burn down the house with the woman inside?

"Well *they* don't call it that," said Jobo. "And they have a choice name for us, too, you may be sure."

"What do *you* call this hamlet?" asked Rigg.

"Not everything has a name," said Bak.

"We call it home," said Jobo. "And I hate talk about evil old customs like house burning."

"It always made a kind of sense to me," said Bak. "His wife sleeps with another man, the husband's house is already destroyed and his wife is already dead to him. Burning down the house just makes it real to everybody."

"They don't burn down the house around adulterous *men*."

Bak merely looked puzzled. "Why would they? He's not going to get pregnant with another bird's egg!"

"You hear how he quotes foolish old sayings!" said Jobo hotly. "Everybody thinks he's so nice, but he's got a cold temper, cold but deep and it never stops till he's satisfied."

She was afraid of him. He bore her tongue well enough, but if he thought he had suffered real injury, he'd seek justice. That's what she feared, and that was what she was trying to impress on Rigg. Just in case he actually was a finder.

Rigg knew he couldn't find the button or the consequences would be terrible. Or at least he couldn't openly find it where it was.

"After lunch, can I lie down and let the finding happen?" asked Rigg.

"He needs to be all alone, except for me," said Ram Odin.

Including you, you old weasel, thought Rigg. But he didn't dare to contradict him—if they ever disputed each other's story, it would cast doubt upon all.

So a half hour later, they were shut up together in a room

with a nice bed, by local standards, and Rigg explained in a soft voice where the button was.

"Don't want to see this house burn down," said Ram Odin.

"Not going to," said Rigg. "I'll get the button and find it somewhere else. Excuse me for a minute."

He took off his sandals—they were noisy on the wood floors—and jumped back in time to the middle of the night. Sure enough, there was Jobo asleep in the bed, but not Bak. He must be sleeping somewhere else in the house.

Rigg crept softly from the room, out of the house—through an open window so he didn't have to open the door—and along behind houses, following the same path that Jobo had used on haying day. He got up right behind the mayor's house and then latched on to Jobo's path as she left on that day. In an instant it was daytime, and Jobo was rushing away, the gap in her blouse showing skin between the bottom button and the three at the top. She had closed the door carefully, but Rigg knew the mayor would soon give up his continuing button search. Sure enough, the front door of the house soon opened and the mayor went out that way.

Now Rigg could go in and find the button. The house was empty and there was no one to hear him open the door and go up the stairs.

He felt around under the wardrobe. He could feel the slats underneath and knew that the button must be resting atop one of them. But he couldn't twist his hand around to find it.

Can't go tipping the wardrobe. What if it fell over? It's a heavy piece of furniture.

So Rigg sighed and watched the scene from haying day four times, until he knew exactly where the button bounced. Then he positioned his hand to catch the button and jumped back about an hour to the exact moment—got it!—and shifted right back to when the house was empty. He was there so fleetingly, thanks to the quick reflexes that the facemask gave him, that even if the mayor's mind hadn't been on other things, he would only have seen him for an eyeblink. And Jobo's back was to him.

Holding the button in his hand, Rigg wondered, not for the first time, if the reason the button never made a sound and came to rest on the floor under the wardrobe was that Rigg had caught it. But he hadn't caught it until it already turned up missing.

That was where thinking about the changes they made always led—to the edge of paradoxical madness. They had long since agreed that nothing was circular. Things couldn't cause themselves. So the button really *had* been lodged up there, setting in motion this entire dilemma, and now it *wasn't* there, but only because Rigg, at the end of the chain of events, had gone back to fetch it.

He went out the back door, closed it carefully, and then jumped back to the night he arrived at the mayor's house. Now, in dark of night, he walked to the main street and followed the many paths out beyond the town toward the hayfields. He knew that because that's where everyone's paths had gone on haying day. He picked a stone beside the track and pushed the button under it so it wasn't visible at all, but still might believably have bounced there.

Then he walked back to Bak's and Jobo's house, climbed in the window, and went back up to Jobo's room. On the way he saw that Bak was sleeping in one of the children's bedrooms. His son's bedroom. The door was closed; Rigg saw him only by his path. But he could see, with his path-sense, that Bak slept little. Could see him lying there staring at the ceiling. Maybe not right now, but for long hours of the night, tonight and the other nights since the button was missed and he left Jobo's bed.

And there was Jobo, faithless woman. Rigg, with his knowledge of all people's paths, knew well enough how common, and how uncommon, such actions were. More common in the city, less common in small villages, where everyone was known and it was hard to do anything unseen. It really took some ingenuity for Jobo and the mayor to betray their spouses here. And it had only happened twice, two months apart—Rigg knew that. Perhaps after this, never again.

Rigg jumped forward to the time right after he left Ram Odin.

"Got it?" Ram Odin asked.

"Moved it to where I'm going to find it," said Rigg. "Took a bit of maneuvering."

"So you're going to help the conspirators get away with it," said Ram Odin.

"This time."

"I'm glad you confined yourself to retrieving the button," said Ram Odin.

"What else could I have done?"

"You could have spooked her so she ran away before she got to his house," said Ram Odin. "You could have gone back to the first time they caught each other's eye and plotted this sort of thing."

"Should I have?"

"If you did, we'd have a devil of a time explaining what we're doing in this room, where no one invited us because nobody lost a button."

"If I had Umbo's talent," said Rigg, "I could have appeared to us on the road and warned us away from this village."

"I thought the facemask let you do everything Umbo does," said Ram Odin.

"No," said Rigg. "Not even close. He can speed up his own perceptions, so time seems to go slower, *and* he can speed up other people's. He did that to me—that's how I first learned that all these paths were really people. The facemask does it for me now—but it can't speed up anybody else's perceptions. And that business with just appearing to people? That's Umbo. I latch on to a person's path and there I am. He *sends* a message somehow. He's the really powerful one, if he only learned to master it, but who can help him? What he does, nobody else does."

"But once he gives a warning, doesn't he have to be sure to give that same warning when he gets to that point in the future?" asked Ram.

"Hasn't an expendable explained that to you?" asked Rigg. "Because of Umbo's warning, we never *get* to that point in the future. It doesn't exist. Everything that happened down that road— the network of cause and effect—it's gone. It never happens."

"So he never sends the message," said Ram Odin, shaking his head.

"I remember thinking the same way," said Rigg. "But what

we've learned by experience is that an effect can't undo its own cause. So the old future just disappears. Never happens. *And* I can never time-shift to a lost time because it leaves no paths in *our* past."

"So why didn't you just disappear when you warned yourself— or I should say, warned Noxon?"

"Because I didn't *warn* Noxon. I'm not Umbo. I couldn't just appear, I *came*. The moment I changed the course of events, Noxon would no longer become the me who had killed you. But that wouldn't erase *me*—because *I* had caused the change in Noxon's path, so I had to remain."

"I hope I'm not the only one to whom this makes no sense."

"It's causality. Conservation of causality. Umbo's messages can cause things in the past to change in such a way that it destroys the future in which he sends those messages. Like the messages from the Odinfold time-senders—because they're sending an object, not going themselves. But a shifter like me and Noxon and Umbo, too, when he actually travels—I can't *go* to the past and change it and destroy myself, because *I* am the causer, still in that past, persisting into the change I made. It makes sense, really."

"No, it doesn't," said Ram Odin. "But if you think you understand it, that's good enough for me."

They rested a little while on the lumpy bed—the master bed of the house, the *best* bed, thought Rigg—long enough to make it convincing. Then they came back out of the room. "I know where the button is," said Rigg. "Let's go get it."

Jobo looked like she was barely containing her terror, but at this point she dared say nothing. Still, Rigg wasn't cruel. "You must have forgotten when you went out toward the hayers. I don't know if you were feeling better and thought to join them, and then changed your mind, or maybe you were just going to see if they were coming back."

"I never went out of the house," said Jobo, too fervently.

"You were ill," said Ram Odin. "You might not remember. It might seem to you to be part of a dream. But if Rigg says he knows where it is, then he knows."

The fear drained from her face, but what replaced it was not relief, but the same contempt she showed when she was sniping at Bak. She thinks I'm a fraud, thought Rigg. Well, let her think that. "Let's go get it," said Rigg. "It has to be you that finds it."

"Why me?" asked Jobo. "I don't think I went out there, so why should I go looking where I never was?"

"We learned a good time ago," said Ram Odin, "that if Rigg's the one as picks up whatever was lost, then folks will whisper that he had it all along, that he stole it in the first place. So he won't come near it. You'll find it."

"I won't."

"But not for lack of trying," said Bak softly. "You *will* try, because it's very important to find that button. I paid good money for it in town. Because my wife should have brass buttons instead of common wooden ones."

"I should never have nagged you for those foolish buttons."

"They were the desire of your heart. And you were proud of them," said Bak. "I try to get you your heart's desire, when it's within my reach."

And in those words Rigg heard a lifetime's tragedy. He didn't know what it was, not without looking. But there was something Jobo had longed for that Bak could not obtain for her. More children than two, perhaps? Or something else unguessed. Rigg could follow the paths back and see the whole story, but he'd found out enough of their secrets for now.

The moment they came out of the house together, the four of them, other people came out of their houses. They were quiet in this hamlet — Rigg didn't hear anyone shouting, though he did see children scampering a bit in the back way behind the houses. But it was pretty much the whole town following them, he could see by the paths. Only a few stay-at-homes — mothers with babies, old people sleeping in the middle of the day. The fieldwork of this place was over for the year, but it was not yet winter. They had been working at the preparatory tasks — cheesing, smoking meat, sausaging, repairing harnesses, making rope, remaking loose chairs, rehanging doors with a catch in them. Whatever work there was, that they could do for themselves, they had been doing. But they set it aside for this. For Jobo's missing button. And Rigg wondered how many of them were coming along just for curiosity, to see if Rigg and Ram Odin were fakes, and how many because they knew perfectly well, or guessed rightly enough, where that button had been lost, and wanted to see if there'd be a housefire today.

Rigg made a show of groping through the air with his eyes closed, though of course he could see his own path from the night before and knew exactly where the button was. He also knew that no other path led near the place since he had put it

97

there, so no one had found it or moved it since then.

Suddenly his eyes popped open, and he whirled and pointed to the exact point where he could see his own path bending over the stone. "There," he said. "It bounced and lodged itself under a stone about this big."

"Oh, really," said Jobo.

"Will you look, or should I?" asked Bak softly. "I think the boy is telling the truth, or he thinks he is. Don't you hope he's right? Wouldn't it be good to find that button here in the road?"

Jobo set her lips and marched to the place. She saw the rock—it was the only one "about this big" at that spot. Instead of bending, she only nudged it over with her foot.

Then she cried out and bent over, reaching for the button.

And then, because sometimes the universe conspired to make things work out perfectly, the wooden button she had sewn into the place of the missing brass one popped right off the blouse. Because she had bent over so far. Popped right off.

Jobo cried out and held up the button for all to see. Bak, though, moved behind his wife and carefully gathered the edges of the blouse together so no skin showed. Rigg had never seen a man so relieved and happy.

"I must have—I thought it was a dream," said Jobo. "Like you said, I thought I was only dreaming that I came to see if you were coming back, only you weren't, and then I felt very faint and I bent over all the way, to hang my head and get blood back into it, and that's when it must have popped off. Oh, how could I have thought it was only a dream, when here's the button to prove that it was real!"

Everyone was listening to her in her rapture, watching Bak in his joy. But Rigg had already seen how Ram Odin had moved over to stand beside the mayor and murmur something softly that no one else could hear.

The mayor heard, and gave a short sharp nod, and then moved away to join the crowd. Ram Odin came back to Rigg.

"You said to him . . ." Rigg prompted.

"I said, 'We saved you this time, but if you ever do it again, I promise you that two houses will burn.'"

"Which would happen how?"

"That's for him to worry about. To watch his own wife and maybe be a little more attentive to her. Or maybe he fears the second house would be some other mistress he's taken in this village. I have no idea. But it sounded very menacing and fine, didn't it?"

"So what have we learned here? Burning up adulterous women in their own house? This children's news service? The way the best man in town is *not* the mayor, but everyone knows which one is best and the mayor can't touch him?"

"All of that," said Ram Odin, "and we still have supper tonight, and a bed to sleep in. Though I imagine we'll be downstairs now in the boy's and girl's bedrooms, because I think that Bak will be in Jobo's bed again."

"How did you know?"

"I saw that the boy's bed had been slept in, and the girl's not, and Jobo's bed in the room with us was the only one big enough for two. It isn't calculus. It's barely arithmetic."

"So you see paths too."

"Of a kind. In my way."

And now the attention turned back to them, and suddenly people were crowding around them. But oddly enough, nobody had anything to find, except a child who had buried a favorite doll, and Rigg easily pointed to the place under a shade tree where the child had knelt for a time a year ago. The doll was there, half-rotted away, but now the children had far more reason to rejoice than over a brass button. Finder of Lost Toys! How his fame would spread.

CHAPTER 6

Undoings

Umbo listened to Loaf and Leaky as they planned the journey to get Leaky a facemask of her very own. He had misgivings, but there was no point in arguing with them. They were going to go, and they needed Umbo because the way Rigg set up the rules, they could only go through the Wall if two of them were together. Two, that is, of the original party, which had included Umbo and Loaf, but not Leaky.

"The good thing about a journey to the Wall right now," said Loaf, "is that nobody's looking for us yet."

"I'm still not used to this," said Leaky. "You say half the kingdom is looking for you, because you escaped from this General Citizen and then helped the queen's daughter and Rigg escape from the People's Revolutionary Council, but it hasn't happened *yet*."

It was only then that Umbo realized that their journey might not be such an easy thing. "I know another thing that hasn't happened yet," said Umbo.

"Your beard?" said Loaf.

"Rigg hasn't taken command of the ships yet. That won't happen for a year, almost. So if we go to the Wall now, the ships' computers won't know to let up on the Wall."

"What's a computer?" asked Leaky.

"If I understood it," said Loaf, "I'd tell you. Whatever it is, it talks but the voice comes out of nowhere, and if it feels like it, it tells you things you need to know. But not *enough* things you need to know."

"Did you hear me?" asked Umbo.

"I'm thinking about that," said Loaf. "And I think what we'll do is go to the Wall, and then you take us into the future, *after* the queen and General Citizen have left, and you'll take us through then. That's after Rigg's order, isn't it?"

"But I can't do that," said Umbo. "Go into the future."

"You do it all the time," said Loaf. "When we all went back to watch the battle between the bare humans and the facemasks, you took us all into the future."

"No," said Umbo. "I *stayed* in the future and brought you all back to me. I was the anchor."

"But when you went to the Visitors' ship, that was years in the future."

"And I didn't do that," said Umbo. "Param did. When she slices time, she can take us into the future very quickly. By thousands of tiny little skips. Then I brought us back to the past in one big leap. That's just what each of us can do."

"Rigg skips into the future, doesn't he?" asked Loaf.

"Noxon is trying to learn how," said Umbo. "And Rigg and Noxon have facemasks. So maybe they can do it, but I can't. And I think they can't, either, because Rigg has always gone into the past by connecting with somebody's path, and the paths are only in the past."

"So we can't go?" asked Leaky.

"I think we can," said Loaf. "I think Umbo just doesn't know all that he can do yet. I think where his time-shifting is concerned, he's like a baby who's become really good at crawling, but he still hasn't tried to get up on his hind legs and walk."

"I wish you were right," said Umbo.

"I think you should try it," said Loaf. "Go into the past, and then come right back to now, while now is still fresh in your mind. I'm not talking about going a year into the past or even a day. Go a minute into the past, then take two steps away and try to pop right back."

"Then there'd be two of me," said Umbo.

"Only for a minute," said Loaf.

"But even if you couldn't *jump* back to the present, you'd only have a minute to wait," said Leaky. "It makes so much sense."

"I have a better idea," said Umbo. "I have an errand to run that's only a few weeks ago. I'll go do that, and then either I'll live through those weeks and come back, or I'll *jump* back, but no matter how much time *I* spend, I'll be back before you know it."

Loaf looked at him suspiciously. "What errand? You're not going to go dig up the jewels again, are you?"

"It's not a prank. But I have some unfinished business back

in Fall Ford." The moment he mentioned his hometown, he knew it was a mistake.

"If you're planning to settle accounts with your father," said Loaf. "He's still bigger than you are. Well, maybe not. But leave well enough alone."

"Loaf," said Leaky. "He isn't going back to get even."

Umbo didn't want to discuss this anymore. "See you within a few hours."

As he said this, he heard Leaky finish her thought. "He's going back to save his brother's life after all."

Then Umbo was gone, so he didn't have to hear Loaf shout at him about how dangerous it was to try to do that. He knew it was dangerous. But he had to try.

Ironic that it was Leaky who remembered Kyokay's death, though she hardly knew Umbo, while Loaf, who had traveled with him for years, thought Umbo would go home for revenge. But maybe it wasn't about who knew Umbo better. Maybe it was just that Loaf was thinking of the kind of thing he himself might do—punish someone who had done wrong—while Leaky was better at remembering personal things, like how Kyokay had died right before Umbo's eyes.

Umbo jumped back easily enough to a time before he had left Fall Ford with Rigg. The real problem was that he was still in Leaky's Landing, and he had to get upriver. It had been a long hike to here, and that was with Rigg, a skilled trapper, providing food along the way.

On the other hand, Umbo had a little money now. Compared to then, in fact, he had a *lot* of money.

He was in the kitchen yard of Loaf's and Leaky's roadhouse and he took a moment to inspect his coins to make sure none of them were new—so new that they wouldn't even be minted for a few more years. He didn't need someone to accuse him of counterfeiting.

Then he heard the kitchen door open and he realized that Leaky would have no idea who he was. And if she saw his face and took him for a thief, she'd remember him when he and Rigg showed up a few months from now, and would never let them in.

Fortunately, he wasn't far from the fence, and it was no problem to vault over it. He didn't even drop his moneypurse or snag it on anything. All she could possibly have seen was his back. And since he was now at least a hand taller than he had been when Leaky first met him, she'd never connect the boy Umbo with the thief she surprised in the kitchen garden.

If it was Leaky. For all he knew, it was a patron staggering to the privy to void himself. But it would have been stupid to turn and look to see who it was, showing his face.

He walked between a couple of buildings to come out on the road, and as he did, he jumped another day back in time, so he could walk right past Loaf's and Leaky's roadhouse without fear of her seeing him and calling him a thief.

There were two boats docked at Leaky's Landing, but they were both heading downriver. That was all right. Umbo knew he had plenty of time to get upriver. He could wait.

As he waited, he thought through the dangers Loaf would surely have warned him of. Saving Kyokay would not be easy. If Umbo saved him by bodily preventing him from going up to the top of the falls, then Rigg wouldn't have needed to drop all his pelts to try to save the boy from falling, and therefore Umbo—younger Umbo—wouldn't have "seen" him push Kyokay from the cliff, and so Rigg wouldn't have been forced to leave town in a hurry, and Umbo certainly wouldn't have felt any need to go with him to make amends for having nearly gotten him mobbed, and . . .

A part of his mind insisted that none of that could possibly change, because—well, because it *hadn't*. But they had made plenty of changes before, and as best they understood the rules of how this sort of thing worked, whoever *made* the change continued to exist, even if his own past was obliterated. But this change would be Umbo's alone, so he was the only one who would be preserved.

It wasn't till the next day—only a few hours before Leaky, or someone else, would catch a glimpse of Umbo jumping over the fence—that a boat came upriver and tied up.

"Not going all the way to Fall Ford," said the pilot.

"How far then?" asked Umbo.

"Bear's Den Crossing," he said.

"Never heard of it," said Umbo.

"I have," said the pilot, looking irritated.

"Left bank or right?" asked Umbo.

"It's Bear's Den *Crossing*," said the pilot. "If you don't like which side of the river I tie up on, you can *cross* to the other side."

"Oh, you mean like you can *ford* the river at Fall Ford?" asked Umbo.

The pilot did know the river top to bottom, so he got the snide joke. Fall Ford hadn't had a usable ford in centuries, but nobody bothered to change the name. The pilot glowered. "Every smart remark just raises the price."

"Then I'll try to make it up to you by being useful on the trip," said Umbo.

The pilot looked him up and down, sizing him up. "Slender arms."

"I sure couldn't pole the boat alone," said Umbo. "But I know how to poke and push and lift a stick, and I also know how to sit the prow and watch for debris coming down and call a warning in plenty of time."

"So you've made the voyage before."

"Only once. Not enough to be an expert like you, sir," said Umbo, "but there were many days of work, and I worked hard all those days."

The pilot named a price, then, and promised some of it back if Umbo worked as he claimed. And that was that.

Except that for some reason, Umbo was reluctant to give his right name. "Ram Odin," he said, when the man asked. And there was a case to be made that whatever was done in this world, Ram Odin had a hand in it.

Umbo worked hard. It was a pleasure, and it kept his mind off of brooding about the impossibility of what he meant to try. Somehow he had to let Kyokay do everything he had done that got him killed, up to and including his fall off the cliff. There was no way that time-shifting could allow Umbo to catch him part-way down. But there were some things he might try.

The key was to find a path to the foot of the falls without

passing through Fall Ford itself, where, even though he was taller, he was bound to be recognized, to the confusion of all. But the road was on the right bank, along with Fall Ford. Umbo had never heard of any kind of road on the left bank, not paralleling the river. If he had Rigg's ability to see paths, then he could easily find paths through the thick forest. But he couldn't see paths. Couldn't fly, either. He might have a knife with the ship-controlling jewels in the hilt, but the Ramfold starship was a long way beyond Upsheer Cliff, and he didn't think that if he called for the flyer he'd get much of a response.

By the time they got to Bear's Den Crossing, he had earned the respect of the pilot and the other boatmen. He had eaten what they ate, and worked as hard as anyone, and made no mistakes. He even fended, by himself, one big water-soaked log that didn't become visible through the morning mist until it was almost too late to avoid a collision. Nobody would have blamed him for not seeing it, the mist was that thick. Instead they thanked him well for quick action and a perfect placement of the ten-foot fending pole.

So when it was time to settle up with the pilot, the man was better than his word. He gave him back his entire fare. "I was planning to hold back only the cost of what you ate," said the pilot, "but the morning you saved my boat, you earned your board. The only reason I'm not paying you a wage is that the owner only authorized me for three boatmen besides myself, and you make the fourth."

"I meant to pay and didn't expect anything back, sir," said Umbo. "I might have saved the boat, but that was my duty that morning, I think, and along with you and your crew and cargo, I also saved myself. But I thank you for being an upright man, and I take back anything I might have said disparaging about Bear's Den Crossing."

"You can disparage it all you like," said the pilot, smiling. "Won't make it any better or worse than it is. And as to your wish to get to Fall Ford, I can't say we're exactly close, but come morning, if you happen to be in the middle of the river, you'll catch a glimpse of Upsheer Cliff afar off to the south. It's still two days on the water, and a good deal more than that afoot, I dare say. But within sight of the cliff is not *very* far, I think."

"I think you're right, sir," said Umbo. "And now will you let me give you back this fenten, not as fare, but for you to buy a few rounds of ale for my crewmates, at a time you think it won't interfere with their duty?"

"I will let you do that indeed, and tonight is that night, and they'll raise a mug in your honor. I take it you don't mean to be there yourself, or you'd do the buying."

"My journey is long, and I'll be setting out today, there still being many hours of light. And you see why you shouldn't have paid me—I wasn't there for the loading, and I won't be here for the unloading either."

"Now I see that you *are* a slacker," said the pilot. "Now be off before I call you a generous man and other such names."

Umbo left the small wharf with a light heart and a brisk foot, though it was strange to be walking on solid ground again. He had been so long in the company of Rigg or Loaf—or Param, who had spent the whole time before she proposed marriage disparaging him—that he hadn't really known that he knew how to talk to a good man and be taken for a good man himself. His height explained them taking him for a man now, but as for the "good," Umbo had earned that himself. He had been so long treated like nothing that he had started half-believing it himself.

Well, no. He knew, in some rational part of his mind, that he fully believed he was nothing without anyone having to treat him very badly at all. And he knew why. If he hadn't fallen hopelessly in love with a princess, and spent hours noticing all the ways he was beneath her, he might not have been so prickly and taken offense at everything that could possibly be construed as looking down on him. *Now* he understood that. But he also knew himself well enough to be pretty sure that when and if he got back with Rigg and Param, he'd still be prickly, even if he tried not to show how easily offended he was.

He did stop for a quick meal and some provender for the journey. He'd be doing no trapping. As often as he had watched Rigg set traps, Umbo still had no idea *where* to set them. Rigg knew the paths the animals used. Umbo would just be setting a trap in some random place, and he was sure that animals would only stumble on his traps out of pity, they'd be so ill-situated.

The travel was not as hard as he feared, but harder than he hoped. There were tracks and traces in the woods, and once a fair reach of fields that the farmers consented to let him walk through—half a day's journey, passing through open ground without brambles and branches trying to leave scars all over his body.

He got to the base of Upsheer not far from the falls, and he was pretty sure that Kyokay had not fallen yet. The trouble was, it might happen tomorrow, and it might happen next week, and if he let his attention wander, the whole thing could happen while he was peeing or napping or eating.

Of course, if he missed it, he could always go back again. But then he'd have to deal with his own lazy self, sitting around getting in the way. Or he could just appear to himself at the right moment, telling himself to get a move on, it was about to happen.

Instead, he picked his way to a stand of trees with a good view across the river, and when a bunch of boys came to the river to swim, despite the cold water and the stiff breeze, he saw Kyokay among them.

Not so much among them as all around them, doing five stunts for every one that another boy tried. Why Kyokay didn't die long before that fall from the cliff, Umbo couldn't understand. He climbed everything, jumped off of everything, swam under or into or through any obstacle in the water, dove deepest and held his breath the longest. He leapt into the water backward, or deliberately splatted in a belly flop, or tried to turn multiple somersaults in the air when he jumped from the highest part of the bank. And it's not as if he was particularly adroit. Kyokay must have hit his head half a dozen times, and one time he yelled for help when he got his arm caught in a floating log that he himself had just pushed free from its entanglement with the bank. Nothing taught him a lesson. Nothing made him more careful.

What will I be saving him *for*? thought Umbo. That boy is doomed to get himself killed.

But not on a day when I was charged with his safety. Especially when I now know that I probably helped to kill him. Or, to be more accurate, made it harder for Rigg to save him. Rigg had risked his life to get out to the perilous rock at the brim of the cliff, but Umbo had slowed time, and included Rigg in it, which was why the path of a long-since-fallen man turned into that very man, blocking Rigg from getting to Kyokay in time to save him. It was the first time Rigg had any notion that paths were really people or animals, and that when Umbo was slowing time for him, the past became solid, and Rigg could touch a man, and push him, or steal a knife from him . . .

And Kyokay had fallen while Umbo prevented Rigg from helping him, though he *thought* he was preventing Rigg from killing him. I judged too quickly, when I couldn't really see what was happening. And not only did Kyokay die, I also came this close to getting Rigg killed by a mob in Fall Ford.

Then Umbo knew his whole plan, all at once. Bits of it had been nibbling at him during the whole voyage. *Maybe* Kyokay hadn't been killed in the fall, maybe he only drowned in the turbulence of the water. So *maybe* Umbo could swim to him and help pull him out.

Or maybe Umbo would get drowned, too, and put an end to his miserable stupid life.

But now Umbo realized that he could do more than just swim out to drag whatever was left of his brother to safety. The very thing he had done to slow down time for Rigg, he could do to Kyokay as he fell. Slow down time so that Kyokay had time to think, to twist around in the air, to get *ready* for his collision with the water. It might make all the difference.

Once Umbo had learned how to shift time the way Rigg did, only without having a path to latch on to, he and everyone else had pretty much forgotten this much feebler ability that he had started with. But it might be just what he needed. And it was something Rigg couldn't do, not even with the facemask: He couldn't project his power to someone else that he wasn't even touching.

If only Umbo could slow down Kyokay himself, so that he settled like a leaf to the water's surface. But no, Kyokay would fall as fast as ever, and hit with the same momentum. The only difference was that the time of the fall would seem slower to Kyokay, giving him time to think.

Not that Kyokay was famous for thinking. But he *was* fearless. And maybe as he fell that fearlessness would allow him to prepare like a cat for the impact. Maybe.

Meanwhile, it wouldn't hurt for Umbo to use the time he had to practice swimming in the dangerous water at the base of the falls. Of course there was no swimming right under them—the bones would be pounded right out of his skin. But he could see just how close he might get. And he'd know how cold the water was, and where was the nearest bank, and . . .

And so off came the clothes, as soon as he was up by the base of the falls, and down into the water he went. He was no Kyokay—he didn't just dive in. Good thing, too, because in the roiling water he could not see where there were submerged rocks. After he got to where he could open his eyes underwater, he realized: There are submerged rocks everywhere, and Kyokay is going to die.

No he isn't. I will get him out of this water alive.

Because to Umbo's surprise, it didn't take him long to adapt to swimming there. The water was icy, but Umbo didn't stay in it very long at a time, and he took care to dry off and warm up thoroughly before going back in.

What he learned was that if he slowed the perception of time for himself, he had plenty of time to orient himself under the water and sense the currents. If Kyokay was alive after he fell, then Umbo had a fair chance of getting him out of the water before he drowned.

Umbo would not enter the water, though, until Kyokay was in it. That's because he had to be up on a good vantage point so he could see where Kyokay went into the water.

Three days later, Umbo wasn't napping, eating, or peeing when he saw Kyokay running along the road to the great stair that climbed up through the rock to the top of Upsheer. And sure enough, after him—too far behind him—came Umbo, looking young and stupid and angry and helpless. What a privick I was, thought Umbo. What a privick I *am*.

But he wasn't there to criticize himself as a boy. He was there to bring his brother back from the dead.

He watched the whole thing unfold. He was so close to the base of the falls that he couldn't see anything that happened up top until Kyokay slipped and clung, and then there was Rigg, pounding at something—but *not* at Kyokay's hand, as Umbo had thought. No, Rigg was pounding at a man that he could see but Umbo could not, because *younger* Umbo had made the path visible to him.

114

And then Kyokay slipped, starting his tumble. That's when Umbo's work began in earnest. With all his concentration he slowed time for his brother as he fell. He was farther from him than his younger self had been from Rigg that day so long ago — today — but all the other things he had done with time-shifting had also strengthened and sharpened this half-forgotten skill. He knew that he was slowing time for Kyokay far more than he had ever been able to do as a lad. And he saw that Kyokay was using his quickened perceptions well.

Kyokay did not land among the rocks closest to the surface. He was in an arms-first diving position by then, and there was water for him to plunge into. Was it deep enough? From above the water, Umbo could not tell, and besides, it was now time for him to be in the water.

He dove from his perch — he had ascertained that it was safe enough to dive at that spot — and swam swiftly and surely toward a spot downstream from where Kyokay had hit the water. Umbo was slowing his own perception of the passage of time — which meant he was speeding up his own reactions and processes — even more powerfully than he had slowed Kyokay's. He quickly saw his mistake: Kyokay was not being carried downstream, he was caught in the roiling water, getting tumbled over and over in the same place.

Umbo instantly changed the direction of his swimming, cursing himself for not having guessed this would happen, because now he had to swim upstream instead of across the current. A few seconds longer for Kyokay to roll around under the water.

As he drew closer, Umbo saw why Kyokay couldn't swim

himself free. The boy was conscious—he was trying to kick—but both arms seemed to have way too many elbows. Those extended arms had saved Kyokay from the certain death of smashing his head into a rock—but the arms had broken in the process.

He couldn't worry about how much pain Kyokay felt. The only thing Umbo could grab was one of those broken arms, and so he did. In water this cold, and with so much terror, Kyokay probably wouldn't notice the pain.

The trouble was that Kyokay couldn't grip him back, couldn't help at all.

No, he *could*. Once Umbo had stopped his spinning and pushed off from a rock to push himself and pull Kyokay out of the turbulence that held him, Kyokay's kicking began to have a purpose. He couldn't hold on to Umbo, but he could join his kicking with Umbo's, and then they were free of the unpredictable cross-currents and into the main stream of the river.

Umbo had left his clothes—and his blankets—at the place where he was pretty sure he'd have to fetch up on the bank, and yes, he was able to get there. He dragged Kyokay out of the water and checked to see if he was breathing. It had all happened quickly enough that Kyokay had not drowned at all. He coughed and sputtered, but there was no water in his lungs.

In moments Kyokay was whimpering, because now he felt his arms. Three breaks in the right arm, four in the left. But all clean and honest breaks—nothing sticking out of the skin. These could be set and splinted, Umbo was reasonably sure.

In Odinfold, they had the doctors and the tools and the drugs to fix him up without any pain at all. But they weren't in Odinfold.

Umbo worked to dry himself first—he needed to get back the full use of his fingers and he couldn't afford to be shivering much as he worked on getting Kyokay dry and warm.

By the time Umbo was able to get his own clothes on, and was wrapping Kyokay in a blanket, Kyokay was capable of speech. "Did you jump after me? How did you get down there so quick?"

Umbo didn't bother trying to explain.

He found that he was large enough now, and strong enough, especially after a couple of weeks of boatwork, to pick Kyokay up like the child he was and carry him down to the ferry.

It wasn't an *attended* ferry—just a boat attached by an iron ring to a hawser that stretched across the river where once a ford had been. There was another boat on the other side. Umbo laid Kyokay in the bottom of the boat and then took the oars. The rope strained to keep the ring from moving forward, but it had been well-greased during the summer and whenever it snagged, on the next pull of the oars it broke loose and slid further out into the stream, and then out of the stream as it came closer to shore, and then the bottom scraped on gravel and Umbo was out of the boat, lifting Kyokay and carrying him toward his family's house.

Mother could nurse him, and there were those in town who had a knowledge of bone-setting and splints. If it left Kyokay just a little bit weaker, then maybe he wouldn't get himself killed next week or next month. Maybe all this would be worth it, if Kyokay had learned something from his terror in the fall.

Unless he thought that his perception that time had slowed was some kind of magic that proved that a kind saint or spirit was watching over him. Then he'd be more of a dares-all than ever.

Umbo knew he couldn't let the family see him. He laid Kyokay on the ground within easy earshot of the house and then jumped back in time a few minutes. Long enough to run out of the way, into a brushy patch where he could watch. In moments, there was himself, carrying Kyokay, laying him down roughly and abruptly.

No, I was *careful.*

But careful did not mean gentle, he could see now. He saw himself wink out of existence. Yes, that is disturbing, he thought. Good thing we try not to let other people see that too often.

Kyokay called out as Umbo had told him to do, and in moments Mother appeared, and soon Kyokay was surrounded by her and the other kids—whom Umbo now realized he missed more than he would have supposed possible. One of them was sent running for help, of course.

Umbo was about to jump back in time even farther, to make his getaway, when he saw Father rushing up, dragging young Umbo by his upper arm and making it almost impossible for the boy to walk or run alongside. "Does that look dead to you!" shouted Father.

"I saw him fall!" said young Umbo, terrified. "How could he live?"

"But you saved me from the water," said Kyokay.

"His arms are broken," said Mother. "Deal with Umbo later, we have to get his arms set."

"We can set Umbo's arms too, while we're at it. We were going to kill Rigg because you said he killed Kyokay, do you know that, you lying little demon!" Father cuffed young Umbo so hard he sprawled out facedown on the ground. But Father wasn't done. He ran into the house and came back, not with a strap as Umbo had expected, but with the heavy knife he used for cutting leather.

"No!" Mother screamed, and rushed to stop him, but Father flung her aside and stood straddling young Umbo. He pulled him up by the hair and Umbo thought he was about to witness his own murder, the knife drawn across his throat like a pig being slaughtered. But no, Father began striking him with the flat of the blade, hitting him on the shoulders and the side of his head, until young Umbo hung limp and unconscious.

By then some men were rushing from town, including Sellet the barber, who was the second best bonesetter in town. They began shouting at Father to put down the knife, put down the boy, be glad that Kyokay was alive, there should be no killing, and after brandishing the knife a while to keep them back, Father finally gave in to Sellet's obvious point that if Father kept him away, he couldn't set Kyokay's bones, which he could see from there were broken in many places.

"I need splints and leather thongs to tie them," said Sellet. "Be a good father and fetch me what I need!"

"Don't tell me how to be a good father!" roared Father, and it might have started up again except now there were six strong men looming around him, making it clear that they would tolerate no more nonsense from him. Two of them went into the house with him.

Sellet went to Kyokay all right, but the others went to young Umbo, who was now being held by his mother. Father might have struck with the flat, but the blade was still there, and it had cut willy-nilly all over young Umbo's head and shoulders and arms.

"Nothing's bleeding hard," one of the men said. "But I think the skull is broken here. Look how it's swelling, but it looks dented anyway."

"I'm sorry, Enene," said one man. "But I don't like the look of his head."

"Umbo saved me," said Kyokay feebly, and then cried out in agony as Sellet pushed one of his bones into place. Father came out with thongs and bracing sticks that Umbo recognized as dismantled frames for stretching leather. He was still angry and Umbo could see that he wanted to kick young Umbo again.

"What are you doing?" said a man. Umbo couldn't remember his name, though once he had known it. "One son all broken up, and this boy saved him, and you already broke his head. He may never be right again, you fool."

"He was never right! He was never my son! I say it out loud—does he look like me? All the others do, but not him! And now he tried to get us to commit murder by his false accusation! That's no son to me!"

They got the splints and thongs out of his hands and then he was roughly walked far from the scene. Mother continued to weep over young Umbo.

Only then did Umbo himself jump back in time just enough to allow him to arrive at the riverbank only moments after he had carried Kyokay up from the boat. With two boats on this side, it was easy enough to hop into the one he had just left and row urgently back to the other side.

Though there *was* no urgency. Only in his own heart and mind. He had all the time in the world, because he was not going to let this happen.

Umbo was coming up out of the water for the last time on his second day of swimming, when he saw a vision of himself standing on the shore only a few feet away.

"I'm not here! I'm not going to make two fools where one will do. You can't do it. It's a disaster."

"What's a disaster? *You're* all right," said Umbo.

The vision of future Umbo seemed distraught, about to cry, but also angry and ashamed and . . . urgent.

"I'm such a fool—and so are you!" cried the vision of Umbo. "It all works, you save him, his bones are broken, you take him home and leave him, but then he says that Umbo saved him, and so it makes me—us—young Umbo, it makes him look like a liar, like he *knew* Kyokay was alive and he lied to try to get them to kill Rigg and Father beat him—us—"

"Young Umbo," prompted Umbo. "Beat him, of course."

"Broke his skull," said vision Umbo. "Maybe he'll die. Maybe he'll live and be . . . simple. Or crippled. But he's sure not going on any trips with Rigg. It's all undone. We just—I just ruined everything. You can't do it! Don't do it! Undo this future, you fool! Let him die!"

And then he was gone.

What could Umbo do but dry himself off and think about what his future self had said? Yes, that was a disaster. Of course Kyokay would know that it was Umbo who saved him. He wouldn't be in any shape to notice how much taller and stronger he was. But Umbo couldn't blame himself for rushing Kyokay home. It's what they always did when Kyokay injured himself. Rush him home, take him to Mother, then let Father yell and beat on somebody for not watching Kyokay, even though everybody else knew that you couldn't watch Kyokay because he would do what he wanted no matter what.

Future Umbo was wrong, though. In the rush of emotion after saving Kyokay, he had hurried home to Mother and that was the disastrous mistake. Not saving Kyokay, but taking him home.

Now that Umbo knew he could save Kyokay, he wasn't going to *unsave* him because future Umbo was a hysterical mess. He had just watched Father beat his younger self. It made Umbo sick with fury even now. He hated that man — *not* his real father at all. Just Tegay, master cobbler, wife beater, child beater, and evil fool.

But *I* didn't see it. *I* didn't just save my brother from the water. I can think more clearly, and I'm going to save Kyokay and leave the future unchanged.

It meant he would skip a bit of practice swimming to make a few more preparations. He would need more blankets. He would need a much heavier knife than his everyday knife, or the jeweled knife that he rarely used and feared to break. But that was a simple matter, to swim across the river in the night and steal the heavy leather-cutting knife from Father's — Tegay's — workbench. Sharp. Yes, Tegay was kind and caring to his tools. Anything it touched, it would cut.

It might also rust, since it got plenty of underwater time as Umbo swam back across. When he stole blankets, though, he had to use the boat to ferry them, then use the pulley line to haul it back across to the far side. Couldn't have wet blankets for this.

He cached everything near the ferry, then went back to swimming and watching.

He saw the tale unfold—Kyokay running to the stone stair, Umbo following after, but too far away. Kyokay laughing, knowing he was doing something stupid and wrong, but delighting in it.

But there was now an added complication. Umbo knew that when he had done this the first time, everything had worked out well enough—broken bones, but alive, not drowned. Now, though, besides trying to concentrate on the things he had planned to do, he had this nagging doubt: Am I doing it exactly as I did it before? Or slower? Or wrong somehow? Will I fail now, though I succeeded before?

Kyokay fell. Umbo slowed him so much he was afraid he might exhaust himself so he'd have nothing left to slow time for himself as he swam. But how could he do less than his strongest, fiercest effort? What good would it do to save strength for later, if he didn't keep Kyokay alive now?

Kyokay twisted himself in midair so his legs would enter the water first. Smart boy, thought Umbo. Don't get your head anywhere near those rocks.

Umbo plunged into the water and swam directly to where Kyokay was being churned by the water. His legs were broken, feebly waving around with extra bendings. And a dark patch spreading from one leg made it clear that a bone had broken the skin. Can't worry about infection now.

He got to Kyokay and the boy was able to grip his hand, then cling to his shoulders as Umbo swam strongly to shore. He dragged him up out of the water and realized at once that he couldn't leave that bone sticking out. He used the jeweled knife to slice open Kyokay's trouser and then he gripped the boy strongly and pulled the bottom of his leg away far enough to put the jutting bone back in place. Then he tied strips of Kyokay's own trouser leg around the wound to keep the leg from moving and to keep the wound closed. It was a ragged job and if it wasn't fixed soon, if the bones knit back together as Umbo had left them, Kyokay would never walk right again. But he was alive.

Kyokay bore the pain well, but the reason was clear. He was trembling, then *shaking* with cold. The numbness helped him bear the crude bone-setting without screaming. But now Umbo had to get him warm and dry.

As for himself, he was used to the cold water, after all that practice, and the exertions involved in setting and binding the leg had kept him warm. So he worked on getting Kyokay as warm as possible.

Some of the shivering probably came from shock. But Umbo couldn't do anything about that. If he was going to get help for Kyokay, he'd have to move fast.

He carried the boy swiftly, knowing that every stop caused him pain. But he had to get away before anybody from Fall Ford started searching for the body of the boy who had fallen.

He laid Kyokay on the gravel landing area at the ferry, then went for the cache of blankets and leather-cutting knife. With the blankets he made a kind of bed and then lifted Kyokay and put him back down in the bottom of the boat. With Kyokay's weight, the boat was now firm on the gravel, though the current tugged at the other end. The rope connecting the boat to the iron ring was slack. So he could cut it without the boat getting away from him.

When the rope was cut—and it took only two swipes with the leather-cutter—Umbo thought of throwing the knife into the middle of the river, so Tegay could never again use it to beat a child. But no, that was one of the tools with which Tegay provided for the family. And in this world, Tegay had not beaten Umbo's brains out. If this worked, would never beat young Umbo again. So Umbo laid the knife in plain sight in the middle of the gravel, where anyone using the ferry would stumble across it. It would get back to Tegay's bench.

Then Umbo pushed the boat out into the water. The current took it so swiftly that Umbo had a few moments of fright as he struggled to climb up and over the side to get in it. Nothing deft about *that* operation. But he finally got into the boat and then laid the rower's plank across the middle and sat with his legs straddling Kyokay, who wasn't shivering as badly now, so maybe it had been only the cold and not the shock of the wound that had him shaking so much before.

"How did you get down into the water so fast?" Kyokay asked.

"You fell very slowly," said Umbo.

"Yes," said Kyokay in wonderment. "I did. But I still hit very hard."

And then he closed his eyes. With all that pain, he couldn't be *asleep*. Unconscious, then. Exhausted. Maybe in shock after all.

But all Umbo could do was row like a demon. The current was fast—Umbo wanted to go faster. What would have been several days' journey upstream might be only a couple of hours going down. He had to get to Bear's Den Crossing before dark, or he'd float right past it and then Kyokay really would be in a dangerous position.

It took till the last light of dusk, but Umbo saw the wharf and tied up at it. The boat he had come up on was gone—of course it was gone, the owner had to keep the boat moving. But when Umbo carried Kyokay into the tavern where he had bought his provisions for the journey to Upsheer, whom should he see at one of the tables but the pilot he had parted with so warmly.

At once the pilot was on his feet, clearing away dishes to let Umbo lay Kyokay on his own table. A bonesetter was called for, and a stitcher too, once they saw the blood-soaked rags binding the wound. The pilot asked no more questions after Umbo said, "I saw him fall, and I knew nowhere to take him but here."

"What about Fall Ford?" asked the pilot.

"We were already downstream of it," said Umbo. "And you— your boat is gone."

"My brother took it back. I'm here waiting for my wife to deliver my firstborn. If she doesn't hurry, I'll take the boat *you* came in and catch up with my brother."

Umbo didn't want to lie to this good man, but he knew he had to, for the future's sake. "This poor boy thinks *I'm* his brother. Kept calling me by his name. Bobo or something like that."

"Whereas you're 'Ram Odin.'" The pilot's tone made it clear that he didn't believe that was Umbo's name, and probably never had.

"On the river, sir, a man is what he does, don't you think?"

The pilot only grinned at him and kept working on warming up the boy's arms and legs.

Next morning, Umbo left a good deal of money with the taverner with instructions to send someone upriver to tell the folk in Fall Ford that they should come fetch one of their children. Umbo knew it would insult the pilot to offer payment to him, and that the man would look in on Kyokay as if he were his own nephew, if not son.

When Umbo got to his little boat, he saw that it had been provisioned for a downriver voyage. A long one. And someone had untied the rope that had once connected the boat to the ring. So it was no longer obvious that it was a stolen ferryboat.

The man didn't know whether my business was fair or foul, but he abetted me in trust that it wouldn't bring him harm.

I already repaid him by *not* undoing the course of events that brought me and Rigg together, and Param, and Loaf and Olivenko. Now it's *their* job to go ahead and save the world. I saved my brother's life, and that's all I can do, and more than I should have attempted, but now it's done.

CHAPTER 7

Paths and Slices

Noxon wasn't despairing yet, exactly. He and Param had accomplished quite a lot. The easiest part was for Noxon to master the stuttering forward jumps that Param did when she sliced time, so that he could race through hours and days in just a few minutes.

But he was not a whit closer to being able to do it backward. Not simply going into the past—he could already make backward leaps just by attaching to some path and joining that person or animal in its time. What he couldn't do was get time flowing the other direction and then slice through it in that direction. He wasn't even sure it was possible.

And Param, for her part, was now better at what she already did—she learned a bit from the way Noxon's facemask helped him slice time in greater and greater swaths. Her gift really was the most remarkable, because alone of the timeshapers she had always been able to make jumps forward rather than back.

The drawback was that her forward jumps were only a fraction of a second at a time; but she did a lot of them in rapid succession, and could keep it up for hours. When she did, though, she remained trapped in the place where she was when she began the process—not visible to others, but if they knew where she was when she disappeared, they could make a good guess where she was now. Her physical movements through space were greatly slowed while she was slicing time, and if someone brought something dense, like a metal bar, and passed it into her body and held it there, she would burn up slowly from the heat of it. And if she came out of her time-slicing with the metal in her, it would tear her apart.

But as Noxon's facemask helped him learn to make longer jumps between slices, and Param learned to do it along with him, it meant that even with a metal bar held in the midst of her body, she spent far less time with it, and surely the would-be murderer was bound to conclude that nothing was happening because she wasn't where he thought she would be.

If they accomplished nothing else, that was a good thing. It made her safer. It also meant that when they had need of her ability to race forward through time, she could do it more quickly and efficiently.

But it wasn't enough. Noxon had half-expected to fail at his task, learning to reverse the flow of time for himself. But he had not expected to fail at helping Param learn how to slice into the past. She wouldn't be reversing the flow of time—in the moments she spent in realtime, she and her body and clothing and whatever else she held with her would still be progressing in the normal direction of timeflow.

She followed him so easily when Noxon sliced forward with facemask efficiency. But when he jumped backward while holding her hand, she had no idea how he had done it. And when he jumped backward in time *without* holding her, he simply left her behind.

"It's all right," she consoled him. Time after time she said it, and Noxon believed she meant it. She, too, had not expected to succeed.

They began to spend more of their time just talking, either about their lives in such different upbringings, or about things they had learned in their studies. They had no one else to talk to, most of the time, because even though they had to depend on the Larfolders for their food, they never knew what time — what year, what month, what day — they would be in when their bodies told them it was time to eat.

Fortunately, they could always slice forward until they saw somebody preparing a meal, and it was a part of Larfolder culture that they always welcomed the unexpected mealtime guest.

One day, after such a meal, which had, in Larfolder fashion, turned into a storytelling session, with lots of singing and chanting of old songs and legends and stories, Noxon could see that Param was tired. "We've had a long day," he said to the Larfolders.

The Larfolders laughed, and one of them said, "How would you know?"

That was a good question. And yet it was one that didn't really matter. They ate when they were hungry and slept when they were tired—those were their times and days and nights, since no calendar or clock could contain them.

Noxon walked away with his sister. She held his arm and leaned on him. "I'm going to sleep as we walk," she said. "And when I wake up tomorrow, I'm going to make you take me back eight hours or ten so I can sleep that time again."

Noxon chuckled. "The Larfolders seem to make the most of their time on land. They have no voices underwater, and no spoken language. They come here to remember being human."

"Oh, I love being with them," said Param. She shuddered. "Their singing drowns out the noise, as much as is possible."

"The noise?"

She shook her head. "I'm so tired I was almost talking to myself."

"But I want to know. The Larfolders aren't all that noisy. It's not as if they have drums or horns."

"Oh, not *their* sounds. I love the sounds of life. And nature. And civilization. Wind in the trees, frogs croaking, crickets chirping. But also crowds of people, the bustle of the city. I love that! I wish I had lived in Odinfold when billions of people lived so close together in their great cities. But now they didn't even exist. They never happened. That makes me sad."

Noxon was almost turned aside to try to console her sadness. But not this time. He was intrigued by her talk of noises. "So there's no noise in a big city?"

She laughed. "Of course there is. That's why I never talk about this thing I call noise. It's not really *noise* because I'm the only one aware of it. At Flacommo's, though, I loved to spend my days in remote parts of the house where nobody had been in years. It was so much quieter there. Never silent, but . . . you know."

Noxon thought he did, though he tried to conceal his excitement, for fear of dashing her hopes if he turned out to be wrong. "So you needed to be away from people."

"Oh, people are *fine*, people drown out the noise! All the talking and clattering, it was such a relief. But in those rooms where people gathered all the time, the noise was almost unbearable when *those* rooms were empty. It's as if the rooms stored up all the noises that had ever been in them, and when there was nothing to distract me, I had all these . . . tunes or rhythms or whatever they were."

"So slicing time was how you got away."

She shook her head against his shoulder and gave one laugh. "No," she said. "That was the worst of all. Not a breath of *real* sound. Just those memories of all the stored-up sounds. I couldn't even sing to myself, except silently in my own head and that didn't actually help much."

"When you're slicing time, there can't possibly be any sound," said Noxon.

"I know that," said Param. "I think my schooling was at least as good as yours, privick boy."

"I wouldn't be too sure. I had Ramex teaching me."

"So did I, under another name. Though not as much as he was with you, of course."

"Did you ever tell him about these noises?"

"I only told *you* by accident. Like I said, they aren't real noises. I think they're a sign that I'm crazy."

"The way I see paths everywhere," said Noxon. "Paths that nobody else sees. I'm definitely out of my mind."

"Yes, just like that," said Param. "Except that it turns out your paths are real. People really *did* move through the world right where you see the paths."

"But I can't shut out the paths by closing my eyes or turning my back," said Noxon. "They're still there. But I don't really *see* them, it's another sense entirely. So they never get in the way of my seeing things that are really there."

"I know," she said. "Just like my noises. They're always there, more in some places than in others, but they don't stop me from hearing *real* noises and sounds and talking and music. And plugging my ears doesn't change them in any way. Only going to rooms with less noise stored up makes the sheer clangor of it ease up and give me some peace."

Noxon stopped walking. "I'm so glad you were tired enough to tell me this," he said.

"Yes, just one more thing that's wrong with poor Param." She said it wryly, but Noxon knew she also meant it.

"I don't think it's anything wrong," said Noxon. "I've always told you that I don't see the paths with my eyes. I just *compare* it to seeing. I use the words of seeing to describe the way I sense them, because there *are* no words for pathsight."

Param was not slow. "But how could I *hear* a *path*?"

"How can I see a tune?" asked Noxon. "For all I know, we're using different words, different *comparisons*, to talk about the exact same thing. As if somebody were trying to describe an orange to someone who had never eaten one. You might try to explain the look of it. Or you might try to talk about the taste or the smell or the *feel* of it in your hand. But it's still an orange that you're talking about."

"But—"

"No, no, Param, don't give me a list of reasons why I can't be right about this. Let's just do the science. Let's compare how these things work. Is the noise just—well, just a porridge? Or can you hear individual—voices? Tunes?"

"Lots of individual ones. Bouncing off all the walls."

"Really? An echo?" asked Noxon.

"No, but coming from different directions and going in different—"

"Like paths through the room."

"No, I don't *see*—"

"Stop saying 'no' and just describe what it's like. You move through the room, and some get louder?"

"Yes. Some get really loud and some are always faint. But when I get closer they all get louder than they were, and then they fade and others rise."

"As if you were crossing a *stream*, with its own particular tune, but then you step from one stream into another."

"I know you're only using 'stream' instead of 'path' so I won't say no."

"I'm trying to find out if you can lay hold on them."

"How do you lay hold on a *sound*?"

"How do I lay hold on a path?" asked Noxon. "My paths never looked like people or animals—but they *were*, when time slowed down. When Umbo sped up my brain processes so the world around me seemed to slow down. Now the facemask does that for me."

"Well, it can't do it for me," said Param. "And I don't want a facemask."

"Yes you do," said Noxon. "You cry yourself to sleep because nobody ever got you one."

"It certainly made *you* prettier."

"Didn't you notice how *my* facemask is so much prettier than Rigg's?"

"Oh, of course you say that now that he's off on his expedition, so nobody can actually compare."

During this banter, Noxon had picked a nearby path — without slowing it down to see who it was. It was at least a century old, but that made it far newer than the few other paths in the vicinity. The Larfolders didn't feel at home in the woods, so few of their paths ever came here.

"So is there any noise here?"

"There's always *some* noise," said Param.

"But I mean, are there any particular noises?"

"A few. Nothing very loud."

"Is there one that's louder than any of the others?"

"Yes," she said instantly. "But it's not *loud* loud."

"Do you know where it's coming from?"

Param thought. "Well, yes. I think I always know. That's how I can avoid them when I just want some peace. It's over this way."

But she closed her eyes when she said this, and her eyes were still closed when she pointed.

She pointed at that newest path.

"Let me see if I can hear it too," said Noxon. "Let's go stand right in the middle of this particular tune." He led her to the path.

"You're seeing a path and you think they're the same."

"No, I'm positive they're not the same at all," said Noxon, "so I'm going to get you to confirm that by telling me we're not standing in the middle of it right now."

"Well we are," said Param. And then she began to gasp. For a moment he thought she was feeling faint. And then he realized she was laughing. No, crying.

"It is not possible," she finally said.

"Let's go to one of those fainter tunes," said Noxon.

"They're not really musical."

"And my paths aren't really colorful. But I *call* the differences among them colors. And you called them tunes, didn't you?"

"That's how I think of them. And yes, we're standing in another of them now."

"It's a very old path," said Noxon. "But you hear it."

"It's not loud, but yes."

"I think it's safe to say that you and I are both pathfinders."

"I can't believe I'm about to say this, but I wish Umbo had ever done his slowing-down trick on me!"

"Every time he dragged you around in time, he was doing it," said Rigg. "You just weren't expecting it to turn your tunes into anything, so you didn't notice."

"I wish he were *here* to do it now!" said Param.

"He'll be back, sooner or later," said Noxon. "But maybe we can do something ourselves. Let's stand here—beside this path.

This tune. Look at my hand. Where I'm placing it. The tune is right *there*, isn't it?"

Param looked at his hand, which he was holding out from his body. "I never realized how *precisely* I knew where they were. You don't expect to know where sounds are, but yes, I always knew which way to go to get away from a particular noise, or the noisiest ones, anyway."

"I'm going to use the facemask to help me see the actual person. I always see the people now, a little. But I'm going to see her clearly."

"Her?"

"Some things are pretty obvious, the way I see paths now. General size and body shape. I'd say it's an old woman. And I want to pick a moment when she's already past this point. Say nothing, do nothing, so we don't alert her and make her turn around and see us."

"There's nobody there."

"I haven't done it yet. But look toward where you know that tune is. Where it passes between those trees."

"I'm looking."

"I can see her now, very clearly, taking a single step. And now I'm bringing us into resonance with her, very precisely, so she's frozen in midstep. You're not going to do something stupid like letting go of my hand, are you?"

"Unless I feel like it."

"No more talking now. We're going to jump to her time."

And with that, Noxon fixed himself on the woman and made the jump into the past.

Param must not have been able to help it. Her gasp was of pure startlement. The woman stopped and started to turn. In fact, she was whirling around to see what was so close behind her. But Noxon had facemask reflexes now, so he saw what she was doing and jumped back a little farther in time, before she could have caught even a glimpse of them. She would think she was startled at nothing, some random forest sound, and laugh at herself for thinking someone was there.

Noxon pulled Param away from the woman's path. "You couldn't have been that surprised," said Noxon. "I told you that you'd see an old woman's back. And she's a Larfolder, so you can hardly have been surprised at her mantle."

"No, no, that's not why I gasped. I'm so sorry I did that, I couldn't help it."

"Tell me why."

"Because I realized that she *was* the tune. The tune was streaming back from behind her. She was *making* the tune."

"Making the path, you mean."

"How could I live all these years without noticing that the tunes were streaming along behind people?" Param sank to the ground. "But I did know. I did realize it. As a little girl, I told Mother, 'I don't like his noise, he has a bad noise,' and she told me to hush and never talk like that again, so I didn't. 'He's not making a noise, don't be rude,' that's what she taught me. So I stopped noticing. Or stopped admitting that I noticed. But there were noises that I definitely associated with people. The noise of Flacommo was all over the house. And I knew Mother's tune by heart, I knew where she had been. But I never thought it was this specific. That she passed by *this* place or *that* place at a certain time."

"But she did. You're not stupid for not realizing all this. Do you think I knew what I was seeing? Father helped me understand it. He didn't know that I could *jump* to those times — Umbo and I discovered that — but he helped me understand that I was seeing — no, that I *perceived* — different people and different animals, and that some were more recent than others. I think of the recent ones as being brighter, but for you they're — "

"Louder," said Param.

"You're such a pathfinder," said Noxon, with mock contempt.

"I need me an Umbo!" she cried out in joking frustration.

"When we jumped, though. Could you feel what we were doing?"

"Not really. I knew *when* we jumped, I know *that* we jumped. But I don't know what you're doing when you do it."

"Just like I didn't know what you were doing as you sliced time. So let's start picking paths and jumping to them, and you see if you can start to get what I'm doing. Because there's no reason to think you don't have the same ability to hold on to a particular point in the path. A particular moment in the tune."

"I see one problem," said Param. "We're going to practice by going back and back, to ever older tunes. Paths. But we don't have Umbo as an anchor, to bring us back."

"We need us an Umbo," he said, echoing her joke. Then he caught himself. "It's not funny. We always needed Umbo. How did we ever make him feel that we didn't?"

"Because I *told* him we didn't," said Param. "And he believed every nasty thing I ever said. How could he still want to marry me, the way I treated him?"

"Because love forgives much. Not all, but a lot."

"I like him now. I'm *used* to him and I like him. And now I see that I need him."

"If he were here, it would be easier. But remember who you are and who I am. So what if we go a few centuries into the past? We'll just slice our way forward again."

"We're already a century in the past," she said.

"How do you know that?" asked Noxon.

"You said."

"Did I? I don't remember. I thought maybe you just knew."

"Maybe I did. I just remember how long it took Umbo and me to slice forward to when the Visitors' ship was here."

"And don't you and I slice ten times faster?"

"More like a hundred times. Let's go back a few more times and then come back to the present."

Noxon laughed. "Param, what in the world does 'present' mean to you? To me, *this* is the present. Wherever I am. But you didn't mean *now*."

"I meant the time and place we just left. The one we've been coming back to."

"We've been back and forth through a hundred different days in the same two-year period."

"One of those, *that's* what I mean. A couple of years before the Visitors come."

"All right. That's the 'present,' and we'll slice back to that after a few more tries."

It took several days of jumping back together, then slicing forward, before Param finally said that she thought she had an idea of what he was doing. Since that was about how long it had taken Noxon to really understand what her slicing was about, he was encouraged.

Then one day, they jumped before he was ready. They didn't jump to the exact moment he had chosen. But they had attached to the same man's path. And Param had done it.

She clung to him and wept in relief and joy.

"Well, you're one of us now for sure," said Noxon, trying to joke her out of her crying.

"I'm not *sad*, I'm happy," she said. "And that's exactly why I was crying. I'm one of you now. I can do what you and Umbo do." And then, as if correcting herself. "*And* Rigg."

"It's all right that you think of me as Rigg. I *am* Rigg. I'm just the one who volunteered to change names so people didn't get confused."

"And it's working," said Param. "I'm never confused." With that she did begin to laugh. A little hysterically, but definitely a laugh.

So Noxon had learned how to slice like Param, and now Param was beginning to take hold of paths, too. What Umbo was actually doing when *he* jumped, Noxon had no idea. Since Umbo never saw paths or heard tunes, apparently he just sort of flung himself into the past. And Umbo was the only one who could affect other people's timeflow without touching them. So Noxon didn't know if anybody else could ever learn Umbo's skill. But all four could now jump into the past.

Noxon had also been practicing, surreptitiously, the little thing that only the Odinfolders had been able to do—move objects in time and space. He had first tried it in the starship in Vadeshfold, soon after he mastered the facemask. He had moved Vadeshex himself—*it*self—just a tiny bit forward in time and in space as well, but if Vadeshex noticed it, he didn't mention the fact.

Since then, Noxon played with it only when no one was watching, moving a pebble or twig or leaf just a little to one side, or a titch into the future. Until it came easily to him, and he began to move these small natural objects farther in both space and time.

So when he returned to the shore, where they usually slept, Noxon would quickly take inventory of items he had moved there. This twig, sent this morning; that colored pebble, which he sent from last week. Then he would throw them away into the distant past of another wallfold, where neither he nor anyone else was likely to take note of the fact. But it was good to get a feel for moving things over great distances and long time periods.

He could not hope to approach the precision of the mice, for if the Odinfolders were to be believed, they had moved genes from one person's cells to another's, across thousands of kilometers. Supposedly that was how Umbo had been conceived, with no genetic contribution at all from his purported father. Noxon was glad to be able to move visible things across relatively trivial distances and timespans, with anything approaching precision. If a pebble was less than a meter from the place whither he meant to send it, Noxon counted it as a bullseye.

And that was about all Noxon could expect to accomplish here on Garden. He had learned what Param knew, and helped

Param learn what *he* knew. He had practiced a crude version of the timeshaping the mice could do. The things he still needed to learn, nobody knew, so nobody could teach him.

All he could do now was get himself back to the moment of transition, when one ship became nineteen. He had to look for that twentieth ship, the one moving backward. It might be the only object in the history of the universe that had *ever* moved upstream through time. It was quite possible that it blew up immediately and didn't actually exist for longer than a microsecond. Or it might be that Noxon could be there in that moment and not see it. Not *perceive* the backward-flowing path.

Maybe the jump through the fold in space would make it impossible for him to see Ram Odin's path. Seeing it, after all, would require spanning a lightyears-wide gap. The only reason he had any hope was that the ship's computer had assured him that in that instant, there was no gap at all. There should be a single continuous path from every one of the nineteen Ram Odins back across the fold to the one original pre-jump Ram Odin. And somewhere — no, *exactly* where the original Ram Odin's path was and reaching back to the Earth he had left behind — there should be another Ram Odin hurtling toward Earth, moving the wrong way through time. That backward Ram should be dancing circles around the forward one.

Either Noxon would see it and seize it, or he would not. But it was time to graduate from his and Param's school of mutual ignorance, and find out whether he could do the only thing he could think of that had a chance of saving this world without wiping out the other.

A few more days of practice with Param, to make sure she really had it without any help from him at all, and then he could go. There was no reason to wait. Not even to say good-bye to Umbo or Rigg or Loaf or Olivenko. They knew he was going, and if he waited for *anything* it would be a sign of his own dread. He couldn't let fear slow him down now.

CHAPTER 8

Negotiating with Mice

"I'd be grateful if you would stay here," said Noxon. "Not *here*, but in this time."

"I'm not afraid of the mice," said Param.

"Foolish of you. They already killed you once."

"But now I can jump back in time."

"Yes—with six pregnant mice hiding in your clothes," said Noxon.

"I heard their tunes," she said.

"We brought them into Larfold, but we mustn't bring them too far into Larfold's past. We dare not take them anywhere else. Or any*when* else."

"So why talk to them?" asked Param.

"To see if I can negotiate a way for them to come with me to Earth."

"So they can wipe out the human race?"

"We don't *know* that," said Noxon.

"You weren't there. The more I think about it, the more certain I am that those mice were sick, and there's no reason to send *only* sick mice on a starship unless you're planning to start a plague. One the humans on Earth will have no defenses against."

Noxon nodded. "I didn't see what you saw. I have to accept your judgment."

"Nobody else does. Loaf made us feel like monsters. Especially Umbo. It really hurt him."

"Loaf is worried that this power is going to our heads. And it is. Because we *can* do these things, we act as if we had a right to. Which is why I have to talk to the mice."

"I don't see the connection. They're treacherous and unpredictable."

"And sneaky and small," said Noxon. "Either we're going to be able to share this world with them, or it's going to be war, and if it's the latter, I think we're likely to lose."

Param thought about that for a while. Noxon liked it that she didn't always have a ready answer.

"They could unleash that plague here on Garden," she said.

"True, and not just in the wallfolds they're in. They can't travel in time, but they can send objects, and not just in time but in space as well. They could seed their plague in every wallfold. They could do it now."

"So what you're really doing is negotiating a treaty with a foreign power."

"With an alien species. One that has a lot of the human genome, but we definitely can't interbreed."

Param pursed her mouth. "I don't know which of the two images that came to my mind is the more disgusting."

"Will you stay here and not follow me into the future?"

"Do I have to decide and take a solemn oath right now? If I don't agree, will you decide not to go?"

"It would be a waste of your time anyway," said Noxon. "You can't hear their high little voices, and they talk very fast."

"They must get so impatient, waiting for humans to finish talking."

"They hold dozens of conversations of their own while we're saying, 'Well, um . . .'"

"Go," she said abruptly. "I need some alone time anyway."

Noxon wasn't sure if she was angry or not. And even if she was, *whom* she was angry at. Him, maybe, for shutting her out of a negotiation. Or herself, for still being afraid of the mice, maybe, or for being inferior to people with facemasks, or some other unfathomable reason. Sometimes Noxon thought that if he had grown up with Param as a sister, he might have turned out even crazier than he was just getting to know her now.

It was a simple matter to return to the time of the mice in Larfold. Once they had brought the mice in, they had propagated so quickly that there wasn't a habitable region of the wallfold that didn't have nests and warrens. And these mice were like humans—they didn't choose just one habitat, they adapted to every possible habitat. They lived in trees, in grass, in burrows that they dug themselves—or burrows that other animals had dug, which the mice expelled them from. They lived beside streams and in dry places, in crags and swamps. They made ordinary mice seem lazy and finicky.

They also bred themselves for particular traits. Within a few generations, the tree mice would be different from rock mice and swamp mice and field mice. But they were all part of the same species, and, like dogs, they could be quite different in size and other traits, yet still interbreed.

Noxon didn't want to talk to them in their billions. He wanted to talk to them only a few generations after they first came to Larfold.

He rapidly sliced his way forward in time until he saw just a few of the distinctive paths of *Mus sapiens*, and then he abruptly stopped. At once the mice in the clearing stopped what they were doing and ran up to him. Several of them scampered up his clothing and perched on his shoulder. "Rigg or Noxon?" one voice asked.

Regular human ears would have heard only a brief squeak. Noxon imagined that a mouse could spout a lot of vilification while a cat was preparing to kill it.

"Noxon," he replied.

"You've been hiding from us." "Where's the girl?" "Why won't you take us with you?" "What are you doing that you don't want us to see?"

The questions came on top of each other, from different mice that were now in various places on his body. He could sort them out because the facemask kept them clear in his memory. Noxon knew that all the questions came from all the mice. He also knew that he should answer only the questions he wanted to answer.

"I'm here to talk to you about taking you with me."

"Into the past?" "What wallfold?" "Vadeshfold!" "Earth?"

"I'm going to try to get to Earth in a peculiar way," said Noxon. "It may not work. It involves hooking onto a backward timeflow, and I may not be able to do it."

"Worth the risk." "We'll be there." "Let us see Earth." "Where you fail, we may succeed later."

"Not that simple," said Noxon. "I said I might take you with me *in the ship*, but that doesn't mean I'm taking you to Earth."

"Where are you going if not Earth?"

"I'm going to take the ship to Earth, but I can't land it on the planet. It'll be in orbit. And when I go to the surface, I may or may not take mice along."

"Then what's the point?" "We've seen spaceships." "We have all the schematics." "A voyage just to stay in the ship?"

"I don't know yet. That's my point. I'm going to go down to the planet and try to learn why they destroy Garden, and then see how I can prevent it. Until I've seen what's going on, I'm not bringing anyone with me. But I may need you. And if I do, I'd like to have some of you there." He did not say: I may need you to destroy the human race, to wreck their ability to come to Garden and destroy us. He knew that they already understood what their task would be.

But that did not mean they were content to let him call the shots. "Why is it all your choice?" "You think you're King-in-the-Tent." "We won't go."

"Then don't go," said Noxon. "I was only inviting you, not commanding you."

"Let us go!" "We want to go!" "Don't leave us all behind!"

They nagged like children. Cute, too, like children. But Noxon knew just how dangerous they were.

"I know that even on the ship, you can cause trouble for me," said Noxon.

"Not us." "Why would we cause trouble?" "We want to help." "Let us help."

"You can send things in time and space. You could kill me in my sleep."

"Why would we do that?" "We aren't killers."

"You most certainly *are* killers," said Noxon. "I saw Param's dead body."

"We never actually did that." "You got her away in time." "We weren't really going to do it."

"You did it, and then we came back and *un*did it." Noxon didn't mention the attempt to infect the whole population of Earth with a plague of some kind, because they hadn't done it yet, and it would be a bitter irony if it was Noxon who gave them the idea. "I'm sure you had very good reasons."

"We knew you'd undo it!" "We were just trying to get you to take action!" "You were all being so complacent!" "Lazy!" "It was time to act."

"I'm sure your motives were pure."

"Irony!" "Lie!"

"Not a lie, and not irony," said Noxon. "You were doing what you thought was right for *Mus sapiens*. It just happened to be inconvenient for Param."

"Queen-in-the-Tent." "We love her." "We revere her."

"You love no human, you revere no human."

Silence.

"Of the biped class," said Noxon. "I recognize you as a kind of human."

"Then we are not *Mus sapiens*, we are *Homo musculus*." A single voice. The distinction was important to them.

"You're right," said Noxon, drawing upon Father's counsel about negotiations: Get your counterpart to agree with you about a common foundation, then build on it. "You are as entitled to the one name as the other. It's really up to you whether you're mice with human traits grafted in, or humans with the gifts that come from being small but many."

"Good." "Very good." "True." Father's advice worked again, as it almost always did. More mice were talking than ever before. Tiny voices, but so many it was like a chord of music, held long on an organ. And instead of arguing with him, they were agreeing, amplifying.

"For all I know, you'll be the key to solving the problem and saving Garden from the Destroyers," said Noxon. "But you have to agree in advance that you'll stay on the ship until I choose to bring you to Earth, and that you'll do no mischief."

Silence for a while, and then a lone voice: "Mischief to you might be survival to us."

"I understand that. I'm asking you to put a lot of trust in me."

"But you are not putting any trust in us." "You try to control us."

"Trust? I'm putting my life in your hands. Once you're on the ship, I can't possibly watch you all the time. You know how to interface with the ship's computers, you could change our course, you could corrupt the life support. You know how to kill a man in his sleep."

"We can't harm you." "You are the one who can take us into the past." "Backflowing time is a trap only you can pull us out of."

"Yes. You know you need *me*, but I don't know yet if I need *you*."

"Whatever you say." "Take us along." "We promise."

There was no way to get any firmer promise than that. What could they stake as collateral to assure their compliance? Noxon had to proceed on the assumption that they *would* try to cheat him eventually, even if they were perfectly sincere in their promises now.

Yet, being human, he couldn't help but try to give the oath as much force as possible.

"I don't know how your society functions," said Noxon. "Do you speak for everyone? Every single homusculus?"

"Definitely." "We all agree."

"If you truly all agree, then I'm not sure you should be considered human," said Noxon. "Total agreement is something humans never achieve."

"Lots of discussion." "Plenty of disagreement." "Many hate the plan."

"The issue is whether this promise will be binding on all the homusculi, even those who disagree."

"Can any human speak for *all* other humans?" asked a lone voice.

"Thank you for your candor. I'm aware that not only is there disagreement among you now, but also there will be generations between now and when I leave, and generations on board the ship. The children may not like being bound by the promises of a previous generation."

"As you said. We are human."

"So you will understand and forgive me, I think, if I treat the mice who come with me as if there were no promise. I will check constantly. I will assume you are trying to cheat on our agreement."

"We never cheat." "We give our word." "You're a fool if you think we're lying."

"I think you're telling the truth," said Noxon. "I think I can trust you enough to take six mice. None of them pregnant."

"Not enough," they said at once. "At least twenty."

And from that Noxon concluded that they needed at least twenty mice in order to . . . what, move objects through space-time? Or simply to establish a viable gene pool? No point in asking; he wouldn't trust the answer to be complete. They always intended many different things at once. It was like trying to blow smoke away. It swirled and eddied but you were never in control of it.

"Bring thirty," Noxon said. "In case I accidentally step on a few of you."

They might or might not have a sense of humor. Whether they took this as irony or as a threat didn't really matter to Noxon at the moment.

"When do we go?" "How long till we go?"

Those were excellent questions. He should say good-bye to Param and let her know she was on her own. Or should he first take her to Olivenko? Or wait until he could unite the whole group?

It was enough if one of them knew that he had gone. Param could tell the others. Noxon was the extra Rigg, the expendable one. No reason to act as if he thought he would be missed. When he left, there would be exactly the right number of Riggs in the world.

"Stay here," he said. "And by that I mean—everybody off me and out of my clothes. That includes the five clinging to the insides of my trouser legs, the three on my arms . . ."

They knew that they couldn't fool the facemask. They scampered or leapt, and in a moment they all stood around him in a circle.

"It isn't very promising when you already try to sneak one stowaway with me."

They put on a good show of consternation, and it's true that the one who was still clinging to the back of his shoe looked small. He might really be as young and foolish as they said. Or he might have been of a small breed.

You can't trust the mice.

It was easy to jump back to Param—he had never lost track of her path. This despite the fact that it had already jumped backward in time twice since his path had left hers. Her path was unbroken—it just got fainter and fainter as she practiced her backward jumps. She was about to do it again, he could see, when he arrived and touched her shoulder. She whirled and then relaxed.

"I'm going," he said. "To Earth, I hope."

"What about me?" she said. "Are you going to leave me here?"

"Yes," he said. He tried not to think what it meant that her only thought was that she would be alone for a while, rather than that he might be going to death or oblivion. "But you'll find your way home."

"I'll miss you," she said, gripping his arm.

"Rigg will soon be back from his wandering."

"You have begun as the same person," said Param. "But you're the one who was so patient. You're the one who realized my sounds and your paths might be the same thing."

"I'll miss you, too," said Noxon. "And not just because you taught me how to slice time effectively."

She kissed him on the cheek.

"You know you'll have to go through the same thing with Rigg when he gets back. He won't be happy till he can slice time this quickly. Umbo too, probably."

"It would never do to give one of you an advantage over the others," said Param. "It's so hard to persuade would-be alpha males to get along."

CHAPTER 9

Getting It Right

So there was Umbo, floating down the river, in no hurry now, so he only used his oar to keep the boat straight in the water. And, to tell the truth, he dragged the oar in the water to slow himself down. Because what was he going to do when he got to Leaky's Landing? At this moment, young Umbo was with Rigg, making their way overland beside the river. *They* wouldn't reach Leaky's Landing for several weeks.

Then there would be the time spent getting to O, their arrest, and Umbo's journey back to Leaky's Landing with Loaf after they got off the boat where they were prisoners. After that, the time Umbo spent struggling to learn to send messages without Rigg's help.

Finally Umbo and Loaf had set out to liberate Rigg. That was the great divide. After that, Umbo had appeared to Leaky again, then brought Loaf to her with his facemask. That's the time he had to return to—and it was a long time from now. Umbo could *feel* how much empty time lay ahead of him. Time that he would have to live through, doing . . . something. Doing nothing that mattered.

If Param had been with him, she could have sliced them forward to the right time. But she was off with Noxon, learning how to time-shift without leaving herself vulnerable to assassins with iron bars. That was more important than the fact that Umbo was now stuck having to live through almost half a year.

No, not "almost half a year." He had a much clearer idea than that.

Umbo couldn't have said the exact number of days, because time wasn't actually divided like that. It wasn't divided at all, except into the huge number of separate causes and effects that determined the direction, if not the speed, of the flow of time. But without being able to name it, he *knew* the amount of time that lay ahead of him. He knew the "place" of those events in the forward sweep of time.

He had visited that narrow period of time often enough—his and Loaf's departure from Leaky's Landing, then his messages to Leaky and his return with Loaf—that it was now a firm anchor in his sense of the flow of time.

He couldn't have charted it on paper—this many days, on this particular date. He didn't keep a calendar in his head, and besides, whatever this time-shifting talent was, it couldn't depend on literacy or calendars because presumably it would simply work, like sight and hearing. Yet he *knew*, the way you know where your hands are when your eyes are closed, just *when* in the future that day would come.

Was that real? Could he use that, the way Rigg used his paths, to journey to that time?

He thought back to the weeks in the roadhouse when he was struggling to find a way to send messages to the past without having Rigg to help him. When he finally began to have success, that was just the beginning. Then the trick was to get a sense of how *far* to reach back in order to send a message to arrive at the right place and time. Gradually, through trial and error, he had learned to have pretty good precision in throwing his image into the past and keeping it there.

At the time, he had thought he was *going* into the past, but now he understood the difference, and could do both. When he needed to push himself back to a few weeks before he and Rigg had left Fall Ford, it was easy to shift back within a day or two of the time he wanted. He didn't have to be more precise than that.

And even though he had fretted about whether he might be asleep or doing something else when the exact moment of Kyokay's death approached, on the day he simply knew it was the day, and at the time, he looked up to see Kyokay running toward the stairs—but why? There by the waterfall he could hear nothing. Why had he looked at that exact moment?

Because he knew. When he was in the future, he knew how to come back to a time before that event, and then when he reached that moment again, coming from the other direction, he *knew* it before his eyes could confirm it.

I have a map of time in my mind, just the way a blind man might learn to keep a map of his house in memory.

And he relied on that map all the time to travel into the past. It wasn't precise to the second, but after so much experience, when he needed it to be, it was precise to the hour, or the half hour, or the ten minutes. He didn't think of it that way—he just concentrated and got more careful when the exact time mattered.

No, he didn't just concentrate. He sped up his perceptions— or slowed down time, as he had always thought of his talent as a child. The more precise he needed to be, the more sharply he made himself perceive the world, and the slower time seemed to flow for him. The map of time got sharper and clearer, the faster his perceptions were working.

He closed his eyes for a few moments at a time, trusting the dragging oar to keep them in the middle of the river, pointed downstream, and slowed time in order to examine his map. It wasn't visual. It really was like the way you can feel your limbs without looking, or your tongue inside your mouth.

He couldn't see the past—he wasn't Rigg—but he could remember it. Not every second of it, but the key moments. Mostly times when he had sent messages or time-shifted, but also a few other events. The death of Kyokay. Jumping off the rock with Param. The moment when he accepted Param's proposal of marriage.

He couldn't see the future—nobody could. How could he have markers in times he had never lived through? But the next few years, though they lay ahead of him at this moment, had once been part of his past. No, they had *often* been part of his past.

159

Those few years that he had already lived through more than once *were* part of his map. If he were ahead of them in the stream of time, he'd have no hesitation in time-shifting *back* to them. Couldn't he use that same timesense to shift to other remembered points in time, even though at this particular moment they now lay in his future?

He had always thought of shifting into the future as a leap off a cliff. Not knowing what the future felt like, what was happening there, to jump into it would be insane. What if he jumped ten years into the future? By then the Destroyers would have come, and the future he entered would be an uninhabitable wasteland. And if by ill luck he should jump into the exact moment in the future when they were burning Garden to a cinder, he would probably die before he could realize that he'd better jump out of there.

But no, not now. Because he had already lived through that time. He had stood on the beach in Larfold and watched the fires begin, before they all jumped back to a safer time.

That moment—the end of the world—was one of those markers in the future that he remembered with all the certainty of the most important times he had lived through or visited in the past.

And because his time map had nothing to do with place—it was a map of whens, not wheres—he could jump to any particular moment in the past, no matter where he was. He'd still be however many hundreds of leagues away that he had been before the time-shift, but he would be *when* he wanted, even if he wasn't yet *where* he wanted. Just as he had done in jumping back to the time before Kyokay's death.

Now Kyokay was alive again, but the day Umbo saved him was the same marker as the day he had failed to save him the first time around.

Maybe I *can* jump into the future. Not slice into it, a fraction of a second at a time, invisible to everyone, yet vulnerable to enemies. *Jump* to it.

Not while I'm out in the middle of the river. I don't want to arrive at exactly the moment a boat is passing through this exact spot.

And what if for some reason the boat didn't come with him? Even if he could shift into the future, there was no guarantee he could take anything with him in that direction. Umbo could swim, but he didn't relish a soaking.

As he pulled the boat onto a firm landing place, it occurred to him that if he couldn't take the boat, what about clothing? The jeweled knife?

No, no, these were foolish fears. Param jumped into the future all the time. A microsecond at a time, but she skipped forward with clothes and whatever she was carrying on her. I'll have everything with me when I get there. If I get there. Won't I?

He stood on the bank, then decided that he'd better do this sitting down. And not just sitting, but sitting inside the boat, holding on to the knife with one hand and the rim of the boat with the other. Just to make it clear to whatever force in the universe controlled time-shifting that this was his stuff and he wanted it with him.

Then he slowed down time—sped up his perceptions—and

found the marker he was looking for. He sharpened his awareness even more, and then chose a time a little bit this side of the time when he left Loaf and Leaky to come on this errand.

And then he jumped.

He opened his eyes. Nothing had happened.

Well, that was disappointing.

He sighed and rose to get out of the boat.

The boat shifted and slid awkwardly under him. He nearly fell.

The solid ground at the riverbank was muddy now. It hadn't been muddy when he landed. He looked at the sky. It was sunny, but he could see the clouds that must have just finished dumping rain here not an hour ago.

It had rained two days before they got to Leaky's Landing.

Of course everything looked unchanged. He was sitting on the riverbank looking at the river. What, exactly, had he thought would be different?

But his timesense didn't lie. When he checked to see when this moment was, he could sense the marker looming only a couple of days from now.

Since he didn't know how far upriver he was from Leaky's Landing, if he was going to arrive when he said, he would have to hurry.

Then he laughed at himself. If he arrived late, he could easily jump *back* to the right time.

I jumped into the future. Not slicing, jumping. To the time I chose. Nobody else can do that. With no external paths, only the map of time I unconsciously formed while doing all this jumping, I was able to jump into a future I had already lived through.

As he got the boat back out into the middle of the stream, he checked his markers again. The end of the world was the farthest in that direction. And in the past, the farthest he had gone—well, the farthest he had pushed anybody—was to almost the exact time when Ram Odin's nineteen ships crashed into Garden, destroying native life almost as thoroughly as the Destroyers would. Rigg had chosen the moment by attaching to the path of the last animal to pass through the space where the Wall would be. Rigg had chosen the animal thinking that it would be the last moment before the Wall was created, but no. After the crash of the nineteen ships, there *were* no large animals to leave paths through the wall. So Rigg had inadvertently taken them almost to the exact moment of the *previous* destruction of life on Garden.

We were the Destroyers that time. Not us exactly, not Rigg and me and the others, but we humans. Ram Odin. The expendables. Garden has had bad luck with living through the arrival of ships from Earth.

Still, this meant that Umbo's map of time extended from the last moment before humans came until nearly the last moments that humans survived. Almost all his time-shifting had been within the past dozen years, but they had gone back to a time only a few centuries after the establishment of the colonies, when they all went to witness, in Vadeshfold, the battle between the people with facemasks and the people without them. That is, they had all gone except Umbo, because he had had to stay behind as their anchor, so they could return to the time they had left.

Now, though, I don't need an anchor. Now I could go with them on such an expedition, and bring us all back. Because the whole history of Garden, up to the end, is the past in my mind.

He reached Leaky's Landing with a few hours to spare. He didn't want to walk into the roadhouse before he left to go save Kyokay, lest he should cause a copy of himself to pop into existence or, worse, deflect his earlier self enough to make it so he did not figure out the plan that worked to save the reckless boy.

He was looking for an out-of-the-way place to wait, one where he wouldn't be noticed by his earlier self while he was waiting for an upriver boat. Then he realized: I don't have to wait. I can jump to the right time. Just because it's only a few hours doesn't make it any less possible.

Umbo chose an out-of-the-way place to make the jump in privacy. Not for the first time he wished for Rigg's path-sense, because Rigg would have known just how heavily trafficked any spot might be. Then again, Rigg couldn't help him in this case because the paths that would be most pertinent had not yet been laid down in this place. Rigg could not see into the future.

Umbo tried to keep from thinking, Rigg can't do what I can do. But the effort not to think it was nothing more than another way to think it, while feeling even more guilty and frustrated.

He made the jump forward to the exact time he wanted. To Loaf and Leaky, he would have been gone only an hour.

He walked to the roadhouse door, opened, came inside. "Well, I'm back," he announced.

Loaf and Leaky looked up from behind the bar, where Loaf was putting away glasses and mugs on the highest shelf.

"Took you long enough," said Loaf.

"Sorry," said Umbo.

"Well, did you save him?" asked Loaf.

"Mostly," said Umbo. "Pulled him out of the water before he drowned. His arms were—no, his legs were broken."

"You can't remember the difference?" asked Loaf. "Remind me not to let you tend to my injuries."

"That's *my* job," said Leaky.

"The first time, he broke his arms. The second time, it happened a little differently. He landed legs-first, so those are what broke."

"So you didn't interfere with events until after everybody thought he had died in the water."

"The first time I was so stupid I carried him home before Rigg and I had even left town, and that wrecked everything. So I had to do it over."

"Well, now that that's done," said Leaky, "Let's set out for the Wall."

"Give the boy a chance to rest," said Loaf.

"He's only been gone an hour," said Leaky impatiently. Then she gave a sheepish grin. "I haven't had as long as you two to get used to how things work now. He's been gone for weeks, hasn't he?"

She said it to Loaf, but spoke it while looking Umbo up and down. "Not a very cleanly expedition, it would seem," she said.

"I haven't done much clotheswashing."

"You never do."

"I keep thinking I'll just jump back to a time when they were clean."

Loaf glowered. "That really doesn't make sense."

"It was a time-shifting joke," said Umbo. "I don't have many people I can tell those to."

"Lucky them," murmured Loaf. "We'll leave for the Wall in the morning."

"One tiny problem," said Umbo. "We can't go through the Wall now."

"Rigg set it up so any two of our group can go through," said Loaf. "That's how we got back here to Ramfold."

Umbo shook his head. "Rigg hasn't set it up that way *yet*. And Vadeshex hasn't even met us. We don't want to arrive with you wearing that facemask. Who knows how differently he'd act if he already knew he would succeed."

"So we do have to wait," said Loaf.

"Not necessarily," said Umbo. "We have two choices. One. We can go back in time to before the Wall was made. Two. We can skip forward to right after we passed through on the way here."

Loaf looked at Umbo for a split second and then began a low chuckle. "You sly barbfeather," he said. "You've learned how to make forward jumps."

"I've been to the end of the world," said Umbo. "All of the future that we can possibly use has already been the past to me. So I can jump there now."

"This," said Loaf to Leaky, "is a very useful boy. I'm not sure any child of ours wouldn't make us feel disappointed at the clever things he *couldn't* do."

"But he'll be bigger, stronger, and not half so smug as this one," said Leaky, "so I'll take ours over *him* any day."

CHAPTER 10
Lord of Walls

"So am I a Finder of Lost Things again here?" asked Rigg.

"Not in Gathuurifold, no." Ram Odin chuckled. "No, for this wallfold you're going to have to go back to the rich-young-man pose you carried off so well in O when you were just starting out."

"I ended up in prison," said Rigg.

"Because they believed you were a royal, not because they *didn't* believe you were rich and educated."

"But I'm not educated in Gathuurifold. I won't know anything about their history or customs."

"Gathuurifold is as large as any other wallfold. You can be from one part of it and know nothing about the other parts. Science you'll know—more of it than they do—and mathematics. As for economics . . ." and here Ram Odin chuckled again, "they'll have a bit to teach *you*, though I hope you don't come away a true believer."

"So I'm a rich young man."

"No, you *act* like a rich young man. What you are, in terms they'll understand, is this. You are my owner. And you, in turn, are directly the property of the Lord of Walls."

"Property!" Rigg was appalled. "They have *slavery* here? That was done away with in Ramfold a thousand years ago. Long before the Sessamoto came out of the northwest."

"Slavery was abolished fifteen separate times in the past eleven thousand years in Ramfold, though admittedly I'm rather proud of Ramfold that this last time it was the whole wallfold that got rid of it, and it hasn't been reinvented yet. Though the People's Revolutionary Council was getting close."

"You're saying slavery is one of those universals."

"When you have wars, what do you do with the prisoners?" asked Ram Odin. "You can kill them all. Bloody work, that, and it encourages your enemies to fight to the death. You can send them all back home again as soon as the war is over, but in the meantime you have to feed them, and after they go home they're a ready-made, fully-trained army."

"I'm getting your point."

"You can sacrifice them to your gods, which makes a difference only if they believe in the same gods. Or you can put them to work as forced labor, to *earn* their keep. Or, let's see . . . keep them in prison camps, not working but having to be fed, until they die of old age. Which is the cruelest course?"

"You've made your point. So Gathuurifold is unusually

warlike? So they're constantly generating new slaves?"

"Not at all. In fact, I'd say Gathuurifold is unusually peaceful. War is quite rare. Because of all the things that slaves have been known to do, provoking wars is rarely one of them."

Rigg thought about this for a moment. "You mean *everybody* in Gathuurifold is a slave?"

"Slavery became pervasive, with this wrinkle, that slaves could own property which did *not* belong to their owners. That meant that slaves can own slaves, who own slaves, who own slaves."

"If you can own property, how are you a slave?" asked Rigg.

"Because your owner can move you to one place or another, can break up your marriage, can sell your children to some other owner, can decide how much education you'll receive, and what work you'll do, and what hours you'll keep."

"And this system persists?" asked Rigg.

"I'm not saying I like it," said Ram Odin. "It's just another way of organizing human life. It's only been like this for fifteen hundred years or so, and Wall-to-Wall for only nine centuries. But in human terms, nine centuries might as well be forever. People here have little idea that society *can* be organized any other way."

"Everybody owns everybody?" Rigg asked.

"Everybody is owned by somebody," said Ram Odin. "There are plenty of people who don't own anybody."

"So who's at the top of this pyramid? Who owns *him*?"

"I own him," said Ram Odin. "Or, properly speaking, you do, since you are now the master of all ships. But since you didn't know about this system, you haven't been giving him any instructions. Therefore he continues to follow the last instructions I gave him. And for our purposes in Gathuurifold, you are posing as *his* slave."

"Gathuuriex," said Rigg. "The Lord of Walls is the expendable."

"Who else?" said Ram Odin. "He never dies. He travels wherever he wants in his flying house, to make sure that his slaves are doing his will. I've instructed him to govern with a light hand. Whenever possible, he adjudicates disputes by making them work it out themselves, within certain parameters. He only goes after the Savages when they become particularly destructive, which he forestalls by making sure there are feeding stations in hard winters and droughts."

"Savages? So not everyone is in this slave system?"

"No system is good for everybody," said Ram Odin. "So yes, some people run away and escape into the wild. But most of them come back. The wild isn't safe. Nobody knows who they belong to, and so there are no rules."

"You make it sound like slavery is a good idea," said Rigg.

"I think slavery is a terrible idea," said Ram Odin. "But the whole idea of the wallfolds was to see what humans would do, what they would become with eleven thousand years of noninterference. Gathuuriex did absolutely nothing to promote slavery. He only stepped in to become the Lord of Walls—at my instructions—when there were getting to be too many murders among the top families."

"How kind of you," said Rigg. "Maybe that would have

brought down the whole system, did you think of that?"

"I did," said Ram Odin. "But this was only two hundred years ago, so I knew the end was coming, and these feuds had turned into wars before during the previous seven centuries of universal slavery. So I sent in Gathuuriex to become the owner of the top owners. He broke up the conspiracies, ended the feuds, arranged a few key divorces, dispersed the children who were the most tyrannical to learn some humility farther down the slave chain. I thought it wouldn't hurt anything to have a few centuries of peace in this place."

"Why not eleven thousand years of peace?"

"I didn't create the slave system," said Ram Odin. "For a long time I truly hated this place worse than any except Vadeshfold. I thought of it as a failure."

"So you intervened."

"No. It had already stopped being such an evil place a couple of thousand years ago. But no more talking about it, Rigg. I could have given you a history lesson about Gathuurifold and heard your tut-tuts and tsk-tsks back in Larfold. We have work to do."

"Work?"

"There are certain responsibilities involved in being a slave directly owned by the Lord of Walls. Because everybody answers to someone who answers to someone who answers to the Lord of Walls, nobody can tell his slaves that they don't have a right to travel wherever they want. But in return, such traveling Wallmen, which by the way is your official title, function as itinerant judges, auditors, inquisitors, and arbiters."

"I have no idea how to do that!"

"Neither does any other human being, yet we do all those jobs, all the time, whenever we get the chance. Rigg, you're the one who wanted to tour all the wallfolds. I can assure you that if you don't travel as a Wallman, you don't travel at all unless you have an owner who sends you on a specific errand. And since you don't belong to anybody, you would only have two choices."

"Become a Savage," said Rigg.

"Which you would not like, and which would not tell you much about how the vast majority of the people in Gathuurifold live."

"And the other choice?"

"Find somebody willing to take you on as his slave."

"And who wouldn't want a fine specimen like me?" asked Rigg.

"A self-assured, independent young man with a mouth on him? They would think your owner had done a bad job of training you and they wouldn't want to bring trouble into their house."

"I was being ironic," said Rigg.

"I wasn't," said Ram Odin.

"Couldn't I be *your* slave?"

"Nobody would send an old man like me out on extended errands. Much more convincing if you're the Wallman, and I'm your old clerk and adviser. If you were the slave, then I'd have to treat you like one, and you would truly, truly hate that. No, if you want freedom of action, you have to be a Wallman, and that means you have to do a Wallman's job. Suck it up, Rigg, and take it like a man."

"But the decisions I make as a judge—"

"Are final. There is no appeal. And you'll have this wise old adviser at your side. Trust me. You'll do as well as any of the *other* Wallmen."

They clattered along in a carriage. The vehicle was well-sprung, but the road was not in good condition, so there was a great deal of jouncing, and for all the clatter, they didn't make that much forward progress. "I'm not impressed with the road maintenance," said Rigg.

"You can take it up with the master of roads," said Ram Odin. "I'm sure you can get a lot of road repair started while you're in the area."

"But it won't continue after I'm gone."

"The master of roads belongs to someone who isn't you. If his master wanted him to fix this stretch of road, it would already be fixed."

"And this system works well enough to be universal?"

"I could have taken you to one of the places where it works best," said Ram Odin. "But then I'd be deceiving you, wouldn't I? No system works well unless good people do their jobs with integrity, and then almost *any* system works well enough."

"It's the problem with authority, at all times," said Ram Odin. "You only know what your subordinates tell you, and your commands are only carried out as long as your subordinates feel like it."

Rigg couldn't argue with that. He had seen enough of that already, and it was one of the principles Father had taught him.

Father. Lord of Walls. The same mechanical men, playing

different roles in different places. What Ram Odin didn't have to say was this: If you want a job to be done by someone you can trust, who won't lie to you, who'll persist in his obedience, get yourself a mechanical slave.

Of course, your mechanical slave will lie to everyone else, in order to achieve your purposes. But I am lying to everybody in Gathuurifold, in order to achieve *my* purposes. Purity is so hard to achieve.

So far Rigg had experienced only the privileges of Wallmen, and none of their duties. They had taken the Larfold flyer to a fairly remote city, where a carriage was waiting for them, along with letters of authority and a complete set of clothing for the journey. Wallmen, it seemed, wore an unbelievably silly style of clothing involving a puffy hat and intricately arranged bright-colored straps across the chest. It could not be put on without the help of a servant. And since Ram Odin had never arranged the straps either, they spent a good deal of time in the flyer, getting instructions from the ship's computer, until they finally got it down.

"I'm too old to learn mechanical tasks like this," said Ram Odin.

"I think this costume is a sort of safety valve," said Rigg. "If they make the wielders of authority look ridiculous, it takes some of the sting out of their authority."

"I don't see how that would help," said Ram Odin. "And you haven't seen yet what the other people wear."

Soon enough he saw that *every* job and every social level had its uniform. The messages were complicated, but the fundamental one was this: At what level of slavery were you, and how prestigious was your owner? A single band around your neck put you at the lowest level. But what was it made of? Leather? A thin red ribbon? A gold chain? A simple string? And when the straps moved away from the neck and onto the arms, then around the chest, it expressed such nuances as your years of education, and where you were schooled, and how highly your master esteemed you, and more, till Rigg's eyes glazed over.

The rules were all so complicated that Ram Odin was now wearing a transmitter in his ear, allowing the ship's computer to prompt him so he could "advise" Rigg. "We'll tell anyone who dares to ask—and almost no one will—that it's a device for delivering medicine very slowly, directly into my brain," said Ram Odin. "This will be taken as a sign that you esteem me highly— thank you for the great honor, O Master—and that the Lord of Walls esteems *you* so highly that he allowed you to festoon your prize servant with such a rare and prized adornment."

"Which no one else in the history of Gathuurifold has ever seen or heard of before."

"That's what makes it rare. But you can be sure that within six months, highly prized servants of very rich slaves will all be wearing intricately decorated ear-thingies. It will probably make them half deaf and give them headaches, but . . . anything for status."

There were no roadhouses, because there were no travelers who were free to stay where they chose. Instead, there were relay stations for changing horses, which only those within a few levels of the Lord of Walls could use, and there were the large houses of the highest-status slave in any town. Rigg, as Wallman, would call upon this person, bring the greetings of the Lord of Walls, and then accept the offer of lodging for as long as he cared to stay. Of course he would be put in the master's own bed and bedroom.

Meanwhile, Ram Odin would stay in the relay station, in a little room over the stable. He assured Rigg that this was very fine treatment for a personal servant, and he rather liked the smell of horses.

Thus they had made their way for a week from town to town, always on their way to somewhere else.

But even so, people were already bringing disputes to Rigg. So far they had all been of the sort where the solution is easy and obvious, but people's egos and anger were so involved that the easy solution was the one that everyone hated most. Rigg's job, in every case, was to impose the easy solution, but to find a way to phrase it so that nobody felt that they had been repudiated or that their arguments had not been heard. It was a game of language more than law. Nobody was necessarily happy, but everyone was mollified, and Ram Odin assured him that they would abide by the decision because, after all, it was the easy and obvious solution.

Ram Odin had almost never had to whisper into Rigg's ear to tell him of some obscure point of law. In fact, the whispering had mostly been to tell him exactly how this or that person should be addressed. Titles were very important in this land of slaves.

Rigg wondered if they could really be called slaves anymore. He already had a pretty good idea that slavery was evolving into something else, without losing the name. People had so much freedom to make economic decisions—to buy whatever they liked, and to assign their slaves to manufacture whatever they wanted. Some masters hired out their slaves to others, for a fee; others allowed their slaves to make their own arrangements to serve here or there as they could find work.

It became much clearer when he began his conversations the next day. They were judicial proceedings, to be sure, but they were *called* conversations and in fact that's how they were conducted. As slaves, they had no rights, but it was always legitimate for slaves to ask for a conversation with a nearby Wallman. If the Wallman then decided to make decisions in the name of the Lord of Walls, well, that was always his option. And if there were any reprisals against a slave whose conversation might have led to unhappy results for someone, then they could be sure that the wrath of the Lord of Walls would come down on them. For it was not right for one slave to take vengeance on another for merely bringing information before the Lord of Walls or his closest servants.

It was a system that begged to become corrupt, Rigg saw at once. He would have been surprised, though, if someone had come to him with the offer of a bribe. The Lord of Walls, after all, was completely incorruptible himself, and would not be susceptible to flattery or deception by his underlings. If someone was certified as a Wallman, it was because the expendable Gathuuriex had found him to be intelligent, morally decent, and completely honest. Rigg wondered if he would have measured up to Gathuuriex's scrutiny, if he had attempted to reach this lofty office through the normal means.

But it was not only because Gathuuriex and his men could not be bribed—it's that every single person would have to account to their owner for what they did with their money. Or so it was, at least, in theory. This first set of conversations was being held in a part of the land that was clearly not held to the same standards as the crisply tended fields and shops they had passed through at first. Everything was just a little raggedy. People moved with less of a hurry. Rigg wondered if they worked with a kind of laziness or carelessness, too. Presumably he had been given the owner's bedroom, as at any of the relay stations. There was running water in the privy room, which Rigg had come to expect in Gathuurifold. But the hot-water knob merely spun, as if it were decorative.

Which it turned out to be. The owner explained that he didn't feel much of a need for hot water in the washbasin in the privy room—only the bathroom needed it, and that was downstairs, a single tub to serve the household. "They make the faucets to fit the specifications of richer folk than we are, sir. So I could only buy one with a cold and a hot. But there's nothing to connect the hot one to, so it spins."

It all made perfect sense. It just felt . . . if not slovenly, then slapdash.

But when it came to the conversations, people took a great deal of care. Most plainants came in with their master, or a steward sent by the master. And there must be some kind of legal training, even if there was no written law—slaves having no rights, except the right to petition. Make sure you say this, the master would whisper. She really meant to say, not that, but *this*, a steward would explain, as the plainant sat there nodding. Yes, yes, that *is* what I meant.

After the plainant was done, Rigg could either send for the misbehaver—there was no presumption of innocence—or simply announce his decision. Sometimes he was tempted to decide against someone whose complaint sounded frivolous, or for someone who was clearly sincere in her grievance. But his expectations from the customs of Stashiland—laws and practices older than the Sessamids and certainly older than the People's Revolution—made this impossible for him.

Every time, he learned something important from the misbehaver. Sometimes it became clear that the actual complaint was merely an excuse for bringing the misbehaver before the Wallman. One swaggering overseer was arrogantly dismissive of the complaint—that he was always rude to the woman in question, even though she tried to serve him well. "She's clumsy, she's stupid, and she doesn't even try," he said. "I'm wasting time I owe to my master, so she not only costs him what she eats without producing anything of worth, now she's making *me* less productive."

Rigg saw at once that the man was blustering to hide some kind of shame. There was something he didn't want to get caught at. At first Rigg thought it might be that the man was unkind to many other servants, and only this one had the courage to come forward. But it would actually be strangely to his credit if he was equally rude to everyone, instead of singling this one out.

"If you don't mind sitting here for a moment," said Rigg, "I'd like to think about something."

"No, no, I don't mind," said the overseer, because what else could he say to a Wallman?

Rigg kept his eyes calmly fixed on the overseer's face, but in fact his attention was directed elsewhere. He followed the overseer's path backward in time. The little factory that he managed was only half a kilometer away, and Rigg studied his pattern of movement through the past day. Two days. Three.

"You're not a very hardworking man," said Rigg. It had taken him only about a minute to do this examination, because the face-mask made everything go so much more quickly.

"I work as hard as I should!"

"It seems to me that you hardly visit the factory floor."

"What did she say about me!" the man said, outraged. "That's not her business. She doesn't own *me*, the master gave me charge over *her*."

Rigg felt Ram Odin's touch on his forearm. So instead of answering, he smiled and turned to Ram.

"My friend," said Ram Odin, "do you think that Wallman Rigg came here without first inquiring of the Lord of Walls whether he had any concerns?"

The man settled down at once. "She only has a right to complain about how I treat *her*," he muttered.

"Do you think Wallman Rigg doesn't know that?" asked Ram Odin. "He knows what he knows—that slave only complained about your rudeness."

"You're not a hardworking man," said Rigg. "You walk *through* the factory in the morning when you arrive—but work has already been going on for some time. If anyone tries to ask you anything or tell you anything, you brush them aside. Too busy for their problems, is that it?"

"They should do their work and not bother me with endless *nothing.*"

"But the slave who complained—she insisted, didn't she? She came to your door and knocked."

"My door is always unlocked."

"But your rudeness is the same as a lock—designed to teach people to leave you alone. She complained that the equipment kept breaking, and some of it couldn't be repaired. Three spinners are idle all the time, because their wheels don't work."

"Then they should call for the repairman!"

"He doesn't answer to them, though, does he? When they send for him, he doesn't come, because it isn't *you* sending for him."

The man opened his mouth to say something, then looked furtively away. He had been about to lie. "I didn't realize it was so serious. You're right, I should have summoned the repairman myself."

"There are a lot of things you should have done yourself," said Rigg. "What do you do, alone in your office, since you aren't doing any of your work for the factory?"

The overseer seemed as if he wanted to protest, but again, he shied away from a quibbling lie. "I sleep," he said.

"I know," said Rigg. "Why don't you sleep at home?"

The man leaned his elbows on the table, put his head in his hands, and began to weep.

"You walk up and down in your rooms. Your children are asleep—why aren't you?"

The man finally mastered himself enough to speak. "She's a good woman, my wife. My master chose very well for me."

"I'm sure he did," said Rigg. "Yet something keeps you from sleeping."

The overseer leaned back in his chair, rubbing his eyes and rocking his head back as if he were looking for something on the ceiling. "She snores," he said at last.

Rigg did not laugh. The man's misery was so sincere that Rigg did not want to make light of it. And this much he knew was true: He was getting no sleep at night.

"Tell me about her snoring."

"Great ronking snores, sir. As if she were calling to geese to come back from their migration. As if she were sawing through great trees. And then in mid-snore, she stops. Stops breathing. And I wait. Because if she doesn't start soon I have to waken her. Then she starts, and the noise is horrible. If she's breathing I can't sleep, if she's not breathing I can't sleep."

"Yet you've said nothing to anyone."

"Because I know how my master will solve the problem," the man said. "I'm not complaining, he's a fair master, but he goes straight to the obvious solution."

"Separate bedrooms so you can sleep?"

"That would be such a bad example!" he said. "If he gives me a separate bedroom because of snoring, every woman he owns will be asking for a separate bedroom because her husband snores. Too expensive."

"And I think you don't want to tell anyone about your wife for fear of shaming her."

"I love her," said the man. "My master would split us up if he knew."

"Split you up?"

"She already has three children, which my master thinks is enough for any of his women. But not for his best men. He'll give me to another woman who doesn't snore, and put her in my wife's place. Everyone will be taken care of, but he can't have me become . . . an unproductive male. His policy is that his best men should make six babies."

"That seems a little imbalanced," said Rigg.

Ram Odin touched his arm.

"Not said as a criticism, just as an observation," said Rigg.

"It's actually very sensible," said the overseer. "Women put their lives at risk with every baby they have. Each one weakens them. But a man puts nothing at risk. It's good to have a father to help with the little ones, good to have a marriage where people care for each other. But when a woman wants to stop, any time after three, he lets them move out right away. Just like that."

"Divorce at the wife's option," said Rigg.

"Most women that love their husband, they stay out the six," said the overseer. "But some die, just as the master fears. His policy is a wise one."

"So if you complain to him about the snoring, he'll assume that you want a divorce."

"He won't care what I want, sir," said the overseer. "Why should he?"

Rigg curbed his anger at this foolish system. "Why doesn't her snoring keep the children awake?"

"The doors are good and solid, sir," said the overseer. "And they sleep like babies, because they are. They had that snoring the whole time they were in the womb, sir."

"And you don't really want to sleep in a separate room because of the times she stops breathing."

"I don't want her to die, sir," and he burst into tears again.

"My first decision," said Rigg, "is that you must go immediately into the room where that spinner is waiting."

"But she'll see me like this," he said.

"I want her to," said Rigg. "Don't you see that she'll think I must have rebuked you severely, to reduce you to tears? That may satisfy her completely, don't you think? Don't *show* her your tears. Try to conceal them. She'll see. Now go."

The man got up at once and went through the door that led to the room where the woman was waiting.

"So you start with the illusion of having punished him," said Ram Odin.

"I don't have any idea what to do."

"One thing you've done is quite remarkable," said Ram Odin. "You got to the heart of the matter. The woman is going to feel remorseful for having made the overseer weep. It's obvious she only complained about his rudeness because the factory is falling apart and she only has a *right* to complain about how he treats *her*."

"I know that," said Rigg. "This is a terrible system, you know?"

"Because in Ramfold, free workers and free managers are never in a situation where the employees are terrified to complain to the owner about how the manager is doing his job?"

Rigg rolled his eyes. "That's different."

"It's the same," said Ram Odin, "under different names. They are both owned by the same master. In Ramfold, they would both work for the same employer. But both would be terrified of losing their position."

"In Ramfold, the owner of the factory can't divorce a man from his wife because he complains about her snoring."

"But in Ramfold," Ram Odin said mildly, "the owner would demand that he explain why he's sleeping during the hours he's paying him to work. If he doesn't fire him out of hand, he'll demand that the manager find a way to sleep or quit his job. So the manager is right where this overseer is—does he act to protect his wife from her apnea? What good will it do her if he loses his position and can't get a good recommendation? They'll lose everything. Out on the street. Disaster. In all likelihood, reduced to poverty and—"

"I get the point. But it still doesn't help me figure out what to do."

"I think you should let me sit with the wife tonight. Let him sleep in my quarters. I'll have the ship listen to her breathing and evaluate her medically and tell me whether the apnea is life-threatening."

Rigg looked at him uncomprehendingly.

"Apnea. Stopping breathing from time to time. It affects a lot of people but very, very few die of it. If we can tell him that she's not going to die, he can go sleep in the children's room."

"Oh," said Rigg.

"And if she really *is* in danger, then we tell the owner that the overseer is torn between protecting his property—the wife—and managing the factory."

"The owner will still make them divorce," said Rigg.

"Not if you forbid him to do that," said Ram Odin. "Remember, the owner is also a slave, and *his* owner is owned by someone who is owned by the Lord of Walls."

"I really hate Gathuurifold."

"No, you're just barely coming to understand it, that's all. You'll find that people are still people and find a way to carve out a life for themselves within whatever rules their culture imposes on them. This master's rules about marriage are actually derived from his religion—the ship was telling me this while you were listening to the overseer. It's a very practical religion, not a lot of ritual but plenty of rules of life and most of them make sense. But as with all rule sets, there are unintended consequences. Like the women who have six babies so they don't have to leave their husbands."

"You're saying that the whole wallfold doesn't have that rule."

"Most people who practice the religion don't actually *follow* that rule. My guess is that rather than obey you about *not* forcing a divorce on them, the owner will sell the factory to someone else."

"Come on," said Rigg. "Sell a factory because your overseer's wife snores and the Wallman said you couldn't split them up?"

"Remember that the factory's in a bit of a mess. Broken equipment. Badly managed."

"So the new owner will get rid of the overseer."

"Probably sell him," said Ram Odin. "He shouldn't be in this line of work anyway. He's a terrible manager."

"Only because he doesn't sleep at night!"

"Oh, Rigg, please. It would take him ten minutes to listen to the woman's complaint and send for the repairman. He hates his job. Probably never asked for it. So yes, he's desperate for sleep, but he's also desperate not to do his job."

"How do you know that?" asked Rigg.

"Experience, my lad," said Ram Odin. "I've known plenty of managers like that. They hate their job, they hate their lives. If I owned the man, I'd make some effort to find out what he actu-ally *likes* to do, and then find a way to let him earn his keep by doing it. But then, I'm probably too soft to be a really effective slaveowner."

"You? Soft?" Rigg shook his head. "I know you better than that."

Ram Odin didn't argue. "Do you agree that I should offer to sit up with the wife tonight and listen to her breathe?"

"Don't you need *your* sleep?" asked Rigg. "If you fall asleep during tomorrow's conversations, I'll have to sell *you* to some-body else."

"Did you notice something else?" asked Ram Odin. "Some-thing personal about their response to you?"

"Yes," said Rigg. "Nobody looks away from my face. I'm apparently much prettier here."

"You're a Wallman," said Ram Odin. "Power and authority make any man handsome."

"I liked being a Finder of Lost Things much better."

Rigg went ahead and held the next conversation. He put in a full day and was exhausted by suppertime. He and Ram Odin ate a pretty good meal, considering that slaves normally didn't have much choice about what they ate, so the culinary arts had no financial incentive to improve.

At breakfast, Ram Odin looked perfectly well rested. "She's not in danger at all," said Ram Odin. "Half an hour in, the ship gave me a full prognosis, and I went in to where the poor fellow was busily trying to sleep in the room with his two boys. I took him into the hall, told him the good news. Of course, I had to phrase it as *your* decision based on *my* medical expertise—that's part of the reason you bring me along. Just in case anyone asks."

"Now you're a doctor."

"I *have* been a doctor, more or less, when I started up the colony in Odinfold. Of course, with the ship's equipment, anybody could be a doctor."

"He believed you?"

"I didn't leave till he was really asleep in the boys' room."

"Now if the wife dies of a heart attack . . ."

"He can't complain," said Ram Odin. "He's a slave. And we did nothing wrong, because we had the best available medical advice. Did you have a better plan?"

"I had no plan at all," said Rigg.

"So what are you thinking? How you ought to shut down the Wall and bring the rampaging Sessamoto legions to do away with this whole repulsive system?"

"Bad as this system is," said Rigg, "I know enough about history—and about the Sessamids—to be skeptical about bringing about any actual improvement. As you pointed out, the system is no worse than the people running it, which is you."

"Indirectly," said Ram Odin.

"And there's a serious danger of the Sessamids liking the idea of universal slavery and importing it to Ramfold."

Ram Odin chuckled. "I hadn't thought of that. They'd fail, but they'd be envious of the idea of owning everybody."

"I think what matters here is that they've accommodated slavery to human proportions. They've adapted it so people can bear to live with it."

Ram Odin gestured for him to go on.

"Slaves owning property, including other slaves. That means that nobody's a pure owner—they're all accountable to somebody above them. With the Lord of Walls and the Wallmen as a court of last appeal. It's a check on the power of ownership."

"But it's still ownership," said Ram Odin.

"Yes. People have surrendered a huge amount of personal choice. But not *economic* choice. They still decide what to spend their money on."

"That's why there's still an economy," said Ram Odin. "Very good."

"Economic freedom means that relative prosperity is still possible—even for the slaves at the bottom of the ownership heap. They can *aspire*. And slavery itself appeals to people who don't want the risks of freedom. If their lives go bad, there's always someone else to blame. They don't have to think and decide and bear the consequences of their own choices."

"Very good," said Ram Odin. "I think of slavery in Gathuurifold as a kind of climax feudalism. As feudalism was *supposed* to work but never did. And this system did *not* work well when there was a small ownership class and bribery was rampant. Corruption sapped all prosperity out of the system and the owners did what they wanted, spreading misery and havoc."

"But that would have led to revolution, eventually," said Rigg. "A revolution that you eliminated by instituting this benign Lord of Walls."

"That's true," said Ram Odin. "And I would be duly ashamed of myself except that near-universal slavery persisted for centuries, corrupt and oppressive in the extreme, and there was no revolution. And then we were getting close enough to the end of the world that I decided that instead of letting millions die in a social upheaval that would not only mean bloody war but also economic dislocations that would lead to poverty and starvation and misery on a large scale, I would simply tidy things up and let all these people have what happiness was possible within this strange, oppressive system, until the Destroyers come and wipe them all out."

"I don't know if that was a good decision," said Rigg. "You could just as easily have decided that since they were going to die anyway, you might as well let them die fighting for freedom as passively waiting like cattle in the slaughterhouse."

"I'll admit that I'm getting old," said Ram Odin. "Struggling for a cause looks like a much better idea to the young than to the old."

"Because you're getting tired?"

"Because I've seen that reforms are never as transformative as the reformers imagine that they'll be. Nothing works as planned. What I did definitely made a bad system better."

"But if Noxon succeeds, and the Destroyers don't come . . ."

"You want me to make the Lord of Walls go on a long vacation."

"I think it's time for you and the expendable Gathuuriex to have the Lord of Walls take a long vacation and let the former Wallmen fight it out among them until the people revolt and make whatever progress toward freedom they can."

"Because Garden cannot survive one-nineteenth slave and eighteen-nineteenths free. A house divided against itself cannot stand!"

"It sounds like you're making a speech."

"Echoing one. So you're thinking the Walls *won't* come down?"

"I'm seeing reasons why they shouldn't *all* come down."

"You'll see more reasons as we continue these tours."

"I want to continue as a Wallman for a few more days."

"Better than being an itinerant Finder of Lost Things?"

"It's the same job," said Rigg. "I go back into the past and find out what actually happened. Then I do something about it."

"Ah, but *what* do you do."

"Any complaints?"

"So far so good."

"I get the idea," said Rigg, "that while I'm judging the wall-folds, you're judging me."

"I already know the wallfolds. You I'm just starting to get acquainted with."

CHAPTER 11

In Reverse

Noxon had all the time in the world, and so he walked to Ramfold. Having spent almost every waking moment with Param for the past few months, it was a relief to be alone. Nothing against his sister. He had come to love her, and perhaps even understand her as well as one person can understand another. But he needed to be alone for a while, and this was that while.

Well, not alone. Mice all over him, but they weren't chatty and that was fine with him. They were sulking because of the rules he had laid out for them. Once they got to Ramfold, they were not free to go off and start trying to populate the place with their species. Because of the facemask, they knew that even when he slept, Noxon was keeping a continuous count, and if he needed to, he could catch them. Well, not so much catch as crush. But that was the deal they made in order to be able to accompany him on the voyage.

It's not that he really had *all* the time in the world—he had more. The world had only a finite number of years. Noxon could have more years than that, if he wanted. He could just keep going back to other times, and live on until he died of old age. People who couldn't shift time were stuck with the life they had. If somebody came and burned all life from the surface of the world, well, that was too bad; they were cheated out of all their potential life after that.

But how was that different from the way the world worked all the time? You could get sick, you could take a fall, someone could kill you, there might be a flood, a drought, starvation. So many ways to die without living out your normal span. Everybody died of *something*, didn't they? The only thing that made the end of Garden so tragic was that everybody met up with the same death at the same time.

No. That wasn't the only thing. It wasn't even the main thing. What made the end of the world so terrible, so vile, so urgent to prevent, were two things.

First, *nobody* would be there to remember. Everything would be lost. You couldn't leave anyone or anything to continue work you had just begun. Any other death would at least leave a memory of what had once been. But not this one.

Second, and worse, was that somebody did it on purpose. It wasn't an act of nature, it wasn't an accident, it wasn't the vicissitudes of chance. It was the murder of a world. Nineteen worlds, nineteen collections of human history and culture.

But during his walk, Noxon didn't just think deep philosophical thoughts about why it was worth risking his life to try to prevent the end of the world. He also replayed old arguments with Father, pondered questions he had never had a chance to answer, thought about what Rigg might do, if Noxon succeeded in his mission—how he might finish out their shared life. If he might marry and have children, and if so, what wallfold he would choose to do it in, since by then he would know them all.

We are no longer the same person now, Rigg and I, thought Noxon. He is getting to know this world; I am leaving it. He has a future on Garden; I will never come back.

Even if he succeeded in changing Earth's future so that the Destroyers did not come, that did not even hint at a possibility that the new future would have room in a starship for Noxon to return to Garden. If by some miracle he managed to arrive on Earth, it would be at the time when Ram Odin's voyage—the first interstellar flight in human history—was just about to launch. He could not *tell* them he was a native of this world, because at that point Garden had not yet been settled, let alone named. Who would believe him if he tried to explain that by some bizarre stroke of fate, Ram Odin's ship was replicated into nineteen forward copies and one backward one, and that they were thrown back in time 11,191 years? From what Rigg had read in Odinfold, most nations on Earth would treat him kindly; few would lock him up as a madman. But certainly no one would believe him, and he would spend a lot of time conversing with doctors whose compassionate purpose would be to bring him back from this delusion of his. He certainly couldn't talk anyone into sending him home to Garden.

Nor could he slice time in order to be invisible and stow away on Ram Odin's original voyage. It would not do for him to run the risk of being noticed by the ship's computers on the outbound voyage, because they would then inform Ram Odin of everything that was going to happen.

Or would they? Did they lie to him, too? Or withhold information that he wouldn't think of asking for? Did all the expendables know from the start what would happen?

No. They would have acted, deliberately or inadvertently, in such a way as to change the future. Or would they?

Was this present time precisely the future that the ship's computers already knew would be reached, because the jewels he carried provided them with knowledge of every single action the computers and expendables would ever take?

There was no answer to this, but it didn't stop Noxon from thinking of possible ways that such things might work — or not work at all. It was a pleasure to be alone with his thoughts. Especially because he did not waste time thinking about the one vital thing: what he would find when he followed Ram Odin's path backward to the moment of the anomaly that created all these copies and plunged them back more than eleven millennia in time.

Either he would be able to detect the paths across that 11,191-year gap, or he would not. Either he would be able to detect the timeflow of the one backward copy of the ship, or he would not. And if he detected that impossible ship, either he would be able to attach himself to it, or he would not.

Fretting about it would not relieve his ignorance or allow him any insight into what it would be like, and how he would deal with it. There was a very good chance—the ship's computer had implied as much several times—that in trying to make any of these possible jumps, Noxon would find himself stranded outside the rational universe and never be able to get back. If this happened in the cold of empty space, his last moments would be mercifully brief. And he would not spend them wishing he could have saved Garden—if he failed and died, it would no longer be his responsibility.

Only if he failed but lived would he need to regret whatever mistakes he might be about to make that would lead to that failure.

Not a productive line of thought.

But as he walked from Larfold to Ramfold, he gradually lost interest in all the thoughts that he had wanted to think, and by the time he reached the Wall, he was weary of the journey. He even got to the point where he started speaking now and then to the twenty mice embedded in his clothing and in his small pack of tools and supplies. They must have been getting bored, too, because they answered now and then. Not that there was any real attempt at conversation. They might be sentient beings with a lot of human genes in common, but they were definitely not of the same village or the same tribe as Noxon. They had little in common, except this mission.

It was no problem for Noxon to pass through the Wall without one of his erstwhile human companions. The computers did not bother distinguishing between the two Riggs, so they were both exempt from the rule. He knew that the ships' computers monitored the Wall continuously, and when he entered Ramfold, that meant the expendable Ramex would be alert to his presence. So in the midst of the Wall he spoke aloud. "I'd like the flyer, please, Father."

Since he had had no itinerary, being content to eat whatever came to hand as he traveled, as he emerged from the Wall he had no idea where in Ramfold he might be, except that he was near the eastern Wall somewhere well to the north of the latitude of Aressa Sessamo. This was wild land, where various villages and tribes lived in an uneasy relationship with the central government. Never conquered and never assimilated into the Stashiland culture, these people paid, not taxes, but tribute. And not very much of that, because they were poor.

Or at least they made themselves *seem* poor when the emissaries of the Sessamids or the taxmen of the People's Revolutionary Council came for a visit. Who knew? A few of their people spoke Stashi; nobody from Stashiland spoke their language.

Except Noxon, since he had passed through the Wall and had all possible human languages instilled in him.

It would have been interesting to get to know these people, as he imagined Rigg was getting to know people in other wallfolds. But that was not his errand. He would rather avoid contact with them.

Yet he could not avoid it in the obvious ways—by slicing time, or jumping back and forth in time as the people's paths made it seem advisable. For if he strayed from this exact timeline, how would the flyer find him?

He saw the path of the man who spotted him, as he watched,

then ran off through the woods to report. He saw the paths of the people gathering to intercept him. Apparently strangers here were rare—or at least, strangers coming from the direction of the Wall. He wondered how long it would take the flyer to reach him. He knew they were fast, but *this* fast? And would the ship send the flyer with urgency? Or at leisure?

Noxon walked to the middle of a large meadow and stood there waiting. Soon they formed a ring around him, out of sight to his eyes, just inside the shelter of the trees.

"I am a visitor from beyond the Wall," said Noxon.

They made no sound, but he imagined their consternation at hearing their own language spoken by a stranger. Especially a stranger with a weird, semi-human face.

Then he saw the arrows coming toward him and realized that people responded to consternation in different ways. One of them was to kill the alarming stranger.

By now he was able to jump into time-slicing almost as quickly as Param. But he did not dare to slice his way too rapidly into the future. He had to remain in this spot until the flyer arrived.

Which was almost immediately, though it might have felt to Noxon like less time than actually passed. Certainly the first wave of arrows had all hit the ground, having passed through seeming nothingness—though Noxon felt them all as heat passing through him. They were very good at hitting what they aimed at. He knew the flyer had arrived by the way the people, who had started walking out into the meadow, suddenly rushed back to the cover of the trees.

A ladder dropped down out of the sky. Noxon stopped his time-slicing, dashed for the ladder, and began to climb. The flyer rose into the air, the ladder rose into the flyer, and they were gone before any arrows could find the range.

Inside the flyer, Noxon found Father waiting for him.

"You timed your arrival well," said Noxon.

"Good thing, too. The flyer was all for leaving when it found you had disappeared."

"Do you mind if I call you Father?"

"You can call me whatever you like," said Father. Or Ramex. "Do you expect me to call you Noxon instead of Rigg?"

"I wish you would. I once was Rigg, back when we spent so many years together, but I've been Noxon for months now and I need to make that identity completely my own."

"As you wish," said Ramex.

Father would never have said that, so this was the obedient expendable, not the domineering tutor.

It took very little time to reach the starship in Ramfold. Noxon watched out the windows and then on the screen that showed what was passing directly under and a little ahead of the flyer. They passed over Upsheer right at the falls. He barely caught a glimpse of the handful of buildings that made up Fall Ford. He couldn't see the stairway but he did see the broken-off nubs of the most recent of the bridges over the top of the falls. The others had long since crumbled away, becoming boulders in the pool at the base of the falls, and eventually becoming ever smaller rocks and stones as one rock broke another.

"You didn't want to linger, did you?" asked Father. "Stop by and say a fond farewell to Nox? I think she'd be flattered that you took her name."

"I think she'd be annoyed. And with this thing on my face, I doubt she'd believe that I'm me."

"She would if I told her to."

"She'd be alarmed to see you back from the dead."

"Less alarmed than you might think," said Father. "I think she has some idea of my seeming immortality. I'm not sure if she believed your story."

"If she had thought I was lying—"

"She would never have protected you, I know. But there's a difference between believing in your honesty and believing in the factuality of the story you were telling. If *you* believed it, then it wasn't a lie, but it wasn't necessarily the truth, either."

"I don't want to stop in and see her."

"I think the flyer would have been hard to conceal from prying eyes," said Father. "But I do miss the old village."

"No you don't," said Noxon. "You just pretend to have feelings like a human being."

"I have much nicer feelings than most."

"I'm sure," said Noxon.

He had wandered for years through the forest on the plateau of the starship's crater. Now it seemed small. They passed over it so quickly, and then straight down the shaft to the starship itself.

The starship of Ramfold was no different from any other. Except for a difference that only Rigg and Noxon could see. *This* one had Ram Odin's continuous path. Not the Ram Odin that was with Rigg, touring the world right now—that was the Ram of Odinfold. No, these paths were of the Ram Odin who had ordered the expendables to kill all the others, and then brought out his colonists when the land was habitable again. This was the Ram Odin who had married, had children who then had children of their own, and so on until that time-traveling gene had made its way into the embryo that grew up to be Noxon.

That Ram's path was all over the inside of the starship, but it was very, very old.

There were several iterations of more recent paths, too—the Ram Odin of Odinfold had visited here now and then over the years. But Noxon could see the faint but detectable differences between the paths of the two Ram Odins. They had begun to diverge once the copies had been made, and now Noxon could tell them apart with only a moment's hesitation, and not just because the Ram of Odinfold had all the recent paths.

Noxon went right to work, finding the very oldest path. It began in the pilot's seat in the small control room—just like the room where Rigg had come to stop Noxon from killing Ram Odin before Ram Odin could come and kill *him*.

But it could not begin in the pilot's seat. "He wasn't born here, in that chair."

"But he arrived here that way. You know your paths are tied to the surface of the planet, not to any vehicle."

"Then I've failed before I even began."

"You don't know that," said Father. "You don't know anything about what the paths do when the starship is not on a planet's surface. Besides, what you're seeing may not be the ship's arrival here. It might be the moment when the ship passed through the fold. Ram Odin was sitting in that chair for that, too."

"If I could see a path for *you*, I might be able to tell."

"But the facemask lets you see more than the mere path. Look closely. Even if you can't see me, you can see whether he's talking to me."

Noxon looked. "He's talking to you in all the paths. Talking to you seems to have been his main activity."

"It was," said Father. "I'm excellent company. Part of my programming."

"And sounding proud of it—that's part of your programming, too?"

"And a bit shy—don't forget that I also had a hint of modesty as well as pride."

"Well done," said Noxon. Now that he knew Father was a machine, he wasn't half so frightening. Nor, to tell the truth, was he trying to dominate Noxon the way he had dominated the child named Rigg.

"After he ordered the killing of the other Ram Odins," said Father, "I recall that he turned around in his seat in *this* direction. Because I was standing here."

Noxon looked at the oldest moments of the path and yes, there was indeed such a turn.

"Of course, I often stood here, and he always turned in that direction to face me, when he felt the need to face me. That time, though, he was looking to see if I was going to kill him—he didn't know if his command was the one with primacy."

"He looks relieved," said Noxon. "It's subtle—Ram Odin

doesn't show much — but the facemask can detect the difference in expression."

"I think we can safely say that the evidence indicates that the paths here in the starship go all the way back to the moment of division."

"The moment after."

"The moment *of* or the moment *after.* That will make a difference, won't it?" said Father.

"When I appear, the computers will read the jewels, won't they?"

"Oh my," said Father. "How full of perplexing possibilities that question is."

"Can the computers detect the jewels if I'm slicing time?"

"Slice away and we'll see," said Father.

Noxon sliced a little, and then moved very quickly. Father did not move, so it was hard to gauge just how far he had gone.

He came out of time-slicing. "Well?" he asked.

"Did you have to do it for a whole day?"

"You didn't move," said Noxon. "It was hard to gauge duration or speed."

"The answer is that for just a few minutes, the jewels were detectable but not readable. Then they became undetectable for the rest of the day."

"So if I slice time at a moderate pace, you can tell that I'm there. But when I really race, you can't."

"Here's a question," said Father. "You can slice time in such a way as to skip over fractions of a second in rapid succession, moving forward in time much faster than normal people do. But can you slice the other way? No, not backward—I know you can do that, too, though not as smoothly. No, I mean can you jump back into the past at the rate of one second every second, so that you freeze in exactly the same moment?"

"Except for the millions of collisions between the atoms of myself that would cause me to burst into flame or explode, yes, I think I could do that."

"Oh," said Father. "That's right. Slicing means you're nearly in the same place for a long time, but never in the same *time* at all. In fact, mostly not there at all."

"You raise an excellent point, though," said Noxon. "When I'm slicing—backward or forward—everything outside of me moves much faster. Which means that I'll have even less time to observe what's going on, at precisely the moment when I need to have as long as possible to observe."

"I'm not sure of the math on this," said Father—which Noxon, by old habit, took to mean that Father was sure to the hundredth decimal place—"but the exact moment of the jump has no duration at all. It isn't a moment. It isn't in time at all."

"That's not encouraging."

"But don't you see? If you can get to that moment, you can stay there as long as you want. Observe everything."

"Or I can be completely obliterated."

"Well, that was your gamble from the start, wasn't it?"

The tone of voice was Father's "what did you think?" and, just as if he were still a child, it made Noxon feel hopelessly stupid.

"It's not as if *you* can do any of this," said Noxon. And, for having responded like a child, he now felt that he *deserved* to feel stupid.

"You can do what you can do," said Father, "and I can do what I can do."

"I don't know what I'm doing," said Noxon.

"No one ever does," said Father. "But at least we expendables always know what we *did*. You humans can't even hold on to your memories, just the echo of a shadow of a dream."

Noxon didn't bother arguing. "You are superior in every way," he said placidly. "I'm content with my second-rate yet biologically active state."

"And every bug is content to be a bug."

"*Proud* to be a bug, and don't you forget it."

"I won't," said Father.

Noxon laughed. "I'm having so much fun, it makes me want to kill and skin a beast of some kind. Just for old times' sake."

"Old times," said Father. "I don't suppose you want to take me back to the beginning with you."

"Then there'd be two of you in Ramfold, and no way to hide you from your old self."

"I just want to know what happens," said Father. "You can understand my curiosity."

"No, I can't," said Noxon. "That's such a human emotion."

"It's in my programming. I have to know."

"And yet you won't."

"But the mice will," said Father.

"If I decide to bring them," said Noxon.

"And if you don't?"

"We can't have them infesting Ramfold," said Noxon. "They know that. So if I go, and I leave them behind, it's your job to make sure they never get off this ship."

"My job to kill them."

"You've done it before," said Noxon. "After all, you're expendable yourself."

"But you're going to take them," said Father.

"I haven't decided."

"But you *are*."

"I've killed and skinned a thousand animals. More. Do you think the deaths of these mice will bother me?"

"Yes," said Father.

"Well, you're right. And I'm taking them. If I die, they die. If I live, they'll share my fate."

"They're not saying anything about your magnanimous decision," said Father.

"They weren't sent on this mission because they were the chattiest of mice," said Noxon. "And I don't imagine they're rejoicing that I'm not going to have you kill them here, but instead I'm going to take them to die with me in oblivion between stars and between millennia."

"Or they weren't expecting to die even if you decided not to take them. You forget how much of my programming they understand."

"Now there's something it's easy to forget, since none of *us* learned anything about your programming," said Noxon.

"The Odinfolders know a lot," said Father. "But the mice know more."

"Do the mice know everything?"

"They know everything that can be known by mice," said Father.

"What does that mean?"

"That it's good to keep them guessing."

"I think I'm going to go now," said Noxon. "It was good to see you again."

"Every time you see any of the expendables, you see me," said Father. "I have all their memories. They have all of mine."

"But I know that you're the one who raised me from a pup."

"You think you know that," said Father. "How do you know we don't swap wallfolds every now and then? How do you know it was the same version of me that came back from every trip?"

"That's right. Shatter my confidence just before I'm really going to need it."

"It's my job," said Father. "Keep him guessing. Never let him feel *too* smart."

"You really are good at that part of your job. So I know this will mean nothing to you. And if it does mean something, you won't tell me anyway. But here it is. I forgive you for lying to me constantly as I was growing up. I thank you for teaching me all the things you taught me, and helping me learn to think the way I think."

"You're quite welcome."

"One more thing," said Noxon.

"Don't say it," said Father.

"Why not?"

"Because you know that if I answer, it will be a lie."

"I don't care whether it is or not," said Noxon. "I love you."

Father sighed. Part of his programming. "I love you too," he said.

Noxon attached to the earliest possible moment on Ram Odin's path, and then jumped just a hair, just a titch, just the tiniest bit beyond it.

Noxon was still on the ship. Still in the cabin. Ram Odin was there, in his pilot's seat. The expendable was standing exactly where Ram Odin would look for him in just a few moments, as soon as the expendable could tell him what had happened.

Only it hadn't happened yet.

Or, more precisely, it was happening right now. In this moment, this infinite unchanging moment, there was only one ship, but there were twenty potential ships coming into existence. It was jumping from one point in space to another that was many lightyears away and yet, at this moment, perfectly adjacent. It was passing from the moment zero of the year zero to a time 11,191 years earlier.

It had been the right guess, that the moment of transition existed but had no duration, and having no duration, therefore could not end. Infinitely brief, yet also infinitely long. Not so much outside of time as deeply within. Full of imminent creation and movement; yet because there was no duration, movement was impossible.

What Noxon had not guessed, and Father had not guessed, and Ram Odin had not guessed, was that in this timeless moment, Noxon could not move. The mice could not move. The electric signals of the computers hesitated and could not move on. Noxon's heart could not beat, he could not take a breath, but he also did not need a breath, did not need a heartbeat, because no cell in his body craved oxygen. All processes were in complete stasis because there was no movement and no causality and no possibility of change.

Yet *something* in him was still functioning. Because he could still see Ram Odin and the expendable. Or could he? Had that image simply frozen on his retina, in the place in his brain where vision was constructed? It could not change but it also could not fade away or leave?

Yet I am *thinking*, thought Noxon.

Only that's not what he thought, because to his surprise he could not form words or even clear ideas. He could not *remember* language. What would have caused him to form the conscious thought "I am thinking" was really an inchoate recognition of himself. And the knowledge that his self-realization contradicted the idea that nothing could happen, because his mind, at some level deeper than the brain, was still functioning.

And even if he could not turn away from the image of Ram Odin and the expendable and the pilot's seat and the different stations that the pilot could move to on his chair, if he could move, Noxon *could* see the paths.

Not *see* the paths. But whatever it was in him that sensed them, could sense them now. He had always been able to see the paths without turning his head. He only had to turn his attention. He could see them through walls. He could see them behind hills, though not as well. He was aware of them.

But the facemask was not helping him see them as he had become used to seeing them. The facemask was as frozen as the rest of his body, and it could not do for him any of the things that it was supposed to do. He was on his own.

What he saw were not the enhanced paths that were really people moving through space and time, as the facemask showed them. Nor were they the paths that he had seen since earliest childhood, a streak of something that he thought of as color, that he thought of as a line or a wind or a memory in the air.

What he saw now had no dimension because it had no duration. It was not a path, but an instantaneous slice of the path. A single moment of path.

He concentrated on that spark of path in Ram Odin. With all his other senses inert, each with its last message frozen in place, Noxon could sort his nonphysical observation of Ram Odin's path from all the physical noise and bring it to the center of his attention.

Still there were no words in his mind, but he was beginning to realize that far from being less clear for the lack of language, his thoughts were more clear. It's as if language itself, along with all the other noise of his senses, all the tumult in his brain, had been a barrier, a fog that kept him from achieving real clarity of thought. Without the necessity of explaining to himself in language, he was able to comprehend that nub of a path as it really was.

There were really twenty-one paths intersecting there.

One led into the past. It was the end of the causal chain that had brought this starship and Ram Odin to the moment of the leap across the fold.

Nineteen of them led forward into the future. He could not see where they led, because in this moment they still led nowhere, but there was causal potential in them: They would yet have more effects, whereas the path that had brought Ram Odin here had spent its causality. It was done.

None of these mattered to Noxon. Though he could not put his mission into words, he had not forgotten it. He knew that going back to the past to the beginning of Ram Odin's outbound voyage was his last resort—he would only follow it if he could not find the twenty-first path.

The twenty-first path was as rich with causality as the others. It was not spent like the past. But it was also somehow their opposite. They each pointed to slightly different destinations. But this one pointed somewhere else entirely, and he could not see or understand where that might be.

Without words, he realized: If I attach to this twenty-first path, then I will truly be cut off from the rest of the universe. But it's what I came for. This is my purpose. This is my gamble in order to save Garden from the Destroyers.

What he felt was not fear—fear was an emotion tied to the body. He *felt* nothing, not in the usual sense. But he knew that attaching to that nub of backward-streaming path could mean utter failure or complete success.

He remembered that there were two of him, and he wondered what the other version of himself might do if he were here instead of Noxon. Rigg was the one who had seen the need to kill Ram Odin, and he had done it. Then Rigg was the one who saw the need *not* to have killed him, and so he undid it. But from this choice there would be no undoing.

Noxon could hesitate as long as he wanted. His body would not decay here. He could not die.

But neither could he live. Neither could he *act* and make changes in the world.

Of course, heading backward he couldn't make changes outside the limits of this starship. It would be a very small world indeed. And who knew if, once caught in that timeflow, the regular stream of causality would not become as invisible as backward-flowing time had been to him till now.

Filled with uncertainty, filled with determination, Noxon mentally attached himself to that nub of a path, that path of a kind and color he had never seen before. He attached to it, and left that moment of nothingness.

The moment he could sense motion again—and it felt completely normal, he felt like himself, nothing had changed, and that infinite moment between everything was now infinitesimal in his memory—in that moment he began to slice time so that he would be invisible and undetectable to the computers.

He did not know if he had acted quickly enough. He did not know how long it would take the computers to be aware of the presence of the jewels he carried with him. Or how long it would take the computers to upload all the contents of the jewels, containing as they did the entire history of the human race in every wallfold of Garden. And the history of Ram Odin on all nineteen starships.

But even if it *had* absorbed every speck of those memories, it didn't matter the way it would have if he had joined with any of the nineteen forward-moving copies of the ship. Because *this* ship was going back to Earth, but undetectably. As it now was, this ship could not have any effect on the rest of the universe.

Noxon's job was to find an appropriate opportunity, after the ship returned to Earth, and take the whole ship with him back into regular time, so that he could learn what motivated the people of Earth to wipe out life on Garden, and prevent it if he could.

For now, though, his only job was to stay alive through the seven-year voyage.

If the expendable knew that there were jewels aboard, he showed nothing. Noxon could not hear the words they were saying, because he was slicing time so sound could not reach him in any intelligible form. But there was only the frustration of realizing that they were the loser in the lottery of ships, that they were the one that would never found a colony, the one that would never reach any destination at all.

Ram Odin was a man so young, so childlike compared to the old man Noxon had known. He and the expendable conversed. Ram got up and talked. The expendable talked. They walked here and there. They did inexplicable things that didn't matter to Noxon at all.

All that Noxon cared about was the place where he could use the jewels to take control of the ship. Of course, it was possible that the ship would not let him take control, since Ram Odin was the commander.

But it was also possible that once Noxon had allowed the ship to upload the contents of the jewels, the ship's computers would realize that Noxon *was* the commander of the only mission that mattered now, and that Noxon was the only person who could possibly bring the ship back into forward-time.

After the huge gamble he had already taken, wouldn't it be ironic if the ship refused to pay off on *this* small bet.

It took Noxon more than a day of ship's time to cross the small room to the jewel station. Then he kept sidling left and right, waiting for Ram to leave the room again.

At last he did.

Instantly Noxon stopped slicing time. His hand was already poised over the reader. He dropped all the jewels at once out of the bag.

They did not bounce off the surface because they were immediately locked in place, held in an invisible field that kept them all moving relative to each other. Noxon remembered the dialogue he had used before, the words he was supposed to say. But the ship's computer did not speak to him.

Instead, it spoke to the mice.

Noxon could hear the high-pitched, rapid words, because the facemask allowed him to. It meant that the ship's computer knew that with the facemask Noxon could understand this language, and therefore the computer used it so Ram Odin could not hear what it was saying. Or it meant that the ship's computer, having reached its own conclusions from whatever was on the jewels, wished only to deal with the mice.

No. The words were to him. "Rigg Noxon," said the ship's computer. "We understand why you are here and we regard you as the commander of this vessel, superceding *this* Ram Odin because the older, better informed, and therefore more authoritative Ram Odin has certified you as his true successor in every one of these jewels. Do not speak because I must use the expendable to explain you to him before he sees you."

"No," said Noxon aloud. "I will explain myself."

"The shock might harm him."

"I have had far too much experience with ships' computers and with expendables to believe that you have actually surrendered control to me, or that you will actually say what I would wish you to say."

"It is unfortunate that you have such an untrusting attitude."

"The mice that are now escaping from this room are to be contained on this ship and not allowed to leave it under any circumstances, until I specifically authorize each instance of their departure."

"Understood."

From down the corridor, he could hear Ram Odin's voice. "I'm hearing a voice and it isn't yours and it isn't mine."

"And you will preserve both my life and Ram Odin's life, from each other and from ourselves as well as from you, the expendable, or any other peril."

"Understood."

Ram Odin came into the room. Noxon turned to face him. Ram Odin looked at him and kept a remarkable degree of composure. Which is to say, he leaned against his chair and then sank into it. But he did not point or shout or ask questions like "Who are you?" and "How did you get here?"

"First," said Noxon, "I am fully human. My face looks like this because I have a symbiotic relationship with a parasite that enhances my perceptions and my reaction time. My name is Noxon."

Ram Odin said nothing.

"Second, I am in control of this ship now."

Ram looked at the expendable. The expendable nodded.

"Third, there are now mice aboard this ship. They are sentient, they are untrustworthy, but they might be quite useful to us at some later time, so do not harm them."

Ram nodded slowly.

"Fourth, you know that we're cut off from the normal flow of time. I was able to join you on this timestream only because I entered this path from the moment of intersection, where all the copies of the ship came to be. I don't know if I *can* get us back onto the normal timestream, but if I can't, nobody can, nothing can. I am your only hope to get back to the world of causality."

Ram Odin kept looking at him.

"That's all I've got," said Noxon. "You can talk now."

Ram Odin shook his head. Then, his voice choked and croaking, he said, "No I can't."

"For what it's worth," said Noxon, "I've met your very old self. One copy of yourself, anyway. I know that you're a sneaky conniving arrogant murderous son-of-a-bitch. I also know that you are willing to sacrifice whatever needs sacrificing in order to save your people. Even though you're not the copy of Ram Odin who actually founded nineteen colonies on the planet Garden, you could have become him. You meant to found a colony. I'm asking you to preserve the results of your own work. The lives of your own children. I'm one of those children.

I'm here to keep your life's work from being obliterated."

Ram Odin nodded. "I'm listening," he said.

So Noxon told him about the world of Garden, and all the things Ram Odin had done, and all the things Noxon and his companions had done. He didn't hurry the telling. The story was spread across several days. When his memory was incomplete or inaccurate, the expendable prompted him, for all these stories were now a part of the ship's memory.

When he was done, Ram Odin said, "I'm in."

"You're in what?" asked Noxon.

"I'm in the game. I'm with you. Let's save the world. Your world. My children's world."

"Garden," said Noxon.

"Right," said Ram Odin. "Let's save Garden."

CHAPTER 12

Choosing Masks

Umbo could have avoided Rigg's rule and taken Loaf and Leaky through the Wall by jumping back before it was created, then leaping forward again in time. But that would be showing off, and besides, who knew what dangers there might be in the world of Garden before the colonizers shattered the biosphere and replaced most of the native life with plants and animals from Earth? Rigg could always see the paths of creatures and avoid anything large and dangerous. Umbo could not.

And since Umbo and Loaf were together, they could pass through the Wall—but not until after Rigg's rule of two-at-a-time went into effect.

Umbo chose the time right after Rigg went back to Vadeshfold, got his facemask, then killed and then unkilled Ram Odin.

Loaf and Leaky and Umbo traveled to the Wall, however,

in the time before Rigg, Umbo, and Loaf had been arrested in O—a time when no one was looking for them. Though it probably wasn't necessary. They would be looking for a boy the age Umbo had been, and a soldierly man just Loaf's size—but with a normal human face. They would not be looking for Leaky at all.

But even if they weren't looking for them as they were now, it was better to travel at a time when nobody was looking for anybody.

They hired a carriage for the part of the journey that went from town to town, but the last part could only be done on foot because no roads led to the Wall. It was then, at the verge of the Wall, that Umbo pulled the others forward into the future moment when Rigg, Noxon, and Ram Odin had just left to rejoin the rest of them near the shore in Larfold. The flyer would be gone, but Vadeshex would be at home.

Passing through the Wall with permission did not involve the agony of anxiety and despair that normally made it impassable. But neither was it completely absent. Several times Umbo saw Loaf take Leaky by the hand and reassure her, because even these pale shadows of the feelings the Wall evoked were clearly upsetting her. Umbo remembered watching Rigg, Olivenko, and Loaf walk this half-league—though *that* time there had been soldiers coming to kill Umbo and Param as Umbo held the others in the past. Umbo also remembered making the walk himself, holding Param's hand. They had just saved each other's lives, and Umbo was in the first throes of falling in love.

All in all, it was a place that filled him with nostalgia, as well as dread.

Umbo half-expected Vadeshex to be there to greet them, as he had been the first time. What he did not expect was to meet himself.

Or at least the image of himself. Loaf was reminding Leaky to step only where he stepped as they came near the first stream, when someone cried out, "Stop!"

They turned and saw Umbo, and knew at once it was a message from the future rather than another copy of Umbo himself, because the background was different around him, and his hair was blowing in a breeze that didn't exist where they were.

"It doesn't work," said the messenger. "Leaky can't master the facemask. We waited a year but she never came out of it."

Leaky was angry. "Are you saying that I'm weak? I'm too weak?"

"It's not about strength of will," said the messenger. "You're plenty strong, but that probably makes it worse."

"What is it, then?" asked Umbo.

The messenger clearly didn't want to say it, but realized that he must. "Loaf thinks it's a matter of self-control. Leaky doesn't have enough of it, and neither do I. Rigg and Loaf do. Go back. There's nothing for any of you here."

And then the messenger—future Umbo—was gone. Gone completely, gone even from the future, because his message made it so that particular future would never exist.

Leaky sank to the ground, Loaf with her, his arm around her. "Why do we have to believe him!" she said.

"Because Umbo doesn't come back and give false messages. Why would he?"

"What if I can do it *this* time because I was warned?" asked Leaky.

"Warning won't help," said Loaf. "I know what it's like to have this thing come over you, get inside you. It was hard for me, and that's with the discipline of a soldier's training. And Rigg, he was schooled by Ramex, taught a kind of self-mastery we can only guess at. It's nothing *wrong* with you, Leaky. Humans weren't designed to have a thing like this attached."

"It makes you stronger! It repaired everything—even your scars are gone!"

"We don't even know that *your* body is the reason we haven't had a baby," said Loaf. "Let's go back and see what happens."

"I *do* know!" she cried. "Because I had a baby once."

Loaf did not move.

"Before we married," she said. "When I was barely a woman. I was too young. The baby was breech and it died trying to be born. They cut it out of me. And I was so torn up inside the midwife said I'd never be able to bear."

"You never told me," murmured Loaf.

"You said you didn't want children, that you couldn't raise children, being liable to go on campaign at any moment. So it didn't matter. But then you left the army and it *did* matter after all."

"You could have told me."

"I was ashamed!" She wept for a while.

Umbo wondered if he should leave. This was clearly a time for husband and wife. Yet by leaving he'd call attention to himself. Of course, he could simply skip forward in time and let them have their privacy. He had to admit to himself that he simply didn't want to. He was fascinated, even though he felt sorry for her pain. *Their* pain.

He noticed that Loaf did not ask who the father had been, or whether Leaky had been married before.

"And now I'm ashamed again," Leaky said more quietly. "Because I have so little *self-control* that I can't master this thing that a *child* like Rigg was able to control."

"Rigg's not a child now," said Loaf. "And even when he *was* a child, he was . . . unusual."

This made Umbo realize that he *should* be feeling resentful of Rigg for being able to bear a facemask when it was certainly out of his own reach.

But no, Umbo might be envious of Rigg for many things, but not for the facemask. Not now. Yes, it made Loaf an astonishingly effective soldier. It gave Rigg and Noxon so much more control over their timeshaping. But the thing was so repulsive and deforming. Umbo had gotten used to seeing it on Loaf. Definitely *not* on Rigg and Noxon. And the thought of having that thing crawl over his own face, push into his ears and nose and mouth, breathing for him, probing every aperture, taking away his eyes: How did they bear it? The horror of such an invasion?

Loaf was a soldier. People had pushed foreign objects into his body from time to time. He had borne pain and horror, and yet kept fighting, kept control of himself. Umbo wasn't exactly a big baby about such things, but he could not stop himself from leaping to conclusions—wrong ones—and acting on them in irrevocable ways. It had got Kyokay killed that day. It had kept Umbo saying things, doing things that showed his pathetic yearning for Param, his childish resentment of Rigg. He knew these things made him look foolish, and yet he had not been able to stop himself.

Rigg was able to plan and calculate. Umbo did everything he did in a rush, on impulse. Even learning to travel in time, to send himself messages—he had done it by brute force rather than by thinking it all through and understanding it. Oh, he *tried* to think, and maybe his thinking helped. Somehow. But mostly it was just taking his power to manipulate people's timeflow and trying to use it in a new way. That's why it had taken months to learn to use it on his own, without Rigg—he had no idea what he was doing, he just flung himself into it, trying different things until one worked.

I learn like a squirrel, thought Umbo. No analysis, no finesse—I just keep leaping until I finally land where I want to.

I will never have a facemask, and I'm perfectly happy. I'd rather be my second-rate self than go through what Loaf and Rigg went through—and then wear that trophy of a face the rest of my life.

But if he said to Leaky, You're better off this way, Umbo had a feeling that her response would cost him a significant portion of his hearing, if not a limb. Because it was true. Leaky did *not* have self-control. That's why it had taken him so many tries before he was able to prepare her properly to meet Loaf again, in his new condition. She could not stop herself from raging long enough to hear the whole message, not until he found exactly the right way to approach her.

Which, of course, he had learned by flinging himself into the past, finding out that one method of telling her about it failed, and then trying again. Rigg probably could have succeeded the first time.

Still, I did figure out how to jump into the future, in a limited way, and I did it without a facemask. Just because I'm not Rigg doesn't mean I'm nothing.

"What you don't know," said Loaf gently, "is whether that midwife was right. It's easy to say, You'll never bear children, but what did she know? If she was a good midwife the baby might have been delivered alive."

At the mention of the baby's death, Leaky's tears came afresh. "I can't believe I told you," she said. And then, "I can't believe I went so long and never told you."

"You've told me now," said Loaf. "So hear me out. We might still have a baby, though it's perilous, because it'll look like me. But if you want to risk adding to the ugly in the world, then let's see if the problem was me. But if the problem is an old injury of yours, then that's the way it is."

"But the facemask could have cured it."

"It's not a cure if it kills you," said Loaf. "If you aren't still my Leaky, then I don't want you to have my babies. And as long as you *are* my Leaky, then I'm happy whether we have babies or not."

She flung her arms around him and wept even more, and finally Umbo did the thing he should have done in the first place, and skipped into the future by a few hours.

They were lying on the ground. Leaky was nestled next to

Loaf, his arm around her. She was asleep. Of course Loaf noticed Umbo's return, but he raised a finger to signal silence. Umbo nodded, walked quietly away.

He took a long walk, and after a while the city came into view. The great empty city with its sad empty towers made of fieldsteel, which never weathered, never wore away. Would the fieldsteel outlast the great burning when all life on Garden was ended? Would they remain as the sole remnant of human life here? No, there were other monuments—the Tower of O was also of fieldsteel. And there were nineteen craters and upthrusts scattered around the world, where starships had crashed deliberately into the crust and changed the planet's speed of rotation, lengthening the day and adding more debris to the Ring in the sky that made it so no clear night on Garden was ever fully dark.

That's all we leave behind us. A few buildings and nineteen deformations of the land.

"Have you come for your facemask?" Vadeshex emerged from the door of the building where he had first served them water.

"For a drink, I suppose," said Umbo. "And water for the others, though I didn't bring their water bags."

"I anticipated that," said Vadeshex. "Being an old friend of the family, so to speak, I thought to welcome Leaky to Vadeshfold with some refreshment, food and drink. But she isn't with you."

"We ran into a messenger. From the future."

"Then the messenger was you."

"Not *me* but yes, a version of me from a future that now will never happen. He warned us that the facemask doesn't

225

work on Leaky. You don't happen to have a milder version, do you? Maybe not so effective, but also easier to adapt to and get control of?"

Vadeshex shook his head. "The one your friends wear is the mildest one I've ever been able to breed. Facemasks are invasive. They're not for everyone."

"How did you choose Loaf?"

"I didn't," said Vadeshex.

"It was just chance?"

"It was Ram Odin who chose. He observed, and he said, Loaf, and no other until Rigg is ready."

"So he judged us and knew who was strong enough."

"It isn't about strength," said Vadesh. "It's about self-mastery."

Umbo chuckled. "And here I thought my future self was terribly wise and analytical, to come up with that."

"He was wise to explain it to you that way, though, don't you think?" asked Vadeshex. "The woman is apt to flare up at anything, isn't she?"

"You don't know her."

"Once you brought the jewels into Ramfold in the era you arrived in, Ramex knew she was important and he went to the roadhouse as a customer. He has seen her temper. It's a marvel to behold, but then she's filled with regret and self-recrimination. Like you."

"We know what self-control looks like in other people," said Umbo, "and wish we had it for ourselves."

"Oh, you have it," said Vadeshex. "It just doesn't kick in until you've already said and done things you can't unsay and can't undo. Though of course *you* can. But it does cut out a chunk of reality and discard it in the invisible dustbin of lost futures."

"You saw me save Kyokay."

"And saw you cause a disastrous change in futures."

"How can you know that?"

"You were carrying the jewels. They came back in time with you when you undid your mistake. Any future in which you carried the jewels—on the knife or in a bag—and then come back with them, we have a record of it, at least the part surrounding you. But when you send a message, the jewels don't come back, so *those* futures are lost."

"If I send a message, I don't run the risk of copying myself. The world can find a use for two Riggs, but I can't even find a use for the one Umbo."

"There you go. You *couldn't* stop yourself from that bit of self-pity."

"I didn't *try* to stop myself."

"But you feel contempt for yourself for having said it, yes?"

Umbo shrugged. "If you have food for them, can you bring it?"

"It's spread on a table," said Vadeshex, "and even though I'm very dextrous by human standards, I'm liable to spill something if I try to carry the whole table out to them."

"Is the flyer available?"

"It will be soon. Meanwhile sit and talk with me."

If Vadeshex had been human, and not a lying and conniving machine, Umbo would have complied. Instead, he said, "No thank you. I think I'll go back to them afoot. You can bring the food when the flyer comes back."

"Let me refill your water bag before you go," said Vadeshex.

Umbo waited. When Vadeshex returned the bag bulging, he also gave Umbo a covered bowl. "You don't need utensils for this. It will keep them till I get there with the main meal."

When Umbo got back, they were sitting up and talking. Umbo opened the bowl and the crisp round pastries were still hot. Each had barely more than a dot of something spicy in the middle. They were delicious.

"That machine can cook," said Loaf.

"What machine?" asked Leaky.

"He'll be here soon with a whole meal," said Umbo.

"Oh, do you mean the man-shaped machine that Rigg thought of as his father?" asked Leaky.

"The same *kind* of machine," said Umbo.

"Supposed to be identical," said Loaf. "Supposed to have all their memories in common."

"I don't believe it," said Umbo. "I knew Rigg's father. He taught *me*, too, a little. I thought of him as a great man. We called him Golden Man. Nox called him Good Teacher. Both true. But Vadeshex? Nothing but lies, manipulation."

"It might be," said Loaf, "you could have swapped them and they would have acted exactly alike in each other's situations. But you get a history with one machine, and a different history with another, it's hard to think of them as being the same."

"How are you doing?" asked Umbo.

Leaky shook her head. "Desolated," she said. "But not dead."

"And that's a good thing," said Loaf.

"Says you," said Leaky.

"Says *me*," said Umbo. "I can only imagine the state Loaf was in, in that future where you failed to come back out of the face-mask trance. If that's how it happened."

"More likely I ran around screaming through the facemask till it finally opened a hole for me to yell through," said Leaky. "I was probably lashing out and breaking things."

"Maybe," said Loaf. "We've only seen one transformation — mine. Rigg did his alone, and none of us saw it. His is newer, so he looks a lot less human than I do."

"Human enough for me," said Leaky.

Vadeshex came not long after, and spread out a picnic for them on the grass in sight of the Wall. He offered the suggestion that some of Leaky's grief might be owing to their having just passed through the emotions induced by the Wall, and to the fact that they were still close to it and bound to be feeling some residual effects.

"Thank you for your suggestion," said Loaf.

"Thank you for the meal," said Umbo. "It was very good."

"I don't often get to check out my culinary routines," said Vadeshex. Shyly? Was he actually trying to conceal a bit of pride? No, it was just the way he was designed. Or a deliberate manipulation, to try to change their attitude toward him. It wasn't going to work.

Wasn't going to work *much*. The food had been very good. And they *had* come to him to get a facemask. The old machine had its uses.

Vadeshex offered to fly them home, and they accepted. They traveled that night; Vadeshex landed them in a field a mile from Leaky's Landing. They were home before midnight.

"I can't believe there's such a machine, to fly through the air. Remember how long we had to ride, how many days, and here we are on the very night."

"People on Earth do this kind of thing all the time," said Umbo.

"Well if we had eleven thousand years here," said Leaky, "and you say that humans on Earth got technologies like this only ten thousand years after inventing agriculture—"

"Ten thousand, give or take," said Loaf.

"Why haven't we done any better?"

"We're blocked," said Umbo. "It's one of the things the expendables do. And the ships' computers. They choke off any line of development that might lead to high technology. Except in Odinfold, and that's because Ram Odin gave it an exemption, up to a point."

"The thing's almost as big as the roadhouse, and it flew," said Leaky again.

"And here we've gotten used to it and think of it as nothing special," said Loaf. "You're reminding me how miraculous it really is."

"Don't go yet, Vadeshex," said Umbo. "I think I may be needing a ride back to Larfold, where my fiancee is waiting."

"Stay with us," said Leaky. "You hardly visited."

"I'll be back," said Umbo. "The question is, when?"

"Give us a couple of years," said Loaf. "That's time enough. Check back and see how we're doing."

"I could go right now into the future and find out."

"Then you'd be tempted to tell us," said Loaf. "No, go somewhere else and have something like a life—whatever's possible with the lovely Queen of Nothing Much and her Kingdom of Nowhere."

"In other words, you'd like me to try to accomplish something before I come back pestering you."

"No, we just don't want you getting jealous of how in love we are," said Loaf.

"Thank you for everything, Umbo," said Leaky. "Especially the warning. I wish it had worked. But I'm glad that you kept me from giving up my life for nothing."

"Thanks for trusting me enough to believe my warning," said Umbo. He turned to Vadeshex. "Take me back to Param?"

"Wherever and whenever she is," said Vadeshex.

"Get me to the where, and I'll work on the when myself."

CHAPTER 13

Where Not to Go

"Have I ever resisted your visiting any of the wallfolds?" asked Ram Odin.

"We've only been to two," said Rigg.

"Well, we happen to have come rather early to the one that I *will* advise you not to visit."

"You understand that it makes me all the more determined to go there."

"I took that into account," said Ram Odin. "But I have no choice. Janefold is as interesting as any of the others. It has only one statistical quirk."

"Which is?"

"The life expectancy is about half that of other wallfolds."

"And why is that?"

"Disease," said Ram Odin. "This is the place where plagues begin."

"Because it's tropical?" asked Rigg.

"I don't know why, though that may be part of it. Some of the diseases are vectored through biting insects, some of them through other mammals. Some originated in animals that thrive in this climate. None of the diseases depend on microbes native to Garden. Nothing smaller than a facemask or a mantle has yet jumped the barrier between the biotas of Earth and of Garden."

"So you don't want me to go there because you're afraid I might die?"

"I'm reasonably sure you *would* die."

"How sure?"

"Your odds of survival are about one in fifty. But that's a guess, since you'd be the first visitor from outside the wallfold since I last visited there about ten thousand years ago, give or take."

"Did you get sick?"

"Almost died. And the really interesting diseases hadn't started up yet. This is the incubator of hellish death, Rigg. If it weren't for the Wall, diseases from Janefold would sweep across the world, killing half each time."

"Then why is there anyone left there at all?" asked Rigg.

"They've built up resistance. Not individually. But each time a new plague comes up, the only survivors are those with natural defenses. The deadly disease that almost killed me is now no more than an itchy rash and a case of sniffles—to the Janefolders. But if it got out of the wallfold, it would probably have the twenty percent kill rate that it had when I caught it."

Rigg thought about this. "If they have resistance to disease, then why is their life expectancy so low?"

"They develop resistance to *each* disease. But the newer the disease, the more people it kills with each resurgence. And some of them mutate, so that people who lived through one iteration have no defense, or little defense, against its successor."

"I hate to be offensive, but this makes me wonder what's hiding there. What you don't want me to see."

"What's hiding there is death, and what I don't want you to see is the inside of your coffin lid."

"So you keep me out of Janefold with a threat of plagues. What will be the excuse the next time you want me not to visit a place? Earthquakes? Really bad weather? Ill-behaved children?"

"This is how the world works," said Ram Odin. "It happened on Earth. There were a couple of places that spawned plagues that covered the world, because trade routes connected them to everybody. But there were other places that were cut off. The Americas didn't spawn a lot of diseases because population density never got that high, and because there weren't a lot of primates to incubate diseases that would be particularly apt to kill humans. When people from Eurasia landed there, those worldwide diseases, in combination, had a killoff of about ninety percent of the locals."

"I read about that."

"Africa was the opposite. It was isolated, too—not a lot of trade, because traders had to cross oceans and deserts. Sick people tended to die before they could spread the diseases to the rest of the world. But when Europeans got there, if they went ashore for a week they simply didn't come back. If they went ashore for a day, they came back to their ship and infected everybody else and some ships were found drifting, with a one hundred percent killoff."

"And you're saying the Wall has protected the rest of the world from Janefold. If I visit there—"

"It would be miraculous if you didn't catch something incurable and highly contagious. And here's the problem. You can't go back in time and change it because you'll have the disease in you already."

"I also have the facemask."

"So you'll have much keener awareness of your symptoms and be able to track the progress of your disease quite clearly, as you die."

"The facemask doesn't help keep me healthy?"

"It helps keep you robust," said Ram Odin. "It doesn't filter out diseases that your immune system can't cope with, because it can only detect disease agents from Earthborn biology if *your* body senses them."

"Yet people live there."

"If they make it through childhood, then they tend to have lives of normal length. Childhood is when disease weeds out the weak and selects for those who adapt well, whose bodies resist. The longer the disease has been around, the more children live through it. But there are some diseases that are less than a thousand years old, and those are still taking a lot of children. So at birth, half the life expectancy. But if you live to adulthood, then the survivors have normal lives."

"Do they have larger families?"

"Some cultures within Janefold do, some don't. Some don't bond with their children until they're older. Some break their hearts loving all their children from the start. Some regions and tribes avoid large concentrations of people. Some keep their children isolated. Some deliberately allow their children to get exposed to everything—I suppose to end the suspense. Some villages, some tribes routinely burn down the houses of families who have a few key symptoms—open sores all over the body, bleeding from eyes, nostrils, and ears, blood in sneezes and coughs, that sort of thing."

"Burn them down with the people inside."

"That's the point."

"So you're just protecting me."

"If somebody comes at you with a knife, you can pop back in time and save yourself. If somebody comes at you with a sneeze, you have nowhere to run."

"But I *don't* breathe," said Rigg. "The facemask does."

"The facemask doesn't have an Earthborn biology. It will pass the disease through to you without noticing it's there."

"You have to understand, Ram Odin. I've been lied to so much."

"Not by me."

"We only just met, and your lie-to-truth ratio is pretty high. Plus most of the expendables' lies originated with you. Or they were invented in order to protect your secrets. What are you protecting in Janefold?"

"The future of the human race on Garden," said Ram Odin. "By not letting that poisonous place kill you."

"The future of the human race here no longer depends on

236

me," said Rigg. "You're thinking of my other self, Noxon."

"We don't know how that mission will turn out. Rigg, please trust me on this one. There are no great secrets in Janefold, except death. Maybe because of systematic isolation, there are a few more languages. Some intriguing philosophies, a few death-worship religions, a lot of fatalism. One religion that for almost a thousand years was almost universal in Janefold, not because the doctrines were so convincing, but because the believers routinely risked their own lives to care for the sick and dying, and to bury the dead."

"That made the religion more attractive?"

"It made the believers seem more sincere, and filled others with gratitude and admiration. Rigg, all the records are open to you. Explore this one from inside the ship and save your legwork for a healthier place."

Because the facemask picked up subtle nuances he would normally have missed, Rigg could trust his judgment more than he used to, when it came to discerning whether people were telling him the truth. He became mostly convinced that Ram Odin meant what he was saying, whether it was true or not.

"So if we skip Janefold," said Rigg, "where next?"

"Anywhere else. When I said this was the only one I'd resist your visiting, I meant it."

"Singhfold," said Rigg.

"An intriguing one. The only wallfold where the crater from the ship's impact is the most level ground. Singhfold is mountainous, with lots of valleys and a huge range of cultures."

"Are the individual tribes very small? That usually implies that the culture isn't going to rise very high."

"There is a broad, well-watered coastal plain where some pretty high civilizations have risen and fallen. But most of the people, most of the time, have lived in those isolated valleys. Shall we give it a go?"

"I reserve the right to come back to Janefold. To do it last."

"Whenever you go there, Rigg," said Ram Odin, "you'll do it last."

What Rigg thought was: I'll go back in time, to when the colony in that wallfold was young, and so were the diseases that infest them. Because people who live in the constant immanence of sudden, miserable death by an invisible hand—it has to change them.

And if we ever have to protect ourselves against the people of Earth . . .

"Ram Odin," said Rigg. "All this information about Janefold was available to the Odinfolders, right?"

"I kept a few secrets, but not that. Yes, they knew."

"And the mice can move things remotely, through space and time. Things as small as DNA molecules."

"Those are big molecules."

"They're still molecules," said Rigg.

"That's how Umbo was made. By genetic manipulation conducted remotely, by the mice."

"So the mice that were boarding the Visitors' ship, the ones that Umbo and Param warned the Visitors about—they could have gotten their diseases from Janefold."

"You don't know if a disease is virulent unless you test it," said Ram Odin. "Janefold is by far the best disease laboratory in the world."

Rigg chuckled at himself. "I wasn't sure if Umbo and Param were right about the mice being sent to Earth to wipe out the human race. Where would they get such a disease? And I didn't believe you, though I didn't *dis*believe you, either. About Janefold."

"But combine the two doubts, and . . . certainty?" asked Ram Odin.

"Not certainty. But a major shift in my view, yes."

"So you'll stay away from Janefold. For real this time, not just an empty promise to placate me?"

"The mice got their species-wrecking plague from somewhere."

"Oh, you might go farther," said Ram Odin. "They probably enhanced it, and tested it in some of the villages."

Rigg took that in for a moment.

"You did understand that the mice are *not* human. They have no more qualms about testing a disease on human subjects than we would have testing it on mice."

"They got their sentience from us," said Rigg.

"And for how many generations should that make them grateful and subservient? But I don't *know* they did this. I'm only guessing from what I know about them. They did kill Param, though."

"That was the Odinfolders' idea, wasn't it?"

"It might have been," said Ram Odin. "But for a long time now, all Odinfolder decisions are based on data that is supplied to them . . ."

"By the mice," said Rigg.

"So whether the mice decided for themselves, or provided shaped data to the Odinfolders so *they* reached the desired conclusion—"

"Nothing much happens in Odinfold unless it's what the mice want," said Rigg.

"I think that's a fair way of summing it up."

"So this business of the Odinfolders reshaping their own bodies into stumpy dung-throwers, into yahoos—"

"They began that before they began mouse-breeding."

"Oh. It just seemed like deliberate humiliation, as if the mice were getting even."

"For what?" asked Ram Odin.

"For making them mice," said Rigg. "They, who have the genes to be human, to have hands, to stand tall. I'd say there's grounds for resentment."

"Irrational grounds."

"Resentment *is* irrational," said Rigg.

"Not always," said Ram Odin. "Like Umbo's resentment of you."

"How is that rational!"

"Now, now, Rigg. Leave out how it makes *you* feel. Umbo doesn't have his feelings in order to annoy or hurt *you*. Umbo has good reason for thinking of himself as perhaps the more talented timeshaper. Yet because of the way you were educated, because you're the son of the king—however empty that title might be—everyone defers to you, and nobody defers to him."

"I do," said Rigg.

"But he thinks of that as condescension."

"Umbo is the only friend I have," said Rigg. "I'm sorry his resentment is ruining that. But that certainly applies to the mice. Humans made them. Why? To have convenient slave-mice. Yet they think of themselves as selves, they see the whole group of them as a people. A great civilization. So it's not unnatural for them to resent humans in general, and Odinfolders in particular."

"And yet we're sending a batch of them along with Noxon to try to save the human race on Garden."

Rigg chuckled at that. "To save Garden. If it also saves the humans, they can put up with that unintended outcome. For a while longer."

"Maybe we've underestimated the danger of the mice," said Ram Odin.

"If Janefold is as dangerous as you say. If all the other wall-folds are as vulnerable as the Americas when the Europeans came. Then the mice already have the power to pick up those plagues and put them wherever they want. In effect, as soon as the mice decide, the Wall is down as far as disease is concerned. They use our timeshaping to save Garden, and *then* get rid of us just as the Destroyers did—only with more finesse. Leaving the mice to inherit the planet."

"Devious," said Ram Odin.

"But possible."

"Using us now, planning to kill us later."

"They really *do* have human genes," said Rigg.

"I wish we hadn't sent them with Noxon," said Ram Odin.

"Maybe sending them with Noxon," said Rigg, "is the only reason the mice allowed him to go. Maybe it's the only reason they're letting us live. Because if all humans are gone before the Visitors arrive, then . . ."

"Then they have no reason to come back and destroy all life on Garden."

"I think we're talking ourselves into a serious case of musophobia," said Rigg.

"Or maybe you go back in time and warn Noxon before he left," said Ram Odin.

"He left?"

"A few days ago. Were you going to have a tearful good-bye?"

Rigg ignored the sarcasm. "Time enough to stop him when the plague starts."

"Maybe they kill you before they start the plague," said Ram Odin.

"The facemask will protect me from the mice, even if it can't protect me from the plague."

"Probably so," said Ram Odin. "And for all we know, the mice are deeply devoted to us."

"Yes," said Rigg. "And whatever xenocide they commit against our species, they'll regret it and sing little mouse songs about it for a thousand years."

Ram Odin looked very earnest. "I would rather Garden survive with mice as the dominant species, and not a human left, than to have no life on this world at all."

"Then you are even less trustworthy than I thought," said Rigg.

CHAPTER 14

Opportunists

"I'm not going to experiment with timeflow on this ship until we're in much closer proximity to Earth."

"We're invisible to them right now," said Ram Odin, "but when we rejoin the normal flow of time, we'll be perfectly visible. And if you don't speed us up or slow us down, we'll also be trying to occupy the same space as the original of this ship."

"I know," said Noxon.

"In fact, anywhere you put us back into the normal timeflow," said Ram Odin, "we're going to make a big explosion, because we'll be exactly, atom for atom, in the same space as the original ship."

"*You're* telling *me* how timeshaping works?" Noxon tried not to sound too scornful, but didn't think he succeeded.

But Ram Odin took it. "Then explain to me why we won't explode."

"I'm not playing with timeflow here because there's not too much I can do. The only paths visible to me are your own—your own *since* the jump, when this version of the ship came into being. Nothing from the outbound voyage."

"And you need these paths to travel in time?"

"I need them to travel into the past. I also suspect I'll need them to get us back into the normal timeflow."

"So you have to get back to where there are more people and therefore more paths."

"Yes. And I need to get to a place where the past is deeper, reaching much farther back."

"That still doesn't solve the exploding starship problem," said Ram Odin.

"If I can find a path at all that's going the right way," said Noxon, "it will be farther in the past. Therefore, when I jump to it, the original ship will already be somewhere else, so we *won't* be in the same space *and time*."

"Oh. Yes, of course."

"If I can do this at all," said Noxon, "I'll make sure I jump us back to a time when there were no starships. No satellites. Nothing for us to collide with. And nobody on Earth prepared to think of this starship as anything other than a point of light—a meteor or planet or previously undiscovered star."

"Yes, that would be a stealthy return to Earth," said Ram Odin. "But then?"

"*If* we're going the right direction, then I can slice time forward so that in a few days, we can return to a more useful time."

"But then the starship will appear in a time when people *will* notice it."

"I didn't say I'd bring the starship forward into the future with us," said Noxon. "We can stash it in the past and go back and get it when we need it again."

Ram Odin shook his head. "I'm just not used to thinking of the past as a place where things can be stashed."

"I've had a few years," said Noxon. "You have no idea how strange it can get."

"Going backward in time was pretty strange. I kept trying to find ways to communicate with myself. You know, the outbound me, the one who—"

"I know who you mean," said Noxon.

"But the ship I'm in isn't the ship he's in. We occupy the same space but not the same . . . direction."

"I'm still trying to figure out the rules myself," said Noxon. "For instance, river travelers leave behind paths, not on their boat, but in the air above the water. Showing their course in relation to the planet's surface. But when I was inside this ship after it crashed on Garden, I could see your paths inside the starship. Including your path right back to the moment you emerged from the fold. But that should have been clear out in space, where the starship was when it jumped between stars."

"Apparently the universe doesn't regard starships as boats," said Ram Odin.

"But why not? Because it's so big? It's nowhere near as big as a planet. And this isn't theoretical. Because when I jump us back into the main timeflow, I think it's going to be very useful if I can take the starship with us."

Ram Odin nodded. "That thing about having air to breathe . . ."

"I can bring vehicles with me. I moved a carriage once. Took it back in time with me. But our paths weren't inside the carriage, they were in the air above the road. Here, though, your path and mine are definitely here in the starship. We're not leaving them behind us in space as we go."

"So the starship acts more planet-like."

"Paths cling to the surface of the planet, rather than haring off into space. Now the paths are clinging to the interior of the starship, as if this were a hollow planet."

"Well, in a way it is," said Ram Odin. "If I had decided against going through the fold, I would have revived the colonists and we would have created a habitat in the ecohold. It would have been the whole world for generations of colonists."

Noxon shook his head. "I can't imagine that the paths would respond to whether there was potential farmland in the ship."

"So maybe they cling because the ship moves in space. Independent of any world."

"I don't know why any of this works," said Noxon.

"Maybe it works the way you need it to," said Ram Odin.

"I wish."

"Maybe you're unconsciously making up the rules as you go along."

"Then why did I have these paths? And Umbo had his ability to speed up his own and other people's perceptions of timeflow, and together that meant we could jump in time. And then

Umbo worked until he was able to shift without me, and eventually I was able to shift without him, and then I helped Param realize that she could see paths in her own way, so she can leap into the past and slice her way forward, and so can I, and . . ."

"I think what you're saying is that it works the way you need it to," said Ram Odin, "only you have to acquire each ability one at a time after a lot of trying."

"That would be nice if it were true," said Noxon. "But somehow I don't think the universe is making special arrangements for me."

"That's how it looks to somebody who can't do the things you do."

Noxon smiled. "Our best guess is that we got these abilities from you."

"Oh please."

"The only two wallfolds that have time-shifting ability are the two that had your genetic participation."

"The only two that you know about."

"The expendables have been watching. *You* were watching, in your guise as the Ram Odin of Odinfold. And it isn't just that. The thing that happened—the time-shift at the fold in spacetime— that wasn't predicted and it still doesn't make sense. The ships' computers and Old Ram came to believe that what made it happen was you. An unconscious ability to relocate yourself in time, which was triggered by the sudden entry into that null moment in spacetime that the ship had to enter to pass across the fold. The ship's computers only knew how to move the ship and its contents into the null moment and out again to a specific location in space. But your mind wasn't prepared for any of it, and during that null moment you gave an instruction that moved twenty copies of the ship not only in space but also in time."

"And changed directions on this one. Why would I do that?"

"You didn't do it consciously. Your latent time-shifting ability probably put time as well as space in flux, and then the ship's computers did what *they* planned, only their calculations didn't take into account even the possibility that the *time* part of spacetime might be up for grabs. So they brought nineteen of the ships out in roughly the same location. Only spaced far enough apart that nothing exploded. And it happened to be 11,191 years in the past."

"And this one stayed in the same moment that I departed from, only now it was heading backward down its own path."

"Your mind didn't choose those specific outcomes. I mean, how could you do such mathematically precise things? But you made it so the computers' calculations did it. Nineteen computers, nineteen separate jumps of the same ship, into roughly the same space and time, but moments apart."

"And what computer did *this*?" He indicated the backward ship around them.

"Somehow the computers calculated, back on Garden, that this ship should exist. So they knew. Or guessed."

"There were twenty computers on the ship," said the expendable.

Noxon and Ram Odin both looked at him. "There are nineteen," said Ram Odin. "Each doing specific jobs in the ordinary running of the ship, but all ganged together on the calculations for the jump through null spacetime."

The expendable said nothing.

"I think he's thinking of himself," said Noxon.

"But you're slaved to the main computer," said Ram Odin to the expendable.

"So were the other computers," said the expendable, not seeming at all perturbed at being contradicted. Or, for that matter, at being "slaved" to the ship's computer.

"Well, he does have a powerful computer in him," said Ram Odin to Noxon. "But it wasn't involved in the calculations of the jump."

"That's true," said the expendable. "So I spent my time calculating how to get back to Earth."

Ram Odin burst out laughing. "Did you click your heels together three times and say, 'There's no place like home'?"

"I have no idea what you're talking about," said Noxon.

The expendable answered. "Ram Odin is alluding to the film version of a fiction by L. Frank Baum called *The Wizard of Oz*."

"It never came up in my studies," said Noxon, "but I guess I couldn't absorb all of Earth culture in a couple of years of spare-time reading."

"It doesn't matter," said Ram Odin. "What matters to me is this: It took me seven years to get from launch to the jump site. I was afraid that if I went into stasis during the trip, the ship might not waken me in time to make the decisions. So I stayed awake the whole time. Now there's no such worry because the ship can't do anything about our predicament. Do we really have to spend all those endless days? You're charming company, but we'll start boring each other very quickly."

"I know that we're moving into your past," said Noxon, "and

that's the direction I normally jump. But the direction we're going in makes that the *future* to us."

"I was actually proposing that we go into stasis here in the ship. Like the colonists. Then the ship wakes us up when we're close to Earth."

Noxon knew at once that he would never consent to this. It required too much trust of the ship and the expendable. And it would leave the mice free to manipulate things as they wanted. But he didn't want to discuss the danger of the mice to Ram Odin, because the man might decide to eradicate the whole problem and Noxon wasn't sure how to stop him.

Still, instead of simply refusing to consider it, Noxon made a show of letting Ram Odin demonstrate the whole process of going into stasis and then reviving out of it.

"Is there any loss of function? After you wake up?" asked Noxon.

"I assume not," said Ram Odin. "Didn't you say that Old Ram did it all the time, in order to skim through the centuries so he's still alive after eleven thousand years?"

"I can't vouch for his not having lost mental function," said Noxon.

"He's old," said Ram Odin. "There's probably mental loss without any damage from the stasis and revival process. But you're inside a field the whole time. And it's designed to protect your memories and reimplant them as you revive. To restore anything that might have been lost. In experiments on Earth the subjects reported that they actually improved in their ability to access memories."

"So it *does* alter function." And Noxon thought: Maybe this is the same kind of field that inserts all human language into our minds when we pass into the Wall. Which made him think of all the other things the fields that made up the Wall could do to his mind.

Finally Ram Odin said, "You're not going to do it, are you?"

"You can do what you want," said Noxon. "I won't interfere, and I'll make sure you wake up on time."

"You'd be alone with *him* for the next seven years," said Ram Odin, indicating the expendable. "You'll be bored out of your mind."

"I wandered the forests of Upsheer with him for my whole childhood. I called him Father and he taught me and tested me constantly. It was hard and sometimes I wished it would stop, but it was never boring."

"I really enjoyed those years," said the expendable.

Ram Odin turned on him. "It wasn't you, it was a copy of you."

The expendable mildly agreed but added, "He brought a complete set of the ships' logs. Nineteen of them, interlocking and verifying that everything he told you was true, within the limits of his knowledge and understanding. I have a complete memory of all the days, all the hours, all the *minutes* that the expendable named Ramex spent in the company of this young man."

"But it wasn't *you.*"

"It *was* me, because I perfectly remember it," said the expendable. "We expendables don't have the same kind of individual identity that biologicals have."

"So it'll be like old times for the two of you," said Ram Odin, more than a little snidely.

It dawned on Noxon that Ram Odin was jealous. Here came Noxon out of nowhere with a far superior claim to intimacy with Ram Odin's companion of the past seven years.

Even though he did not say this aloud, Ram Odin reacted as if he had. "I am *not* jealous of you!" Then he drummed on the console in front of him. "All right, I'm human. I couldn't help bonding with this asinine machine and so yes, I was *briefly* and irrationally annoyed, but I'm over it."

Everything about his tone and expression said that he was definitely not over it.

"You're welcome to stay awake with us," said Noxon.

"Seven years of *aging*," said Ram Odin. "It's not just the mind-numbing boredom."

"I can promise that you age very well," said Noxon.

"So if you won't go into stasis and turn the ship over to the computers, why not try what your sister does? Slicing forward in time?"

"I sliced time when I first got here, hiding from the ship. But now I'm in the open. If I bring you with me, I risk bringing the ship as well. That would take us out of sync with the original ship."

"But you already saw that the paths travel *with* the ship. So you won't take the ship with us."

"But if I can't take the ship with us, we're going to stay in this backward timeflow forever."

"That's a different kind of timeshaping, and it's in the future," said Ram Odin. "When we're closer to Earth. Right?

So by then, maybe Earth's gravity will make it so you *can* take the ship with you."

Noxon put his face in his hands. "I'm scared to try it."

"You'd be insane not to be scared," said Ram Odin.

"He'd be insane to try it," said the expendable, "when there's no recourse if your guess is wrong."

"There's no recourse no matter what we do," said Ram Odin. "We're cut off from the whole universe, and you're worried that something might go *wrong*?" He turned to Noxon. "Just slice time for a little bit. Take my hand—that's how you take me with you, right? And take us a second into the future."

"A second or an hour," said Noxon, "if we get out of sync with the original ship, it might get ugly."

"Just do it," said Ram Odin. "I believe that whatever you do, it won't destroy you, because you're the causer. Right?"

"Terrible things can happen to us," said Noxon. "Being the causer only means that we can't accidentally wink ourselves out of existence by changing our own past."

"Take my hand," said Ram Odin. "Slice time. See if it destroys us."

Noxon took his hand and, with only a moment's hesitation, sliced forward for only a second of perceived time.

But because he and Param had practiced slicing forward at a very fast pace, his "second" was more than an hour.

Nothing blew up. They were both there. And the expendable was exactly where they had left him.

"Well," said Noxon. "I guess now we know that we can do that."

"Please don't do it again," said the expendable.

"Missed us?" asked Ram Odin.

"No," said the expendable. "The moment you disappeared, the mice started attacking the ship's computers, trying to take control. They're very good at it and very quick. They ignored my commands to stop. So I had the life support system drop oxygen levels so low that they all fainted. Then I found them all, put them in that box, restored the oxygen levels, and came back here to wait for you."

Ram Odin gave a little bark of laughter. He thought it was funny, apparently, but that's because he didn't know the mice.

Noxon walked to the box, sat beside it, and leaned his head against it so he would be able to hear their tiny high voices, if they should feel inclined to try to explain themselves. "Well," said Noxon, "you violated our agreement the moment you thought you could get away with it. I think you know what that means."

There was begging and pleading, all the voices at once. And then one emerged stronger than the others. "You don't tell us your plans, we don't tell you ours."

And another mouse voice: "We didn't try to attack you. We could have."

"Not twenty of you," said Noxon. "And you know I slice much more finely than Param did back when you killed her."

"And I would have removed any metal they placed in your space," said the expendable. "They knew that, of course."

"I assume you're talking to the mice," said Ram Odin.

"Human ears can't hear their conversation," said Noxon.

"But your facemask —"

"Loaf's ability to hear the mice and keep track of them was

one of the reasons I knew I needed to have a facemask of my own. For this voyage."

"Kill them," said Ram Odin. "I know they're not ordinary mice, but this was treason."

"I'm not king," said Noxon. "Well, technically I suppose I am, in Aressa Sessamo, but that's a dangerous thing to be. I'm not going to kill them. I might need them."

"For what?" asked Ram Odin. "You can't trust them."

"I can trust them to do what they think is in their own interest," said Noxon.

"In the interest of the world of Garden," said a mouse.

"In the interest of the *mice* of Garden," Noxon corrected him. There was no argument from the mice.

"But now I'm sure that I *will* slice time with you," said Noxon to Ram Odin. "Only we'll bring the mice with us. The less time they have to figure out ways to fiddle with the ship, the better off we'll be." Then Noxon turned to the expendable. "Thank you for your quick action."

"It was the obvious thing to do," said the expendable. "Remember that I have a complete record of all the things the mice have done. Including the attempt to send a devastating plague to Earth, and the murder of Param. I have been watching the mice continuously since you appeared here. I recognized them as soon as the memory transfer was complete."

"Thank you for taking the *obvious* action, then," said Noxon.

The expendable nodded graciously.

"Give me your hand," said Noxon to Ram Odin. Noxon scooped up the box of mice, tucking it against his body. "By the way," Noxon asked the expendable, "why did you happen to have an empty box lying around?"

"This is a colony ship," said the expendable. "We have hundreds of containers of various sizes for the use of the colonists."

"They can't chew through this, can they?" asked Noxon.

"It would break their little teeth," said the expendable.

"Then by all means," said Noxon to the mice, "go ahead and give it a try."

"I've seen people talk to their pets before," said Ram Odin, "but you're the first person who actually got answers."

"Not this time," said Noxon. "I think they're pouting."

"They had a near-death experience," said Ram Odin. "I think I know just how low our friend here took the oxygen level. They were desperate for air."

"As *we* will be," said Noxon, "if I can't take the ship with us back to regular time."

"Cheer up," said Ram Odin. "You probably won't be able to *find* regular time, so it's a moot question. But let's get close to Earth and see."

Noxon turned to the expendable. "We'll be moving very quickly. What should I look at to know when we're nearing the gravity well of Earth, but are still outside it?"

"Gravity goes on forever," said the expendable. "The Earth is already exerting a faint but noticeable tug on this ship. What threshold am I looking for?"

"I don't know," said Noxon.

"When we come within the average orbital distance of Pluto," said Ram Odin.

"I didn't even think about the outer planets," said Noxon. "What if one of them captures our timeflow?"

"We don't come in through the plane of the ecliptic. Our course brings us toward Earth from the North Pole. Or rather toward L5, a point balanced between the gravity wells of Earth and the Moon."

"No," said Noxon. "I don't think this will work if we're at such a point of balance."

"As we approach," said Ram Odin reassuringly, "Earth will have a much stronger pull on us than the Moon, until right before we arrive at the point where this ship was built."

Noxon thought of something else. "Do you have any control over this ship?" he asked.

The expendable cocked his head. "The other computers and I *are* the ship."

"No. I mean . . . can you make the ship go where you want?"

"I haven't tried to change it," said the expendable.

"We're facing the wrong way," said Ram Odin. "If we could deploy our ram scoop it would still be behind us. So we're not capable of gathering fuel. The engines seem to be running, but I don't know how."

"Our best calculation," said the expendable, "is that as hydrogen dust is consumed in the engines of the outbound ship, it powers the movement of both ships, the outbound and the inbound."

"So matter *is* crossing over."

"No," said the expendable. "It remains entirely in the normal timeflow."

"Then energy is crossing."

"No," said the expendable. "Energy and matter are the same thing, in a fusion engine."

"*Something* is crossing over," said Ram Odin impatiently.

"As near as we can tell," said the expendable, "and that's not very near, because there is no way to measure this, the only thing crossing over is momentum."

"Is momentum actually a thing, in physics?" asked Noxon.

"It is not," said the expendable, "at least not the way we're using the term. Our hypothesis is that there's some unknown force binding the subatomic particles to each other, forward and backward."

"You know what?" asked Ram Odin. "I don't actually care how it works. I only know that when and if we do break free and jump back into ordinary time, we'll be hurtling toward Earth *in reverse*. That's another argument in favor of making the switch before we come too close to Earth."

"Yet if we try it too far out, we can't bring the ship with us," said Noxon.

"That's all we were doing," said a mouse. "Trying to figure these things out in advance."

"I believe you completely," said Noxon to the mice.

"No you don't," said the mouse.

"Apparently you don't believe *me*," said Noxon.

"I will alert you by standing exactly here and raising my arm like this when we're approaching Earth but are still well back from it. Maybe a week or two out. Would that be good?"

"Yes," said Noxon. "Make it three weeks. I want to see when

I start getting a sense of paths that are tied to Earth rather than to spaceships. And that means I need to start looking well before the point of no return."

"So shall we slice time?" asked Ram Odin. "I'm looking forward to my first actual time-shift."

"You just had one."

"Only an hour or so. And I didn't feel anything."

"You *won't* feel anything. Nothing in the ship will change, unless *he* moves around. We'll be moving, of course, but if I do this right, we won't complete even a single step."

"Then let's *do* it," said Ram Odin. "We have nothing to lose but seven years of mind-numbing boredom."

"All right," said Noxon, and he took a step as he sliced forward.

CHAPTER 15

Building a House

Singhfold wasn't *all* up-and-down, mountains and valleys — there was a coastal plain, and some high plateaus. But the level ground was in the rain shadow of the mountains, and those who lived there scratched out a living by damming the occasional streams and laboriously irrigating the fields.

In most of the mountain valleys, however, rain fell often, and snow-fed streams never disappeared. The ground was rarely level, and farming required terracing. But nimble goats and sheep thrived on the grass that grew wherever the snow abated, and if winters were long, there were many labors that resulted in artifacts for trade. It was a good life for people who were willing to work hard, and each community learned to be self-sufficient.

Singhfold was also a linguist's heaven, or would be, if anyone but Singhex traveled enough to realize how many languages were spoken, and how they revealed deep secrets of history by the groups and families of languages, and how they were interlaced among the valleys.

Along with the languages came a variety of folkways—from which valley the young people of a village might seek a spouse, and into which it was forbidden to marry. Some villages practiced strict exogamy; some regarded "foreign" spouses with suspicion and treated their children and grandchildren as strangers.

"I love Singhfold," said Ram Odin. "My regret is that because I've tried to prolong my life by sleeping through the years in stasis, I never have time to visit here for more than a few days. It's the life I think humans were meant to lead—intensely involved with a community that knows you too well, that's always in your face and in your business."

"I think those sound like reasons *not* to like the life here," said Rigg.

"People don't understand how evolution has shaped us to hunger for human company," said Ram Odin. "Even the shyest of introverts suffer from being alone."

"Meaning yourself," said Rigg. "Because what human on Garden has been as much alone as you?"

"I *feel* it more than most, it's true," said Ram Odin. "But that doesn't mean my observation isn't true. Shy people might take their doses of companionship like an ill-tasting medicine, but they need it, and they suffer a thousand maladies, physical and mental, if they don't have it."

"Well, then, this must be the healthiest place in the world," said Rigg.

"It is," said Ram Odin. "Partly because there's no anonymity. Everybody is always with people who know who they are."

"No traveling merchants or peddlers? No show people, no bards? No wars to force one village to bow to another?"

"At different times and places such people have arisen, and such events have happened. It's in human nature to come to blows sometimes. Every few generations, one of the cities of the plain, weary of the struggle to live with little water, gets the grand idea of conquering the mountain valleys."

"But they fail?"

"Oh, they succeed easily. The valleys don't have enough people to defend them against a relentless enemy. But the valleys farther in take the refugees, and the people of the plain don't know how to work the land, or what crops grow. And when do you stop? Which valley is the last one you'll conquer? Whatever place you choose, the people in all the nearby valleys will shun your trade, and if you've been particularly brutal, the neighboring valleys conduct a relentless guerrilla campaign. If the conquerors leave a small force, it will be killed one by one. If they leave a large one, it will starve or freeze."

"So their history is the same thing over and over," said Rigg.

"All history is the same thing over and over," said Ram Odin. "The technology may change, but the behavior is still human. We are who we are. Individuals learn, grow up, get better, wiser, stronger, healthier, kinder—or the opposite. As a group, though, we keep inventing the same behaviors. Some work, some don't. In the valleys of Singhfold, most of the villages and hamlets have found and held on to customs that allow the most happiness for the most people."

"First you tell me that there's infinite variety here, and then—"

"The superficial customs vary extravagantly," said Ram Odin. "But the underlying principles of village civilization are still served by all of them. Which is why Singhfold could reward a lifetime's study—and can be discovered almost completely in a few days."

"But if they don't have peddlers or bards, what are *we*?"

"Priests," said Ram Odin. "It's one of the ways they amuse themselves—there are more religions than languages. Organized and disorganized, proselytizing and localized, every possible religion."

"Each valley has its own?"

"Some valleys are mostly one thing or another, and others are so eclectic there are hardly enough believers in any sect to make it worth building a meetinghouse."

"And what religion, exactly, are we preaching?" asked Rigg. "Are they mostly monotheists? Partisans of favorites in a pantheon?"

"It almost doesn't matter. Because traveling priests are all treated respectfully, but none is expected to do anything in particular. Some are silent and very holy. Others pitch in and join the village in all their labors, talking about their gods as they do. We can belong to the Church of Finding Out How People Think, and simply ask questions."

"That might make us the most annoying of all," said Rigg.

"Your face will make us annoying and disturbing," said Ram Odin.

"If there's one thing we've learned, people get used to me if

263

they look long enough. And this lovely facemask of mine might make me seem all the holier."

"Then let's do it," said Ram Odin. "These valleys are secure enough that they don't have any habit of killing strangers. The worst that can happen is that they'll escort us to a pass and encourage us to move on to another valley."

"Well, then, human nature is *not* the same here as everywhere else."

"You'll see," said Ram Odin. "They don't have to kill us, because expulsion, to them, is worse than death. To be alive, but have no home, no village, no people you belong to — booting out strangers is, to them, worse than killing them, but also kinder."

"There have to be exceptions," said Rigg.

"There are," said Ram Odin. "But we're not going to those places."

"Those," said Rigg, "are precisely the places where I want to go."

"Because you like being depressed and angry," said Ram Odin.

"Because if the Wall comes down, the danger to other wall-folds is likely to come from the people who aren't happy and nice and kind to all living things."

"Well, then," said Ram Odin. "Let's by all means find a bitter, suspicious village and invite them to prove me wrong about how they only exile the people who annoy them."

In their own language, their name for the valley and the village was the same: "Good People's Home." Of course this rolled off the wallwalkers' tongues as if it were in their native speech: Woox-taka-exu. This meant that simply speaking the name was praise and nostalgia and affection, even for people who had never lived there.

At Rigg's insistence, they joined in with the work that was going on, which at present was beginning to move indoors, as the winds rose, the sky was slate, and snow flurries came often and unpredictably. Not hard winter yet, because the snow could pile up to rooftop level in those storms. But the promise of winter, the warning of it. Get your flocks in from the hills, make sure your hay is stored up high in the barn, slaughter the excess geese and sheep and goats, smoke or dry or salt or sausage away the meat, grind bones into fertilizer.

Gather fallen wood for fires—it took less than Rigg might have thought, because the fires were never very hot or bright. With houses insulated by snow and no one going outside most of the winter, body heat and small, steady fires kept people as warm as they needed or wanted to be. But woe to the family that ran out, because no one else would have very much to spare. Usually, instead of sharing their firewood, the neighbors would take in this or that family member for the rest of the winter, and then mock the householders mercilessly when spring came.

Rigg liked to work alongside people. Much better than being a judge—he didn't like arriving with an office that kept him distant. He realized that Ram Odin might be right—Rigg didn't need to *talk* to people, but he needed to be near them as they talked to each other. They saw that Rigg was trying to learn and that he worked hard—he certainly wasn't accepted enough to marry one of their daughters, but they trusted him enough to talk in front of him.

Ram Odin, on the other hand, gravitated toward the old men who gathered in the Cave, which was not a cave, but rather a house-sized building with few interior walls. It served as town hall, church, court, and ballroom by turns. And it was the gathering place of the old men who got cold too easily and left all the last-minute winter preparation to younger folk. "I plan to die this winter," said one of the men. "So what do I care if there's firewood? I won't be using it."

"You say that every year," another retorted.

"Not bending over to pick up sticks is why I didn't die."

Ram Odin soon joined in with a dry witticism or two, and after a while began discussing various philosophies with them, in a folksy way.

Rigg and Ram soon learned the same thing: why this village was a sad and suspicious place. A girl had been lost fifteen years ago, and not in winter—it was spring when she disappeared. No one saw her leave. She was simply gone at suppertime one day, and no one knew what happened to her.

All their children were known to all, and loved more or less according to their character. But this girl, Onishtu, was spoken of with reverence. Not only was she an extraordinarily beautiful girl—"Like the sun when she first comes warm in spring to melt the snow"—but she was also kind and generous, loved by all, and if any of the other children envied her, they kept it to themselves because no one wanted to hear ill of Onishtu.

"*They* took her," said someone, and with each person there

seemed a different idea of who "they" were. Mostly, though, the candidates were the people of this or that nearby village. "Took her, they did, and stuffed up her mouth so she couldn't cry out, and carried her off."

To be somebody's wife. To be everybody's wife. To be disfigured. To be kept in a cellar and fed as little as possible until she became scrawny and sour. "They'll give her back to us then, when she's an ugly hag, bitter and mean. Then they'll say, 'You were so proud of her, do you like her now?'"

And people would nod as if they agreed. Only they'd nod again at the next theory.

Rigg got the idea that they didn't talk about Onishtu all that often — but it was a story so central to their lives these days that even after fifteen years, it was an open wound, and the arrival of a stranger meant that the tale *had* to be told, in all its details, from every angle.

When Rigg and Ram Odin were alone in the haybarn where they would spend the night, Ram Odin preempted any discussion by saying, "You're not the finder of lost things here."

"I'm the only person who can solve this mystery."

"It's not a mystery, it's a tragedy."

"It's a tragedy that they can't find the answer to the mystery."

"It's a tragedy that a beloved child was lost. It's become a part of how they define themselves — we're the people that someone envied so much that they did *this* to us. They're actually quite proud of it. It sets them apart."

"I think they'd rather have the girl back."

"Would they?" asked Ram Odin. "Are you sure?"

"Do you think that if I asked them, any of them would say no?"

"Do you think that just because that's what they *say* they want, what they *believe* they want, it must be what they *really* want?"

"Why do you have to fight me on something so obvious?" asked Rigg. "Aren't you glad I went back and prevented *your* killing?"

"It's precisely because you have that experience that I'm afraid your do-good soul will triumph over your see-ahead brain, which teaches you caution."

"I'll be cautious."

"Meaning what? The way you were cautious in Ramfold? Constantly fiddling with the past, having no idea what the consequences might be?"

"Everything turned out fine."

"As far as we know. So far."

"That goes without saying. The Umbo that warned us of future danger always disappeared when we took his advice and did a different thing."

"Yes," said Ram Odin. "I'll keep that in mind. Just promise me something—and not an idle promise, not an 'agree so he'll stop talking' promise."

"What's the promise?"

"That you won't go back into the past and *change* things without talking to me first. No, talking to me and *listening* to what I say."

"I've never had to consult you on these things and I've done well enough."

"Yes, you have," said Ram Odin. "And I admire your self-restraint—that you've never used your ability to rule over other people, or for vengeance. Mostly it's been to help you accomplish a good and honorable task. But promise me all the same."

"Yes," said Rigg. "I promise. It won't hurt—I always have time to talk things through before I act."

"Then play this out and see what you find," said Ram Odin. "I'm curious, too."

Rigg began right after breakfast the next morning. "Would it be wrong of me to meet Onishtu's family?"

"You already have," he was told.

"I mean . . . would they mind if I asked them about her?"

"Maybe they would and maybe they wouldn't," he was told.

"How can I find out?"

"Ask them about her and see what happens."

So when the father was pointed out to him among the men bringing in the bees, Rigg waited till he finished with one of the hives and then took him aside. "I don't mean to give offense," said Rigg. "But I believe that people leave behind a kind of aura, a trace of the path they took through the world. Your daughter Onishtu sounds like a person who would leave a path of joy, and if I can see where she lived, perhaps I can gain some bit of grace for having met her, even across all these years."

Couching it in religious terms did the trick. The father wasn't satisfying idle curiosity, he was allowing his long-missing daughter to give a gift to—and perhaps be admired and remembered by—this young stranger, ugly as his face might be.

So after supper, Rigg and Ram Odin went to their house, to

the second story. All the houses had two stories, so when the bottom floor was completely buried in snow, they could still get out of the house and tend to the animals and other tasks.

"This was her room," said the father. "It's full of grandchildren at the moment."

"We kept it for her for a few years," said the mother, "but we couldn't afford to keep the room out of a hopeless hope, when there were people here with us who had need of it." She sounded stern as she said it—as if she was rebuking herself for regretting the necessity.

Rigg found the girl's path easily—it filled the place, during the years it had been her room. Rigg followed the most common routes—to the bed, to the window, to the small washstand, to the chest where clothes were kept. Now that he knew which path was hers, the facemask helped him see what she looked like. A gracious child, her hair long in gentle waves of ebony, her smile wide and welcoming. He saw her when she was alone, when she was with company. He saw how her path intertwined with others, and without leaving the room, traced her pattern of friendships.

"She had many friends," said Rigg.

"Everyone loved her," said her father.

"Don't pretend to 'feel' what everybody already told you," said the mother scornfully.

Rigg smiled at her. "I want nothing from you. She's beautiful. I can feel that wide smile of hers shining in this room, that's all. It's what I came for. She's gone, but some of her beauty remains, and I am taking joy in it. I'm sorry if you thought I meant to exploit your love for her. I don't." He turned to Ram Odin. "We've troubled this good family enough. Let's be on our way to bed."

At the door to her room, the father put a hand on Rigg's chest and said, "I think your gift is real and you know where she went."

"My gift is real," said Rigg, "and I *don't* know where she went."

But even as he said it, he was finding out. Without even meaning to, he was tracing the youngest of her paths in the room. Sensing where it went. "It was lambing time when she went, wasn't it?" he asked.

"It was."

"And the snow was still far down the slopes, so the flocks were close by."

"A din and a stink," said the mother. "It was her favorite time of year. How could she leave during lambing?"

Rigg saw her follow a path she had taken many times before. It wound among the houses and went up through the ruins of a couple of collapsed houses. "Why are there so many abandoned houses here?" Rigg asked.

"Not abandoned," said the father. "Never finished. Never had the second story or a roof."

Ram Odin explained. "While you were working to earn our keep," he said, "I was gossiping with the old men. It's how folks marry here. A man builds a house for a particular woman. If she says yes, then they put on the second floor and thatch the roof together and they're wed. But if she refuses him, then he can't offer that shell of a house to another—it would be wrong. So the walls stand as a monument to false hopes."

"Not false," said the father. "The hopes were true, but the girl is free to say no."

"It shames the fellow, though, doesn't it?" asked Rigg.

"They say not," said Ram Odin. "They say nobody knows who built what house, or who it was for."

Rigg cocked his head a little. "I think maybe everyone *pretends* not to know."

The father nodded ruefully. "We always know who's building," said the father. "But not always who he's a-building for."

Rigg nodded. "Did anyone build a house for Onishtu?"

"She was too young," said the mother quickly.

"I would have torn down such a house with my bare hands," said the father. "A girl her age, there should have been no house built for her."

"A man usually won't build a house unless he has a good idea the girl has her eye on him," said the mother. "But what has any of this to do with our Onishtu?"

"I think she liked to wander among the empty roofless houses, that's all," said Rigg. "I think she dreamed of marrying."

"As all girls do," said the mother. "Will it be a good man and a happy house? Or a sad one, or an angry one."

"We had a ewe once who always went within walls to lamb," said the father. "At lambing time, you follow where the ewes have gone to bear. I think if she wandered among the houses, it was looking for that ewe."

"I'd forgotten that crazy old sheep," said the mother. "She was Onishtu's favorite. And she being the oldest, she was fully able to help with lambing by herself. We thought that's where she

272

had gone that day, but we found the ewe, still full, and we never found Onishtu however much we searched." She had tears down her cheeks now.

"I'm sorry to have made you cry," said Rigg. "I wish now that I hadn't troubled you."

"Pay no heed to the crying," said the father. "Tears come easy, no matter how many years go by. When you have a child of your own someday, if some girl is willing to see past your face, you'll know what I'm saying. You lose a child, and the tears are always just inside your eyes waiting to spill. But it's a joy to remember her, too, and we're not ashamed to cry, nor any sadder for it."

"I'm crying to think of how she loved that sheep and how she cared for the lambs. She had a loving touch with the sheep, but she hated the goats!"

And the two parents burst into laughter, perhaps remembering a particular event in Onishtu's childhood.

"It's late all the same," said Ram Odin. "Glad we are that we've not brought you grief, but it's time for us to leave you to your sleep, and go take ours. Rigg has a lot of work to do tomorrow, and I have another day of faith-talk ahead of me."

"Your boy works as hard as any man," said the father, "and no one begrudges what he eats. Many a stick that keeps the family warm will have his handprints on it, as they say."

With such polite talk they made their goodbyes and Rigg and Ram Odin spoke not at all as they walked back through the sharp cold of the night breeze. Only when they were inside the haybarn, and Rigg had assured Ram Odin that no one was inside with them, or even near enough to overhear, did Ram Odin ask, "Well? What happened to her?"

"There was a man who followed her. Always at a distance. I've scanned all their paths and he was close, but never beside her. I don't think they ever spoke until the end."

"Let me guess. He was subtle enough about it that nobody accused him of stalking her like prey."

"Everyone had their eye on her, but no, I don't get a sense that anyone was wary of him. He's still here in the village. Nobody knows that he's a rapist and a murderer. He only did it the once."

Ram Odin covered his face with his hands.

"I didn't expect you to be so moved," said Rigg.

"I'm hiding my eyes from the future. I don't have to have any time-shifting ability to know what you're planning to do."

"I have no plan yet, so you can't possibly know."

"I *do* know," said Ram Odin, "even if you don't know it yet yourself."

"Oh," said Rigg. "What am I planning, then?"

"There are two courses of action you could follow," said Ram Odin. "The first is to find her body, wherever it's buried—I assume it's buried, and that you know where."

"Yes and yes," said Rigg.

"You find it—tomorrow, say—and then the family has an answer to the mystery. She's dead, and here in the village, not in some other town. But you won't like that plan because it leaves more questions than it answers."

"And also, if I go finding the body, people will think I put it there."

"I suppose they might," said Ram Odin. "Though you'd have to have been no older than five at the time."

"They can't read my age through this mask," said Rigg. "Finding the body is just too hard to explain."

"I wish you'd do it that way, though, compared to the other thing."

"You think I'll go back in time and prevent it," said Rigg. "And you have a powerful argument against it, yes?"

"I think saving the life of a young girl, keeping her from being raped and murdered—I'm always for that. Even if she's *not* extraordinarily pretty. Is she, by the way? Or is that just fond memory that has made her flawless?"

"She's more beautiful than I imagined. Extraordinary. Unforgettable."

"Now you're teasing," said Ram Odin.

"I'm not," said Rigg. "The man had built a house for her. She was kind and gentle but she said no. Maybe he took her attitude for coyness, but he tried to kiss her and she was still too young and small to put up much of a fight. When he was done with the rape, she was crying and her clothing was torn. There was no way that people wouldn't know what he had done. I haven't actually *gone* back and listened, by the way. I'm just telling you what I *saw*. He actually tried to comfort her. Maybe he was apologizing. But she turned away from him and at one point tried to get out of the shell of the house he had built for her. I wish I could say that he killed her accidentally, in the heat of the moment. But no. He dragged her back into the house and she was sitting on the floor, crying again. It took him a while—several minutes—to make up his mind, but then he dragged her to her feet and strangled her. It was brutal. He held her up and she flailed and kicked but her arms weren't long enough to reach his eyes and her kicking him did no good. When she stopped struggling, he kissed her. Then he pulled away stones from the wall under a window, put her into the earth behind them, and piled the stones back in place. There was already a space there for the body. He didn't have to dig. I think he planned to kill her if she said no to him. I think he had already decided that if he couldn't have her, no one would."

"It's a bitter story."

"The man built another house years later, and he has five children now."

"Is it someone we know? Not our host, I hope."

"You've talked with him some in the Cave," said Rigg. "He's never said a word to me, but he has friends, a normal life. She was his one obsession, and he never did such a thing again."

"So much for having no anonymity here in these villages," said Ram Odin.

"This house-building thing," said Rigg. "If they all pretend not to know who's a-building, that means they don't cast their eyes toward a house under construction. The first floor of these houses is always half buried, so once a man has dug the hole, he's out of sight. But they know who's gathering stones from old abandoned houses and reusing them. If I even said, 'It was a man who had built a house for her,' I'll bet they'd figure out who it was, pretty quick."

"They just wouldn't be able to figure out how you knew," said Ram Odin.

"Exactly. But if I go back in time, I can prevent it."

"Really? How?"

Rigg knew Ram Odin was taunting him. "There are plenty of ways. Distract her and keep her from going after the ewe that day."

"He'd just wait for another day. You plan on spending your life watching her?"

"Maybe I'd have a talk with him. He's bigger than me but with the facemask I'm a match for anyone."

"A match? How would such a fight end?"

"I wouldn't have any qualms about killing a murderer."

"But when you do it, he won't *be* a murderer yet."

"Even if he hasn't done it yet, he built that house with space behind the wall to hide a corpse."

"I'm surprised the stink of putrefaction didn't bring them."

Rigg shook his head. "The body wouldn't have rotted yet when they went searching. And people avoid a house under construction that hasn't been offered yet. I would have to actually *go* to that time to know whether the house was finished at the time, but I'm guessing not. I think he took her to a house that only had the walls up to ground level, say, and he said, 'I'm building this for you, say you'll marry me,' but after she went missing, he still had months of work to do on it. So they'd think he hadn't asked a girl yet, and the girl he wanted was one of the ones of age. If he was smart, he'd wait until a likely girl accepted another man's house, and then stop his own building. So nobody would think he built the house for Onishtu."

"What you're really saying," said Ram Odin, "is that you

prefer to kill this man. You think he deserves to die. And I agree—today, even after all these years, he deserves whatever penalty these people put on a rapist and cold-blooded murderer. But when you go back in time, Rigg, he won't *be* a murderer."

"No, he'll just be a man planning murder."

"But at that point, he still might not do it. He might even believe that he won't really do it, even as he hollows out that space for her body."

"It doesn't matter. I *know* he does it."

"You know, from here, that he did it. But when you're there, do you see his future path?"

"Of course not."

"You can't just go killing people because you know they're going to do something terrible."

"Explain to me why not," said Rigg.

"Because until he does the murder, he doesn't deserve to die."

Rigg shook his head. "But I *know*."

"But justice *doesn't* know," said Ram Odin. "Look at it the other way. In your own life, when you did something stupid and wrong, Umbo would appear to you and warn you not to do it after all. So you were constantly undoing your own actions and trying something else. So . . . did you do those bad things, or didn't you?"

"The me-that-was did them, but *I* didn't."

"Should you be punished for your misdeeds? How many times did Umbo and Loaf try to break into that bank to get the missing jewel back? Are they thieves?"

Rigg shook his head.

"And why not? Say it, Rigg Sessamekesh."

"Because they didn't actually do it. The realities in which they did are gone."

"And the reality in which this man killed Onishtu also doesn't exist, at the time you plan to kill him."

"It's not the same." Rigg understood his point, but he couldn't doubt the reality of what he knew about this man. And how much more valuable Onishtu's life was than any justice owed to her murderer.

"Fine," said Ram Odin. "I see you're not convinced, but I don't mind, because that's not my real argument."

"You have another?" Rigg almost laughed. "A *stronger* one?"

"Yes," said Ram Odin. "If you save her, will she *never* die?"

"No, of course she'll die. But she might never be raped."

"Do you plan to undo all the rapes and murders that ever happened in Singhfold?"

"If that's your argument, then—"

"That's groundwork. Listen up. You don't know if saving her from this admittedly terrible death will prolong her life for a week or ninety years. You don't know if the life you're giving her will be happy or sad."

"I don't even *care* about that," said Rigg. "All I care about is that she have the right to choose her own life."

"Because the life she chooses to live, that's who she is, yes? She'll decide whether to be joyful or sad within the events and years of her life, yes?"

"That's what life *is*."

"That's what life is, unless a timeshaper comes along," said Ram Odin.

"Oh, come on," said Rigg. "I'm not going to make her do anything."

"You're going to make this murderer die without having raped or murdered anybody," said Ram Odin. "So what happens to this man's eventual wife and children?"

"She marries somebody else."

"So those children never exist."

Rigg had no answer that sounded right in his own mind. But he said one of them, anyway. "Never existing is not the same thing as murdering somebody."

"But you'll be taking away all those choices in life. Those children will never exist so they'll never have those experiences, they'll never become anybody at all. At least Onishtu had years enough to win the hearts of a village, to live on in their memory, to color the way the whole valley looks at the world outside. But now they'll never become who they are."

"Suspicious and resentful and sad," said Rigg.

"Have they gone to war over it? Made a revenge raid on another village? Killed one girl in each of the other valleys in order to retaliate?"

"They *suffer*."

"They have a wistful memory of an extraordinary child whom they all loved and whose disappearance shattered them. But they've turned it into something rather ennobling and fine, even if it looks like a shadow to you. They all share this grief. It helps unite them."

"Including the man who actually did it."

"Maybe it tortures him," said Ram Odin. "Maybe he doesn't

care. What difference does that make to the *other* people? That girl's life changed them all, and her death changed them all. People see the world differently because she's gone. I don't know how that changed their behavior, their decisions, and neither do you. But maybe there are marriages that didn't happen, jobs that were done differently, or not done at all, because of the shadow of Onishtu's life and disappearance. You don't know how their lives and choices would be different. But you arrogantly assume that because her death was awful, that gives *you* the right to take away all the lives that have been lived in this valley since she was buried under that window."

Rigg sat very still, thinking, thinking. "It's what the Odinfolders did—sent back messages that wiped out billions of lives."

"Their lives! Their *own* lives. And they chose to send back the Future Book in order to save the world. A knowing sacrifice. Who is getting a choice if you save this one girl from her murderer?"

"*She* is."

"And nobody else. Give one girl a few more years, and *obliterate* all the other lives that have been lived after her death—including the children of her murderer and his wife. Do *they* deserve to die for a crime their father committed before they were born?"

"That's not what I'm—"

"That's exactly what you're doing. You can lie to yourself but don't lie to me. Because remember, you think of me as a murderer even though I never killed you—but you *did* kill *me*. Noxon didn't, because you came back and prevented him. So tell me,

Rigg. Are you and Noxon *both* killers? I won't say murderers, because according to your story you acted in self-defense—and I believe you, I know I was thinking about it, I had decided to do it, but this man talking to you right now, Rigg, *this* me never made the final decision to take your life. But *you* are the very one who deliberately, calculatedly went back in time and killed me first, before I could kill *you*. And then you regretted it."

"I killed you because I believed that it was you, alone, who triggered the destruction of Garden. Not just because you tried to kill *me*. I could have dodged you forever, to keep *myself* alive. I killed you to *save the world*."

"But it turns out you were wrong and I didn't blow up Garden and obliterate the life that I had been tending for eleven thousand years! What a shock! How could you have guessed!"

"I undid the killing," said Rigg, quieting himself. The last thing they needed to do was let their shouting in the cold night air bring curious people to the barn. "I was wrong, and I undid it, and I believe you are not dead, sir."

"And this murderer—I wonder if, after a while, he came to wish he hadn't done it. I wonder if he might not have chosen to go back in time and stop himself from killing her—even at the risk of causing two copies of himself to exist."

"He can't. Nobody can. Just me and Noxon and Umbo. And the mice, in their own way. Everybody else is stuck with whatever choices they made. I know."

"So you think because you can *un*do a terrible mistake like killing an innocent man—me, because I never killed anybody and I did not destroy the world—because you can undo it, you're *not* a murderer. You're an *ex*-killer, a former killer, but you unkilled me so — "

"I get your point. Two points. One, that I don't have the right to wipe out all the things this village has done in response to Onishtu's death. Two, that I don't have the right to kill him before *he* has killed. You think people have the right to be vile before they get punished for their vileness. By that reckoning, do we have to let the Destroyers wipe out all life on Garden before we take action to prevent them?"

"If you can't see the difference . . ."

"I can see lots of differences. I can see differences between all your comparisons."

"Think, Rigg. When Umbo and Param prevented those plague-infected mice from boarding the Visitors' ship, they made the decision that saving human life on Garden was *not* worth wiping out human life on Earth. There's actually a limit to what they would allow the mice to do in order to save our world."

"Noxon's going to take mice with him."

"Not plague mice, Rigg," said Ram Odin. "I'm telling you that yes, you can prevent the destruction of Garden and yes, in the process there may be people you have to kill or cause not to exist in order to prevent the death of a world. But you try to make as little change as possible. You don't just decide that to save this one girl, you can wipe out innocent children and make it so their lives never happen."

Rigg just sat there, not really thinking, because he knew that he wasn't going to prevent Onishtu's death after all, but he hated himself for listening to Ram Odin, and he now felt as ashamed as if he had stood at the door and watched the murder and had done nothing to prevent it. Because that was pretty much how things stood. He had the power to stop the rape and murder, and he wasn't going to stop it, and it *hurt*.

"Rigg," said Ram Odin. "I'm only urging you to follow the course you and Umbo have followed all along. Minimal change. All the things you did affected mostly yourselves, and nobody else's life was going to be all that changed by it. And you were contained within Ramfold, so nothing you did could possibly transform any of the other wallfolds. Noxon and Param went off by themselves to practice chronomancy, so they wouldn't go back in time where it might change the course of the Larfolders' lives. And in Yinfold, you didn't prevent the adulterous pair and you didn't even tell on them. In fact, you covered up their betrayal so that greater evil wouldn't come from it."

"Adultery is not the rape and murder of a child."

"I know that," said Ram Odin. "And so do you. I'm talking about the principle of minimal change."

"To be able to stop it, and choose not to, that makes me *complicit*."

"No!" said Ram Odin sharply. "You have this godlike power to force other people not to do evil, but to choose *not* to use it doesn't make *you* evil. It says that you respect other people's freedom enough to allow them to choose to do terrible things. To reveal who they are by the choices they actually make, the things they actually do. If you didn't have this godlike power, if you had lived in this village and realized what the murderer was going to do, and you came and saw what he was doing and decided to let it happen, *then* you'd be complicit. But you *have* a godlike power to compel people to be better—or at least less awful—than they wish to be. How many people can you keep from being moral monsters? You children are going to try to stop the destruction of a world—but even then, there are limits to how you'll go about doing it. There are limits! The only reason you can be trusted with this power is that *there are limits.*"

"So you stopping *me* from doing something, that's all right, but I—"

"I'm not stopping you, foolish boy. I'm trying to *persuade* you. But I know perfectly well that at any second you could leap back in time, go prevent the murder, and come back here to rejoin this conversation right where we left off."

"I actually can't. I'd have to slice my way back."

"You'd get back here. If you wanted. You could also leave me behind whenever you want. But you don't do those things."

"Maybe I should."

"But you haven't and I think you won't. You sat here and listened to my arguments for one reason and one reason only."

"I know."

"Tell me the reason."

"You're not my father. You don't have the right to quiz me."

"You listened to me because you know I'm right. No, more than that. You *already* knew I was right, and you let me talk you out of it because you already mistrusted your decision to save the girl. You just needed me to help you do the right thing."

"Yes," said Rigg. "You nailed it. And now I'm going to sleep."

He lay down in the hay, his coat under his head to keep bits of straw out of his nostrils while he slept. But he did not sleep until he had exhausted himself with weeping. For the beautiful dead girl whose path was still present even when he shut his eyes, whose face was always before him because he could not stop himself from examining her path.

In the morning, Rigg went to work with the other men — sausage-making today, because it was beginning to snow, and it might turn into a real storm, and nobody should be caught out in the woods when the world went invisible and white.

"I had a dream last night," said Rigg. "After imagining that poor girl's path through the world. I dreamed that I saw her dead."

One of the other men grunted. Nobody said anything.

"I know I'm a stranger here, and I have no right to anything to do with that girl. I don't have a right to say her name, if you don't consent to it."

"Onishtu," said one of the men. "You can say it."

"Dreams are dreams," said Rigg. "They mean nothing except that's what was on my mind. Only I do believe that people leave paths in the world, and I do believe those paths enter into my mind sometimes. And I wouldn't mention it even now, except that I also happened to see the very house I dreamed that she was buried in, and if *that* was real . . ."

All work stopped. "House?" asked a man.

"One of the empty houses," said Rigg. "In my dream, it had been built for her."

"She was too young," said a man. "Nobody would build a house for her."

"I know, her father said so last night — I'm sure that's why it was on my mind. Forget that I said anything. It was just . . . such a vivid dream."

Silence for a long time. They got back to work. Rigg kept grinding the meat and fat that would go into the sausages — the bloodiest and most menial task, but he didn't mind.

As Rigg expected, the silence was finally broken by a man asking, "Which house?"

They didn't leave their task until it was almost time for the noon meal. They would all eat together, so they didn't have to change out of their bloody clothes. But they had to wash their hands, at least, before putting food into their mouths, and for that they went to one man's dooryard. And when they were clean, the man said, "Food's not quite ready. Suppose you point out the house in your dream."

"No, no," said Rigg, but they insisted.

On the way, they passed the Cave, and the old men who were spry enough came out and walked with them, and a few curious women joined them, so there were about twenty people when Rigg got to where he had a clear view of the house that was Onishtu's grave and marker. They were still a good hundred meters from it, but he could point and there would be no ambiguity about the house he meant.

"Let's go have a look," said a woman, who had been filled in on what they were doing in quiet conversation along the way.

"Not me," said Rigg.

"You said she was buried there, in your dream," said one of the sausagemakers. "Where?"

"Behind the wall under a window," said Rigg. "The west-facing window."

"*Behind* the stone? Not in the floor?"

"That's right," said Rigg. "But is that even possible?"

"We'll see," said a man. And they went on ahead.

Ram Odin was among the men who had come out of the Cave. He didn't go into the house, either. "So you decided to tell them your . . . dream."

"Naming no names," said Rigg. "They'll know whose house or they won't. They'll accuse him or they won't. He'll break down and confess what he did, or not. But her parents will have her body and know she didn't leave them and run off somewhere. No one carried her off. They'll know."

"Small comfort, if they knew *how* she died."

"After all these years, I think the comfort will be more than small. But I'm not telling them how she died, or what was done to her first. I'm making the *minimal* change, and leaving them free to make of it what they will."

They were a deliberate people—after all, despite years of suspicion, they had never taken any action against the villages they suspected of taking Onishtu. The girl's parents were given a chance to wail over the body, and they buried the body in a real grave, among her ancestors, with a marker, before anyone started open inquiries about who had built the house.

It took only a few minutes to get past the "nobody knows

who builds them" objection, and then it was only a few moments before they had named aloud the man who built it. The murderer kept his silence, except to say, "I'm angry that the killer hid her in the house I was building."

And they took that at face value for a while.

But finally the question came. "Who did you build it for?"

He would not tell them. "A man doesn't have to tell. Shouldn't tell. She chose another."

They started ticking off the women who had accepted houses during that year. They all agreed—for by now the whole town had assembled—that the man had not shown special attention to any of those women.

"Did you never offer it?" asked a man.

"She already took another," said the murderer.

"Who, then? Because if it's one of these, she never knew."

"I'm a shy man," he said. "I was afraid to speak, and then it was too late."

"You never even looked at any of the women of Woox-taka-exu," someone pointed out. "Was she an outsider?"

"When would I see an outsider girl?"

"Who was it?" they demanded.

He named one of the women who had accepted a house at the time.

"You never looked at me, you never talked to me," the woman said.

"I was afraid you wouldn't like me," said the murderer.

"Then why did you build a house for me?" she asked. "Who builds a house for a woman he thinks won't like him?"

"I hoped you would like the house."

They all looked at the house. "It is a fine one," said the woman, "but what kind of empty-headed fool would marry a man she didn't love because the house he built was so sturdy?"

"I hoped you would," said the murderer. "Now I'm going home with my family."

He reached for his wife, who had been there when the conversation started. But she was gone. With the children.

"She must have gone ahead to prepare the table," the murderer said.

Only then did the murderer seem to realize that his outward calm was no longer in place. He looked tense. He looked as if he was barely controlling himself. So now he let go with an emotion he thought might explain his nervousness. "Why are you asking me these questions? Are you accusing me?"

"She wasn't wearing her clothes, they were wrapped around her," said a woman. "I think someone tore them off and then wound them around her dead body."

"Not me!" said the murderer.

No one looked at him.

"Not! Me!"

"Why isn't your wife standing by you?" asked a woman. "I'd stand by my husband, if such things were being said or even thought. Because I know he doesn't have it in him."

"She knows I don't have it in me, either," said the murderer. "Do you think she'd have married me and stayed with me all these years if she did?"

That was when some men came back with the wife, who

hadn't gone far. "Found her crying just around the corner there," one of them said.

"You know something," said a woman. "Tell us all."

"She knows I'm innocent!" said the murderer.

Reluctantly, the murderer's wife spoke. "I had my eye on him for a long time. When he built his first house, I hoped it was for me. But it wasn't. I knew it wasn't because he never looked at me. He never looked at any girl but one. And her too young for a house."

"If you're accusing me," said the murderer, "how can I stay married to you?"

"He kept building on it after she disappeared," said his wife. "But maybe that was just for show."

"I'm the father of your children," he said quietly.

"I think you need to winter in another house," she said.

Those words hung in the silent air. Snow once again started drifting down, but there was no wind and it looked like just a flurry.

"I think you need to winter in another *valley*," said a man.

There was a murmur of assent.

The murderer visibly sagged. "Do you even care that I didn't do this?"

Rigg became conscious of the many eyes that were now glancing at him. Or openly watching him.

"You're a kind of holy man," said a sausagemaker. "Do you think we'd be doing a wrong if we held this man to account?"

Rigg did not know how to answer. So he just looked at the murderer. A long, steady gaze.

"You'll believe a stranger over *me*?" he shouted. "He comes into the village and suddenly he knows where she's buried! Don't you think that's suspicious?"

"Hard to guess his age," said a woman, "but he's young. I think he would have been under ten years old when she died. So no, I don't think that's suspicious. I think it's the Sight. He said he sees the paths people take in their lives, and he saw where her path ended."

"Did he do it?" another man asked Rigg.

"The boy is not a judge," said Ram Odin. "He had a dream. You found the body that he saw buried in that dream."

"But did he see who buried her?" demanded a man. There were open declarations of agreement.

"I would never accuse a man on the basis of a dream," said Rigg. "I don't know which dreams are true and which are merely dreams. I'm sorry this one turned out to be true."

"You didn't answer," said a woman. "Was he in your dream?"

"In my dream," said Rigg, "the cavity behind the wall under the window had already been dug out to receive the body before she died."

"You can't know that!" shouted the man. "He doesn't know what he's talking about! And even if it's true, somebody else could have done it!"

"We would have known," said a woman, "if a man started digging in another man's marriage house."

The assent was resounding.

"Will you give him a night to pack his things?" asked his wife. "The man who did this murder deserves nothing, but my children

292

will be uneasy if their father goes away empty-handed, with winter coming on."

"You can't believe I did this!" the murderer cried to his wife.

"I know she was the only girl you ever loved," she answered him. "And never me. Even when you built a house for me, your heart belonged to her. I've seen you staring at this house over all these years and I knew who it was you had built it for, even though she was still too young. I knew who you were thinking of. But it never crossed my mind that you were looking at her grave. Her clothes were torn off. Did you have her the once before she died?" The wife was taking no pleasure in this. She was being more ruthless with herself than with the murderer. "When you stare at this house of a night or of a morning, are you grieving for her? Or remembering that you were the only man ever to possess that beautiful child?"

There was a growl of rage now among the men. Not at the wife, but at what the wife had seen and what her words meant.

Ram Odin strode to the murderer and put an arm across his shoulder. "Let me take you back home, sir. You have some work to do tonight, I think."

He wasn't out of earshot when other women offered to take in the children and the wife herself for the night. The murderer would have his own house to himself.

This much goes to his credit: He did not kill himself inside the house, or in any other place where it would be one of his children who found him. He went into the smokehouse during the night and hanged himself from a short rope tied to one of the hooks.

Rigg and Ram Odin left the next day, walking on toward the next village. "We thought you'd winter here," said Onishtu's father.

"We owe you much," said Onishtu's mother. "Winter with us."

"We have a place farther on," said Ram Odin, "but your offer is kind."

Rigg silently agreed, for he could not bear the thought of staying in this place. Justice had been served, he believed. But he also knew the repercussions would be long and hard. He had spared the lives of the murderer's children by not changing the past in such a way that they would never be conceived, but their lives would be forever altered by the knowledge of what their father did, and that it was their mother's testimony that condemned him in the eyes of the village.

As they walked toward the mountain pass that led to the next village, Rigg said, "I can't figure out if he finally felt remorse at the end, or if he had felt it all along."

"I don't think he ever felt anything like remorse," said Ram Odin. "I think he treasured the memory of the rape and the murder, both, indistinguishably."

"Then why did he kill himself?"

"Because he couldn't conceive of life outside his own village."

CHAPTER 16

Near Earth

Noxon had sliced this fast before, practicing with Param. And, a few times, had sliced through more years. He had even watched for a marker—a stone he placed on top of another stone. When he saw it stacked up, he knew he had arrived at the target time, and stopped. The expendable's arm would be as good a signal.

It felt like no more than five minutes, at the rate Noxon was slicing. But five minutes of absolute silence can seem long indeed. Noxon could have taken them even faster, but he didn't want to overshoot too far from the time he saw the signal to the time he stopped.

The expendable's arm went up. Noxon stopped slicing. Just like that, they were back to one second per second.

"Whee," said one of the mice.

"So you enjoyed yourself?" asked Noxon.

"Did we skip seven years of unchanging travel? Then yes," said Ram.

"Sorry, I was talking to the mice. They were getting sarcastic about how much fun they had."

"We're in a box," said a mouse.

"So are we," said Noxon. And then he repeated to Ram what the mouse had said.

"What matters, I think," said the expendable, "is whether you can sense any of the paths on Earth. Inside Pluto's orbit makes Earth a nearly-invisible dot."

"So we should have picked Neptune?" said Ram. "Jupiter? I'd suggest Uranus, but you don't have one."

"I actually have an anus," said the expendable, "because the lack of it would make it too easy to tell that I'm not human, and it's important that I be able to pass for human for sustained periods of time."

"Does it work?" asked Ram.

Noxon knew perfectly well that it worked—Father had done his business in the woods every day, like clockwork. If you had a clock that pooped. All very authentic. "Could we please stay with the subject? Can you point out where Earth is?"

"Are you asking him or me or the mice?" asked Ram.

"The expendable." Noxon almost said "Father," but that was an old reflex, and not that hard to suppress.

"Good thing," said a mouse. "Cause we're in a box."

"We can't do astronomy from here," said another.

"Only boxonomy."

Noxon didn't bother reminding them that their own malfeasance got them there.

"While we were moving forward," said Noxon, "I was thinking about all the things that can go wrong. For instance, all the paths on Earth are moving the direction I need to latch on to in order to return to normal time. But the path of the outbound Ram Odin is in this starship, moving the right direction in time. If I can't see it now, what makes me think I can see any other path moving that direction?"

"What an excellent question," said Ram Odin.

"Now you think of it," said a mouse.

"It's not as if I had any wrong-direction paths to practice on, back on Garden," said Noxon. He couldn't keep his irritation out of his voice.

"Ignore the mice," said the expendable. "They have nothing like your ability. It merely amuses them to snipe at you."

"I know," said Noxon. But Father's reassurance made him feel better. *That* hadn't changed, although he knew "Father" was a machine.

"Have you looked for the outbound path?" asked Ram Odin.

"I don't *have* to look for paths," said Noxon. "They're just there."

"But this one isn't. So now you do have to look for it. And that may be why you haven't seen it, because you aren't used to having to look for paths."

"I have to search out individuals among the mesh of intersecting paths," said Noxon. "But they're always visible. Or *present*, anyway."

"I get it that you don't see them with your eyes," said Ram. "But since we don't have words for the ability to sense people's passages through time and space, just use the words for vision."

"All right, yes, of course," said Noxon. That's what he and Umbo had always done.

"So what I'm thinking is, you won't see a path, because causality is going the other direction," said Ram.

"That's what I'm thinking, too," said Noxon. "But that would imply that we're doomed."

"It's not *all* I was thinking, if you want to hear the rest," said Ram Odin.

"Oh, we do, we do!" cried the mice in their chirpy sarcastic voices.

"People moving through time the same direction as you, they make a path the way movies do it—one instant hasn't faded out before the next one begins."

"Because instants don't exist," said Noxon.

"Well, they *do*," said the expendable. "You just can't distinguish them."

"Continuity, that's my point," said Ram. "But when they're running backward, you don't get any continuity at all. Still, that doesn't mean you can't see each—forgive me, each *instant*—but only *for* an instant."

"I don't see any," said Noxon.

"You haven't looked," said Ram. "You've looked for continuous paths. But what happened when Umbo slowed you down in time? Your perception of paths changed. They started individuating. You could see that they were people. You could see faces.

298

The slower you went, the more clearly you saw them."

"Because the whole continuity was there," said Noxon. "No matter how slow I go, they still connect, they still make a continuous movement."

"Exactly my point," said Ram. "Maybe the most you can sense of backward paths is momentary slices. No continuity."

"How can I see those? They don't exist long enough to *be* seen."

"You don't know that," said Ram, "because you haven't looked."

Noxon shook his head. "How can I slow myself down enough to sense something whose existence in our timeflow has no duration?"

Ram shrugged. "Got any better ideas?"

"The ship has been calculating," said the expendable, "and your physics is correct. Each instant of the backward path would have no duration. Except that this is also true of forward paths, and you see *those*."

"Because of causal continuity," said Noxon.

"That's your guess," said the expendable. "It's a good guess, unless it's wrong. But I think you're probably right. That doesn't change anything. The other timeflow also has causal continuity. So what's to say there isn't a lingering image? Not an after-image, as with ordinary timeflow, but a pre-image, a semi-physical memory of what is about to happen, because in that timeflow, it already happened. Each instant caused the next and the next. Maybe there's enough of causality clinging to each instant of a human life that it becomes visible."

"If that were true," said Noxon, "I should see them already."

"No," said the expendable. "Because they're *un*happening. Causality is unraveling, in the direction we're going. Each instant is unmade as you sense it. So instead of a path, a continuity of events, it's a series of discontinuities. An unpath."

"Clever naming," said Noxon. "But you don't know what you're talking about."

"On the contrary," said the expendable. "I don't know what *you're* talking about, because I've never sensed these paths. But when we're talking about the logic of causality and time, my guess is no worse than yours. And even if I'm wrong, my wrong guess will be more *precise* than yours."

Ram barked a laugh. "See what I put up with for all those years in space?"

"See what *I* put up with, day after day in the forest," said Noxon.

"I don't expect *you* to understand what *I* put up with," said the expendable.

"We're in a box," said a mouse. "That's something to put up with."

"If he's right about this," said Ram, "and it's not as if I know anything here, but if he's right, then at least you'd know where to look for these not-quite-instantaneous instants of my outbound path. My life was pretty much limited to sitting in that chair. Or lying on that bed. Or exercising in there. I swivelled the chair a lot. Not like a little kid spinning around, but from station to station. To do different jobs. I don't know what you need—motion or stillness. That chair is where I sat still most of the time. Or if you need me walking, I only followed certain paths, but I did them over and over."

"Do you think I haven't been looking for *anything* anomalous since I got on this ship?"

"No," said the expendable. "I think you have *not* been looking for this because you didn't know what to look for. Looking for 'something anomalous' is identical to just scanning around and hoping something slaps you in the face."

And there was Father's note of scorn.

"Yes, that's right," admitted Noxon.

"Have a plan," said Father. The expendable.

"A plan to do something that nobody in the history of the universe has ever done."

"You don't know that," said the expendable.

"If they did, I didn't read the report," said Noxon.

"What made paths turn into visible people to you? Slowing down," said Ram. "And then attaching to them."

"Attaching to them brought me into their timeflow," said Noxon. "That's the last thing I want to do, until we're in a place where I can take the ship with us safely."

"Right, no attaching," said Ram. "But when you came *here*, when you first latched on to this timeflow, how did that feel?"

"I wasn't in any timeflow. I wasn't in time at all."

"You were fully stopped," said Ram.

"But *I* didn't stop me," said Noxon. "The fold was a place of no movement. I just hung there, unmoving, until I attached."

"The ship's computers got us to that place, somehow," said the expendable. "But since we didn't know that the fold would be a place without motion, time, or causality, we had no plan for emerging from the fold. We might have inadvertently created the twenty possible causal paths. But we think it was Ram Odin who did what *you* did—only instead of picking one, he attached to all of the causal potentialities and the whole ship took all of them at once."

"I did no such thing," said Ram.

"Nobody thinks you were conscious of it," said the expendable. "What we *do* know is that the only successful time-shifting of living people and animals we've ever seen has been done by human timeshapers. You were the only conscious human, Ram Odin. We think you were choosing *forward*, and so the whole ship moved forward in all the available directions."

Noxon was thinking aloud now. "I was in a place with no movement at all. Nineteen paths started along the regular line of time. One path went the other way. I took the strange one."

"Strange in what way?" asked Ram Odin.

"It led into a potential future, but it tracked into the past."

"So you *do* know what a backward path looks like," said Ram.

"The others weren't paths either. You're right, what I saw then is what I'm looking for now. It's like . . . the promise of a path. Like seeing underbrush get lighter and darker long before the person swinging the lantern comes along."

"But the one going the wrong way was different. How?"

Noxon shook his head. He couldn't remember.

But the facemask did. It couldn't sense paths itself, but it could re-create Noxon's brainstate at the time he was in that frozen moment. At the wish to remember it, the facemask re-created that brainstate and Noxon was there again.

The trouble was that along with the brainstate of what he was observing, he could only think the thoughts he was thinking then. And he was also aware of being completely unable to take any action, except to choose a path and attach to it. Only now he wasn't seeing paths, he was *remembering* seeing paths. So there was no escape. He couldn't even put together a coherent thought along the lines of: Help! Get me out of this loop!

There was no sense of duration in that brainstate. He didn't know how long he stood there, utterly immobile and incapable of action. He only knew that eventually it ended and he could think and move again. "That was unpleasant," said Noxon.

"What was?" asked Ram.

"Being unable to move. To *do* anything."

"When did *that* happen?" asked Ram.

"So the facemask didn't allow it to go on long enough for you to notice. That's good."

"You just got the memory back?"

"Not *my* memory. The facemask's memory of what my brain was doing at that moment. I could only think what I thought then."

"Except you were able to worry that it might go on too long," said Ram.

"That wasn't a conscious thought. That was the behind-thought. The watcher. The one without any words who's always listening to what I think consciously in language and evaluating it."

Ram nodded wisely. "It's terrifying how well I know what you mean."

"It was a good refresher, once it actually ended," said Noxon.

303

"I didn't stay there forever, though it felt like it. And now I have a much clearer memory of what I experienced at the time. How paths look when they're not moving. The nineteen with the potential to move away from me into the future. And the one with the potential to move into the past."

"What about the one that got me to that point?" asked Ram.

"The others all attached to that one," said Noxon. "They were all continuations of that."

"So you saw some going back and some forward," said Ram.

"That's not the difference. They were all going into *a* future. But this one was heading into . . . an unproductive future. A place with no causal potential."

"So look for that."

"But at that point I wasn't seeing paths at all. Nothing was moving. They were all alike—I can't explain why the one was different from the others. It just was. The point is that I know what an unpath looks like, a slice of path, because they all looked like that. But in order to see it, I have to be completely stopped in time."

"Still as death," said a mouse.

"Yes," said Noxon.

"And how do you come back from that?" asked a mouse.

Such a good question. Not sarcastic at all. Well, a *little* sarcastic, as if a human could hardly be expected to come up with such an important question on his own.

"The way I got out of that moment was to attach to one of the paths. The one going the wrong way."

"Answering the mice?" asked Ram.

The expendable explained, ending with, "So there's a good chance that if Noxon can slow down enough to see the paths, it'll be impossible for him to come out of it without attaching."

"But I don't know if I even *can* get to that point myself," said Noxon. "Remember that I got there by following Ram Odin's path backward—the path of the Ram from Ramfold. I could never have slowed myself down that much."

"So if you have to be completely stopped," said the expendable, "then there can be no experimentation. You have to do it holding on to the mice, to Ram Odin, and to the ship and all its contents, and you have to do it at the time when it's most convenient to make the jump, and you have to attach to exactly the right path so we jump into the past, long before spaceships."

"Except that I have no idea if I can slow down enough to get to that condition."

"So the alternative," said the expendable, "is that you will start to detect the backward path of outbound Ram—the individual nubs of each instant—before you get to a complete stop in time. If you can slow down to such a degree, but not lose the ability to snap yourself back to *this* timeflow, then we'll know that this venture is possible."

"Might be possible."

"But if you can't slow down enough to see his path," said the expendable, "then we'll know that's an approach that doesn't work."

"And then I'd have to figure out how to get myself to a complete stop."

"Death," suggested one of the helpful mice. "Works every time."

"From your expression," said Ram, "a mouse said something you didn't like."

"It was very funny," said Noxon. "To anybody who didn't actually have to do this."

"So are you going to do the experiment?" asked Ram.

"I'm going to try," said Noxon. "The trouble is that speeding up is easy, now that I learned how from Param. Slowing down— I always do that by sort of watching the paths and doing whatever I do that makes them visible. It was really hard to learn. It's the thing Umbo does naturally."

"So follow my path. Here in the ship. Or your own."

Noxon grimaced. "I hate using my own path to slow down. I have to see myself. And I'm always worried that I'll attach and then there'll be two of me."

"Umbo slows himself down and sends himself messages," said the expendable.

"Because he can't see the paths," said Noxon. "He can't actually see in advance if the person he's talking to is there. He finds the exact time another way, some inner time sense, and then he speaks the message to the place where he knows the person will be. At least that's how it was for him, starting out. It's why it was always easiest for him to send messages to himself, because he knew where he had been."

"So he has no risk of attaching to himself," said Ram.

"But if I use my own path, I always risk attaching to myself and making two of me," said Noxon.

"So use *my* path," said Ram. "Would it help if I sat in the pilot's chair? Or near it?"

"It doesn't matter what you do right now. It's your past self that I'm working with."

"So I can sing? Dance?"

"I thought all the sarcastic ones were in the box," said Noxon. Ram began, "I'll be as quiet as —"

"A mouse," said the expendable. "Your sense of when to drag out some old saying is deplorable—and the saying is contradicted, I might add, by the mice we have with us, who are not quiet."

"We are right now," said a mouse. "We don't want Noxon to get distracted and screw this up."

Noxon held up a hand. "I'm not going to attach to the path. But that's my reflex, so I have to concentrate on *not* attaching. Which means staying completely calm."

"Unlikely," said the expendable. "Your vital signs are showing all kinds of stress."

"As calm as possible," said Noxon, "but thanks for instilling me with confidence."

"You needed to know," said the expendable.

"The warning would have been necessary *if* I didn't have the facemask to calm all my vital signs whenever I need it to," said Noxon. "And to shut out all sensory information from you folks, if I need it to."

"Very useful," said Ram.

Then Noxon heard nothing, saw nothing. The facemask responded, not to his words, but to his will. All he could sense now was Ram Odin's path through the ship.

It had been only a few days since the time of splitting, so the paths weren't all that extensive. That was good. Fewer alternate paths to distract him.

Noxon watched but did *not* attach. He concentrated on making the path into a person, and then into a person who was moving very, very slowly.

What he had never thought about before was whether his path-sense had something like peripheral vision. Could he be concentrating on one path, and yet still be able to sense other paths? Or were they all shut out?

Or was the facemask shutting them out?

Noxon didn't have to put it into words. He only felt the need to be able to sense all the paths without losing track of the one that was slowing him. The facemask responded.

But not instantly, because of course it was slowing down along with him. Or . . . the question that had bothered him and Umbo from the start . . . were he and the facemask speeding up relative to the timeflow of the path? Speeding up, not by slicing time the way Param did, which meant skipping over microchunks of time, but really speeding up, five moments per moment, experiencing every bit of time and causality, but moving so rapidly compared to the normal timeflow that it seemed slower and slower to him.

It didn't matter what was *actually* happening. He saw the path resolve into Ram Odin, and then Ram moved more and more slowly, until he was almost not moving at all.

Hold me at this speed, thought Noxon.

And the facemask responded, as quickly as a reflex. Noxon no longer had to concentrate on holding this relative speed and now he could look for something else.

He almost missed it. Because the little nubs of backward time were not human-sized or human-shaped. And they didn't flicker. It was nothing like the paths. Except in color.

Only it wasn't color. It was the attribute that Noxon thought of as color, because that's how he described it to Father when he first started quizzing him about it. As a child he had even thought of them as blue and green, yellow and red. But it wasn't color at all. It was something else, the attribute that made every person's path just a little different from everybody else's. And markedly different from the paths of animals, and the more-intelligent animals sharply divergent from those with lesser minds.

It's the consciousness itself that I'm seeing. Not the molecules of the body passing through space and time, but the mind itself. Without physical substance, and yet inextricably tied to the body and brain. It had no dimension, but it had location—like the theoretical point in geometry. Only the color made it detectable at all. A thread of it. Wherever he paid attention to it, it became detectable for only the tiniest distance—the tiniest duration in time.

It was so hard not to reach out with his mind and attach to it. Because this seemed to him to be the purest path of all, the path within the path. He had to know if it was really a person or just something he was making up because he wanted so badly to see something.

Disaster if it *was* something, and he attached, and the molecules of his body were annihilated. Or if he simply appeared in the outbound ship, in the normal timeflow, and then had to explain himself to *that* Ram Odin, which would change all of the history of Garden, maybe cause it not to exist at all. And Ram and the mice, trapped in the backward flow—they would just see him disappear. All this effort wasted.

He held himself back. He did not attach. Instead, he let the facemask know that it was time to ease back to the regular speed of time.

He opened his eyes.

"Tell us when you're going to start," said Ram Odin.

"He's already finished," said the expendable. "Did it work?"

"Yes," said Noxon. "I can do this. Once we're close enough to Earth. And *if* I can bring the ship along with me. I think I can do this."

"Then what are we waiting for?" asked Ram Odin. "Slice us forward in time."

Noxon didn't know why he hated the idea. "What's the hurry?" asked Noxon.

"What's the delay for?" asked Ram Odin.

"It's life!" said Noxon, frustrated. "Things take time. That's how it's supposed to work."

"For everybody else. But look what you can do!"

"Yes, I can speed and skip and go back and all kinds of things, and you know what? Most of the time I don't gain anything by hurrying."

"After years on this voyage," said Ram Odin, "I can tell you that you don't gain all that much by waiting, either."

"Not *waiting*," said Noxon. "You didn't *wait*. You read. You talked with *him*."

"I didn't accomplish anything," said Ram, "except to avoid being comatose for the jump."

"You didn't learn anything? None of your thoughts were worth having? None of your conversations had value?"

"It was *boring*," said Ram Odin.

"You seemed interested enough at the time," said the expendable. "Maybe it's only boring to remember."

"I've had enough adventures," said Noxon, "to know that boredom is the closest thing to happiness. Boredom means that there's nothing wrong. You're not hungry, you're not in pain. Nobody's making any demands on you. Your mind is free to think whatever you want. The only thing that makes boredom unpleasant is if you're impatient for something else to happen."

"Which I am," said Ram Odin.

"And I'm not," said Noxon. "Because when we get there, I'll find the nub of some path that's two or twelve or a hundred years old, and I'll attach to it, and then either the ship will come with me when I take us back to the forward timestream, or it won't."

"It will."

"You don't know that. If it doesn't, then we'll be up there in space, dead in seconds."

"I *do* know," said Ram Odin. "It's the only thing that makes sense. Supposedly, *I* caused the twenty-way leap in time—nineteen forward, one back."

"You took the ship and the colonists through and out of the fold," said Noxon. "The computers caused the duplications."

"Didn't the ships come along on every one of those jumps? And I wasn't sitting there chanting, 'Bring the ship, bring the ship,' because I didn't know there was going to *be* a shift in time."

"The ship just came."

"And I wasn't even near a planet," said Ram Odin. "My path was tied to the ship, you've proven that, so the ship was massive enough to hold on to my path the way planets usually do. Yet it still made the jump with me. So it's going to make the time jump with you, too."

"Maybe, yes, probably," said Noxon. "Though there are a lot of variables that may or may not be significant."

"So what? So we die. Poof, the ship disappears around us, and we become tiny momentary sparks of fire in the night sky as our corpses enter the atmosphere. We won't be the only humans to die that day, because dozens of people die each *second*. It won't even extinguish our identities, because you've got a copy of you under the name of Rigg back on Garden, and I've got a copy of *me*, only about forty years older."

"But *I'll* be gone."

"You'll be gone someday anyway. Get over it."

"You're not afraid to die?" asked Noxon.

"Of course I am," said Ram Odin. "But I volunteered to be the pilot of the first human starship, the founder of the first colony in another solar system. I don't let my fear of death keep me from doing the things that make my life interesting and, maybe, worth living."

"You're so brave," said Noxon, sounding a little sarcastic, but also meaning it.

"Me? *Nothing* I've done compares with that business you did right after your mechanical father pretended to die. Leaping on rocks over a waterfall current that could have swept you to your death if *anything* went wrong. All to save a stupid kid whose idiocy was going to get him killed someday anyway. That was *brave.*"

"I was like a machine, acting by reflex. The job needed doing, I moved, I didn't think. But this time I've done nothing *but* think."

"And you want *more* time in order to do more thinking? That's going to be helpful in some way?"

"And there's more at stake," said Noxon. "I was trying to save one kid back then. Now it's a whole world."

"You were trying to save somebody who *wasn't you*, and you risked everything you had and ever would have—to wit: your life. Your life is the same thing you're risking now, and all the people you're maybe going to save are equally *not you.* It's the same thing, except now you're getting cold feet."

"The point I'm making," said Noxon, "is that I've been really *tense* and maybe it would be good for me to have a few more days as we approach Earth to maybe wind down a little. Read a book. Maybe watch that *Wizard of Oz* movie."

"I don't know if we even have it on board," said Ram Odin.

"We do," said the expendable.

"If you want the time, take the time," said Ram Odin.

"Thank you," said Noxon with exaggerated politeness.

Then they sat there for about five seconds, as Noxon realized how impossible it would be for him to concentrate on anything, knowing what he had to do as soon as they got to Earth.

"Silbom's left elbow," said Noxon. He picked up the box of mice. "I was forgetting the mice. I couldn't very well ask them to wait inside that box for days on end. But I'm also not letting them out. So it's only fair to speed things up."

"For the sake of the mice," said Ram Odin.

"Right."

"And not because you realized that neither of us could possibly stand to read books or watch vids or even converse about anything until we succeed in getting back to the right timeflow."

"Not because of that at all," said Noxon. "That never crossed my mind. I don't even care about that. I'm truly only thinking of the mice. You'd feel the same way, if you had known them as long as I have."

"As brief as my acquaintance with the mice has been," said Ram Odin, "I already feel that I know their deep inner essence, which consists of a ruthless survival instinct hidden behind clouds of deviousness and hypocrisy."

"That's pretty much it," said Noxon.

"We're trying to learn civilized behavior from you," said a mouse. "But it's hard to know when we're seeing anything particularly civilized."

"Everything we do is civilized," said Noxon.

"Talking to the mice again?" asked Ram Odin. "I'll step outside so you can converse in private. Oh, wait. I can't."

"All right, hold on to me," said Noxon. "Father . . . Ramex . . . expendable. Would you be so kind as to raise your hand again when this ship is firmly docked, as it was just after Ram Odin boarded it with all supplies and colonists ready for the voyage?"

"I won't know when that is," said the expendable. "They'll all be invisible to the ship's sensors."

"You'll know that the ship is in the dock because it won't be moving," said Noxon. "Raise your arm then."

314

Ram Odin put his arm around Noxon's shoulder, while Noxon held tightly to the box of mice, and then Noxon sliced them all forward at such a clip that within only a minute or two, the expendable's arm rose.

"We're here," said the expendable. "Are you?"

"Yes, I'm here," said Noxon. "Give me a minute to unwind from the slicing. It uses a completely different approach and I'm kind of exhausted. Mentally. Physically I didn't even break a sweat."

"Take all the time you need," said Ram Odin.

"Thank you for your completely insincere expression of patience," said Noxon. "I've never been to Earth before, expendable. Is there some way of getting a view from here?"

There was a pause. "Noxon," said the expendable, "you *do* understand that we're the only objects in the universe moving backward in time."

Noxon felt like an idiot. "I just thought that—planets would be visible."

"Not even stars," said the expendable. "We can't even detect gravity. Nothing."

"Then how did you know when we were inside the orbit of—"

"We have a perfect record of the exact moment when the outbound ship reached each distance," said the expendable. "Since we're locked to that ship, we're assuming that our clock will tell us when we've reached any particular point along the way."

"So our only navigational instrument is a clock," said Noxon.

"The clock was the only means that sailors in the old days were able to tell their longitude," said Ram Odin. "There are precedents."

"But if the clocks are off—"

"Why would they be?" asked the expendable. "We have the same clock now that we had then. Only our direction in time has changed, not our velocity."

"As far as you can tell," said Noxon.

"We might be inside a sparrow's eyeball for all we know," said Ram Odin. "But we assume we're not. By the only means we have of estimating our location, the ship says we're in place for you to start looking for forward-moving paths so you can get us going in the right direction . . . a few centuries ago. If you don't find the paths, then we'll know something's wrong."

"All right, of course, yes," said Noxon. "I think that this time, you won't need to hold on to me. Either the ship will come with me or it won't. If it does, you'll come along with it. If it doesn't, then at least you won't be stranded in space without a ship."

"That's dumb in sixty ways," said Ram Odin. "If we're *not* sure that the ship will come with you, why would we want to stay with the ship? I'm hanging on to you for dear life, my boy, though if you want to try your experiment with the mice, I don't mind. That's what mice are for."

Noxon held on to the box of mice.

"Excuse us," said a mouse, "and I know this will sound self-serving and you'll interpret it as an attempt to finagle our way out of the box, which it is, but we would feel a lot safer about this change in time direction if we had direct contact with your skin the way Ram Odin does."

Noxon understood at once and, despite his annoyance with and distrust of them, he opened the box and let the mice crawl up inside his sleeves and pantlegs and down the neck of his shirt.

"Thank you," several of them murmured. Noxon appreciated the politeness, though he also knew that once they got back into forward-time—if they did—he'd wish there were a way to make them get back in the box—which there wasn't. Short of stripping naked and having the expendable pick them off his body one by one. And who knew how much damage they could cause before he was able to carry out such a plan?

They had served their time in prison, and now they were free again, and he would have to deal with them like the sentient beings they were.

"All right," said Noxon. "I don't know how long it will take me to find an appropriate path. Earth is a long way off, hundreds of thousands of kilometers even now. And the nubs of paths are very small even close up. This may take me a while. It may not even be possible."

"We won't interrupt you," said Ram Odin.

The first challenge was to find paths at all—or, rather, the nubs that implied the presence of a path. Noxon began with near-contemporary paths in the construction station itself. He quickly found a few, then a lot of them. He began spotting paths that must be in nearby ships and shuttles, and then in farther ones.

It got harder and harder, the farther they were. And none of them were all that far.

He realized that there was no chance he could spot any individual paths on Earth, especially since they would all be mere nubs anyway.

"I need a second plan," said Noxon. "I can see the nearby

paths in the station and ships but Earth is just too far."

For a few moments, there was silence.

"Well," said Ram, "that's useful information."

"Can we start up our engines and move away from here, closer to the surface?" asked Noxon.

"Theoretically," said the expendable. "But we've been in an atom-for-atom lock with the structural components of the outbound ship. The energy cost of breaking away might be too high. We don't understand the nature of those bonds, since they've never been detected or measured in nature. Nor can we be sure in which direction Earth might lie. Or how far we've traveled in relation to it."

"Clear enough answer," said Noxon, who understood little of the physics but knew what "probably not" sounded like when he heard it.

"The new plan is obvious," said a mouse.

"The mice think it's obvious," said Noxon.

"The mice can come live in my butt," said Ram Odin.

"No need to be crude," said a mouse.

"He's being hospitable," said another.

"What's your obvious plan?" asked Noxon.

"Slice onward until the time when they haven't yet started constructing the outbound ship."

The expendable heard this, too, of course, and immediately began working it out. "Looking at the ship's memory, which includes all the reports on the construction process, the ship was finished on—"

"No," said Noxon. "We need a time when there was *nothing* in the space we occupy, but there *were* people up here so I can attach to their paths."

"If it's at all possible," said Ram Odin, "can you seek out a time, about twenty-five years, when there were no paths at all, and choose a path *before* that break?"

"Why?" asked Noxon. "What's the gap?"

"The comet that came so close it threw the Moon out of its orbit. Tidal forces then tore chunks out of the Moon, which formed a ring that destroyed everything that was orbiting Earth. I'd really like us not to reappear during that time. And before it would be better than after."

"Why? Either way, we'll be seen."

"I don't want you to be disappointed in the dingy little runt of a Moon we have left," said Ram Odin. "You need to see the glorious Moon under whose influence the human species evolved."

"I'm pretty sure I'll see both versions of the Moon, if this works at all," said Noxon. "So here's what I'll do. I'll take us forward to a time before this ship was built. Then I'll attach to a forward-moving path out here in space. I'll switch the whole ship to that timeflow. If it works, then I'll immediately jump us further into the past without looking for a path at all."

"I thought you couldn't do it without a path."

"I can't go to a *particular* time without a path. But in this case, once I get us facing the right direction, I'll simply slice my way backward as fast as possible, like closing my eyes and throwing us all into a time before space travel. Preferably before telescopes. Once we get there, we can figure out when we are."

"Close your eyes and jump," suggested Ram Odin. "Like Icarus learning to fly."

"Icarus fell to earth, burning, as I remember from my reading in Odinfold," said Noxon. "That *is* the legend you were referring to, right?"

"Just trying to think what people on Earth will think of this new, fast-moving star."

"Once we get back to the right direction," said Noxon, "I don't actually care much about what people on Earth think of us. We'll be visible here for a second or so, but no longer. Maybe nobody will be looking, but there are bound to be instruments that register our presence."

"They'll call it a computer glitch," said the expendable. "It happens all the time. And since the ship won't be there for them to discover, I'm betting that nobody will suggest that what they saw was a ship moving backward in time that flipped directions and then threw itself backward like a child diving into a swimming pool."

"Because that would be insane," agreed Noxon.

"Maybe this is a better plan than the original one," said Ram Odin. "The distance from the surface of Earth to L5 is actually farther than from the surface of Earth to the near surface of the Moon. It's safer to move an object the size of this ship when we're not all that close to Earth and its corrosive atmosphere."

"I never really understood how far things were in space," said Noxon. "I knew I could sense paths that were much farther away than I could actually see. But distances on a planet's surface are trivial compared to distances in space."

"Words like 'near' and 'far' take on completely different

meanings out here," said Ram Odin. "Just the fact that I say 'out here' instead of 'up here' shows something. On a mountain, you're up high. But in space, you're far away, you're *outside*."

"So I was naive to think I could find a two-hundred-year-old path from space," said Noxon. "But what if I hadn't spent all those months working with Param to figure out how to back-slice? I'd be helpless now. Umbo might have done it, because he doesn't need paths, but until Param and I trained each other, I couldn't have done it."

"Then it's a good thing you took the time to learn," said Ram Odin.

"Just do it," said a mouse. "Slice us on into the past, please, so we can get moving in the right direction."

Even the mice were impatient with him. Noxon wanted to yell at them all, mice and human and expendable: Don't you see that I have no idea what I'm doing? I'm going to kill us all, or strand us in some impossible place and time, or even if I get us on the right timestream I'll still fail at finding a way to save Garden. So what is your hurry?

Instead he closed his eyes. "Shut up, everybody, please."

He had only sliced a moment or two when he realized that closing his eyes wasn't going to help, considering that he had to see the expendable's signal when he had reached a point before the ship was built.

The expendable's arm was already up.

"You started time slicing with your eyes closed," said the expendable, "and I was beginning to wonder if you left them that way."

"Only for a moment," said Noxon, "but that was too long. Sorry."

"The ship's computers have concluded that we are no longer bonded with the outbound ship," said the expendable. "As far as we can tell, it doesn't exist. The question is, did you bring us to a time before anyone was up here at L5 preparing to build it?"

"The only way to answer that," said Noxon, "is to see if I can find the nub of somebody's path."

At first glance, Noxon thought he had gone too far—there was nobody up here in space. But maybe he had gotten them into that twenty-five-year gap in which Moon debris was wrecking everything everywhere. Maybe there was something big and rocky headed for them right now.

Then he found a few nubs. Not terribly close. But if he attached . . . if the ship came with him . . .

He gripped Ram Odin a little tighter. With the other hand he pressed against the instrument panel, as if this would help ensure that the ship came with him. "Hang on, mice," he said. Then he attached to the nearest path.

He felt it, a great wrenching feeling. This was not the simple matter it had been when he first switched to this backward direction. It was as if he were walking through chest-high water. And why shouldn't it feel that way? He had to drag the whole ship with him, change its moment, lever it back to its right place—all without a fulcrum, without any place to stand.

When he opened his eyes, the ship was still there. So were Ram and the expendable and he could feel the mice's feet against his skin. They were not stranded in space. They had air.

Of course, they had had all those things before he tried to jump.

"Did anything happen?" he asked.

The expendable took just a moment before he replied—no doubt waiting for a full report from the ship's computers. "We have joined the normal universe. I believe there was something in your plan about not lingering here for more than a second?"

"Yes! Yes, I just . . . I had to know . . ." And then, feeling foolish in spite of his having succeeded at the most important task, Noxon began to slice time backward, and this time—finally—"backward" was taking him into the past, the real past, the one full of humans and hope.

CHAPTER 17

Saving the Baby

When Loaf and Leaky returned to the roadhouse at Leaky's Landing, they invited Umbo to stay, for a few days at least, before he began his journey back to join Rigg, Param, and Olivenko in Larfold.

Umbo was happy to stay with them. He told them that the food was good, and he was tired of traveling. But they all knew there was more to their friendship than that. Umbo was without a family, but not beyond the need of one. Loaf was not just friend but father to him, and while he knew Leaky far less well, Umbo had helped to restore them to each other.

The roadhouse was beginning to fill up with the evening's customers. Umbo offered to help serve them, but Leaky bluntly told him no. "You don't know any of the work of the kitchen or the table, except to eat. So eat, or don't, but stay out of the way till the work is done." But she softened her words with a pat on the shoulder. Well, what passed for a pat with Leaky—to someone else it might have looked like a shove, but since it didn't actually knock Umbo into a wall or onto the floor, it counted as gentle.

Taking a heel of bread and a bit of cheese with him, Umbo stepped out onto the street and began to walk. He didn't have any great plan in mind as he headed south, though he knew it was the road by which he and Rigg had first come to Leaky's Landing. Perhaps nostalgia was all that drew him there.

His thoughts turned to the future. He wondered for a time about Rigg—both Riggs, but most especially Noxon, the Rigg that had modestly chosen to designate himself as the mere copy, though he was as much the original Rigg as the other one. Noxon, who had come to know and serve Param far better than Umbo. Noxon, who had left Garden, perhaps never to return, in pursuit of one faint possibility of saving the world.

Saving it for what? For whom? What was the world even for, that it was worth saving? Especially if, like Noxon, you were unlikely to be saving it for yourself?

For me? What will I do with this world, if it's saved? What will anybody do? Just what they've always done. They mate, they bear children in hopes that those children will grow up and have children of their own. The replication of genes. Is that all it is?

Maybe it's enough. We evolved so that our greatest pleasure comes from sex, and our greatest joy comes from reproductive success, from bonds with our children and with their children.

Param has chosen me to share her throne, to help her win power in a great kingdom, but aren't Loaf and Leaky the ones with the better goal? They want children, and perhaps, with his facemask, Loaf will now be able to father some with Leaky.

Perhaps? Why should Umbo wonder, when all he would need to do is jump forward in time and see?

He had only just discovered the ability to jump ahead at will, to any point in time that he had already lived in. But now that he could do it, why shouldn't he? He could find out if they have children, and if he learns that they do, well, he'll know that they were going to be happy. And if they don't, then . . . then he would keep that information to himself.

In other words, there was nothing useful he could *do* with the information, once he got it, except to know it. This wasn't like the times when he had sent messages back into the past to prevent himself or others from pursuing a disastrous course. This would be nothing better than spying or eavesdropping or reading someone else's letters. If he told no one, he'd get no joy from the knowledge; it would be hard work to conceal what he knew, good or bad.

And yet the urge to know was insatiable, especially because he knew he could find out without anyone else being the wiser.

He took his last bite of bread and, chewing, stepped off the road into a copse of trees, like any traveler needing to relieve himself. Stands of trees were planted near well-traveled roads for just that purpose.

He stood for a moment to make sure he marked this exact moment on his inner timeline, so he could return to it just after he left. No observer, seeing him emerge from the trees in a few minutes, would know that he had traveled forward in time by several years, stayed for however long he wanted, and then returned.

And with that, Umbo jumped himself forward in time. A couple of years. Just to see.

He chose to return to Leaky's Landing in early afternoon, a warm spring day. He couldn't go to the roadhouse; it would be embarrassing to admit that he was Umbo-from-the-past, checking on the future to see how things turned out. Besides, what if he ran into himself and inadvertently made a useless copy?

As he walked back toward town, he saw that several of the houses were gone. No, the standing chimneys, the blackened stubs of walls, the collapsed and charred roofs showed that they had burned down.

Closer in, several of the tradesmen's shops were boarded up, or stood empty and hollow walled. Glass windows had been broken out. Shutters had been torn off and lay on the ground.

Yet others seemed to be prosperous enough. Clearly, there was more to be learned here than whether Loaf and Leaky succeeded in conceiving a child.

Umbo saw that the shop of a garrulous old cabinet maker seemed still to be in trade. He heard the sound of a saw being drawn across wood. Inside the shop it took a moment for Umbo's eyes to adjust, but yes, there was the old man, methodically pulling a miter saw at an exact angle across a slice of fine hardwood.

The man would not know Umbo, though he might remember seeing him. Umbo was not one to linger in a workingman's shop, not if he had no business. Now his business was information, and he was reasonably sure the man would have it.

"I see that hard times haven't taken you out of business, sir," said Umbo.

The man looked up slowly. "Heard you coming. I'm not deaf."

Since Umbo hadn't been talking particularly loudly, he had no idea why the man had thought that Umbo might have thought that he was deaf.

"Hard times," said the man contemptuously.

"Shops standing empty," said Umbo. "What else am I to think?"

"Times are no harder here than anywhere."

"Then why are those shops out of trade?" asked Umbo.

The man spat on the floor. "Think you can trap me into saying what I shouldn't?"

"I have no trap in mind, sir. I've been in the forests beyond Upsheer, and kept to myself downriver."

"You didn't come down the river, you came along the road."

So apparently the carpenter had not been sawing the whole time Umbo approached, since the road was not visible from the workbench.

"I walked the last bit," said Umbo. "I'm young and my legs are quick enough. I saved myself a ping at least, which I hope to spend on my supper tonight."

"I don't serve food," said the carpenter. He started to saw again.

"I didn't think you would," said Umbo. "I plan to eat at Leaky's roadhouse."

"Oh, do you?" asked the man. "Good luck with that."

"Why?" asked Umbo, dread coming upon him. "Are they out of business, too?"

"You might say so," said the carpenter. "Most customers prefer not to be waited on by the dead, or spend the night in the murder house."

"Dead," said Umbo softly.

"Then you really have been away a long time," said the old carpenter. "Happened late last fall. Near six months ago."

"Sickness?"

"The man, Loaf, that old soldier, *he* died of sickness, in a way. Came back from his travels with an ugly fungus growing on his face. Didn't seem to harm him—if anything he was stronger than before. But he wasn't pretty, and some traveler must have complained about a monster who had taken control of a roadhouse upriver, because soldiers came."

"Soldiers?"

"Of King Haddamander, nobody local, you can be sure. They came here to try to get me to accuse Loaf of something. Anything. I don't think they cared what the charge was, but they wanted *some* pretext, since being ugly isn't against the law when last I heard. They didn't like hearing that from me, so I got knocked down and kicked a little for my trouble."

"I'm sorry," said Umbo.

"Not your fault, unless you're with the king, and you don't look to be one of his, since they're all rich—either started rich or got made so."

"I can be sorry without taking blame, sir," said Umbo.

"And be blamed without being sorry, nor guilty either," said the old carpenter. "Report me for saying so if you want, I'm only a step away from not caring."

"I'm not a spy," said Umbo.

"Just like a spy, to say that," said the carpenter.

"And also just like an honest man," said Umbo calmly. "If they found no charge against old Loaf—"

"Treason was the charge," said the carpenter. "Accused him of being the Rebel King's Captain Toad, the one as leads raids all over Stashiland. Which was known to all of us to be a lie. Never a more doting father than that one, Loaf didn't stray farther from the roadhouse than to buy groceries and other such supply. When could he have gone raiding? I know the Toad is supposed to be ugly but you'd think they'd want more proof than that."

Umbo noticed that he referred to Loaf as a doting father. But the questions that raised could wait a little. "They arrested him, then?" asked Umbo.

"Arrested? You're thinking of the old days under the Council. They don't have trials now, nor jails, nor arrestings. At first old Loaf put up a fight but then they dragged out his wife, her so scared she was silent, if you can believe it. Once they had her down on the ground, Loaf got docile enough, though even then he didn't beg, not for his life and not for hers. They took him out on the dock, cut his throat, and threw him in the river. We all saw—they routed us all out so we could see King Haddamander's justice. Well, we saw it. And we saw how Leaky howled and fought, but the king's men didn't even argue with her, just put a sword in and said, 'She was a rebel too, you saw her fight against the king.' We watched it all without a word, you may be sure, because enough houses had already burned down, enough shop-keepers had already disappeared in the night with never a word, only their windows broke or shutters torn down. But when they threw the baby out the upstairs window, we turned away, we had witnessed enough for that day. I think the captain knew he'd gone too far. Didn't want a revolt on his hands. So he let us walk away, return to our homes. But he did shout something about how the children of monsters could not be allowed to live. Not sure if he meant the monster to be Loaf, because he looked so ugly, or the both of them, because they were accused of fighting against the king."

"So Loaf and Leaky had a baby," said Umbo.

The old carpenter looked at him and there was something sly about him. "How could you not know that?"

"Two years gone," said Umbo—a bit of an understatement, but close enough. He could have named the time to the hour.

"Yes, they had a baby," said the carpenter. "About old enough to toddle about. But not able to fly, poor boy. Had no wings, not him, and so he broke on the ground, and they threw him into the river along with his ma and da. The river must be near full of the king's justice by now. They must have a dam of such justice right across the mouth of it, down at Aressa Sessamo."

"By Silbom," murmured Umbo. "I didn't know it was like that."

"How can you get from Upsheer all the way to here, and not know how it is? Did you fly?"

"I slept, mostly," said Umbo, "and the rivermen were not disposed to converse with me. Now I think I see why. Not knowing who might be hearing with the king's ears, or seeing with his eyes."

The old carpenter grunted and turned back to his saw. "Report me if you want. I'm nearly ready for the river as it is, without any help from the king's men, nor the queen's either. My children live far away now, but not far enough. The Wall itself isn't far enough to suit me."

I have a way through that Wall, thought Umbo. But not one that I can share with you. Nor would your life be all that much better if you left this wallfold.

Yes it would. Because now Umbo understood it all, or supposed that he must. Stabbing Loaf wouldn't have killed him. The facemask would have healed him by the time he reached the farther shore. But it would have done nothing for Leaky or their son. They would be dead.

Then Loaf would have gone in search of one of the timeshapers. Then he would go out raiding in the name of the Rebel King, going back in time in order to . . .

Who is the Rebel King, if not Param's husband? Wouldn't that be me?

Or has Rigg decided to claim the throne as firstborn child of Knosso Sissamik and Queen Hagia Sessamin?

Why not the Rebel Queen? Had something happened to Param? Or was this one of the places that preferred a King-in-the-Tent to a Queen?

But no, that wasn't why it all seemed wrong to Umbo. This whole thing was not possible because as long as there was a timeshaper in the world, this would not be allowed to stand.

All of them were friends of Loaf's. Once they learned what Haddamander Citizen had done, one of them would have gone to Loaf and Leaky and warned them to take their son and flee.

Umbo's first thought had been that Loaf, with his facemask, must have been the person who, serving the Rebel King, had given rise to the stories of Captain Toad. But the only way Loaf could have traveled back in time to lead raids against Haddamander Citizen would have been with the help of a timeshaper, and any timeshaper would already have prevented the deaths of Leaky and her firstborn son.

So Captain Toad could only have been Rigg. Descriptions of his facemask would match Loaf's well enough to explain the soldiers' certainty that they had found their man. It would not excuse what they did, but it would explain why Loaf was targeted for retribution.

Umbo understood it all now, or enough of it. Now it was time to set about undoing this disastrous outcome. If he could save his reckless younger brother, he could save his most beloved friends.

Someone came to the door of the carpenter's shop. The carpenter nodded.

Fearing a trap, Umbo whirled around. But it was only a woman. By no means old enough to be the carpenter's wife. She held a bundle under one arm.

Not a bundle. A baby. Wrapped so as to look more like a package than a child.

"You have to take him," said the carpenter.

Umbo said nothing.

"The soldiers didn't know about their second child," said

the carpenter softly. "Leaky couldn't nurse, so the boy was at Dariah's house during the roadhouse working hours. Only the older boy was home, because he was early weaned. We've kept this little one safe and not a soul has breathed a word, but he's a danger to us all the same."

"Why are you telling me?" asked Umbo. "How can you trust me?"

"Do you think I don't know you?" asked the carpenter. "So many times you stayed with Loaf and Leaky."

"In the old days I did," said Umbo. "But as I said, not for—"

The carpenter grew fierce. "If I was going to betray you, it would have been King Haddamander's men, and not Dariah at the door. We know who the Rebel King is, Queen Param's husband, the true master of Stashiland. The bane of the Sissaminka. I've said it. If you have to kill me now, do what you must. But take this child, the last that's left of Loaf and Leaky. And then go on until you bring down this evil king and serve him as he served Loaf and Leaky and their older boy."

So I *am* the Rebel King. But how do they know it? What have I been doing during these years? How could my face be known to them? Or how could they guess that the boy who periodically stayed with Loaf and Leaky was now the Rebel King?

If they know, others know. General Citizen must have learned of the connection between me and Loaf—that was why they died, not because of mistaken identity.

But now, this baby. How could Umbo explain that he didn't need to take the baby, that he would merely go back in time and prevent the murders in the first place?

Then again, how could he know that if he went back and warned them, it might not prevent the birth of this child after all. They might have *some* child, but once they left Leaky's Landing, as they surely would, their second child would not be conceived at the same time, and the same sperm was unlikely to fertilize the egg. Umbo would save Loaf and Leaky, and might save their firstborn, if he had already been conceived, but *this* child would never come into existence.

Umbo reached out his hands and took the child. The baby was not a newborn, as he had expected—but of course he wasn't, Leaky had been killed nearly half a year ago, and so the newborn had grown since then. "Not weaned?" asked Umbo.

"You'll have to find somebody," said the woman, Dariah. "He's a good baby. Sleeps well. Eats hearty."

"You're willing to let him go?" asked Umbo.

"To save his life? How could I say I love him if I did otherwise?"

The baby regarded Umbo steadily. There was intelligence in his gaze, but no fear and yet also no particular eagerness to please.

"What's his name?" asked Umbo.

"Do you dare to use it?" asked the old carpenter.

"I should know it, all the same," said Umbo.

"They were strange folk," said Dariah. "Their own names were proof of that. So I guess nobody was surprised when they named their first boy Round, the name of a shape. And then they named this one Square. But I've never called him that."

"What do you call him?" asked Umbo. "What name has he heard?"

335

Dariah looked embarrassed. "Well, because his father was named Loaf, you see. I just started calling him Biscuit. Not a name, just a pet name, a silly play name."

"It's the name he knows. I'll call him by neither one for now, but I'll remember both, and one day he'll know."

"I think you'd better go," said the carpenter. "There are spies in this village, as in all villages. You were no doubt seen coming here, and I know Dariah and the baby would have been seen. They might know all about this baby, and it might be bait for a trap."

Umbo thought of going back out on the road with a baby in his arms, walking the mile or so back to the copse where he had made the jump in time. If there really was a trap, there was a chance of an arrow out of hiding. Even if he and the baby were uninjured, he might have to make a jump in time right in front of would-be captors. If he and the others had kept the secret of time-shifting all this time, it would be a shame to let it be discovered by their enemies.

"I know a way of escaping," said Umbo, "that won't require me to go back out on the road."

The carpenter nodded. Dariah's eyes grew a little wider. And brighter.

"We've heard that you can disappear, sir," she said. "Go invisible, like smoke in a high wind."

"I don't want you to see what happens," said Umbo. "You should have a look of honesty in your eyes when you say, 'The boy who visited here only asked questions about Loaf and Leaky, and then he left, I don't know how or where he went.'"

"They'll ask about the baby," said the carpenter.

"Dariah, everyone knows you were wet-nursing for someone," said Umbo. "Can't you say the family sent for the baby and you gave it back?"

"We'll say something," said the carpenter. "You pay no heed to that, it's our affair. With luck nobody saw you or Dariah today, and there'll be no questions."

"I hope you don't end up paying a price for this," said Umbo.

"Put Queen Param in the Tent of Light in her mother's place, and your own skinny buttocks on King Haddamander's horse, and it will be worth whatever price we pay," said the carpenter.

"St. Silbom care for the baby, and the Wandering Saint bless you on your road," said Dariah. Then she bent and kissed the baby again.

"Stay here and chat together for a while," said Umbo. "Perhaps share some bread, so there's a reason for you to have lingered here. I'll go out through the back room."

"I keep that door locked against thieves," said the carpenter.

"Then you must have locked it again after I left," said Umbo. "If anyone asks."

What Umbo *wanted* to ask was for a time, not long after the moment when Umbo took his walk away from Leaky's roadhouse, when nobody would be present in this shop, so he'd have a safe moment to jump back to undiscovered. If he had Rigg's and Noxon's gift, he could look for paths and pick a time when the carpenter stepped out. Instead, he'd have no choice but to guess and hope he picked a good moment. If he guessed wrong, then he'd jump again so quickly that the observer wouldn't know for sure what he had seen, if anything at all.

He walked into the back room, which was mostly used for storing boards and tools and hardware, and closed the door behind him. He looked for a place that would be unlikely to have furniture moved into it during the intervening years, and settled on a spot just inside the locked outside door.

Then he jumped back to a time six hours after the moment he had come from. It had been first dark when he left; now it was the deepest of dark night, a few hours before dawn. He stood in silence, holding the silent baby in the dark, listening. An old man's breathing from a room upstairs. The breath of sleep.

Umbo had assumed he would have to go out the front, but no. This was a simpler time, before General Citizen had imposed his authority as King Haddamander. There was no lock on the back door, only a simple latch, clearly visible in the ringlight coming through a high window, which had been left uncurtained and unshuttered.

He raised the latch. It was a fine carpenter's latch, and a fine carpenter's door. Everything moved silently and smoothly. Umbo closed the door behind him and then carried the baby behind the row of shops to where the alley debouched into the square. Umbo did not hurry and did not act furtive. He walked easily and naturally to the roadhouse door.

It was barred, of course—no reason to invite thieves or burglars. Ordinarily, Umbo would simply have jumped the fence around the kitchen garden, but that wasn't likely to work out well with a baby in his arms. Umbo walked around the corner of the fence to a spot not visible to passersby on the square, nor from any windows in the nearby shops and houses. Then he shifted himself back to the afternoon, a few moments after he walked into that copse a mile or two out on the south road.

Now the roadhouse was open for business, people coming and going, and this early in the night it was safe for him to pull the rope that rang a bell in the kitchen, announcing a delivery.

He could hear Leaky start cursing in the kitchen. Then she bellowed out the back door. "Come back tomorrow! No more deliveries tonight!"

"I'll just leave it at the gate then!" he shouted back.

At once the kitchen door flew open and Leaky's heavy footsteps strode along the path. "I can't believe what I put up with!" she was shouting, but when she opened the gate she looked worried. She must have recognized his voice. Her eyes took in the bundle in his arms.

"You have *not* had time to get a girl *this* pregnant since you left this house," she said softly.

"This would be pretty pregnant," Umbo agreed.

"Come in, you daft boy," said Leaky. "I assume that as a kidnapper you don't wish to be observed?"

"Not a kidnapper," said Umbo, "but yes, I'd like to get upstairs without anyone noticing this package."

She led him into the kitchen, where she wrapped the baby loosely in a washed floursack and handed him back to Umbo. "Take that upstairs and leave it in my room, but mind you I know where everything is!" She spoke loudly enough that Umbo knew she was giving him a reason to hurry upstairs, and enough of an explanation for the bundle in his arms to satisfy the eaters and drinkers who might see him come out of the kitchen and hurry up the stairs.

Umbo unwrapped the baby. The flour sacking came in handy, because little Biscuit stank and all Umbo could think to do, lacking a fresh diaper, was to take off all the baby's clothes, tear the sack in half, wipe him thoroughly with one half, and then using the other to wrap him more or less securely. Through it, Biscuit watched Umbo's eyes, only occasionally glancing around the room. Umbo kept up a murmuring commentary.

It was a couple of hours, and the room downstairs was markedly quieter, when the door flew open and Leaky stalked in, half-dragging a frightened young woman behind her.

It was Dariah.

Umbo almost spoke her name, but recovered in time. This was Dariah before she ever heard of Biscuit.

"This is Dariah," said Leaky. "She has a new baby of her own, and look at those teats. She could feed four babies this size."

"I don't think I—"

Leaky didn't let Dariah finish. "You're perfect for a wet nurse and you need the money," said Leaky. "If you don't like it, you can quit, but not tonight, and not till I find somebody else, understood?"

Dariah nodded and reached for the baby.

"Smells like poo," said Leaky. "You already cleaned him up?"

Umbo wondered how she knew the baby's sex. Or maybe she called all babies "he" till she knew better.

"As best I could, but he needs a clean diaper," said Umbo. "I

VISITORS

don't think that flour sack is going to be absorbent enough."

"It is, if you fold it properly," said Leaky. "I thought you had younger brothers and sisters."

"And a mother who did the diapering and a father who said that baby care was women's work and no son of *his* would fertilize his hands with baby manure."

"You haven't missed much," said Dariah.

"He misses almost everything," said Leaky. "Not an observant boy. What's the baby's name?"

For a moment Umbo thought Leaky had been asking Dariah, and he waited for her to answer.

"Well *I* don't know," said Dariah impatiently.

Umbo thought of how Leaky had named the baby, and how naming happened in the land she came from. "I've been calling him Square Meal, since that's all he seems to need to be happy."

"I didn't ask what you've been calling him," said Leaky. "I asked his name."

"Then his *name* is Square Meal," said Umbo. "But you can call him Biscuit."

"That's only a snack," said Leaky.

"He's only a baby," said Umbo, meeting her gaze.

"Do you want to nurse him here?" asked Leaky. "Not you, Umbo, I've seen you with your shirt off and your teats aren't good for anything."

"I'll give him a quick supper and then take him home." She looked at Umbo. "Is that all right with His Majesty here?"

Because he thought of her as knowing that he was the Rebel King, Umbo was taken aback. "I'm not a—"

Dariah burst into giggles. "Isn't he precious? Doesn't recognize a joke when he hears it."

"Do I need to go with you?" asked Umbo.

"No, you don't," said Leaky. "She needs to go with her brothers, who are waiting downstairs. And you need to come help me in the kitchen garden."

"It's full dark," said Umbo.

"The crop we're planting thrives best by ringlight," said Leaky.

When they got downstairs and out the back, Loaf was already waiting for them.

"You have some answering to do," said Loaf.

"And I'll give you all those answers," said Umbo. "I'm eager to do it, when the time is right."

"And when, in your feeble imagination, do you think the time will be right?" asked Leaky.

"When you answer a couple of my questions," said Umbo.

"If you think—" began Leaky.

Loaf raised a hand. "Leaky, I know this look on his face, and I know this man. Whatever he's done, it was for a good purpose, and if he needs us to answer questions, we will if we can."

"It's going to sound personal, offensive, and irrelevant," said Umbo.

"That describes most of your questions," said Loaf, "leaving out only 'impertinent' and 'incomprehensible.'"

Umbo nodded, acknowledging the remark as having some justification. "I only need to know. Leaky, are you pregnant yet?"

The question wasn't completely out of the blue. Given the age the carpenter had told him for the child named Round, it was highly likely that he had been conceived before they went to Vadeshfold, and was already a couple of months along.

"None of your —" said Leaky.

"Yes," said Loaf. "She is."

Umbo nodded. "It's a boy," he said. "You're planning to name him Round. That's a horrible name, by the way."

"It's a fine name," said Loaf mildly. "Far nobler to be named for a geometrical abstract than for a hunk of bread."

"I'm sure it is," said Umbo.

"You knew I was pregnant," said Leaky. "You went into the future and you knew. Is that our baby she's suckling upstairs?"

"It's not the baby you're pregnant with right now," said Umbo, "but it's yours all right. This second one you named Square."

"Why did you kidnap him?" asked Loaf — surprisingly mild about it.

"I didn't," said Umbo. "A later version of Dariah kept him safe after the two of you were killed."

That got their attention, and they listened without interruption as he told the story.

"General Citizen had them kill the baby?" asked Leaky, her voice soft.

"Yes," said Umbo. "Or so they said. I have no reason to doubt them."

"And Dariah kept this baby safe," said Leaky.

"A version of her. A later version," said Umbo. "But in the future we're making now, she never will, because you'll be long gone before your first son is born, let alone the second."

"Not so hasty," said Loaf. "These troubles begin more than a year from now."

"But we don't know when surveillance started," said Umbo.

"It'll arouse suspicion if we simply walk away," said Loaf. "I need to make a good-faith effort to sell this place. The money will be useful, but mostly it's so that life goes on normally here, but without us in it. If we can't sell it in a few weeks, *then* we'll walk away, because . . . Leaky's mother is dying."

"I have no idea if she's alive or dead at this point," said Leaky.

"Well, mine is definitely dead, if anybody even believes I *had* a mother," said Loaf. "So it has to be yours." He looked searchingly at Umbo. "This really is our baby?"

"It's ugly and has the personality of grass," said Umbo. "How can you doubt?"

"Here's what we'll do," said Loaf. "You'll go to the Wall and summon a flyer. You'll park it somewhere nearby—in the past, if you need to—and then come get us just after we conclude the sale or give up trying."

"How will I know when that is?"

"You'll keep checking in till the answer is yes," said Leaky impatiently. "If you can't think of things like that, I'm in awe that you can even dress yourself."

It took two weeks to find a buyer for the roadhouse. They didn't even suggest bringing Dariah with them, because, as Leaky said, "There are breasts full of milk in Larfold, too, and Dariah's in no danger with us gone."

When they arrived at the meeting beach in Larfold, Rigg and Ram Odin had just arrived themselves.

"I'd comment on the coincidence," said Umbo, "only I'm betting that Ramex told some expendable or another where we were."

"Not many people have authority to call for a flyer," said Rigg. "I always planned to get back here just before you arrived."

"I think we need to get General Citizen out of the Tent of Light," said Param. "Is that what the rest of you think?"

It was.

"Then we need to make a plan," said Param. "Rigg as Captain Toad and Umbo as Rebel King sound fine. But that's only the start of it. Did anybody think to bring Olivenko? It's time for whatever military wisdom he's acquired."

CHAPTER 18

Hiding from the Future

Noxon was not as relieved as he should have been. The first stage of his quest had been a complete success. He had managed to get the starship—and therefore Ram Odin and the mice and all the sleeping colonists—back into the normal stream of time, moving from past into future.

Yet now, orbiting Earth, Noxon realized that this had been a mere mechanical hurdle. The real purpose of his journey still lay ahead of him. He had to get into position and observe the return of the Visitors from Garden, so he could find out why Earth then sent the Destroyers to wipe out all life on Garden. What difference would it make that he had flipped the timeflow of a lost starship, if he failed to save Garden?

"It's not easy to figure out exactly *when* it is on Earth right now," said Ram Odin. "We're before any kind of electronic signals, so we can't mine a datastream and get time and date."

"I'm sorry I couldn't bring us back to a pre-measured time," said Noxon, "but I was jumping blind."

"Nobody's criticizing you," said Ram Odin.

"We are," said a mouse very near to Noxon's ear. Maybe it was joking.

But no. The mice clinging to his body clamored, and the face-mask sorted out the voices.

"Why waste time figuring out when we are right now?"

"We can't stay in this time, whenever it is."

"We're a new star and somebody's going to notice."

"Just because they don't have spaceships doesn't mean they don't *see* us."

"Where are you going to hide the ship? That's the question!"

Noxon had to silence them just to hear himself think. "Wait, stop," he said.

"Talking to the mice?" asked Ram Odin.

The expendable explained. "The mice are very excitable."

"They have a valid point," said Noxon. "It doesn't matter what time we're in right now. What matters is that we need to figure out how we're going to hide this ship and then get to the future and figure out why the human race decided to destroy Garden."

"Hide the ship?" Ram Odin said. "If they don't have tele-scopes . . ."

"We have to leave the ship somewhere while we travel into the future," said Noxon. "We can't leave it in orbit."

"Agreed," said the expendable. "Even if we station ourselves in geosynchronous orbit over the Pacific, we become a fixed star to the Polynesians. And once the Europeans get there, we are the most intensely studied object in the sky."

"Once humans get space travel," said Ram Odin, "this ship is the first thing they'll visit, long before they have the technology to build anything like it. Leaving the ship in space will change everything."

"It may already have changed things," said the expendable, "and every minute spent debating about it creates new folklore about this strange star in the sky."

"At least we're not geosynchronous over Bethlehem," said Ram Odin.

"Palestine is too far north of the equator for that," said the expendable. "And the ship now has a tentative date, based on settlement patterns and existing technology. No railroads, no significant canals. But Constantinople's new buildings are Turkish and there are European settlements in the Americas. For all we know, Galileo is studying us on each orbital pass. We don't want Copernicus to try to work us into his heliocentric model."

"Take us farther back," said Ram Odin.

"I still can't find anybody's path from this far out," said Noxon.

"Just fling us back again," said Ram Odin. "Only farther. A lot farther."

Noxon gripped a handhold on the wall, and reached out to Ram Odin.

"Do we have to do that every time?" asked Ram Odin.

"I don't know," said Noxon. "What if we don't do it, and it turns out we should have?"

Ram Odin took Noxon's hand. "Are the mice all still attached to you?"

"Their little footprints are all over my body," said Noxon. Then he sliced rapidly into the past.

Again, there was nothing to see—inside the starship, there were no observation windows. After a little while, though, the ship's computers put up a display of the huge swath of Earth that was visible from their orbit about three hundred kilometers above the surface.

"It's very white," said Noxon. "Is it an unusually cloudy day?"

"We're over the northern hemisphere," said the expendable, "and we appear to be in a glacial maximum."

"An ice age," said Ram Odin. "Any idea which one?"

"There would be humans all over the place," said the expendable. "Sapiens *and* Neanderthal, during the most recent one, but it was nearly a hundred thousand years long and so it'll take a few passes to get a clear fix. And if it's an earlier glacial maximum we'll still have *Homo erectus*, and they got control of fire about half a million years ago."

"The last ice age ended more than ten thousand years ago," said Ram Odin to Noxon. "So you definitely took us a long way back."

"I was aiming for at least eleven thousand years," said Noxon. "Like when I followed a barbfeather's path before you crashed nineteen starships into Garden."

"Not *me*," said Ram Odin. "It was a copy of me did all that."

"What matters is that astronomical observations from this era aren't going to be remembered and written down," said the expendable. "But we still have to deal with the problem of concealment."

Because the Moon was so large and strange to Noxon, and because it showed only one face to Earth, his first thought was to put the starship on the back side of it. But Ram Odin laughed out loud. "Humans had satellites going behind the Moon taking pictures long before this ship was built. And then there's the little matter of half the moon getting sucked away."

"So we can't leave it anywhere in space," said Noxon. "But it's not as if we can lay it down on Earth, either. By the time this ship gets built, the surface of Earth will have been fully explored, won't it?"

"Satellite photography even finds buried civilizations after thousands of years, by the traces of their irrigation ditches and house foundations," said the expendable.

"So we can't even bury the ship," said Noxon.

"And the hull can't withstand underwater pressures," said Ram Odin. "So we can't drop it into the ocean without risk of debris washing up on shore and getting discovered."

"Even with the fields that protected it from impact with the surface of Garden?" asked Noxon.

"The energy cost of maintaining that strong a field can only be paid once, using the heat gathered during reentry. In the ocean, it would have to last thousands of years under relentless pressure. And it still might be found."

"It might be found *because* of the fields," said the expendable. "Don't forget that it's technology from Earth that creates those fields. There is no chance that such a field anywhere on or under the planet's surface will go undetected once we get close to the time when the ship was built."

Again, the mice were full of suggestions. Noxon sorted them out and relayed the most cogent one. "The mice keep saying to put it under the ice."

"We can go back in time before the top hundred meters of Antarctic ice formed," agreed the expendable. "But either the ice will crush the ship, or the fields that prevent the ice from doing so will give away our location years before this starship was built."

Noxon and Ram Odin looked at each other in glum silence.

Inside Noxon's clothing, the mice gathered and murmured to each other and then settled into a chant: "Stupid stupid stupid."

"The mice are saying that we're stupid," said Noxon. To the mice he said, "Do you include yourselves in that? Or do you have some obvious solution that we've overlooked?"

The explanation, when Noxon understood it, was charmingly simple. "Oh, of course," he said, and then relayed it to Ram Odin. "The mice suggest that the ship doesn't have to survive intact. Park it a hundred thousand years back, at the beginning of the last glacial period, and then let the ice crush it and grind it. We aren't going to use it at the *end* of that period, we just need it not to be found, and not to give off detectable signals or heat or fields of any kind."

Ram Odin nodded. "We're going to go back in time and pick it up right after we left it there. When it's still virtually brand-new. So what happens to the ship a week after we park it there is irrelevant."

"Not completely," said Noxon. "For instance, if we left the mice on the ship and they took it over, they could lift it off the surface long before the ice formed any kind of impediment. Then they could destroy the human race before it became numerous, and have the planet to themselves."

The howls of protest from the mice were loud enough that Ram Odin could hear them, though he couldn't distinguish any of their words.

"They're saying," said Noxon, "that they would never do that and it didn't even cross their minds and shame on you for thinking them capable of such treachery."

"You believe them?" said Ram Odin.

"I'm quite sure that's exactly what they were planning," said Noxon. "Their only goal all along has been to get to Earth and prevent the destruction of Garden. Keeping the human race from evolving in the first place would do the job."

Again, the howls from the mice. But they were both angrier and briefer in their protests. Which Noxon took as a sign that his guess was dead on.

"Still, their point is valid," said Noxon. "We don't have to leave a living ship to be picked up in the high-technology future. We're going to come back to the beginning of the ice age to pick it up. So whatever happens between the time we leave the ship and the far future, when we find out why the Visitors attack Garden, doesn't matter."

"You're suggesting that we kill everybody aboard?" said Ram Odin.

"Without stasis fields, all the colonists will rot away within a few decades, no matter how strong the seal on their sleep chambers is," said the expendable.

"So the kindest thing," said Ram Odin to the expendable, "would be to park the ship where we know the ice will form, kill everybody aboard, leave you awake long enough to make sure it's fully covered with ice, and then you shut everything down permanently."

Killing everybody aboard would obviously include the mice, unless Noxon took them with him into the future. Which he clearly had no intention of doing, since they could not be trusted.

The mice started a few feeble protests. But Noxon could hear them convincing each other that the plan made sense.

"There isn't a hundred thousand years of life support for us, even though our needs are few," said a spokesman for the mice. "Covered with ice, it would be very difficult to do the necessary air exchange. But instead of killing us, you should bring us with you."

"Nice try," said Noxon. "Even if you don't take over the ship, all you have to do is start having babies while humans are still evolving, and if you permit us to survive at all, I have a feeling it will still be a world run by mice."

"We promise we won't!" cried the mouse in despair.

"I think they have to get back in the box," said Noxon. "Then we give them a week, to give us time to get back from the future, send for the flyer, and return to take off again. So, my dear expendable," he said, "will you take care of shutting down all life support on the ship a week after we leave?"

"Will I really have to do it?" said the expendable. "Won't you be back before the week is up?"

Noxon shook his head. "You have to live through the version of events in which we *don't* come back. But when we *do* come back, the version of you that we meet will never experience the complete shutdown, so that version will be sure that you never had to kill the mice and the colonists."

"That doesn't make sense," said Ram Odin. "I take your word for it, but . . ."

"I exist at all," said Noxon, "because there was a version of me, Rigg Sessamekesh, that killed a version of you, Ram Odin—a much older version—in order to keep him from killing me first. That actually happened, and the version of me that is still called Rigg actually did the killing. Just as a version of the expendable will shut down the life support and observe as the mice and all the colonists die."

"So does that mean there'll be two of me?" asked the expendable.

"No," said Noxon. "Because once this ship goes cold, it's completely out of the causal chain. When we return, nothing that happened after we left will have affected Ram and me in any way. So the dead version of the ship won't exist once we make the change."

"You say that as if you knew what you were talking about," said Ram Odin.

"Because I do know," said Noxon. "The only person who gets copied is the one who is part of the causal chain. So when Rigg prevented himself from killing that older version of you, Ram, it created a second Rigg—me, the one that *didn't* kill you—but not a second Ram Odin."

"Except here I am," said Ram Odin.

"You're the twentieth Ram Odin left over from an earlier division, and you know it," said Noxon. "You're just being frivolous."

"I am," said Ram Odin. "I think the plan will work."

"You talk about trusting us!" cried the mice. "But how can we trust *you*!"

"The mice are having trust issues," said Noxon.

"The first time they tried to take over the ship, they signed their death warrants," said Ram Odin. "Even if we never come back, they've had a day of life that they didn't deserve."

"Here's why you can trust us," said Noxon to the mice. "First, unlike you, we haven't broken our word over and over again. Second, I could have you killed at any time and I haven't, so why would I need to go to all this elaborate preparation to kill you now? If I don't want you alive, you're dead whenever I want. You can't hide on my body if I take off my clothes, and you can't hide anywhere else because the expendable can turn off the life support."

"So I'm giving you continuous evidence that I am committed to your survival—provided you don't endanger the survival of the human race, which means you stay in this ship and die with it."

"I don't know why you brought the mice along in the first place," said Ram Odin.

"Because two of the wallfolds on Garden are shared with billions of sentient mice. I may need these as witnesses of what we do here. Or if I conclude that we *do* have to destroy the human race on Earth, then the mice can do it more easily and thoroughly than I can."

"You're the version of Rigg that *isn't* murderous?" said Ram Odin.

"I'm here to save Garden," said Noxon. "And it's humans from Earth who destroy it. You do the math."

"It's ironic, that's all," said Ram Odin. "We created colony ships because that comet came so close to the kind of impact that would destroy all life on Earth. We had to create a colony so humans would exist on more than one world. And now you come back and destroy the human race on Earth."

"I've come back to find out why Earth decided to destroy Garden," said Noxon, "and talk them out of it, if I can. But I'm going to save the nineteen wallfolds of Garden, one way or another. Humanity may have arisen here, but that doesn't mean they have a right to destroy Garden after 11,191 years of history there."

"I agree," said Ram Odin. "I'm just noting the irony."

"Noted," said Noxon.

"I'm afraid to die," said one of the mice.

"You would hardly be sentient if you weren't," said Noxon. "But you *are* sentient, and that's why I'm not going to leave you here, dead. I'm going to change the future if I can. Either way, I'll come back and get you. Just remember that you *will* die, the first time through. But when I retrieve you, you'll have no memory of that death. And you'll know, once again, that I keep my word—even though you don't."

"So it's settled," said Ram Odin. "We park the ship where ice will cover it. Then you and I leave the ship and use the flyer to get us to a place that will someday be reasonably well-inhabited.

From there we travel into the future, while the flyer—and our expendable friend—go back to the starship, kill everybody, and shut down all the systems. But we return in time to stop any of that from happening."

"That's the plan," said Noxon.

"Only one problem," said Ram Odin. "Fuel."

"Oh?" asked Noxon.

"This ship *can* set down on a planetary surface," said Ram Odin. "But on Garden, it was a bit of a sharp collision, right?"

"An extinction-level event," said the expendable. "By design."

"If we land more gently and nondestructively, can we get back up into space?" asked Ram Odin.

"We have been performing those calculations during your discussion of the ethics of temporary musicide," said the expendable. "Since we made the return voyage to Earth without expending any fuel at all, and we began that voyage halfway through the huge energy expenditure of creating the fold and leaping into it, we definitely have enough fuel for a trivial task like rising from the surface of a small rocky planet and getting back to scoop velocity."

Noxon had learned enough to know this meant the speed at which the powerful collection field could be extended to gather interstellar hydrogen and other dust to turn it into the plasma that fueled the ship.

"Then I think we're all set," said Noxon. "All that remains is to choose the right time. For that, Ram and I need to leave the ship for a while. And that means that the mice go back into the box."

"No it doesn't," said a mouse.

Noxon took Ram Odin's hand. "Expendable, please pick the mice off my body so I can begin time-slicing while you reduce the oxygen inside the ship to zero. It will mean I can't come back and revive the mice, but that's their decision."

The mice scampered off his body and returned to the box, which the expendable was holding open for them. "You see we're complying," said a mouse.

"I'll keep my word," said Noxon, "but since I know you won't, I can't leave you in a position to alter the ship's programming."

"We already gave our word, but we understand your lack of trust," said the mouse. "We'll look forward to your return."

"Come with us to the flyer," said Noxon to the expendable.

When they were inside the flyer, Noxon ordered a complete disconnection from the ship.

"Now it's time for you to tell us," said Noxon. "Did the mice already alter the ship's programming so that my instructions won't be obeyed after I leave here?"

"They did not," said the expendable.

Noxon thought for a moment, remembering how many times in the past Vadeshex and other expendables had told lies while adhering to the strict truth.

"I think I asked the wrong question," said Noxon. "They wouldn't *have* to alter the ship's programming to make it so my instructions would be disobeyed, because I'm not the commander of this ship."

The expendable said nothing.

"Ram Odin is the commander," said Noxon. "Right?"

"Yes," said the expendable.

"So any instructions I give are not binding. And he hasn't given you any. So you could set the mice free, give them complete control of the ship, and you wouldn't be violating any of your programming."

"That is certainly possible," said the expendable.

Ram Odin sighed. "I order you to obey all the instructions Rigg Noxon gave you, as if I had given them to you myself."

"Yes, Ram Odin," said the expendable.

"Now let me return to Noxon's original question," said Ram Odin. "Did the mice alter the ship's programming, or *your* programming, so that once I'm away from the ship, you can disobey me?"

"No," said the expendable.

"Try it again," said Noxon. "They may not have altered the *programs*. All they would have to do is invoke a protocol naming them as your successors in command of the ship from the moment you physically leave it."

"Is that what they did?" Ram Odin asked the expendable.

"If they did, the ship's computers haven't informed me of it," said the expendable.

"Here on the flyer, with the doors sealed," said Noxon, "is Ram Odin already considered to be away from the ship?"

"Yes," said the expendable.

"Reconnect me to the ship," said Ram Odin.

"Yes," said the expendable.

Connections were reestablished. Doors opened.

"I don't think you can come with me," said Noxon.

359

"Oh, I think I can," said Ram Odin. "There's just something I need to do first." Ram Odin led the way back onto the ship and into the room where the box of mice was sitting.

In their absence, the ship had apparently caused a second copy of the expendable to assemble itself. It was standing beside the box.

"Have you allowed any of the mice to leave the box?" asked Ram Odin.

"Not yet," said the new expendable. "But those were the orders I was given."

"Now that I'm back, am I in full command of the ship?" asked Ram Odin.

"Yes," answered both expendables, and the ship's computer voice as well.

To the second expendable, Ram Odin said, "Go back and have yourself disassembled and restowed."

The expendable left the room.

"Ship," said Ram Odin. "I designate Rigg Noxon as my only successor in the event I'm disabled and can't command the ship. In the absence of myself and Rigg Noxon, there is no other substitute commander. You will continue to follow my instructions. The mice, individually and collectively, are permanently barred from any command role on this vessel."

"Yes," said the ship's computer.

"And since I know they have reprogrammed you to say that, even though you intend to disobey me, I order you to restore yourself to the condition you were in prior to any alteration the mice made."

It took two seconds. "Done," said the ship's computer.

"Is it really done?" Ram Odin asked the expendable.

"Do you wish the ship to reacquire the data from the ship's logs that Noxon brought aboard?" asked the expendable.

"Will any of that data cause the ship to accept orders or data from the mice?"

"The logs from Odinfold and Larfold will both have that result."

"Restore only the logs that do not give the mice any control or influence on this ship."

"That will leave gaps in our data," said the expendable.

"Gaps that will be alleviated *after* we return from our attempt to change the future," said Ram Odin.

"Good job," said the expendable. "You finally asked the right questions." He turned to Noxon. "Beginning with you."

"I appreciate your congratulations," said Noxon. "But I'm not sure I believe you. How can we be sure the mice didn't instruct you merely to pretend to follow Ram's instructions, so that we'd leave?"

"We aren't infinitely devious," said a mouse from inside the box.

"You do understand why I will never trust you," said Noxon.

"That is a very wise decision," said the mouse. "And one that will cost us dearly, I'm afraid."

"Maybe," said Noxon. "And maybe not. That's still up to you."

"You mean you're not going to kill them even now?" asked Ram Odin.

"I'm not," said Noxon. "But I'm also not leaving them with the ship."

Noxon carried the mice aboard the flyer, but left the expendable on the ship. Ram and Noxon then had the flyer take them down to Earth, to a tectonically stable plateau in what would one day be Peru. Someday, the Nazca lines would be marked out by human inhabitants. But right now, the ground was smooth.

Since humans hadn't yet spread to this area, it was simple enough to pick their spot, pile up a few stones, and then find an animal's path to link to in order to get back to the target time at the beginning of this glacial maximum. At that point, a hundred thousand years in the past, Noxon, Ram Odin, and the expendable spent several days laying out an arrangement of stones large enough to be picked up by the instruments on an orbiting ship a few hundred kilometers up.

They buried the box of mice at one end of the stone figure they had created.

Then they went forward again about eighty thousand years, to the time when they had made that first small pile of stones. They checked to make sure that their large arrangement of stones had lasted for the intervening eighty thousand years. It had. It would be continuously visible from space.

They rode the flyer back up to the ship. Noxon made several huge jumps back in time until their large marker stopped being visible, then made much smaller jumps into the future until it finally showed up again.

They took the ship through atmospheric entry and landed it on a grassy plateau in Antarctica. It was hard to believe that in a few thousand years this spot would be under at least a hundred meters of ice, but the expendable assured them that the spot had been carefully noted and it was ideal for concealing a dead ship.

They left the ship there and took the flyer back to the place where they had buried the box of mice. Then they sent the flyer back to the ship.

Noxon and Ram stood over the burial place. "Think they're still alive in there?" asked Noxon.

"How long since we buried them?" asked Ram Odin.

"Not sure how precisely we handled our return time, but I'm betting they're still in there," said Noxon.

"If you open the box to see," said Ram Odin, "they'll be out of it in a second and we'll never get them back."

"Oh, I have no intention of letting them out," said Noxon. "What I'm wondering is, what are the odds that as soon as we slice forward in time from here, the flyer will return and the expendable will dig them up?"

"I think seventy-five percent against it," said Ram Odin. "But it's impossible to be sure."

"In my experience, the only creatures more devious than the mice are the expendables."

"To be fair," said Ram Odin, "their deviousness on Garden could have been due to their following Old Ram's instructions."

"They're very good at giving truthful answers to the wrong questions," said Noxon.

"And humans are very good at coming up with all the wrong questions," said Ram Odin.

"We never have complete control over anything," said Noxon.

"No," said Ram Odin. "Because at some point, we have to trust machines and people to do what they say they'll do."

"And every now and then," said Noxon, "their disobedience is actually wiser than if they had done what we commanded. Because they have their own wisdom, and we have no guarantee that ours is wiser."

"Trust and obedience," said Ram Odin. "Every cruel dictator in history has only had the power to do evil because so many other people were willing to obey him and carry out his orders."

"And every wise and good leader has been repeatedly stymied," said Noxon, "because no matter how wise his commands, some bureaucrat somewhere believed that it wasn't in his self-interest to carry them out."

"So what are you going to do about this?" asked Ram Odin.

"Well," said Noxon. "I *could* stay here with you and slice time for a few months, watching to see if the flyer returns. We wouldn't leave the surface here until we were sure the mice were dead."

"We'd also see that we didn't return from the future during that time," said Ram Odin.

"The first time through, we'd see that," said Noxon. "The problem is that the second time through, we *would* see ourselves come back, and that would change our behavior, and therefore it would create two new copies of the two of us because we would then behave differently."

"At least we'd know the mice and the expendables hadn't disobeyed us," said Ram Odin.

"There are enough copies of me in the universe," said Noxon, "and way past enough copies of you."

"I can only agree," said Ram Odin.

"So I think our best course of action," said Noxon, "is to assume the mice are still alive, assume the flyer won't return to liberate them, and get out of here so our future selves have time to get here and dig them up alive if the expendable hasn't already done it."

"And if the mice happen to be dead already?" asked Ram Odin.

"We'll shed a gentle tear or two, and move on," said Noxon. "It'll only matter if it turns out we needed them. And if we *really* need them, we can always come back to the moment right after we buried them and flew away."

"Which is another reason not to dig them up right now," said Ram Odin.

"I really don't want to know whether they're still there," said Noxon. "Because if they're gone, it means our mission failed and we needed them to destroy the human race."

"So we don't wait for the flyer," said Ram Odin.

"It's time for us to get on with our mission," said Noxon. He held out his hand. Ram Odin took it.

Noxon sliced rapidly forward in huge leaps, until he reached a time with human paths nearby. Then he sliced his way ahead until their original marker appeared. And beyond. And beyond. Until there were paths of people in airplanes flying overhead. Lots of them.

That was when they hiked their way out. Within a half hour, they were among tourists.

"Of course, we don't have passports," said Ram Odin.

"What's a passport?" asked Noxon.

"Believe me, Noxon, up to now we've only been dealing with time-shifting, the laws of causality, computers that lie, and perfidious talking mice. Now we'll be dealing with bureaucrats. *This* is when it gets complicated."

CHAPTER 19

Council of War

The time-shifters and their friends gathered beside the stream where the Larfolders assembled to tell tales, to learn to walk, and to make decisions that required speech. Their intention was only to greet each other, as Olivenko returned to them from Odinfold, and Umbo, Loaf, and Leaky from Ramfold.

Inevitably, they gave an account of themselves. Loaf and Leaky had a baby to explain—though of course it was Umbo who did the explaining, because he had rescued Square before removing the future in which he had been born. That tale could not be told without a mention of the Rebel King, and of Captain Toad, the ugly soldier who was leading raids all over Stashiland.

"I don't know if we should go to war," said Param, "merely because it seems we've already done so."

"I think we always intended to," said Rigg. "Why else did

we send Olivenko to study military history and strategy? Why else did you need to learn to slice backward as well as forward in time?"

"But now that we're face to face with it," said Param, "I don't know if I have the stomach for it."

"Maybe that's why the people I met spoke only of the Rebel King," said Umbo.

"Even *that* is significant," said Olivenko. "Rigg's the son of King Knosso. Shouldn't they be calling him 'the rightful king'?"

"Only after we win," said Umbo. "Right now, if Haddamander's soldier came through town and somebody remembered you ever saying 'the rightful king' about Rigg Sessamekesh . . .'"

"You're missing the point," said Loaf. "'The Rebel King' isn't referring to Rigg. Rigg is obviously Captain Toad, and he isn't making any claim to the Tent of Light. The Rebel King is the husband of Queen Param."

"I was afraid of that," said Umbo.

"Though at some point," said Rigg, "Param and you really should make it official. The sooner you have an heir, the better."

"That's . . . practical," said Umbo.

"And really intrusive," said Param.

"You know you have to go to war," said Olivenko. "Rigg and Ram Odin decided the Walls aren't coming down — we all agreed to that, once we heard the things they learned. But we still have to live *somewhere*. For now, the Larfolders are providing us a refuge, mostly because they don't spend that much time on land. But Larfold has mice all over it."

"Not to mention mermasks in the water," said Param. "If we

tried to live here, our children or grandchildren would envy the Larfolders their life in the sea, and they'd ask for mermasks and leave the land and become . . ."

"Become a different kind of human being," said Rigg. "It wouldn't be a tragedy, but it's not wrong for us, as land dwellers, to want our children to build lives on the land."

"Vadeshfold is empty," said Loaf.

"But it has wild facemasks in the water," said Umbo.

"There's an obvious solution to that," said Loaf. "Anyone who has a facemask like mine will be immune to the wild facemasks."

"But not everyone can bear them," said Leaky. Her tone of voice was emotional, bordering on anger.

"I'm only saying," said Loaf, "that we shouldn't think of Vadeshfold as empty." He touched his facemask, which was still obvious, even though it had gone so far toward converging with a natural human face. "Someday, there may be people who want to live with these as closely as the Larfolders live with their mermasks. Vadeshfold should belong to them."

"All of this is pointless," said Param, "if Noxon doesn't prevent the destruction of Garden."

"True," said Loaf. "But only in the sense that nothing we do will last for more than a few years. That doesn't mean we shouldn't fight to give the people of Ramfold some hope of relief from General Citizen."

"From Mother, you mean," said Param.

"We don't know how much influence your mother still has," said Olivenko. "She might be as much a prisoner now as ever."

"Wouldn't it be nice to imagine that she isn't guilty of any of King Haddamander's oppression," said Rigg.

"We know better," said Param. "If anything, she's the one goading him to be more and more cruel."

"That's not an unreasonable guess," said Rigg. "But the people Umbo met spoke only of King Haddamander, just as they spoke only of the Rebel King and Captain Toad."

"Meaning that Mother and I have become unimportant," said Param.

"Meaning that war is the business of men," said Olivenko, "as it always has been, even when women fight alongside us."

"What worries me," said Loaf, "is that we might move in circles here. Umbo went into the future and learned that there's a Rebel King, and a Captain Toad who leads raids all over Stashiland. But we still haven't decided if putting Umbo forward as king is a good idea, or that our war should consist of doing a bunch of raiding. The Sessamids didn't conquer and unite all of Stashiland—the whole of Ramfold, eventually—by raiding. Raiding is what they did when they were still a tribe of horse-riding nomads from the northwest."

"It would be easy to take note of the decision we apparently already made, and spare ourselves the trouble of discussing it," said Ram Odin.

"I'm not quite sure that you are part of the decision," said Param.

"I forgot that I was speaking to a queen," said Ram Odin.

"What you forgot," said Param, "is that you are not part of our company. You tried to kill Rigg. *He* may have forgiven you, but I don't trust you or whatever advice you give."

"He hasn't forgiven me," said Ram Odin. "Because he also killed *me*, and whereas I have no memory of my attempt on his life, he has a very clear memory of—what did you do? Stab me? Break my neck?"

Rigg sighed. "He's teasing us both," said Rigg. "And we'd be fools not to listen to his counsel, because he knows far more than we do about Ramfold and all the others."

"But he also lies, and tells the expendables to lie to us."

"True," said Rigg. "So let's ask another source of information. Olivenko, what would you advise us to do, as our student of military history?"

"I came with two plans," said Olivenko. "And the guerrilla campaign by Captain Toad was one of them, though the name isn't one I would have chosen."

"How is that plan supposed to work, since there's at least one version of the future in which we chose it?"

"Guerrilla campaigns can't bring victory by themselves," said Olivenko. "But if you run it properly, you can win over the people while humiliating and terrifying the government. The foolish way to do it is to force the villages to feed your men and assassinate anyone who opposes you, so that all the villagers obey you out of fear—and betray you the first chance they get."

"That's why I was surprised to learn we had chosen it," said Rigg.

"I doubt that you did, because, as I said, it's foolish. Fools resort to those tactics because they expect the people to support them voluntarily, and when they don't, the rebels become angry and take vengeance. But you're not fools. You know that the villagers can't pay taxes to King Haddamander *and* to the Rebel King. When they hid their meager supplies from Haddamander's tax collectors, they weren't saving it for us and our army."

"So what is Captain Toad doing in his raids?" asked Rigg. "Considering that if I'm Captain Toad, I'm no soldier."

"You could be," said Loaf. "It takes training, but if there's one thing we have, it's time enough to do whatever we want."

"Training would be good," said Olivenko, "but what I had in mind was a place of refuge and a source of supplies. And here's where Ram Odin becomes part of whatever we do. In ordinary guerrilla campaigns, the rebels have to hide. Since they're constantly being betrayed by people who want the reward money, they have to move frequently. They can't bring their wives and children. They can't farm or even store up food against the winter."

"You want a safe refuge on the far side of the Wall," said Ram Odin.

"Where Ramfold, Vadeshfold, and Larfold come together, the land is fertile and there's plenty of rain and good streams."

"Some have facemask spores in them," said Ram Odin.

"I think you're perfectly capable of eradicating them from any stream you choose," said Olivenko. "All I ask is that you pull back the boundary of Vadeshfold and make an enclave that isn't inside any of the three wallfolds. Then when we recruit fighters for the rebel army, they bring their families. They farm. They hunt. They make weapons. They train. They stockpile food."

"That could take years," said Loaf.

"But you can always give yourself years," said Olivenko. "Don't make this enclave *now*. Make it ten years ago. The people we recruit will be the ones who are angry—their number will increase, but we can start small. The first recruits will clear land. They'll have children. One village will turn into two or three or four."

"Ten years ago," said Loaf, "the People's Revolutionary Council was the government, and the only people who hated them and wanted to rebel were former nobles like General Citizen and Param's mother."

"But we won't recruit people ten years ago," said Olivenko. "That's just where we go to build up supplies. You bring the first recruits to the place ten years ago; then you bring later recruits to nine years ago, and eight, with each new increment clearing more land, farming more food, mining more ore, making more weapons. Your raids capture food and weapons and you bring them back to whatever time you need them. So the earliest recruits will have ten years in the enclave, but the newest will only arrive when there's plenty for them to eat, and only with time enough to train them."

"So we raid today, then bring the supplies to the enclave at the time we need them," said Umbo.

"Your timeshaping is what sets you apart from other rebels, you see," said Olivenko. "There's no reason not to use your abilities. General Citizen or whatever he's calling himself—he can hunt for you all he wants, but you're not only outside the wallfold between raids, you're also three or five or eight years in the past."

"It's going to take some real care not to bring people back to a time before they came to the enclave," said Umbo. "It won't do to have them meet themselves. Or to have you or any of us making new copies of ourselves."

"We'll keep a calendar," said Rigg. "We'll organize each cohort according to their time of recruitment, and make sure we always bring a group home from a raid to some time after they left on that raid."

"Everything in proper order," said Olivenko. "And we'll also schedule the raids on various arsenals and stockpiles for times when they're not looked for."

"What would happen," said Umbo, "if our first raid were the most recent—say, last Thursday—and our next raid was a week before that, and the next was two weeks earlier. So that every raid is the first one and we always have surprise."

"I don't know," said Rigg. "Wouldn't that make it so they were ready for us on the earlier raids after all?"

"Not if a timeshaper is always with each cohort," said Umbo. "The successful raid already happened in the timestream of the timeshaper, and it can't be changed by having the next raid take place earlier. Can it?"

Rigg pressed fingers to his forehead. "Just when I think I'm beginning to understand how this works, there's some crazy new idea that changes everything."

"It's simple enough," said Param. "Do one raid, and then do the next one earlier, and see if it changes the previous-but-later raid."

"I'm still not in love with raiding, even if it works," said Rigg. "I'm not really a killer. I only did it once, and I didn't like it."

"But that's the whole point," said Olivenko. "If it's always a surprise, you might be able to arrange every raid so that you don't have to kill anybody. You can look for a time of minimal wariness. Nobody watching. Everybody drunk or half the garrison out of town. Or it could be a herd of cattle being driven to where the meat will be butchered to feed Haddamander's army."

Umbo laughed. "Oh, I think we're going to *love* trying to move whole herds of cattle through time."

"We still have to get them across all this country," said Loaf. "With all the times we've used the flyers, you may not understand yet how very big each wallfold is. If you raid on the opposite side, it can take weeks. And the whole country is settled."

"It's settled *now*," said Rigg. "But we *could* move the herds or the soldiers or the families or the weapons far in the past. During the years when the colony was new. Nobody would discover us because we'd slice time a little, just enough to disappear."

"There'd be a stretch of country where all the grass was gone and cow pies were everywhere," said Loaf. "You've never seen the ground behind a military supply herd."

"By the time any colonists see it," said Rigg, "it'll be nothing but meadows with some very fertile patches."

"Exactly," said Olivenko. "By shaping time the way you do, you can avoid all the things that make rebels angry and desperate. You can keep killing to a minimum. But it *will* happen. Somebody will be a hero and you'll have to kill him. This is war, and no matter how careful we are, people will die. And not always soldiers who oppose us. Besides, plenty of soldiers will wish they could join us, but they'll still have to fight us when we show up."

"I'm trying to imagine this," said Umbo. "Say we've done fifty raids, and the most recent one, as far as Haddamander and the queen are concerned, is really the very first one we did. When we did it, we took the garrison completely by surprise, because they didn't even know there *was* a rebellion, because they knew of no previous raids. But *now* it's the fiftieth raid, so they had to be aware of it—and yet the actual events can't be changed, because the timeshaper was there and so the outcome can't be undone."

Rigg tried to imagine it. "I wonder if they'll behave, during the actual raid, exactly as they did when it really happened— with them knowing nothing. But afterward, they'll remember that they *should* have been alert against possible raids because there had already been forty-nine. They won't have any explanation for King Haddamander. 'I don't know why the men weren't on alert, O King-in-the-Tent. I warned them, I posted them, but when the raiders came, nobody was at his post and everybody acted as if there had never been a raid before.'"

"Off with his head," murmured Param.

"By the fiftieth raid," said Umbo, "maybe General Citizen will be used to the fact that we *always* achieve surprise and he'll stop executing the commanders for their inexplicable lack of preparation."

"So when our fifth raid turns the first one into the one that Haddamander *thinks* is fifth, he'll execute the commanders who let him down. But then when our twentieth raid, much earlier, turns that first one into the twentieth raid, they'll already know the pattern and that first commander won't be killed after all."

"The more raids we do, the more lives we'll save," said Param.

"What matters," said Olivenko, "is that it will be General Citizen who's executing his own officers and men. He'll be made to look like a fool, and his soldiers will be frantic with despair, because no matter how much they prepare, they're always taken by surprise."

"If the physics of it actually work the way we're supposing it might," said Rigg.

"It feels like cheating," said Leaky.

"It's war," said Loaf. "Any time I can find a way to cheat so I win without losing so many of my men, I'll do it."

Olivenko smiled at Leaky. "I've read a lot of military history, Mistress Leaky."

"Leaky. No 'mistress,'" said Leaky.

"The commanders who are called geniuses are the ones who won by maneuver rather than brute force battles. The ones who thought up ways to surprise the enemy and get them to surrender or run away. The ones who ended up with an intact, undamaged army while the other side is captured or dispersed, hopelessly disorganized."

"So this will save lives on both sides," said Param.

"It might," said Olivenko. "And the fact that in the future Umbo visited, they talk about raids all over Stashiland, it suggests that we liked the outcomes enough to keep doing them."

"This is all good," said Loaf. "It gets us supplies and demoralizes them, but it doesn't win the war. In fact, our most experienced raiders will be the ones in the very *first* raids that Haddamander's army runs into."

"This is just a way to build up our strength while we train.

To gather supplies, demoralize and confuse the enemy," said Olivenko. "Remember that those experienced raiders who take part in the raids that Haddamander thinks are the earliest ones don't come back to the enclave at that earlier time. They always come back after they left. So our soldiers will experience everything in the right order. So at the end of our ten years of raiding and training and building up supplies and weapons, it will have been only a couple of years in Stashiland. That's when we suddenly show up with a large, well-trained army, only a few weeks *after* the raid we did first, which they think was most recent."

"So there'll still be a battle," said Param.

"Probably more than one," said Olivenko, "though we'll do our best to win a decisive victory the first time. But when you actually commit to battle, you can't predict the outcome. We might lose. Again and again."

"But if we lose," said Umbo, "couldn't we go back and fight it again, using what we learned?"

"You tell *me*," said Olivenko. "I'm not a timeshaper."

"This is where King Umbo comes in," said Loaf. "Instead of taking the whole army back in time—which would hardly work, considering that it doesn't do any good to take the bodies of the dead back in time—instead of that, Umbo, you simply appear to yourself before the battle and tell yourself—the way you always have—what went wrong, so we can take countermeasures and try it again. That will erase the battle we lost so it never happened."

Param nodded. "So the raids will all happen and be remembered. But when the battles come, we'll keep repeating each battle until we get it right."

"Unless Umbo is killed," said Rigg.

"Well, he can't be," said Olivenko. "He has to stay in a protected location."

"If I'm in a protected location, how will I know how the
battle went?" said Umbo.

"Not a protected *location*," said Param. "He and I will be in
the midst of everything, but slicing time so that we're invisible.
If we lose, I slice us forward even faster till it's all done, and *then*
we go to the place where he can warn himself what's about to go
wrong."

"And then you continue to live in that future where you lost,"
said Ram Odin.

"No," said Loaf. "Maybe a version of her will, but she will
definitely be with us when we get Umbo's warning, and so the
real Queen Param Sessamin will always come through in fine
shape. Look, I must have been beaten up, arrested, probably
killed dozens of times, judging from Umbo's warnings. But here
I am. If there are versions of me living out a very terrible life to
the bitter end, I don't know about it because those versions of
reality don't exist anymore."

Param laughed cynically. "Is the same thing true of the end
of life on Garden? If Noxon succeeds in figuring out why the
Destroyers come from Earth, and stops them, does that mean
that only one version of the future has a happy ending, but there
are still dozens of versions in which everybody dies?"

"I don't know," said Loaf, "and I don't care. Because *I'll* be living in the one where Noxon saved the world. Just as I'll be living
in the version of history in which the Rebel King Umbo and the

rightful Queen Param Sessamin prevailed over the pretender King Haddamander and the Mad Killer Queen Hagia Sessaminiak."

"Sessaminiak," said Param. It was the title of a Sessamid ruler who was rightfully deposed because of crimes or madness. It had happened only a few times, and in each case the Sessaminiak former King- or Queen-in-the-Tent was killed in a gruesome, lingering way.

"We don't have to treat your mother the way the other Sessaminiaks were treated," said Olivenko.

"Yes we do," said Loaf. "Or the people will think she deserved leniency, in which case, why was she deposed? Or they might think that somehow her life was saved and you'll be facing pretenders for the rest of your lives, and your children after you. There's a reason for ruthlessness in the business of government and war. But don't worry, Param. You won't have to do it yourself."

"I will stand and watch whatever is done," said Param. "Or I'm not worthy to be Queen-in-the-Tent."

"This whole royalty business is the crappiest job I can imagine," said Umbo.

"The job of captured Rebel King is much worse," said Loaf. "And the job of Param's husband might be pretty good."

To Rigg's surprise, Param reached out and took Umbo's hand. Apparently something like real affection had grown between them while he was gone. That was good. But it was also sad. Because so much could still go wrong, and one of them might easily die. The more they loved each other, the harder it would be to bear.

Or maybe not. Maybe it would make everything better, for one to lose the other knowing there was a strong bond of love between them. Rigg had never loved anyone that way. Except his love for Father. It had nearly destroyed him to lose Father. Even though it turned out to be a lie, it was real enough for at least a year, before Vadeshex met them beyond the Wall and told them that Father was only a machine called Ramex.

It's better to lose someone you love, thought Rigg, *than to have no one to lose.*

"I think," said Loaf, "that it's about time we heard the other plan."

"What?" asked Umbo.

"Olivenko said he came with two plans. He told this one first because in the future you saw, it seems to be the plan we chose. But there's another plan."

"It's simple enough," said Olivenko. "We still build the enclave. We still gather soldiers from the time when Haddamander's oppression does the recruiting for us. We still bring their families with them. We go ten years into the past and build up supplies and an arsenal and we train the soldiers into a superb fighting force. But we give not a breath of a hint of where we are or who we are or what we're doing. People disappear, but nobody knows where they've gone, and there's not a single raid. Then one day an army appears out of nowhere, and Haddamander is completely unprepared and he's destroyed in a single shocking battle."

"Yes!" cried Param. "I choose that one!"

"No you don't," said Loaf, "and Olivenko knows why."

Everyone turned to Olivenko, who shrugged. "I *said* that we train the soldiers into a superb fighting force. But of course that's not possible. You can train them to be athletically robust, but if that battle against Haddamander's soldiers is the first time our men see combat, chances are very good that they'll break and run at the first sign of blood."

"But the training," said Param.

"Training doesn't prepare you for the man standing in front of you trying to kill you," said Loaf. "It doesn't prepare you for the arrows hailing down on you and there's nowhere to hide but you have to stand your ground or the battle is lost before it begins."

"So we go back and try again," said Param.

"That only works if your army is already hardened and experienced. If the only problem was a failure of tactics or strategy, and by changing that, using the same soldiers, you can change the outcome. But if the problem is the soldiers themselves, then the warnings don't work. They won't remember the battle they lost. It will still be the first time they face an enemy."

"But will the raids really prepare them?" asked Rigg.

"Yes," said Loaf. "I've led men in battle. They don't have to have fought a huge army. They just have to have fought *somebody*. They have to know what it means to stand their ground, to fight loyally beside their comrades. To depend on each other. And to win."

"So there *will* be killing in the raids," said Rigg.

"There'll be *fighting*," said Loaf. "That's all we need. Yes, a few will die—with luck, only the enemy. But we'll train our men *not* to charge in and slaughter the enemy. We'll train them to disarm captives and control them. We'll train them for as bloodless a victory as possible. Out of those defeated, demoralized soldiers, we might find many recruits for our own cause. But yes, if they face soldiers who stand and fight, then our men will have to kill them until the rest of them *stop* fighting. Or nobody's standing." Loaf looked around at the others, as if the fierceness of his gaze would convince them.

Olivenko was nodding. "Loaf has fought in war. I never have. But I've read about battles till I nearly went blind, and it's the simple truth. Training is essential, but it's not enough. You have to blood your soldiers. Maybe not all of them, but enough to hold the fabric together on the battlefield. Things don't always go your way, even if you achieve surprise. There has to be a cadre that will stand their ground, someone that the others can rally around. That brave cadre is never composed of green troops. It's always composed of tough veterans."

"So the raids are to gather supplies and weapons and demoralize the enemy," said Param. "But they're also to turn some of our soldiers into those tough veterans."

"Then there's no choice at all," said Umbo.

"There's a choice," said Olivenko. "If we take the second path—a green army that appears out of nowhere—I think we have a good chance of winning. Better than even odds. But Haddamander's soldiers have experience—even if it's only terrorizing villagers or beating down pathetic village revolts. They'll know the sight of blood. And they'll know the terrible things they've done, so they'll believe that their enemy will have no mercy on them if they lose. There's a chance *they'll* have the cadre of veterans that the rest of the army rallies around. I give them one chance in three of winning."

"Not good enough," said Rigg.

"If we have a thousand soldiers who've taken part in raids," said Loaf, "what does that do to our odds in that battle?"

"Less of a surprise," said Olivenko, "because Haddamander will know that there have been fifty raids. But we'll still choose the time and place of battle. It'll still be the first time we came with ten thousand men instead of fifty or a hundred. And we'll have a core of a thousand veterans. I think our odds are four out of five."

"Four out of five isn't that much better than two out of three," said Param, sounding a little outraged.

"It's war," said Olivenko. "Nothing is certain."

"Besides," said Loaf, "Olivenko's making up those numbers anyway."

Olivenko chuckled. "Yes. I'm putting numbers on my gut feelings. And even though so much depends on what the individual soldiers do, it also depends on how they're led. On how much they love the Rebel King and the Young Queen. On how much they trust Captain Toad, who led them on all those miraculous raids. On how much Captain Loaf shouted at them and terrified them during training. And on how well we plan the battle itself."

"Which is where you'll come into it," said Rigg.

"I'm a scholar of war now," said Olivenko. "Not a commander."

"But the key adviser in our councils of war," said Rigg.

"None of us can match your knowledge of past wars," said Umbo. "Just as none of us can match Loaf's experience in battle."

"After a few dozen raids," said Loaf, "you'll pass me right up.

It's not as if I took part in any great war. I've done some bloody fighting, but there were never more than a few hundred on each side. And I never commanded more than a few score of men, and even that was only after the real commander died and I took over in the field. The logistics of a truly massive army —"

"Another reason to learn from raiding," said Olivenko.

"And something else we'll have to learn," said Rigg. "I seem to have been nominated to lead troops in combat, and I don't know if I can do it. I'm not a fighter. Father raised me to be a diplomat. Or maybe just a bureaucrat."

Loaf barked out a laugh. "What do you think the commander of an army *is*? It's ninety percent bureaucracy—babysitting petulant commanders and dealing with their rivalries, planning where everybody will go and how and when they'll march to get there, making sure their weapons and their food all arrive where they're supposed to go. We'll find men and train them to help you, but then you'll have to manage *them* and their ambition and their fear."

"Do you imagine that you're encouraging me?" asked Rigg.

"I'm telling you that it's the job that Ramex trained you for," said Loaf.

Maybe they were right, thought Rigg. Maybe he would find out he was up to the job. Or maybe he wouldn't.

Rigg turned to Ram Odin. "You've been awfully quiet, Ram Odin."

Ram Odin nodded gravely. "I didn't want you to think I pushed you one way or another."

"Well, now we need to know. What do you think?"

"I've spent ten thousand years or so, popping in and out, visiting here and there. All the wallfolds. I've seen bad governments and good ones. Ugly wars and fairly clean ones, as wars go. I think your plan is as good as any I've seen, and I think you won't just be trading one group of thugs for another. My only new advice is this. Don't choose the officers who'll serve under you solely on the basis of their military ability. They can't be idiots, of course, you have to be able to count on them. But when the war is over, your highest commanders are the ones who will know how to go about bringing down a government and setting themselves up at the head of a new one."

"How do we test them for lack of ambition?" asked Rigg.

"Oh, I'm not suggesting you choose men who won't try to do that," said Ram Odin. "I'm suggesting that you choose men who, if they rebel and succeed in killing Param and Umbo and you and starting a new dynasty, they'll be likely to govern fairly and well."

"So even if it's a personal disaster for us," said Rigg, "it won't be a disaster for Stashiland."

"It's the least you can do for the people, don't you think?" said Ram Odin.

CHAPTER 20
Allies

Noxon and Ram Odin rode down from the high Andes in a rattletrap truck with a family of Indians. Noxon had to do all the talking, since he was the one who had passed through the Wall and was therefore fluent in the exact dialect of Quechua that the family spoke.

This was Ram Odin's native era on Earth, and he was able to get a duplicate copy of the credit chip belonging to his younger self. That took care of paying for their plane tickets. All Noxon had to do was pretend to be a Quechua boy as Ram explained that he was taking fifteen-year-old Noxon to Atlanta to consult with a plastic surgeon "to see if anything can be done for him."

The story explained Noxon's obvious ignorance of airport procedures, made the deformity of his facemask into an asset rather than a liability, got them a lot of sympathy from airline personnel, and allowed Noxon to get through security without identification papers. As Ram whispered to him as they walked through the terminal to the gate, "Behind that facemask you could be fifteen or fifty. But nobody expects a fifteen-year-old Indian kid from the high Andes to have identification."

Meanwhile, Noxon looked at everything and everyone they passed. This was his first view of the Earth that would soon send the Destroyers to kill Garden; he had to learn who these people were.

He knew of high technology from the starships that were buried in each wallfold of Garden. He had conversed with computers, he had been raised by a mechanical man, and he had flown from place to place in flyers. He had seen the library in Odinfold, and the empty ruins of their great cities. But he had not been prepared for the degree to which technology pervaded the lives of ordinary people on Earth.

"Everybody's rich," said Noxon to Ram Odin, as they sat together on an airplane flying from Lima to Atlanta.

"Shhh," said Ram Odin softly. "They think they're poor, because they know that somebody somewhere has something they don't have."

"Anybody can buy passage on a flyer here," said Noxon softly.

"To be fair, this is only an airplane," said Ram Odin. "It can't go into space."

"They can talk to anybody, anywhere in the world, and it takes no time at all. Where I come from, rulers and generals have to send messengers, and it takes days to get a reply."

"Remember, please, that high technology was deliberately suppressed where you come from," whispered Ram Odin. "In eleven thousand years, you would certainly have surpassed this level of technology, if you hadn't been so closely watched. The Odinfolders did."

"It's better to be a commoner here than a king in Aressa Sessamo," said Noxon.

"Kings in Aressa Sessamo tend to be killed," said Ram Odin, "so I can't disagree with your point. Just remember how close Earth came to being destroyed by a comet only a few decades ago."

"And remember how few years will pass before Garden is —"

A flight attendant interrupted them. "Can I bring you anything to drink?" she asked Ram Odin. Then, to Noxon, she said, "I'm afraid I can't offer you anything alcoholic, young man, but we have a good selection of soft drinks and juices."

Noxon only smiled at her. He had no idea what to ask for.

"He'll have apple juice," said Ram Odin, "and so will I."

"You have to keep yourself in shape, I know," said the flight attendant.

Ram Odin grinned at her.

"Why did she say that?" asked Noxon. "It seems presumptuous of her."

"I think I picked the wrong time to travel," said Ram Odin. "I've already been named as one of the possible pilots of the foldship, so people who are following the starship program know who I am."

"A pilot is famous?" asked Noxon.

"A very low level of fame," said Ram Odin. "It won't get crazy until I'm selected as *the* pilot."

"We could have sliced our way through this trip," said Noxon. "They would never have known we were on the airplane, and the trip would have been over in a few minutes."

"Next time," said Ram Odin. "I have to admit that I'm enjoying being home on Earth. I like having money and something to spend it on."

"Are you rich here?"

"I make a decent living," said Ram. "But no, not rich."

Noxon had had his misgivings when they boarded the plane. But he couldn't say anything at the time, since officially he could speak only Quechua. "Isn't the pre-voyage version of yourself going to find out you're here?"

Ram Odin grinned. "He's going to find out that somebody got a duplicate of his credit chip. My guess is that the police will be waiting to arrest me as an identity thief when we land in Atlanta."

"How does that help us accomplish our purpose here?" asked Noxon.

"It doesn't. So we *will* slice our way *off* the plane."

In Atlanta, the police boarded the plane before any passengers were allowed to leave. But by then, Noxon's and Ram Odin's seats appeared to be empty. Because time slicing slowed down their movements so much, they were the last ones off the plane before the door closed, and by the time they got to the head of the ramp into the terminal, the police had abandoned their search.

Inside the terminal, Noxon sliced them forward by several

days. Ram Odin quickly abandoned his credit chip. "Sorry," he said to Noxon. "I won't do that again."

"You're going to be recognized," said Noxon.

"I really am about twelve years older now than I was at this point in the past. My face is thicker and as you can see, I'm letting my beard grow. Plus, I expect to spend a lot of time invisible, thanks to you."

"I have a better idea," said Noxon. He took Ram's hand, attached to a path, and popped back to the year before. "Are you famous now?" asked Noxon.

"No," said Ram Odin. "But it still doesn't solve the money problem. We can't afford to walk to where we're going, and without money, we can't get transportation."

"Why can't we walk?" asked Noxon. "If it takes too long, when we arrive I'll take us back in time."

"It's not the time, or not *just* the time it takes to walk. It's that nobody does it. There aren't roads with places for pedestrians."

"Can't we work somewhere for a few days and earn passage?" asked Noxon. "Loaf and Umbo did that on a riverboat."

"You have to have a certified identity to get hired anywhere, for any job," said Ram. "And we don't have any."

"How do we get them?"

"Be born on Earth, and don't have a duplicate of yourself running around getting resentful when you claim to be him."

"How do *we* get identities?" asked Noxon.

"We don't," said Ram Odin. "We sneak aboard public transportation and ride in discomfort, for free."

Fortunately, Noxon's time-slicing was now so effective that

they could get on a bus and walk slowly up the aisle and back to the door during the five-hour ride to Huntsville. To them it took only three minutes and a few steps.

"I warn you," said Noxon, as they walked through town. "We can't steal food while we're slicing, because our hands just go right through anything we're picking up."

"Why don't we sink into the ground?" asked Ram Odin.

"Because we don't," said Noxon. "For the same reason that paths stay in a fixed position relative to a spinning planet. I don't understand the rules, but we stay on the surface."

Noxon was used to walking hundreds of miles in a row, stopping only for sleep and meals. Ram Odin was not. So when they reached the door of the house Ram was looking for, miles from the bus station, he was sweaty and exhausted, while Noxon wasn't even tired.

"Why do you think these people will help us?" asked Noxon.

"Because we have something to trade," said Ram Odin.

"What do we have?" asked Noxon.

"Time travel," said Ram Odin.

"This already sounds like a bad idea," said Noxon.

"It's a brilliant idea, and I think you'll enjoy every minute of it. Well, maybe not the first few minutes, but all the rest of them."

"What happens in the first few minutes?"

"We have to prove to them that we're not insane."

The door was answered by a young woman wearing large opaque glasses. "I don't think I know you. Do you have an appointment?"

"A long-standing one, and you *do* know me, Deborah Wheaton. I'm betting you left your glasses in reading mode."

"I did. But it can't be you, Cousin Ram, because you're in Houston training and competing to be pilot of the first starship."

"Oh, I'm definitely there right now. I remember it well. But to *me* that was nine years ago, I think. And I'm quite sure your father wants to talk to me, with or without an appointment."

"That's always true," said Deborah. "And with or without your right mind."

"He's never had a right mind," said a man behind her, a thin, spectral figure with ordinary glasses and disheveled hair, as if he often ran his hands through it, but never a comb.

"Uncle Georgia," said Ram.

"Who's your friend?" asked Uncle Georgia.

"This is Rigg Noxon. He's been pretending to be a Quechua from Peru, here to consult with a plastic surgeon."

Georgia leaned in close to study Noxon's face. "Odd placement of the eyes, and they seem protuberant. I don't see brow ridges at all. Do those eyes actually work?"

"Yes," said Noxon. "Since you're not my uncle, what do I call you?"

"I'm not *his* uncle, either. I'm Professor Wheaton, to my students. 'Wheat' to my colleagues. 'Georgia' was a nickname given to me within the family, when I first showed interest in primitive anthropes. After an action-movie archaeologist named Ohio Jackson or something. As if archaeologists had anything to do with anthropes."

"So you're from Georgia?" asked Noxon.

393

"I'm from Iowa," said Wheaton. "I think my cousins enjoyed calling me Georgia. It was a slur on my masculinity. Naturally, to overcompensate, I went into erectology."

Ram chuckled, and explained to Noxon. "Nothing to do with urology. Uncle Georgia studies *Homo erectus*."

"The first true humans," said Wheaton. "Or so I have tried to prove. They had complete mastery of fire. They evolved the articulate hand, the running foot. They had also mastered weaving and wore clothing, though not for the purposes we use it for now. And agriculture—not just cultivation—at least two hundred thousand years before anybody else believes it started, and maybe a million. Just because Western civilization used cereal grains doesn't mean that's how agriculture began. It was yams, young man! Yams and taro root, legumes and berries. Nothing that would show up in the fossil record, but the signs are in the teeth! Small ones. Can't evolve small teeth unless you're eating soft food!"

"We're still standing on the porch," said Ram Odin.

"Is that my fault? Is the door locked? Don't your feet work? Come in, uninvited visitors. I was just thinking of peeing when the doorbell rang, and I'm of that age when it doesn't pay to ignore nature's call." Wheaton disappeared inside the house. Deborah ushered Noxon and Ram into what might have been a library. It was lined with books, books and journals were stacked everywhere, and on top of most stacks were fossils inside acrylic boxes.

"It feels like home," said Ram Odin.

"It looks like the basement of an ill-run museum," said Deborah, "but I think that's what you meant."

Noxon picked up an acrylic box with a bone inside.

"Please leave things where they are, without fresh finger-prints," said Deborah. "What's with your face?"

The question seemed quite direct, but Noxon knew how to answer. "What's with yours?"

"I asked you first," said Deborah. "But mine is easy to explain. A car crash and a fire. I lost both eyes and my face is one big scar. Plastic surgeons were able to give me a nose and you might see that around my mouth, they've grown me new lips and the musculature needed to make them work properly. But they can't regrow eyes. I opted for digital glasses. Your turn."

"It's a parasite," said Noxon. "A specially bred variant of a creature called 'facemask,' designed for symbiosis with humans."

"So your having it wasn't an accident," said Deborah.

"I asked for it," said Noxon. "It augments the human brain and body. Speeds up reactions, maintains health, sharpens per-ceptions."

"Your eyes are out of place. Too far apart."

"The first thing the facemask takes is the eyes. Then it grows new ones, better than before. But it's a little careless about placement. It takes a few years for them to migrate to the normal positions."

"The skin seems repulsively unnatural," said Deborah. "Or is that just an artifact of my glasses?"

"No, you're seeing rightly enough," said Noxon. "At least the facemask did a good job of matching my skin color."

"What race *are* you?" asked Deborah. "Too light for African or Dravidian, too dark for Malay. And you're not big enough for Fijian."

"I'm the same color as everyone else in my homeland. I think we may be the original race. That is, we represent a complete mixing of the deliberately diverse sampling of nationalities of the colonists on the starship that Ram Odin is going to pilot."

"That's such a bizarre assertion that I'm wondering if it might be truthful, and if so, how."

"I'm sure Ram is explaining everything to your . . . father?"

"He's my father, yes. Now. He's actually an uncle that took me in. My parents died in the crash that blinded me. I don't remember them, I wasn't yet two years old."

"Do you even remember seeing through regular eyes?" asked Noxon.

"I have memories, but I don't know if they're really from that time, or manufactured in dreams and imagination. Where are you from?"

"Not Peru," said Noxon.

"Ram admitted as much when he said you were pretending to be a Quechua speaker."

"I'm not pretending *that*," said Noxon. "I'm fluent in Quechua."

"But not from Peru."

"I'm from Ramfold, one of the nineteen wallfolds on the planet Garden."

"Planet," said Deborah.

"The colony world that Ram Odin founded. The younger Ram Odin, the one that's going to pilot the starship in a few years."

"So there are two Rams."

"More than that," said Noxon. "There are two of me, as well. The other one kept the original name, Rigg. I go by Noxon so our friends know which one they're talking about."

"I don't mean to quibble," said Deborah. "But if Ram hasn't founded the colony yet, how can you be from there? And how has there been time for the races to mix so thoroughly that you think you've recovered the original skin color of the human species."

"*Homo sapiens.* I have no idea about *Homo erectus.*"

"Nobody does," said Deborah. "So what's your claim? How can this be true? A time machine?"

"Not a machine. More like an inborn ability."

"You just naturally hop around in time?"

So Noxon explained his original ability with paths, and how Umbo's time-slowing talent showed him that the paths were people from the past. And now the facemask allowed him to latch on to paths without any help from Umbo.

She heard him out. And then said nothing.

"You don't believe me," said Noxon.

"I'm trying to decide whether *you* believe you. Between your dispassionate face and my fake eyes, I can't tell if I'm missing your tells."

"I have a simple remedy," said Noxon. He started to get up from the chair he was sitting in, and as he moved, he sliced time. He didn't slice very much—just enough to disappear—and he took only a couple of steps before he stopped slicing. While he was invisible, moving slower than the rest of the world, he saw Deborah reach out to where he had been—where, in fact, he still was—then stand up and walk through him. He felt the heat of her passage, speeding up his slicing a little as she intersected his space, so neither of them would be damaged. She walked to the window, looked outside, then turned around and surveyed the whole room. Perhaps she was wondering where he would be when he reappeared. If he reappeared.

And then he reappeared.

"Neat trick," she said, showing no surprise.

"Not a trick," said Noxon.

"I've seen people seem to disappear before."

"I've seen people move through the space where I'm walking, too, but it never gets old," said Noxon.

"You were really there the whole time."

"I was," said Noxon. "It's one of the reasons why time-slicing isn't useful as a getaway technique. If your enemy knows what you're doing, all he needs to do is put a slab of metal into the space where you are. The heat of a billion atomic collisions cooks you to death."

"You've seen this?"

"My sister died that way, once," said Noxon.

Deborah looked stricken.

"No, it's all right. As soon as we knew what had happened, we went back in time and rescued her before it happened."

"So she didn't die."

"She was dead when we found her," said Noxon. "That's the nice thing about timeshaping. You can sometimes undo some really bad things."

Those words hung in the air.

"You're thinking of your parents," said Noxon.

"I didn't really know them," said Deborah. "And I'm trying to think what would happen if you went back and saved them."

"If *I* went back, alone, then I would change your whole life. Everything you've done since the accident will unhappen. You won't remember any of this, because the toddler who was saved from that fiery wreck will have her normal face and eyes, and her parents, and no reason to be so close with Uncle Georgia."

"How do I know if that other life would be better than the life I've led? Yes, my parents were cheated out of raising me. Or maybe they were spared an ugly divorce. Or maybe I'd hate my serial killer little brother."

"Such a dark imagination."

"But if I went back *with* you," she said. "You seemed to imply there were two alternatives."

"If I took you into the past and you were causally connected to the change in behavior that saved your parents and the toddler version of yourself, then you would continue to exist, with all your memories. The two-year-old would also be you. There'd be two copies. The way there are two copies of me, this one on Earth and the one still back on Garden."

"But Father?"

"Professor Wheaton would have no idea who you are. He wouldn't have raised the little burned and blind girl who survived the wreck. He'd be a different man. And you'd be a stranger."

"So I would survive, but I'd be lifted out of my own life."

"Not really—you'd just be erased from theirs."

Deborah shook her head. "I don't think so. I must be a horrible human being, not to want to save my parents, but . . . this timeshaping thing you do, it can't save everybody. Death still comes."

"Eventually," said Noxon. "But you're right. My friend Umbo has always regretted that we couldn't go back and save his little brother Kyokay, but it was his death that brought us together to discover what we could do."

"Wouldn't the two of you still exist?"

"Now I know that we would. There'd just be a copy of Umbo back in Fall Ford, getting beaten by his father until he either runs away or kills the man. And there'd be a version of me who didn't meet up with Umbo and so had no idea of what it meant to see these paths." Then Noxon shuddered. "And I would have gone back in time to save my dead father. That's when I would have found out he wasn't a man at all."

"A woman?"

"Not human. An expendable."

"But that's illegal. For an expendable to pass for human."

"It may be illegal, but that's what they're designed for. Complete with an anus that passes convincing feces. I lived with him in the forest for months at a time. If he hadn't seemed perfectly normal in every way, I would have known."

"Designed to pass for human. I didn't know. They wear special uniforms and talk in these leaden voices so that you can always tell."

"My father—all the expendables—they spoke perfectly normally. They seemed like people. You'd have no reason to doubt them until you noticed that they live forever and don't get older."

"That's such a crime."

"There are worse crimes," said Noxon. "Like sending a fleet to blow up a planet and kill billions of people."

"Who would do that?" asked Deborah.

"That's why I'm here," said Noxon. "Because that's what the people of Earth do to the people of Garden."

"But your colony is the hope of humanity! After the comet tore up the Moon and nearly ended life on Earth, we knew we had to establish ourselves on another world so that one cosmic accident wouldn't wipe us out. And the fact that you exist proves that it worked."

"I know," said Noxon. "Nobody knew that he'd not only leap the fold but go back 11,191 years into the past. Nobody knew that there'd be nineteen colonies on that one world, instead of one. Nobody knew that in those eleven millennia, we'd develop merpeople and this facemask and talking mice."

"And timeshapers."

"The Visitors who come to evaluate Garden don't know about us," said Noxon. Then he laughed at his own stupidity. "No, of course they know about us. We're all over the ships' logs. They definitely know about us. That's probably why they destroy the planet—to eliminate the people who can go into the past and make erasures."

"I can imagine they might find that terrifying."

"But they would know that we already know about the destruction of Garden—that's in the ship's log from Odinfold. So they must expect that we'd attempt what I'm doing right now."

"You have to admit that your return to Earth is a little improbable," said Deborah.

"Yes," said Noxon. "They might think they're acting so fast that we wouldn't have time to send one of us to Earth."

"But it still seems . . . so drastic," said Deborah. "We send out the ship. Seven years later, it leaps the fold. Then we invent faster-than-light starships and get to Garden at a time when we think you won't even have had time to get there yet—it was supposed to take another seven years from the fold. Only you've already been there longer than the total of human history since the last glacial maximum."

"Lots of surprises."

"But to us, only fifteen years. How do they get the whole human race behind such a wanton slaughter? Genocide of our colonists."

"The whole human race?" asked Noxon. "Why would they tell the whole human race?"

Deborah looked surprised. "Because we're a worldwide democracy now. Lots of different nations, but everybody votes. On something as big as this, they'd—"

"They'd tell nobody," said Noxon. "They'd destroy Garden for the good of the human race, report that the colony failed, and then use faster-than-light ships to establish new colonies. Lots of them. People wouldn't know about us, not for a long time, maybe not ever. Purge the computer records so our logs never show up."

"It's hard to keep a secret like that."

"Once Garden is gone, it can't be undestroyed."

"Except by you," said Deborah.

"I hope. I wish. I can hardly believe we've succeeded this far."

"Why did you come to us?"

"I'm sure Ram is in the other room, asking your father to let us hide here and eat your food while we see what happens when the Visitors return from Garden."

"But if you're right," said Deborah, "they won't tell anybody what they found. And it's not as if Father would be in on any of the secrets. He's a great scientist but he doesn't know any politicians."

"That would be our job," said Noxon. "Well, really, mine. To get to know politicians. It's what I was raised to do."

"But—you're a kid."

"I have no idea how old I am," said Noxon. "But yes, I'm young. But I'll get older."

"And you have . . . that face."

"I saw it on my friend Loaf. The face gets more and more normal—it's still fairly new on me. Even if it doesn't, though, so what? I'll just keep coming back until I find a road in. If I need to. Because the first thing we'll do is slice forward to the time when the Visitors return and see what actually happens. Only then will we have any idea of which organizations I need to infiltrate."

"Why you? Why the kid?"

"Because Ram Odin's face is known throughout the world. Not yet, but it will be. He can't very well show up while his ship is supposedly out there starting a colony."

"I suppose it's too late to invent a twin brother for him," said Deborah. She laughed. "They do that kind of thing on television all the time."

"Well, I invented a twin brother for myself, so it actually can happen," said Noxon.

Silence between them for a few moments.

"You know what I want?" said Deborah.

"Do you really want me to guess?" asked Noxon.

"I want your mission to be completely successful. Then I want to get on a starship with you, one of the faster-than-light ones, and go to Garden and get one of those facemasks for myself."

"You do see how ugly and inhuman it makes me," said Noxon.

"Have you seen *my* face? I want eyes, Rigg Noxon. Even if they're too far apart and one of them sags a little down onto my cheek. I want real eyes instead of something that plugs into my brain and gives me a digital raster image."

"You don't look so bad right now," said Noxon. "They did good work with you. I've seen burn scars and you don't look like that."

"Noxon," said Deborah, "that is a complete load of horse pucky."

"It's true."

"I saw your face when you first looked at me at the door. It was as if you were looking at a train wreck."

"I was trying to figure out what happened, that's all," said Noxon.

"I'm sure that's what everybody thinks they're doing. From my side, though, it looks like horrified staring. Because that's what it is."

"I know," said Noxon, "because I get the same looks. Followed by pity when Ram tells them about my tropical parasite."

"So my choice isn't to be pretty or not," said Deborah. "My choice is to have eyes or not. And I want the eyes."

"I don't know if I'm going back," said Noxon.

"Why wouldn't you? Is Earth so charming that you can't bear to part with it?"

"I have a starship buried under the ice of Antarctica. It's been there for a hundred thousand years. There are some sentient mice in a box in Peru. I have responsibilities."

"So you *have* a ship already," she said.

"One that splits into twenty pieces when it leaps through the fold."

"That's something to think about," said Deborah.

"You can't tell anyone about us, you know."

Deborah laughed aloud. *"Now* you think of that? You don't swear me to secrecy, you just blurt it all out, you give me a demonstration, and *now* you warn me not to tell? Rigg Noxon, I'm already strange. I don't have to add crazy to the list. I can't tell this to anybody."

"I know," said Noxon, feeling foolish. "I just . . . I'm not completely used to this either, you know. The things I can do. And Father taught me—the expendable Ramex taught me never to tell, and that's still nagging at the back of my mind."

"What I'm trying to figure out is why *my* father is taking so long to give Ram Odin an answer. Of course he'll say yes."

"There's no 'of course' about it," said Noxon. "Ram might be recognized. I'm kind of unforgettable. People might wonder, they might investigate."

"But of course you don't understand Ram Odin's plan yet, do you," said Deborah. "He's not asking for a *favor* here. He's bound to be offering Father a trade."

"What do we have to trade?" Noxon thought of the jewels, but here on Earth they would immediately be recognized as memory crystals. Incredibly valuable, but also extremely dangerous.

"You," said Deborah. "He's offering *you*. To take Father back to see for himself whether his hypotheses about *Homo erectus* are true or not."

"Oh," said Noxon. "Of course. I could do that."

"Then let's go tell them that the deal is on." Deborah held out her hand. Noxon took it. She led him out of the room and down a hall, to Professor Wheaton's study, where Ram Odin was napping on a sofa and Wheaton was typing into a computer.

"Oh, are you done?" asked Wheaton. "Is it set?"

"He's agreed to take you back in time to see for yourself," said Deborah. "Of course, you can't write any scholarly papers on it."

"But at least from then on my guesses will all be *right*."

"They always have been, Father," said Deborah.

Wheaton held out his hand to Noxon. They shook.

"You mean the two of you were waiting for *us*?" asked Noxon.

"Ram explained things very quickly, and we agreed that if you could convince Deborah and make the deal, we'd be set."

"But Ram never told me that's what I was supposed to do."

"And I never told Deborah," said Wheaton. "But . . . two smart young people, drawn together by shared experiences and mutual curiosity—*that's* a negotiation that has gone on only a few billion times in human history."

"We didn't agree to mate and make babies," said Deborah testily.

"No hurry," said Wheaton. "Timeshaping will do for now."

CHAPTER 21

Neanderthals

"All I care about is Erectus," said Wheaton. "But yes, of course I'd like a chance to look at Neanderthals. They *are* ancestral to all post-African humans."

"You're curious about everything," said Ram. "You always have been."

"But I wouldn't waste my time going back to meet—whomever. Galileo. Jesus."

"Maybe you would," said Noxon, "if you could pass through the Wall and acquire their languages. So you could converse normally with them."

Wheaton barked out a laugh. "I might at that. People always forget the language barrier when they imagine having dinner with some ancient celebrity. Socrates! What a miserable dinner *that* would be. Fifteen minutes in, he'd expose me as a fool, and

I'm not sure I'm ready for that much brutal self-discovery."

"Which is why you would choose him," said Ram. "And why you're willing to make our trial run with Neanderthals. Because that was your first college thesis."

"I do want to know if bullfighting and bull-leaping are Sapient reenactments of Neanderthal hunting techniques."

"And if it turns out that they aren't," said Ram, "will that count as brutal self-discovery?"

"It will count as finding out that my hypothesis was wrong," said Wheaton. "And *that* is at the heart of science. Anyone who hides from the possibility of his hypothesis being wrong is not a scientist at all."

"So brutal self-discovery is the core experience of science," said Deborah.

"I raised her well, didn't I?" said Wheaton.

"I discovered that entirely on my own," said Deborah.

Noxon chuckled.

"Do you doubt the possibility of adequate self-education?" asked Deborah—so sweetly that it was clear she was hoping for a quarrel.

"All education is self-education," said Noxon. "And all self-education builds on the foundation provided by your teachers."

"I'll make sure that's inscribed in stone somewhere," said Deborah. "Your headstone, for instance."

"I can't escape the teachings of my father," said Noxon. "Everything I figure out by myself, I find him underneath it, holding it up. I find him ahead of me, leading me to where I can see new things and understand them."

"Well, *your* father was an expendable," said Deborah. "Mine was an absent-minded professor. I had to pair his socks for him. I had to lay out his underwear while he showered, so he'd remember to put some on."

"That's a myth," said Wheaton. "Please, take us into the past so I can escape this conversation."

"I can move us in time," said Noxon. "And I can move *things* in space, just a little. But it won't do us any good to go back in time until we're in the *place* where you'll be able to see the things you want to see."

"You're right. All the Neanderthals were dead by the time Sapiens reached America."

"A trip to Europe," said Deborah. "I've been urging that for years."

Ram sighed. "Noxon and I will have to make the flight invisibly. No identification."

"Not a problem, though, with time-slicing," said Noxon. "It's boring because we can't talk to each other or hear anything that anybody else is saying. But I'll slice us fast enough that we won't be in that state for very long."

"Can you slice me with you?" asked Deborah.

"It's not good for you to disappear in a closed space like a plane," said Noxon. "People will notice you're not there."

"I'll go to the bathroom, and then you come to the door and take me out through it."

"We move very slowly in slicetime," said Noxon. "Do you think it's fair to the other passengers to tie up a bathroom that long?"

409

"Then I'll go *as if* toward the bathroom, and we'll slice without leaving a closed bathroom door behind us."

Deborah seemed so eager, but Noxon wondered how long that eagerness would last, in the boredom of slicing time. He thought of Param, who had sliced her way through so many hours, days, months of her youth, and the price she had paid for it. But Deborah has also paid a price; even with mechanical eyes, she has lacked many normal experiences. Perhaps her excitement over timeshaping is a welcome relief from an otherwise tedious life.

With this thought, Noxon looked at Deborah's uncle, to see what he was making of her attitude.

Wheaton seemed to take Noxon's glance as a cue to speak. "I'm glad you're treating this scientific expedition so seriously," he said. Sarcastically, of course, but also affectionately, or so it seemed to Noxon.

"They're children," said Ram. "Let them play."

So Deborah passed most of the trans-Atlantic flight invisible, and Noxon made the time flow around them very quickly, so that the whole voyage only took a few dozen steps. But he returned her to regular time as the airport approach began, or the attendant would have noticed that she wasn't there for the landing.

Once they were out of the airport and checked into a hotel, the first order of business was to figure out where their leap into the past should take place. Noxon's pathfinding should allow them to pick exactly the spot they wanted—but there was a lot of Europe to search through. No point in going to all this trouble just to watch a Neanderthal take a long hike.

"I don't know what a pathfinder can see," said Wheaton. "But what I need is a time and place where Neanderthals were hunting bulls. Aurochs, probably, the giant Ice Age bovine."

"But they weren't entirely prehistoric," said Deborah. "The last of them died in Poland in 1627. They seem to be ancestral to modern cattle. Both Asian zebus and Western taurines."

"A fount of knowledge," said Wheaton.

"I'm telling him that we're not looking for *cows*," said Deborah. "We're looking for *this*." She held out a tablet with a photo of an aurochs skeleton. "Note that the horns bend forward. That's what led Father to guess that—"

"Hypothesize," said Wheaton.

"Take a wild stab-in-the-dark *guess*," Deborah recorrected him, "that the ancient Cretan depictions of bull-leaping show a sport that would have made far more sense with aurochsen rather than taurine bulls. You need to have those forward-reaching horns if you're going to grab them and leap onto the creature's back."

"The *real* source of the hypothesis," said Wheaton, "is the fact that Neanderthals seem to have made no projectile weapons. Their spears were useful only for stabbing. And the terrain they lived in didn't lend itself to open running, the way Erectus hunted. I don't care how stealthy you are, you can't sneak close enough to an aurochs to jab it between the ribs. The last distance has to be crossed in a run, and then the Neanderthal had to jump on its back and stab it at the base of the skull, severing the spinal column."

"And the aurochs held still for this," said Ram.

"It bucked and ran like a son-of-a-bitch," said Wheaton. "But Neanderthals are *strong*. They gripped with their thighs long enough to ram that spear into the spine and bring the beast crashing down."

"Though Father's guesswork," said Deborah, "doesn't explain how you jump onto a bull's back over the horns and somehow end up facing *forward*."

"They were very agile," said Wheaton.

"Let's go find out," said Noxon. "Perhaps you can get me to a place where you know that aurochses were hunted."

"Not *aurochses*," said Deborah. "'Aurochs' is singular *and* plural."

"But Deborah uses the pseudo-Germanic plural 'aurochsen' when she wants to show off," said Wheaton.

"Like 'ox' and 'oxen,'" she said.

"A place where you know they were eating aurochsoto," said Noxon, using a plural from the trade language of the Stashi riverlands. "Then I can hunt for paths with a reasonable hope of success."

The place turned out to be in Slovenia, a tiny nation. But it had one of the better Neanderthal settlement sites, occupied for thousands of years. What Noxon quickly realized was that it was actually occupied six times for a single season each. But there was no way the anthropologists could have seen the discontinuities.

Noxon found paths that seemed to be hunters returning from a large kill—their arrival was followed by a feast and then a lot of meat-smoking—and then sensed where they had acquired their kill. That first attempt was a dead end, though—the hunters had found a dead aurochs, brought down by a combination of dire wolves and disease.

But his second try brought the hunters back to the path of a living aurochs, and Noxon could sense that one Neanderthal's path did indeed take him onto the aurochs's back while it was still alive. Then he looked over the map, fitting the paths onto it as best he could. "No roads take us any closer than we already are," he said. "So we've got about ten kilometers of walking to do."

"How old is the event?" asked Wheaton.

"It's the oldest group that spent a season here," said Noxon. "Isn't there already a date? Carbon 14, at least?"

"The oldest fire built here dates from ninety thousand years ago," said Wheaton.

"That sounds about right," said Noxon. "My view of the paths doesn't come with a calendar. But that ninety-thousand-year figure gives me a benchmark."

"Ten kilometers," said Ram wearily.

"You walk almost as far changing planes at the airport," said Noxon.

"Not even close," said Ram.

"Then stay here," said Noxon. "You can watch over the stuff we don't need, so we don't have to carry it all with us."

"We'll lock that in the boot," said Ram. "I'm not going to *miss* this."

"No, you're just going to complain the whole way. Those Neanderthals, so thoughtless—hunting uri where they happen to be, instead of hoping they'll wander closer."

"Uri?" asked Deborah.

"The Latinized plural of the root word 'urus,'" said Noxon. "I think it's a better name than *aurochs* anyway."

"See, Father?" said Deborah. "There are worse language wonks in the world than I am."

"He's not *from* this world," said Wheaton.

The hike was difficult—lots of ups and downs, scrambling into ravines and out again, and scraping their way through thickets. But they had dressed for hiking and when they got to the site, they were tired but not exhausted.

"If Neanderthals were careful hunters," said Noxon, "there's *no* chance we could suddenly appear without their noticing us. So I'm thinking that I bring us to that time behind this rise, and then I slice us forward as we climb the hill. I won't slice us very fast, so we'll see their actions speeded up but it won't be a blur."

"Will my camera be able to record the images?" asked Wheaton.

"If our eyes can see, the camera can record it," said Noxon. "Images move quickly enough not to lose coherency when we time-slice. Not like sound, which turns into meaningless ragged waves."

"Then that sounds like an excellent plan," said Wheaton.

With the clarity that his facemask brought him, Noxon easily brought them to the moment that he chose and then sliced them with precision as they moved up the rise to perch on the crest. It was close enough for a good clear view, but not so close that they'd have to worry about Neanderthals walking through them.

The hunting was a long, slow process, and several times Noxon sped up the time-slicing so it didn't get too uncomfortable waiting there on the crest. It wasn't just about boredom: Somebody would need to empty bladder or bowel if it took too long.

The four Neanderthals approached the grazing herd with infinite patience. It was incredible how slow their movements were, how utterly still they could remain while holding awkward poses. Each Neanderthal man—two seeming to be in their twenties, two in their teens—had a short spear strapped to his back, stone tip near the man's head. Their hands were empty.

Unlike wolves and hunting cats, they had not sought out an old, ailing, or especially young aurochs. Instead, they had chosen the most powerful male. Apparently they liked a challenge—or they figured that if they were going to take the time to hunt, they should bring home enough meat for it to be worth the effort.

Finally the hunters got near enough that the aurochs began to get nervous. If there was some signal among the hunters, it had to be by sound, because there was nothing visible to the party of Sapient watchers. But the hunters all leapt up at once. The three that were not directly in front of the aurochs pulled their spears as they ran and prepared to jab at the animal's sides. But the one in front kept his hands empty and open as he ran directly at the great horned head, waving his arms and, judging from his open mouth, shouting.

The other members of the aurochs herd began to move away nervously; some of them broke into a run. But the big bull turned to face the shouting man rushing toward him; the bull lowered its head and began to move forward, clearly intending to catch the man on its horns and gore him or toss him out of the way.

The lead hunter's gaze never left those horns. At the last moment, the horns went down and the head turned slightly, to point one horn directly at the hunter. He caught that horn with one hand and then, as he vaulted upward, caught the other horn with the other hand.

The bull tossed him, and the hunter swiveled around in midair, so that when he landed astride the animal's back, he faced forward. It wasn't a crotch-crushing impact—the man's feet landed first, and his legs slid downward, already gripping so that when the man's crotch came in contact with the bony ridge of the bull's spine, his downward momentum was almost nil.

It was the most perfectly controlled athletic move Noxon had ever seen.

At the exact moment that the lead hunter was perfectly astride the aurochs, the three other hunters jabbed at one shoulder and both rear thighs, striking deeply enough that they did not try to withdraw the spears. The wounds would not be fatal in themselves, but because they left their spears in place, Noxon could imagine that if the lead hunter failed to bring down the beast, it would leave a trail of blood as it ran away, and would become weaker and weaker, so the hunters would be sure of a kill even if it wasn't a quick one.

But the lead hunter was no novice. As he settled onto the bull's back, his hands were already pulling the spear upward out of its binding. As the bull began to react to the wounds inflicted by the other hunters, the rider jabbed downward with enormous power, and the spear seemed to go twenty centimeters into the animal's spine.

It shuddered once and then flopped sideways, having lost all control of its muscles when its spinal cord was severed.

As it fell, the lead hunter sprang from its back, so he was not pinned under it.

Noxon thought back through what the man had done. In a single fluid motion, he had caught the bull's horns, vaulted into the air, spun halfway around, landed on his feet, slid down into a tight-gripping straddle, withdrawing his spear and stabbing in the exact place with all his strength and leverage, and then leapt clear of the animal. In realtime it hadn't been as rapid as it seemed in slicetime, but Noxon hadn't been slicing *that* fast. It really had been unbelievably quick.

The other three hunters fell on the fallen animal instantly, using small stone blades to slice open the throat and belly. They disemboweled the animal and skinned it in smooth, practiced movements, each man knowing and doing his job. Noxon sped up his time-slicing enough that they could see the whole process before they needed to leave. When the men had the main cuts of beef and the aurochs hide wrapped in skins, and their spears and knives were fastened again to their bodies, Wheaton pumped his fist and Noxon and the others rose up and walked down the back slope of the hill they had watched from.

Noxon stopped slicing time, so they could talk again. "Need to see any more?"

In answer, Wheaton played back his own recording of the event. "I hope I can slow it down or at least take it frame by frame because there's so much to see," he said. "But I got it. A thing of beauty."

They had been speaking in low tones. But the Neanderthals hadn't survived this long by being careless or unobservant. Noxon looked over and saw that the beef-bearing hunters had spotted them. And, enhanced as his hearing was by the face-mask, he could hear them talking. It wasn't a highly advanced language—it consisted of names and single words. "Who." "What." "Enemy." "Kill."

How the Wall had given him the ability to understand such fragmented speech—from Neanderthals rather than Sapiens—would be a matter for Noxon to speculate about later.

"Disappear but stay in this time?" asked Noxon. "Or return to the future?"

"I have everything I need here," said Wheaton.

The Neanderthals had already dropped their burdens of beef and, with spears in hand, were running toward the observation party.

"Future it is," said Noxon. "I might be able to do this without holding your hands, but let's be safe."

They took each other's hands. The Neanderthals were so fast—Noxon could already smell them, not just their bodies but their breath, when he made a random jump forward in time.

They returned a few days before they had first arrived in the car. Not wanting to go through the tedium of time-slicing, Noxon flung them forward again. But the jump was imprecise enough that he overshot—now there were policemen and a tow truck at their car. They could probably have talked their way through the situation, but they would have had to explain why Noxon was fluent in Slovenian and how they had managed to camp for however many days the car had been abandoned. And then there was that lack-of-identification problem.

So Noxon jumped them back to a time soon after their own paths had disappeared over a hill, and they returned to the car long before their earlier selves would have reached the site of the Neanderthal aurochs hunt.

"We can't *prove* that modern humans ever saw Neanderthals hunt that way," said Deborah. "But Sapiens and Neanderthals coexisted so long that it would strain credulity to claim that they did not."

"I agree," said Wheaton. "My hypothesis isn't proven, but this certainly didn't contradict it. Right down to the picadors, that was a bullfight. *And* the birth of the sport of bull-leaping. Though the Minoan vase paintings show the bull-leapers going clean over the bull. Nobody seems to have tried to *ride* the things."

"That had to wait for the rodeo," said Deborah. "Such strength, such control, such patience. How could *Homo sapiens* have ever defeated these people?"

"They didn't have to *defeat* them," said Wheaton. "The fact that *Homo sapiens* has no mitochondrial DNA from Neanderthals suggests that if there were head-to-head battles, the Neanderthals *always* won, and their males mated with the Sapient women, never the other way around."

"Or Neanderthal women were so strong that they broke the necks of any gracile humans who tried to mate with them," said Deborah.

Noxon wasn't sure he liked the relish with which she said that.

"Seeing all that bloody beef made me hungry," said Deborah.

"Why?" asked Wheaton. "You always like your beef cooked into a flavorless stringy mass."

"But I know that it *begins* with those great bloody haunches and sides," said Deborah, "and I could do with a nice parmentier about now. Or a hamburger."

"Well, Noxon," said Wheaton, "in all honesty, today's work completely pays for the easy half of the bargain—providing you with a place to stay while you wait to see why the people of Earth decide to wipe out your world. So if you want to stop taking me into the distant past, I'd still consider us more than even."

"None of us would be happy without a visit to *Homo erectus*," said Noxon. "Today's excursion was its own reward."

Wheaton laughed. "Here I am marveling at the athleticism of Neanderthal hunters, while the only reason I could witness it was because the human race has evolved an ability that *nobody* could have foreseen."

"Cameras?" asked Noxon, feigning innocence.

Wheaton only laughed. While Deborah took Noxon's hand and squeezed it. So it wasn't all neck-breaking with her.

They decided not to fly back to the United States. Instead, they would go directly to Africa, and search for the paths of an early Erectus tribe. Not ninety thousand years, but nine hundred thousand, at least. Maybe twice that.

And this time, they would want to watch for days, not an hour or so. Neanderthal-watching had left Noxon exhausted. Erectus-watching would be far harder. But . . . it was all part of saving the world. And he was almost as eager to see what they might learn as Wheaton and Deborah were.

At the back of the plane to Nairobi, when they took a toilet break from time-slicing, Ram Odin asked him, "Are you up to this? It looked like that expedition really wore you out."

"In Africa, maybe we won't have to hike so far," said Noxon. "And we'll just watch for a few hours a day, then return to camp in the present. I won't push myself too hard. And this"—he tapped the facemask—"helps keep me strong."

"It doesn't replace food, water, and rest," said Ram.

"It seems you want to talk," said Noxon. "But I need that toilet."

Ram gestured him toward the open bathroom door. Noxon went inside and marveled, once again, at the machinery of daily life that humans of this era of Earth regarded as minimal acceptable conditions. Only a few hours on the plane, but these people had to replace several rows of seats with contraptions for carrying away bodily waste, and with galleys for the preparation of food and drink.

Few of these people could last three days in the wilderness where Noxon had spent his childhood. But they had, and would soon use, the power to wipe the world of Garden out of existence. These feeble toilet-using snack-eating destructive babies—but, like the weaker, possibly stupider Sapients whose superior weapons out-hunted and, maybe, outfought the Neanderthals, they had moved their evolution away from their bodies and onto their tools. They didn't have to be individually clever or strong, patient or wise, or skilled at either peace or war. They could never have wiped out the Neanderthals hand-to-hand. But once arrows and spear-throwers joined their toolkit, the Sapients would use machines to do their killing from a safe distance.

CHAPTER 22

Finding a Home for Square

"What I'm about to ask may seem unpleasant to you," said Auntie Wind.

Umbo responded more to her tone than her words; her tone said that everything was fine, and Umbo would be delighted. "Ask and we'll see," he said.

"I'm concerned about the baby you brought from the future. The little boy called Square."

Umbo was puzzled. "How do you know about him?"

"Your friend Loaf passed him into our care a few weeks ago," Auntie Wind answered. "I assumed you knew."

"Loaf tells me only what he thinks I need to know."

"Well, no matter what *he* thinks, *I* think you need to know, because as the timeshaper you are the one who saved the boy's life and brought him into our time."

"I do care what happens to him," said Umbo.

"Loaf told us that the boy's mother does not regard him as her own," said Auntie Wind. "I understand this, in that she has no memory of carrying him in her womb. Though I do not understand why she cannot take him into her heart as any woman would take an orphan in need of care."

"Leaky can't make herself feel what doesn't come to her naturally." Or keep herself from feeling what *does* come; Umbo had too many painful memories of trying to get her to curb her emotions long enough to simply hear him out.

"That is unfortunate in a full-grown person," said Auntie Wind. "Our difficulty is that our lives are spent in the sea, but caring for Square means that we must keep one nursing mother or another on land for extended periods. Since Square's mother won't have him, I ask consent to introduce him to a mantle and take him into the sea with us. It's a good life."

"I don't think Loaf would want that," said Umbo, "and yet I think it's hard to ask Larfolders to stay on land. Let me talk to him."

"I was hoping for a quick answer," said Auntie Wind. "I'm facing a bit of a rebellion, I'm afraid—there's already so much resentment over the mice that you brought in to possess our land, and some are saying now, Let the baby drink mousemilk, and leave us out of it."

Umbo had heard nothing about resentment of the mice. As far as he knew, the Larfolders hadn't even noticed them.

"Underwater," said Auntie Wind, "it would be an easy matter to care for him. Even on land, with a mantle he wouldn't need diapering."

"The mantle makes it so you don't have to . . ." Umbo was uncomfortable referring to defecation.

"No, but the mantle reaches down and cleans the baby, then washes itself. It's very sanitary. Our mantles have had thousands of years to become habituated to our needs."

Umbo sighed. "I understand your urgency. But remember what I can do. I'll go ask Loaf, but I'll return to you within an hour from now."

"Will you?" she asked mildly.

Umbo was annoyed at her doubt. "If I don't," said Umbo, "it'll be because I'm dead."

"I wasn't doubting your word," said Auntie Wind, amused but kind. "I didn't understand you to have so much precision in your movement in time."

"It's fairly recently acquired," said Umbo. "But now, yes, I can place myself in time with some exactness, especially if it's near a time where I remember having been. Like now."

"Then I will wait here," said Auntie Wind, "though it's dry and hot and you have many days' travel ahead of you."

Let her think what she will, Umbo decided. He had no interest in taking days to find Loaf. He had the knife, which was also a "phone"—a communicator that could call for the Larfold flyer. So he walked only a mile from the shore before the flyer came to him. He didn't bother making it find a landing spot; it lowered a ladder and he stepped onto it and waited as it drew itself—and him—upward through the floor of the vehicle.

Thus it was not even nightfall on the same day when Umbo

came to the settlement between folds where Loaf trained soldiers for Umbo's army. It was inconvenient that whenever Umbo arrived there, he was treated as king. Fortunately, he had refused to allow much folderol to develop, because, as he pointed out, Param was the reigning Queen-in-the-Tent, and he was merely King Consort. So the greetings were only a distraction as he searched for Loaf; there were no time-consuming visits to be paid for protocol's sake.

He could hear Loaf barking orders to a field of clumsy oafs trying to master the use of the short spear. Apparently these were town-born recruits, because they didn't even know the rudiments of quarterstaff and staff fighting that any child in Fall Ford would know just from rough play with the other children. Even privick girls learned how to defend themselves with the quarter, even if the full staff was too long for them to do more than vault streams with it.

Loaf would not be happy to be interrupted, so Umbo didn't interrupt him. There was no urgency — Umbo had taken the flyer out of laziness and a desire not to expend more of his own life in meaningless walking, not because there was any time pressure. No matter how long this errand took, he would return to Larfold at the time he promised, or earlier.

Loaf noticed him right away, but Umbo deliberately looked off in another direction, then sat on the ground, sending a clear signal that he did not intend to interrupt. Loaf nodded to him, then returned to his work.

It was near sunset when he dismissed the weary, bruised, limping men to go off and have some of the glorious stew Leaky and her crew would have waiting for them. Some of the men complained about "stew *every* day," but Loaf and Leaky had worked that out as the best way to make sure that food was always ready, no matter when Loaf dismissed the men from their training. Since other squads were training elsewhere, and would arrive for meals at different times, stew was the best solution for all.

And it wasn't the *same* stew. Leaky made sure they had multiple cauldrons at multiple hearths, and when one stew ran out, she had the pot washed thoroughly. There were cooks who claimed that never washing the pot, merely adding new water and new ingredients, "enriched" the flavor of the stew. But Leaky said, "I wouldn't serve my customers a stew with ingredients older than their grandmothers, which is why our roadhouse was worth building a town around!"

Loaf made his way to Umbo with much more vigor than any of his men showed. "Is Rigg in need of these men?" he asked. "Because they're not ready."

"No, no, I haven't seen Rigg," said Umbo. "Nor do I need them. Unless one of them has teats full of milk."

"I beat that out of them, if any of them is heavy with milk," said Loaf with a smile. Then he made the connection. "You were in Larfold. Is something wrong with Square?"

"I can't believe you sent him to the Larfolders," said Umbo. "The burden of staying on land for him is becoming onerous."

"I assumed that they'd take turns," said Loaf. "Auntie Wind could have said no."

"She said yes," said Umbo, "but others are now saying no,

and I need to bring your answer to her earlier this afternoon."

"Answer to what?"

"She wants to put a mantle on the boy."

Loaf shook his head. "That would make him a Larfolder for-ever," he said. "It would cut him off from his brother."

"Hasn't Leaky already done that?" asked Umbo.

Loaf nodded. "I love her, and she's worthy of more love than I can give. But I admit that her rejection of Square took me by surprise. Even if she didn't accept him as her true son, I thought at least she'd take care of him as an orphan."

Umbo shrugged. "But he's not an orphan, and that compli-cates everything."

"The woman who bore him," said Loaf, "will never exist in this timestream, even if she was named Leaky. I don't know what to do. I can't take Square to Ramfold again, because that makes him a hostage if Haddamander and Hagia ever find out who he is. And I don't think I'd want him among the Odinfolders."

"Auntie Wind said that some were saying we should entrust him to the mice that we allowed to infest Larfold," said Umbo.

Loaf nodded slowly. "So. They noticed, and they're not delighted."

"I think that even though they don't till the soil, they still thought of it as their own land."

"Well, now it isn't," said Loaf. "I don't think we'd have much luck if we tried to gather up the mice *now*."

"We could ask them to stay out of a zone near the shore," said Umbo. "I think they might."

"Or they might say, Let the Larfolders make us move, if they want us gone."

"With their mantles, the Larfolders are the only people in Garden who can all spot the mice no matter how they try to hide and make themselves small."

"And the Larfolders are the only ones who can escape the mice completely, by going into the ocean," said Loaf. "They'll work it out, and we should stay out of it. But I can see Auntie Wind's point. Their mantles are bred to be gentle with children, to grow up with them, so to speak. The child is master of his own body."

"So you think Square should be given a mantle?" asked Umbo.

"I don't want to try to raise a son who can hide from me under the sea," said Loaf.

"So you do plan to raise him?"

"He's going to know he has a father," said Loaf. "Even if it's an ugly old facemasker like me."

"Why not keep him here?"

Loaf shook his head. "You know we tried it. But caring for the son of the . . . whatever I am . . . Sergeant-at-Arms, maybe . . . it was becoming bad for the women, bad for their husbands, and bad for the boy. Spoiled. I meant to leave him with the Larfolders for only a day or two, but I'm so busy here . . ."

"Auntie Wind isn't angry," said Umbo, "and the only person she's critical of is Leaky, for reasons you can understand even though you don't agree."

"I do agree," said Loaf. "By Silbom's left elbow, you'd think

Leaky would take the boy in for my sake, if not for his own."

"But she won't, and you don't want to fight that war."

"So I have no choice but to take him back here," said Loaf, "even if it complicates camp life and keeps Leaky in a perpetual sulk."

Umbo had suspected that all the other reasons for exiling Square had been a mask for this one—that as long as Square was in camp, Leaky was surly and that made Loaf nervous and edgy, which damaged his ability to work well with the men. It was as if Square were Loaf's bastard child by another woman. Which he almost was, in a way, but definitely was not, in another.

"I think I should take as much responsibility for the boy as you," said Umbo. "I'm the one who brought him home to you. I didn't have to. I could have taken him to any number of childless couples."

"You had to bring him to us because he was ours, he *is* ours, even if Leaky is too insane to understand that," said Loaf. "Of course if you ever quote me as having said that, I'll kill you. You can't time-shift fast enough to get away from me."

"Yes I can," said Umbo, "but I would never tell her because Leaky would kill *you*, and then who would train these miserable revolutionary troops?"

"They're more like refugees than an army, though a few of them are really trying to become more soldierlike. Fortunately, since all our attacks come as a complete surprise, coming previous to all the other attacks, we always win with very little fighting, just by showing our numbers and having men who look as if they know how to use their weapons, even if they don't. If we actually had to fight, I fear any halfway competent regiment could slaughter these poor geese."

"But then, Haddamander has a way of removing halfway competent officers because they might pose a threat to him."

"I wish we could rely on him to remove all his good officers. But he still has many, and most are at least adequate, and that's likely to be enough to stop these clowns. But that's how it looks this week, with this group. Who knows what they'll be two years from now?"

"Sick of *you*, I bet," said Umbo.

"Oh, they're already there, I promise you."

"They're annoyed with you, a bit resentful, but they're also proud of the skills they're acquiring. That makes them grateful, too. They won't really hate you until it dawns on them that no matter how hard they work and how much they learn, you'll never be pleased."

"I'll be pleased when I believe that some of them will stand up against a trained army."

"As I said."

"What do I do about Square?" said Loaf. "What with all the talk of the Rebel King and the revolution in Ramfold, I think any orphan child would be viewed with suspicion. *Whose* orphan, they'll ask. What trouble will it bring down on our house, to take him in? I'd ask those questions, and I wouldn't want to give him to anyone so stupid they *didn't* think of that." Loaf pursed his lips and sat in silence a moment. "I don't want to give him to anyone, anyway. Not Larfolders, not Ramfolders, not the mice, not this rebel army. I want him to grow up in the same family with his little brother."

"His older brother," corrected Umbo.

"In a timestream that doesn't exist," said Loaf. "In *this* reality, Square is obviously older, bigger . . . that might be what Leaky's afraid of. That by being older, Square will supplant Round, take away his rights as her firstborn child."

"What I'm thinking," said Umbo, "if you want to hear it . . ."

"From your tone of voice, I assume I'm going to *hate* to hear it."

"The Larfolders' mantles don't take over their babies. They join with them, nurture them, protect them, and surrender to their control as they mature."

"You're not arguing for giving him a mantle," said Loaf.

"I'm arguing for giving him a facemask," said Umbo.

"If Leaky couldn't even bear a facemask—"

"Leaky is a woman who is already barely capable of controlling her physical impulses," said Umbo. "How can we be surprised that the facemask took away such control as she has? But Vadesh learned some things from the Larfold mantles, as he designed this batch of facemasks. And maybe the facemasks act differently when they symbionize with a child."

"And maybe they don't," said Loaf. "I'm not going to let my baby be destroyed in some insane experiment."

"Loaf," said Umbo. "We can always prevent ourselves from doing it, if it fails. Just as we did with Leaky."

"Even with a facemask, it hardly solves our problem," said Loaf. "He's a baby, he needs care."

"The mantles take care of everything for the Larfold babies," said Umbo. "I'm betting that if there was no milk to be had, the facemask could wean him. And if not, it would allow him to suckle from a goat or a sheep or a cow."

"Or mice?" asked Loaf.

"I have to take an answer to Auntie Wind," said Umbo. "I made a suggestion, something we could *try*. And there's this: If it works, then you'll have one son with a facemask like yours, and one without."

"And wouldn't Leaky wreak havoc about that," said Loaf. "Always accusing me of having a favorite and it wouldn't be *her* favorite."

"Accuse her first of favoring Round," said Umbo. "It'll have the virtue of being the simple truth, long before a facemask was involved."

"Don't you know that my being *right* only makes Leaky more stubborn?"

"For a while," said Umbo. "But she's smart and she's fair, and when the anger calms, the argument will hold. She chose a favorite first."

"Worth a try," said Loaf. "Let's go get the baby, and then see what Vadesh says."

"I can bring the baby," said Umbo.

"The Larfolders don't know about diapers," said Loaf. "He shits everywhere."

"I've been turded by yahoos," said Umbo. "I can take it."

"No, I'll bring him," said Loaf. "I'm his father."

"You've already put in a full day," said Umbo.

"I'll sleep in the flyer," said Loaf. "I'm certainly not *walking* to Larfold."

"Can we eat first?" asked Umbo.

"Good idea," said Loaf, "as long as you don't even hint to

432

Leaky about what we're doing. Let's face her rage as sinners, rather than as mere contemplators of a sin."

Umbo smiled his understanding.

But he did not understand. His wife was Queen-in-the-Tent, and she caused him far, far less worry, far less conflict than Leaky caused Loaf.

Then again, thought Umbo, that's probably because she doesn't actually care what I do. She married me only to keep my timeshaping abilities in the royal family. Whereas Leaky is really devoted to Loaf, which is why his actions can make her go crazy.

Don't think like that, Umbo told himself. Maybe Param loves you as much as she's capable of love. She's certainly kinder to you than she could ever have learned from her mother, the Monster Queen Hagia. As royal marriages go, ours is already above average: I haven't been murdered, I haven't had to flee her presence, and if we haven't actually done anything together that might conceive a child, that's only because her being pregnant would be inconvenient and, potentially, dangerous, since we don't know what time-slicing might do to a fetus in the womb.

They ate. Leaky and Loaf were perfectly at ease with each other. Umbo was relieved yet also vaguely disappointed at how easy it was for Loaf to hide his intentions from her.

But he didn't discuss this with Loaf. He knew the topic would probably be off-limits forever. And it was just as well that husbands and wives could keep secrets from each other, when the thing being concealed was necessary and right, and nothing would be gained from quarreling about it. A soldier always has things he needs to conceal from his family. It's a good thing that he *can*, without diminishing the love between them.

When they reached the shore, it was only ten minutes or so after Umbo had left—but Auntie Wind already had baby Square there with her. And no nursing mother. She knew that the baby would be taken away, not because she had any foreknowledge or any timeshaping ability, but because she knew that there was no solution to the problem that would involve leaving Square in Larfold for even one more day.

"Better than your word," said Auntie Wind to Umbo as he and Loaf approached.

"And you have been better than yours," said Loaf. "I never meant to leave the boy with you this long."

"You're preparing for war," said Auntie Wind. "And you're a man. Now you've come to take responsibility, and so there are no hard feelings. We'll remember this boy fondly. He's funny and smart and clever and good, insofar as toddlers *can* be."

"We're going to try a facemask on him," said Umbo.

"I think that's wise," said Auntie Wind.

"And if it destroys him, Umbo will go back and prevent it," said Loaf.

"It will go well," said Auntie Wind. "Even in their original state, the mantles and facemasks are gentler on babies. Babies have little control over their bodies—but their will is terrifyingly strong. They get control over the parasite right along with getting control over the body. You'll see."

I hope you're right, thought Umbo.

And, in the flyer, Loaf echoed the thought. "I hope she's right."

"If she isn't," said Umbo, "we'll try something else."

And then, because he thought of it, and because it was Loaf that he was with, he added, "Square is alive because strangers have cared for him when it was inconvenient. Dangerous. I think Garden wants this boy to live. And with a facemask, and the body you and Leaky made for him, he'll be a force to reckon with."

Loaf heard this in silence.

After a while, though, Loaf said, "If this works, I think I'll seek out some adults and invite them to wear facemasks. You can go back and prevent the ones who fail. Then you can take a colony of successful facemaskers a few hundred years into the past and let them be the citizens of Vadeshfold. Let the colony grow. Far from the city where we first arrived there, but . . . a colony of facemaskers would be the true heirs of the wallfold, don't you think?"

"No mice," said Umbo.

"Wouldn't matter," said Loaf. "With facemasks, the Vadeshfolders could see all the mice, and catch them if they want. Use the mice to sing lullabies to their children. And squish their little mousy heads if they got out of line."

"Once the mice get into the millions," said Umbo, "it would be time-consuming to catch them all. Especially if they developed a disease that weakens facemaskers or slows them down. Or kills the facemask."

"All right," said Loaf. "No mice."

"What about timeshapers?" asked Umbo.

"Rigg already has a facemask."

"But maybe he should be the only one," said Umbo. "Facemasks are one kind of power, timeshaping another. I'm thinking we should keep timeshaping out of the Vadeshfold gene pool."

"Can't be done," said Loaf. "Timeshaping is already in the Ramfold gene pool, and we have no way to screen it out. It's going to crop up eventually among the facemaskers."

"What we timeshapers do is already so dangerous," said Umbo. "Undoing vast swaths of history just because we decide to. With facemasks, there'd be no stopping us. We've got no guarantee that other timeshaping facemaskers would be as nice as Rigg."

"Something to think about," said Loaf. "But not for you and me to decide just between us. If we actually get a colony of facemaskers in Vadeshfold, they should have a voice on such a decision, too."

Umbo shook his head. "It's all right for us to call them into existence, but . . ."

"But once they exist," said Loaf, "they have a right to be consulted about what genetic traits we do and don't allow into their population."

"So sometimes we get to decide for everybody, and sometimes we have to ask their consent."

"That about sums it up," said Loaf.

"And who decides which times are which?" asked Umbo.

"Me," said Loaf. "Because you're an idiot."

CHAPTER 23

Erectids

They had learned a few things from their experience with the Neanderthals. Once Noxon identified which paths belonged to Erectids, he chose an apparent settlement site that was just over a low rise from a very comfortable hotel. The only thing separating them was a hundred meters and a million and a half years.

It was April at the hotel—the rainy season, so there were plenty of rooms available and not a lot of observers. It was a simple matter to leave the hotel, cross a little-used road, follow a walking path over a rise till they were in sight of the little river, and then, when they were out of sight from the hotel, link hands and jump back to the exact time they chose.

They chose to visit the Erectids during the dry season, so even if they arrived wet with rain, they were dry soon enough.

Erectids built no permanent structures, and because they still had a considerable amount of body hair, they did not particularly seek out shade. They knew better than to live right beside the stream—too many animals gathered there to drink, day and night, but especially at dawn and dusk. Better to be a little ways off.

The Erectids organized themselves for protection, and they needed it constantly. Hyenas, savage and relentless, arrived at different times and from different directions, but they did not miss a day. Their favorite prey was untended babies of any mammal species—enough meat to be worth catching, yet small enough to grab and carry off for later dining.

That meant that Wheaton got to observe them in defensive action all the time. When the men were in camp, they used stones and sharpened sticks—not stone-headed spears, not yet—to repel the hyena incursions. But when the young, strong hunters were gone, the adult women, the old folks, and the older children were fierce and savage in defense of the babies.

Noxon loved to watch the babies and toddlers. Walking was already a skill the little ones aspired to from a very early age; Wheaton said that it was a necessity because Erectid arms were already too short to walk on all fours the way chimps and gorillas did.

The little ones crawled and then walked as soon as they could, exploring farther and farther from their mothers—their sole source of food, when they were so young, so they never quite lost sight of her. No wonder the hyenas, watching from a distance, grew hopeful. The little ones weren't exactly fearless, but what they had were monkey fears—spiders bothered them more than animals that were trying to eat them.

But the alertness of the adults and older children never flagged. The Erectids had somehow marked out just how far a child could be allowed to roam before someone swooped in to carry it back to safety, and by the time a child was walking, he or she knew just how far was considered safe. This didn't mean that they never crossed over that invisible line—but as soon as they approached it, they would begin checking to see if any adult was watching them. For the surest way to get adult attention was to stray beyond the line. But the children themselves had no desire to cross the line and actually get away with it—that would be dangerous. They knew that they should only "go too far" when someone older would be sure to notice and rescue them.

The babies also tussled with each other, the males constantly practicing for later struggles—warfare with other tribes, contests with animals, but, most importantly, battles for supremacy within the tribe.

For this Erectid tribe was still divided between alpha and non-alpha populations. They were on the verge of the forest, where dry dead trees showed that the wooded land had once reached much farther out into the savannah. The dead trees provided the savannah-dwellers with fuel for their fires and sticks for their prodding weapons; yet it wasn't so very far to walk into greener woods, where the leaf-eating branch of the tribe still lived with the alpha male and his harem of closely-watched females.

But it was the group that lived fulltime on the savannah, in the grassland, dealing with predators, walking upright all the time, hunting for their food, twisting grasses into twines and weaving them into baskets—they were the ones that Professor Wheaton insisted they must watch. "Because these are the ones heading toward becoming humans."

"Not because they *want* to," said Deborah. "It just happens when they aren't paying attention."

"Less than two million years till the tee shirt," said Ram Odin. "And starflight."

"But right now they don't have the slightest interest in either," said Deborah. "They just want to eat, pee, get laid, and keep the babies alive."

"My little girl," said Professor Wheaton. But he didn't look at her. He only watched the vids they had taken of camp life.

They only visited the camp while slicing time—invisibility was essential. But they set up video cameras and changed out the memory cards several times a day.

"I don't see the point," said Ram. "You can't show them to anybody. You can't use them to prove anything you might write about."

Wheaton didn't even bother to answer.

"Father's already at the peak of his profession," Deborah explained to Noxon later. "He doesn't need to publish this stuff. It just makes him happy to *know* it. He and I will watch these vids later. He's already told me to erase them when he dies."

They did not visit sequential days. From the Erectids' paths, Noxon knew that this encampment remained for three years, before prey animals grew too sparse and they moved on. So each day, they visited a different point in time, noticing how the children had grown, how courtship patterns had changed.

"Not monogamous yet," said Wheaton. "But it's starting. Repeated pairings between the same couple. And because females have to be larger and stronger to defend against hyenas, they're also strong enough to resist being kidnapped and sequestered."

"Raped," Deborah corrected.

"'Raped' carries criminal connotations," said Wheaton. "Because of the progress the Erectids are making, we can afford to criminalize it now, *must* do so. But they inherited chimplike behavior patterns in which rape was one of the few ways around the dominance of the alpha male. It was the only way non-alphas could get their genes into the next generation."

"And now we still can't expunge that old pattern," said Deborah to Noxon. "Even though 'kidnap-and-sequester' has been criminalized in most cultures for thousands of years."

"Civilization only became possible as monogamous pair-bonding emerged," said Wheaton, "which it's only just starting to do in this tribe. The females are getting a real advantage from being larger, and in a while they'll be in a position to start objecting and making their objections stick. Besides, alpha males can tolerate a little genetic insertion by stealthy beta males, but an uxorious male has only one mate, and he can't afford any genetic imposition from other males. Our Erectids are just taking their first steps on the road to sapience and civilization."

"And even then, alphas and stalkers and rapists still keep popping up."

"Because those behaviors still succeed, reproductively, often enough to keep the genes active." Wheaton held out his hands, as if asking for something. "Give 'em a break. These kids are still sixty or seventy thousand generations away from equal treatment of the sexes."

"'These kids,'" said Ram.

"Kids with a new car. Just learning how to pilot this upright body." Wheaton turned away, finished with discussion of an issue he must have resolved in his own mind decades ago. "Noxon, we've observed and recorded nearly their whole time at this site. Can we please follow them on a hunt?"

"They run for a living. We can't keep up with them, especially not if we're slicing time, which makes them faster, us slower. None of us is fit enough to stay with them on a hunt."

"Pick a short chase," said Deborah. "We'll saunter to the kill site, and then you'll bump us back in time to when the prey arrives with our friends in hot pursuit."

"So all you want is to be there for the kill," said Noxon.

"They always leave the females behind. I'll be the first woman to witness their triumph. See if the stories they tell about it are true."

"They don't tell stories," said Wheaton.

"They move their mouths," said Deborah. "They're anthropes. They must be lying."

There was no sound in sliced time, so as long as they remained invisible, they couldn't tell whether the sounds the Erectids made were anything like language.

"There's one kill site we could drive to," said Noxon. "It's near a public parking lot."

"Even better," said Ram. "We astronauts are so out of shape, after sitting around in a starship for a few years."

"You should see the shape your twin is in, after going in and out of stasis for eleven thousand years."

"He's still alive," said Ram. "Good for him."

The next morning they drove to the parking lot early. It was at a ranger station, and it was also a jumping-off point for photographic safaris. So there were plenty of other people. But they were all gathered around the hovercars that would carry them out into the savannah. Only one ranger noticed that the Wheaton group was heading out on foot.

"Not safe," said the ranger. "The lions stay away from the station but not very far away. And they aren't the only dangerous animals."

"We aren't going far. Just wanted a brief glimpse without a car around us."

"There's a reason we send people out in cars," said the ranger.

"An excellent reason, and more than just one," said Deborah. "I assure you I'm a coward, and I'll have us back in ten minutes."

"I won't be keeping track of time," said the ranger. "No matter how long before you come back, we will *not* send anyone out to search for you. With luck, we'll find your bodies while your passports are still legible."

Noxon smiled. "Now she'll hold my hand very tightly, sir. Thank you."

The ranger shook his head and moved away.

"He was really making sure we weren't armed," said Wheaton. "There are still people who think 'safari' requires that you bring home trophies from animals you killed yourself."

"Whereas we only want to watch our ancestors bring down a . . . something," said Ram. Then, to Noxon: "Do you know what the prey is?"

"Not sure," said Noxon. "I mean, I can *see* glimpses of it. Might be ancestral to a gnu. Large grazer from a smallish herd, anyway."

"And is it a weak one? An old one?" asked Wheaton.

"I don't think so," said Noxon. "They don't go for the old and sickly, or the babies. Since they know how to smoke the meat to preserve it, it's worth the extra work to bring down large, healthy prey. They have enough men to carry home most of the meat."

"It's pretty remarkable," said Wheaton. "Males hunting cooperatively. Wish we could hear whether they talk to each other during the hunt."

"I'll jump us back without slicing," said Noxon. "To five minutes or so before they arrive. If we hide, we can hear if they're calling out on the approach."

"Will you know if it's language?" asked Wheaton. "I mean, the ability to translate that you got from the Wall on Garden — will it work?"

"I don't know," said Noxon. "If it's a human language, then I'm supposed to be able to make sense of it. But who knows where that line is drawn?"

"It's a good plan," said Ram. "As long as we all remain very still, and hold hands continuously so that when we need to go invisible, Noxon can carry us along."

"It's more than that," said Noxon. "When I start slicing, we have to move. We only become invisible if we're in motion."

"We've done this about ten times now," said Deborah. "We know that."

Noxon shook his head. "You know it, but it's not a reflex for you, the way it is for me. I've had to drag you to get you moving several times."

"Once," said Deborah.

"She thinks because she has no eyes, she's already invisible," said Wheaton.

"Maybe I did when I was little," said Deborah, "but I can see *now*."

"The kill happens right over there. At that time, there must be a little gully, because the prey goes down a little and they take it on the uphill slope on the other side. Nothing deep, but it slows the prey down enough."

"Where should we be watching as they approach?" asked Wheaton.

"The prey comes from over there," said Noxon. "The wing men are there and there. The followers form a U shape right behind the prey. Most of the way, the prey kept leaving them behind, then stopping to breathe and rest and recover while they just kept jogging along. But the wing men—they're real runners. Fast and steady, so the prey can never turn very far out of the direct line of the hunters behind them."

"And where will we hide?" asked Ram. "Right now this is pretty open land."

"Well, first we'll hide by ducking down in the grass," said Noxon, "so safari tourists won't take a vid of us simply vanishing. And I won't know for sure where we can hide from the Erectids till we're in that time. Trees and bushes don't leave clear enough paths for me to see them after five hundred years, let alone a million and a half."

A minute or so later, holding hands, facing toward where Noxon could see the path of the approaching prey, they all sank to the ground and Noxon jumped them back in time.

It was almost a relief not to be slicing—to hear normal sounds and not be in that state of eerie deafness that Param had spent so much of her life in. Noxon had gotten used to it when he and Param were practicing together constantly, but since then it had grown strange and uncomfortable again. Now, in the million-year past, they could hear insects, could hear each other's small noises.

"We don't have to keep particularly silent right now," said Noxon. "There are no predators near us, and no Erectids, either."

"How long?" asked Wheaton.

"Getting impatient?" asked Ram.

"Father was born impatient," said Deborah. "With everything and everybody except me."

"Except you," said Wheaton, right along with her. "She says that, but of course I was impatient with her all the time. What a little brat."

"As bad as the disobedient little Erectids?" asked Deborah.

"Much worse, because you had such a mouth on you, and if you ever were getting the worst in an argument, you'd act extra blind. What a cheater."

"How does a person act 'extra blind'?" asked Deborah.

"Deliberately reaching out toward me but in a direction where you knew perfectly well I was *not* standing," said Wheaton. "Deliberately tripping a little when you walked. Bumping into the furniture—but I noticed you always chose upholstered or lightweight items."

"The real question," said Noxon, "is whether 'extra blind' kept working for very long."

"It worked every time," said Wheaton. "Every single time."

"That's a lie," said Deborah. "I never got my way."

"But I felt horribly guilty about it," said Wheaton.

"I didn't want you to feel guilty, I wanted you to give in."

"That wasn't one of the options," said Wheaton. "If I ever let you *win* you would have become a monster."

"Instead, I thought I was being raised by one," said Deborah.

Noxon could see that they meant what they were saying, to a point. But under it all was the clear message that they loved each other, that they had loved each other even then.

The conversation ended abruptly when they began to hear shouts from far out on the savannah.

"Shouldn't we hide now?" asked Deborah.

"Shhh," hissed Noxon. "Let me hear their shouting." He noticed that Wheaton was holding up a camera—vid with sound, Noxon assumed. So he could study their utterances later.

Not language, or at least not a language Noxon could understand. The cries were so short.

But then, as he watched, he could see how the men responded to the shouts—the wing men beginning to close in from the sides, the chasers sprinting. And then some of the cries began to have meanings. The leader—one of the chasers, the one with a bit of grey in his hair—was saying a word that meant "gully" and others that meant "run" and "catch." Nothing like sentences, no syntax. Just commands, all of them. Even "gully" was a command.

"They know this land," said Noxon softly. "They all know that there's a gully up here, and they know they'll catch the !a! there."

"Catch the what?" asked Ram.

"Click tones," said Wheaton. "It's a language, and it uses clicks."

"It's *words*," corrected Noxon. "No syntax. All commands. Time for us to hide. They're moving pretty fast."

He had been thinking about what he was hearing and seeing and it was already too late to keep from being seen. The nearest wing man had spotted them and had veered toward them. Now he would see them disappear. Noxon wondered what he would think he saw—a shape like what he would think of as "people," but mostly hairless, and wearing fabrics. And Deborah's artificial eyes. Now you see us, now you don't.

Except that the wing man kept heading right toward them, *looking* at them instead of looking back at the prey animal. Was he merely remembering where they *had* been?

No. Deborah was fumbling with *her* sound recorder. She was not holding Ram's hand. She was not slicing with them. She was completely visible to the wing man.

And while Noxon was focused on Deborah, the wing man brought up an arm. Noxon finally saw it because the facemask saw it and forced his attention from Deborah to what the Erectid hunter was doing. He had a fist-sized stone in his hand and he was bringing back his arm and before Noxon could come out of sliced time to shout at Deborah the stone was already in the air, moving faster than any bird—though not so quickly that the facemask could not bring every moment of its flight to Noxon's attention.

The trajectory was inevitable. It struck Deborah on the side of the head—she wasn't looking at the wing man who threw at her—and dropped her instantly.

Noxon immediately stopped slicing time—he couldn't stay invisible and bring her along with him. She would have to *move* to disappear that way. So now all three of the Sapient men were revealed to the wing man.

He didn't even register surprise. He was already drawing another stone out of the bag tightly bound around his waist. Survival instinct—strange animals that looked like people, but not from his tribe. There was a constant state of war among Erectid tribes; if they ever had truces, Noxon had seen no evidence of it in their paths.

"Both of you hold on to me and Deborah," said Noxon.

The wing man's arm was going back for another throw.

Noxon jumped them all back to the future.

Wheaton was kneeling beside his daughter, checking her vital signs. He began to press on her chest, then breathe into her mouth.

"It's no good," said Noxon. "She's dead."

"People come back from heart stoppages," said Wheaton as he pushed on her chest again.

"She's dead," said Noxon. "No path."

After a half-minute this finally registered on Wheaton. He stopped trying to revive her. He just knelt there gasping.

"Calm down," said Ram. "Remember what Noxon is. What he can do. She isn't *permanently* dead. He can go back in time and prevent this."

That was true, of course, and Noxon was already thinking about *when* he should intervene in the past in order to prevent it.

"Think of something," said Wheaton. "Because I can't bear to stay here much longer, looking down at her dead body."

Noxon concentrated on Deborah's corpse and pushed this lifeless object back about two hundred years.

Wheaton looked up in dismay. "What did you do!"

"What you asked me to do," said Noxon.

"I know," said Wheaton. "But now I know that there's something worse than seeing her dead!"

"Quiet, quiet," said Ram. "There are other people out here. In hovercars, yes, but they have mikes picking up sounds on the savannah."

"How can you think about being *quiet* when . . ." But then Wheaton nodded. "I know. To you, she's not really dead because she's not going to *stay* dead. So let's do it. Let's go back and—"

"We can't just go back," said Noxon. "I mean, we *can*. But if the three of us appear to the *four* of us in the hotel, before we leave, it'll change the paths of the *past* versions of ourselves, but as the agents of change *we'll* still exist."

"So there'll be two copies of all of us," said Ram.

"Except Deborah," said Wheaton. "Worth it."

"Seven of us to live on your already small income," said Noxon.

"It's Deborah's life!" said Wheaton.

"I'm not proposing that we leave her dead," said Noxon. "I'm just trying to think of a way to change the past without *going* there. So we don't get copied."

"Slice time and write a note," said Ram. "You said you and your sister used to communicate that way."

"If I'm there when the change happens, then whether it's a note or a conversation, I'm still the agent of change, still present at the moment of change. I promise you, that's how copying happens."

"Then sneak in during the night and leave yourself a note that you'll find in the morning," said Wheaton.

"All right, yes," said Noxon. "That's good. But what should the note say? 'Don't go on the hunt'? 'Make Deborah hold hands every second or she'll be killed'?"

Ram asked Wheaton quite earnestly, "Would it work, just to warn her that not holding hands will result in her death? I mean, I'm sure she'd promise to comply, but in the moment, with that guy running at us with a stone in his hand—would she even *think* of her vulnerability?"

"I don't know," said Wheaton. "She thinks about whatever she's thinking about, and not the things she's not thinking about. She's human."

"So we forbid her to go?" asked Ram.

"Not sure she'd obey that," said Noxon. "And if it isn't her, it might be one of us."

"We all held hands," said Ram.

"But we were all distracted. Thinking and talking about language. He should never have seen us at *all.* I should have disappeared us much sooner. If I had done that, nothing would have gone wrong."

"If if if," said Wheaton.

"I'm a timeshaper," said Noxon. "My life is all about ifs.

451

When we make changes, it's always in the belief that we understand what caused the problem and what the consequences of the changes we make will be. But nothing ever has just one cause, and nothing ever has just the predicted results."

"So you fail all the time?" asked Wheaton.

"We mostly succeed," said Noxon. "But the edges of everything we do are fuzzy. Nothing is really sharp and clear. So we spend a little time trying to think it through so we think of more choices and then choose the one we think is best."

Ram and Wheaton fell silent then, for a few moments.

"If I were Umbo, I could just appear to myself in a vision," said Noxon.

"You keep talking about the amazing powers of this mythical Umbo," said Ram. "But he's not here."

"What I have to do is the *equivalent* of that. Like a vision. So yes, I think leaving a note *is* the best plan. But a long note. I'm going to lay out exactly what happened here and suggest several changes. I'll tell us that their calls are language-like, and I'll include the chip that has the recording. But then I'll say, slice time from the moment you arrive there, and stay together."

"Will that do it?" asked Ram.

"I don't know," said Noxon. "Because we don't know what Erectids can see. It seemed to me that while he saw Deborah most clearly, because she wasn't slicing time at all, he also saw us, or never lost track of where we were. I think I need to tell myself to slice time much more deeply, and trust the cameras to record everything. Which means we need to arrive much earlier and place cameras. I'll tell us to do that."

"We should have done that in the first place," said Wheaton bitterly.

"What happens to *us* then, after you leave that note. Do we just . . . disappear?"

"I don't know," said Noxon.

"You said Umbo did this all the time," said Ram.

"Yes, but you see, I've always been the guy who *gets* the warning," said Noxon. "When we change our behavior, does that *eliminate* the timestream of the selves that sent the warning? Or merely diverge from it, leaving *them* to live with the bitter consequences of the mistakes they warned us not to make?"

"You mean I might still be here, with my daughter dead?" asked Wheaton.

"I just don't know," said Noxon.

"Well, what if we find out that it's so. Can we go back and give a *different* warning? Or appear to ourselves even before we got the note, and this time accept that yes, we'll copy ourselves?"

"You don't want to copy yourself," said Noxon. "I *know* that."

"You say that with absolute certainty," said Wheaton, "but you're the copy. You *exist* because of copying."

"No," said Noxon. "I'm the original. I'm the one who never murdered Ram Odin—a future version of him. I'm the one who got warned. *Rigg* was the one who had to live with the consequences of having done such a killing. *He* was the one who wasn't saved."

"None of us killed Deborah," said Wheaton. "Unless you want to use some oblique causal chain that starts with 'if I hadn't insisted on seeing *Homo erectus*.' But I tell you this: I don't want to save my *former* self from seeing her dead, while *I* have to go on living in this world that doesn't include her."

"So you want to copy yourself?" asked Noxon.

"I don't know what I want, except I want *every* version of myself to live in a world that includes a living Deborah!"

"There's another choice," said Ram. "We could leave Africa, go back to the States, and then go back in time and prevent the traffic accident that killed Deborah's parents and blinded her."

Wheaton thought about that for a long moment. "In that world, I wouldn't raise her. I would hardly know her. I wasn't really all that close to my brother, and Deborah's mother never cared for me. Deborah would just be an annoying little kid that I avoided because I'd have no responsibility for her." He grabbed his ears and squeezed hard against them, as if trying to crush his own head. "What kind of man am I? I don't want to save Deborah, I want to save myself from losing her. And losing her by having her parents live, saving her eyesight—I hate that thought almost as much as losing her to an Erectid stone. I'm a monster."

"For what it's worth," said Noxon, "it's not a bad thing, to find out a few of the monsters living inside us. Because you know you won't act on that preference."

"Well, one thing's certain," said Wheaton. "If we save Deborah's parents and preserve her sight, she would certainly *not* be with us on this expedition. She'd be at home with her family. Or away at school. And probably not even interested in anthropology, because that would just be something her eccentric uncle did."

"We can't do that," said Ram. "Because it changes too much. We don't know all the influence raising Deborah had on Uncle Georgia. Without her grounding him, giving him a meaningful personal life, a purpose, who knows whether he would have been all that successful in his career? Or even alive? Men living alone don't always take care of themselves."

Wheaton shrugged. "So I allow Deborah's family to die and her to suffer in order to avoid damaging my *career*?"

"I don't care about your career all that much," said Ram, "except that it's your career that gives you the money *and* the privacy for us to hide out with you while we wait for the Visitors to come back from Garden and somehow persuade the people of Earth to commit planetwide genocide."

"Thank you for reminding me of what I'm here to do," said Noxon. "I can't afford to lose track of that. But something Umbo and I learned early on, though we didn't realize we had learned it for a long time: No matter what grand purposes and causes we enlist in, we still have to be decent and good to the people we meet along the way. People like Professor Wheaton here. And Deborah."

"So what's best for Deborah, that still allows Uncle Georgia to be helpful to our cause?" asked Ram.

They were silent for another long while.

"Here's what I'm going to do," said Noxon.

"You just *decide*?" said Wheaton. "Without any kind of discussion or vote?"

"It's always my decision," said Noxon. "Because I'm the one who actually *does* it. So I'm the one who bears the responsibility."

"But without *advice*?"

"Hear me out and then give all the advice you want," said Noxon.

Noxon woke up in the morning and joined the others, who were having room service breakfast. Ram fluttered a two-page note toward Noxon. "Read it," he said. "It's from future you. Apparently our expedition today didn't turn out too well the first time around."

"Because apparently I'm an idiot," said Deborah. "Apparently my dead body appeared out there in the grass about two hundred years ago, and hyenas already had their way with me."

"Let the man read," said Ram Odin.

Noxon read.

"So the thing to decide," said Noxon, "is whether to go out there at all, and trust that we'll do better, or just go back to watching the camp."

"I say we go," said Deborah, "and I just won't be an idiot."

"He lays it out—*you* lay it out pretty clearly, Noxon," said Ram. "Slice time from the start, place cameras to record everything, then watch from invisibility the way we always do."

"Makes sense to me," said Noxon. "But what about his other suggestion?"

"*His?*"

"Future me wrote this note," said Noxon. "I didn't. So it's *his* suggestion, not mine."

"I don't remember my parents," said Deborah to Professor Wheaton. "Not enough to want to trade them for you."

"It's not a trade," said Noxon. "What he's suggesting will copy us. You—the you of right now, eyeless and brilliant and semi-annoying—"

"Thanks for that 'semi,'" said Deborah.

"*You* will still exist," said Noxon. "But that *other* you, the baby with parents and eyes, *that* version of you will continue. And live a completely different life. She'll never know you existed."

"She'll probably get hit by a bus at age twelve," said Ram. "There are no guarantees."

"Or her parents might get divorced. Or all kinds of bad things. But she'll have that life, and whatever happens, she'll see it happening with her own eyes," said Noxon. "And meanwhile, the four of us will still exist because we're the agents of change. And we'll jump forward in time and go calling on the other version of Professor Wheaton, and he'll take us in because he's a generous guy."

"I'll be living in a garret somewhere," said Wheaton. "Or a homeless shelter. Or I'll be dead."

"And if you are, then the four of us will find some *other* way to survive," said Noxon. "It isn't hard for me to make a killing on the stock market. We don't need some version of Professor Wheaton's pension. That's just the simpler way."

"Why are we even *thinking* of going back to save my parents?" asked Deborah. "That was never part of the plan."

"It's what future Noxon said," Wheaton answered her. "We saw you dead. And we couldn't help but think, as long as we're saving her life, why not save her *original* life?"

"We don't have to do that," said Deborah. "We can prevent my death out on the savannah today—or a million and a half

457

years ago, or whatever. And then we just go home and wait for the human race to monstrify ourselves."

"That's one choice," said Ram Odin.

"But it's the one I'm going to make," said Noxon. "Because my friend Umbo—"

"The legendary Umbo," said Ram quietly.

"Never forgot about his brother who died when we first started messing with time. And if I know Umbo, he's probably already found some stupid elaborate way to save Kyokay's life. Because he couldn't go on unless he did."

"But that hardly applies to you, Noxon," said Wheaton.

"And it certainly doesn't apply to me," said Deborah, "because I think I turned out just fine."

"Oh, you did," said Ram. "You are superb. If Noxon proposes anything that might get rid of you, I'll strangle him first."

"We've already proven you aren't quick enough to kill me," said Noxon. "And any change I make, I'll be sure to keep you around, eyeless and mean as ever."

"I'm not mean," said Deborah, sounding a little hurt.

"I meant it in the nicest possible way," said Noxon.

"None of the possible ways to mean that are nice at all," said Deborah.

"He means that he's halfway to being in love with you," said Ram. "And I agree, that isn't a very nice thing to contemplate, what with that incredibly ugly face of his."

"Enough," said Noxon. "Let's go watch a gnu get slaughtered and butchered by Erectids. And then go back and save a little girl from being a blind orphan for the rest of her life. And *then* we can figure out how to save a faraway planet from destruction. I'm not putting it to a vote, and any of you who wants to can opt out of any step along the way, and choose your own consequences. But those are the changes I'm going to make."

"You do realize that the simplest choice would have been to leave me dead," said Deborah. "Why did they even leave this note to warn us? You can still accomplish your mission whether I'm there or not."

"Because Professor Wheaton couldn't bear to live in a world in which you were dead," said Noxon. "Future me explained it very clearly."

"So it isn't me, it's Father who caused all this annoyance," said Deborah.

"My fault," said Wheaton. "I take full responsibility."

"Are you coming with me, or not?" asked Noxon.

They followed him out the door of the hotel room. They arrived at the parking lot much later than before, and now two rangers tried to persuade them not to go. But they went, and saw the prey stunned by two expertly thrown cobblestones, and then killed with the jab of a wooden spear into the spine. They watched the Erectids flake small blades from their seedstones, and flay and section the body while the blood was still warm, then bind the haunches and slabs of meat with twine and start jogging back toward the camp, where the fires would be waiting, and the women and children and old men were hungry for the meat, which would mean the survival of the tribe for another few days.

CHAPTER 24

Motherless Boy

"Something doesn't feel right to me," said Square to Umbo.

Umbo looked at the young man but said nothing. It wasn't Umbo's job to draw him out. Square would say what he had to say, when he was ready to say it. If Umbo spoke now, it would become Umbo's conversation, and since he had no idea what the conversation would be about, it didn't seem likely to be productive.

"I'm trying to think through everything that everybody has taught me about what's right and wrong," said Square. "I know it doesn't mean legal or illegal—it's usually right to obey the law, because that's how civilization works best, but not always. I mean, over in Ramfold, either you're King-in-the-Tent because you're married to Param Sessamin and her mother is Sessaminiak, the rightfully deposed queen, or you're a traitor and a rebel because you and Param make that claim but Hagia is still Sessamin, and

Haddamander is King-in-the-Tent and all his actions are right."

"Is that what you're trying to make up your mind about?"

"Oh, not at all," said Square. "I was just showing my thinking about right and wrong versus legal and illegal."

"I'm not Rigg, and he only demands that from you because that's how *he* was raised, one long oral examination."

"But it's a good education. I know so much now that I finally understand how little I know."

"Very wise. But I was born knowing that."

"Having your supposed father tell you that you're stupid every hour of the day is not the same thing," said Square.

"He swore he was teaching me a lesson," said Umbo. "I was defrauded."

"The thing that doesn't feel right," said Square, "is having Rigg at the head of your army of traitorous rebels."

"He isn't, actually," said Umbo. "Olivenko is the overall commander."

"But it's actually worse the way it is, having Rigg lead every raiding party. He hates fighting."

"No," said Umbo. "He hates killing."

"You can't keep this up forever. Having each of his raids take place *before* all the others, so each one becomes the first one. Always taking the enemy completely by surprise. Eventually you're going to go back so far that nobody will want to join the rebellion because it'll be before Haddamander and Hagia did anything bad. Back when the People's Revolutionary Council ruled and nobody really hated *them* all that much, except the royalists."

"Good grasp of history," said Umbo.

"Well, it's not really history, is it? Since at *this* moment, here in Vadeshfold, those events are still a few centuries ahead. *You* aren't even born yet."

"Nor are you," said Umbo. "And on the timeline that exists now in Ramfold, you never will be."

"It was kind of you to save me from temporal oblivion," said Square.

"Sometimes you talk way too much like Rigg."

"He's your best friend," said Square.

"Maybe you are, now," said Umbo.

"Well, maybe I'm *his* best friend, too. Because he sees the end of these raids coming. And then it'll be time for *real* war, against prepared enemies, and a lot of people will die."

"They all volunteered," said Umbo.

"That doesn't mean dying isn't just as dead," said Square. "And when they kill Haddamander's soldiers, won't it be even worse, because they volunteered to do it?"

"No, Haddamander's soldiers won't be any deader because they were slain by volunteers," said Umbo.

"Morally worse," said Square. "Wronger. I think that's how it feels to Rigg."

Umbo knew he was right, and so said nothing.

"Why can't you admit when you're wrong?" said Square.

"You were right," said Umbo, "but I wasn't wrong, because I didn't disagree with you."

"But you can't say it."

It was time to prod him back onto the topic. "What is it that doesn't feel right to you, Square?"

"For Rigg to have to keep leading raids as Captain Toad."

Now Umbo understood what Square was getting at. "We're not bringing any more facemasks into Ramfold."

"You won't be," said Square. "I'm not talking about bringing any more of my people there."

"Your people!" said Umbo. "There are only six of you who got the masks as babies, and you're the oldest."

"I'm not the one who decided *when* they should arrive here. But you know I'm talking about my future people. The ones who got facemasks as adults, because they wanted to be like Loaf. What are they training for, if not to fight in Ramfold?"

"*If* we need them," said Umbo. "If we can't win any other way."

"Because what's wrong becomes right when the need is great," said Square.

"Because what's perilous becomes worth the risk when alternatives reduce to zero," said Umbo. "Not every decision can be framed as right and wrong."

"Well, actually, every decision *can* be framed as right or wrong, including the decision whether to frame the decision as right versus wrong."

"Please, please stop trying to be just like Rigg," said Umbo. "We had two of him for a while, and we couldn't stand it so we kicked one of them off the planet."

"Not even close to true. Rigg told me what really happened."

"You can't take Rigg's place, Square. He may not like war, but Loaf trained him for it and he's very good."

"The facemask makes him good," said Square. "And I have—"

"No training whatsoever," said Umbo.

"Loaf has trained me a lot."

"Loaf has trained you how to fight like a child."

"I'm older than you are," said Square.

"You know there's no way to prove that," said Umbo.

"Not my fault you skip around in time so much you have no idea how old you are. But I'm taller than you."

"That's heredity. I'm not overly tall and I was slow to grow. You must have had tall parents."

"I think you know who my parents are."

"I know they must have been annoying and stubborn, which is probably why they got killed."

"'Stubborn' just means you don't want to do something somebody else wants you to do, and 'annoying' just means somebody else is frustrated that you won't obey them."

"Excellent on vocabulary, failing grade on getting the point," said Umbo.

"Before you try to change the subject," said Square.

"Too late."

"Look at this."

"At what?"

Square didn't show him anything. Umbo checked both hands, glanced around the meadow where they were sitting. When he turned back to Square, the young man was pointing at his own face.

Except it wasn't his own face. It was Rigg's face. Not Rigg's real face, not his original face. It looked exactly like Rigg's face with the mask on. It had grown a lot more normal looking in the past year, but he still deserved the moniker "Captain Toad," and Square's facemask was shaped exactly like Rigg's.

This was especially surprising because Square didn't have that abnormal facemask look. The facemasks that were applied to babies didn't look toadlike and deformed. By age three, they looked like perfectly normal children. There was no way to guess whether they looked the way the child would have appeared if no facemask had ever been applied, but they didn't look strange, and they didn't all look like each other, either.

"You can change the way it looks?"

"I've been working on it for a few weeks," said Square. "I made my pal memorize Rigg's face the way it looked the last time he was here, and then shape himself to fit. I've been checking every reflective surface and tweaking it where it needed, and now I can pop into Rigg's look whenever I want, and stay that way without even thinking about it."

"Just because you can look like Rigg doesn't mean you're ready to—"

"I can sound like him, too," said Square, in a voice that was identical to Rigg's. "I have his voice inside my head, and also the way he talks."

"Rigg has led men in battle," said Umbo.

"He did it a first time, didn't he?"

"The men will know you're not really him because you don't even know them."

"Don't lie to them," said Square. "Tell them who I really am."

"A boy from another wallfold, with a facemask like Rigg's?"

"Who I *really* am," said Square. "They all know Loaf and

Leaky. They know Loaf is a great warrior. Tell them I'm their son."

Umbo was so unprepared he couldn't answer for a moment, and that was all the confession that a man with a facemask needed.

"Did you think that I'd never guess? I'm taller than you *or* Rigg, and besides, you don't look at me the way Loaf does. I'm his height now. He's *proud* of me when I put in a good day of combat training with him. And don't kid yourself that he's not really training me. Loaf doesn't know how to do anything halfway."

"I'm not confirming or denying anything," said Umbo.

"Come on," said Square. "You and Rigg can visit me back here two hundred years before the war, because you can both timeshape however you want. But Loaf can't. Why does *he* come here, then? One of you always has to send him, and then pick him up and bring him back. I wondered about it when I was little, but when I got as tall as him, it's the only story that made sense."

"I told you the truth," said Umbo.

"I believe you did. I believe you stumbled on a future where Loaf and Leaky had been killed, leaving a baby behind, and that was me. You went back and prevented their deaths, but you took me with you so I wouldn't be wiped out in the causal shift. But Leaky didn't want me."

"Square, that's not something—"

"Loaf wanted me and so he chose to have me raised by Vadesh and the nursewomen brought here to Vadeshfold. He visits me a lot—as often as he can get one of you to send him. He's as good a dad as he can be. And you and Rigg are helping him so I never feel alone. But if Leaky wanted to visit me, she could, and she doesn't, so she doesn't."

Umbo had his own inner debate now, about what was right— to keep his promise, or to break it because it was right for Square to know the truth. Truth won. "Square, she had the son she bore out of her own body. That she *remembered* bearing. His name is Round. But you were a baby who came out of nowhere. She didn't doubt my story, but it wasn't *her*, it was another woman in another timestream. That's how it felt to her."

"I already forgave her long ago," said Square. "If I had a mother who loved me, would you have been able to put a face-mask on me?"

"Rigg and I loved you," said Umbo. "If the facemask had been disastrous, we would have gone back and prevented the attempt."

"How do you know it *wasn't* disastrous?" asked Square. "How do you know I'm the human baby all grown up, and not a facemask that had a real chance to control the human it was given to control?"

"Is that what you want me to think?" asked Umbo.

"I just wondered when you became sure that you had made the right choice?"

Umbo had no answer for that.

Square began to laugh. "By Silbom's right buttcheek, you haven't decided *yet*, have you!"

"Mostly," said Umbo. "We mostly think you're mostly human."

"Except when?" asked Square. "What are my inhuman things?"

"Nothing. Just . . . Loaf only has doubts because he says you're way smarter than either him or Leaky, and Rigg assures him that you aren't smart at all, and I tell them everybody's smarter than them."

"When it's really just because my pal helps me remember things," said Square. "I know the difference between me and him. He's not in control."

"I know he's not," said Umbo. "I know that you really are yourself. It's not that we ever picked a day and said, 'Today we decide whether Square is human or not.' You're as human as Rigg or Loaf, or anybody else who made it through the face-mask as an adult. Only you and the other babies, you didn't have any struggle over it. It was peaceful all the way. Which is why we finally believe Vadeshex isn't a failure. Yes, the first few generations here wiped each other out, but those weren't *these* facemasks, and they didn't get them as babies, the way the Larfolders do."

"So *we're* the real Vadeshfolders, right?" asked Square. "Me and the children, here, now. Not those adults a couple of centuries from now who took on facemasks to become supersoldiers like Loaf and Rigg."

"That's right. In fact, we're talking about offering you and the other kids a chance to go back to a time soon after humans in Vadeshfold became extinct, and let you have almost the whole eleven thousand years. You just have to promise to leave this area empty, so they don't interfere with us bringing *you* here."

"When are you going to offer that?" asked Square.

"When the other kids are old enough to decide," said Umbo. "And when you take a mate and we find the best way to get facemasks on your babies."

Square got solemn. "These are my sisters," he said.

"We've been worried about that."

"I need to find somebody from outside. Somebody who takes the facemask as an adult."

"They won't be pretty," said Umbo.

"You think I haven't seen Rigg and Loaf? I don't care about pretty, I care about not mating with somebody I grew up with."

"I agree with your sentiments. So does the whole civilized species."

"So my plan really *is* the best one."

"I'm *shocked* that you think you've proven your point when I'm not aware of your having done any such thing."

"Which means you're *not* shocked, you just think it's amusing the way I leap to conclusions and don't show you my reasoning. You're as bad as Rigg about that, in your own way."

"I'm so glad to hear it," said Umbo.

"Here's my thinking. You can't decide to bump us back ten thousand years till the younger ones are old enough to make a rational decision. That's going to be years from now. Meanwhile, you have to test mating, and since I'm the oldest, that means you need *me* to mate. But I'm not going to mate until I find somebody from outside Vadeshfold, which means you have to take me out of here and then we have to see if the person who falls in love with me can take a facemask."

"Another few months," agreed Umbo.

"And during that time, what better way for me to occupy my time than to go along with Rigg on a couple of raids, really get my imitation of him down perfectly, and also learn how he leads other men in war. So I can do it in his place."

"What makes you think you'll like killing people any more than Rigg does?" asked Umbo.

"Maybe I'll hate it," said Square. "But I'm Loaf's son, and he went for a soldier, didn't he? He's a good man, isn't he? But he's killed other men willingly enough, and it didn't make him a monster."

"No," said Umbo. "He's the best man I know, and I know some good men."

"Am I a good man?" asked Square.

Umbo didn't hesitate this time. "You are," he said, "though you haven't faced all the tests that will show who you are."

"Well, here's a test that will show who *you* are," said Square. "I want to prepare to take Rigg's place as Captain Toad. For Rigg's sake, to spare him all the killing that's going to come. And for my sake, so that I'll know a wider world before I decide to go back and found a colony. You and Rigg and Loaf have taught me a lot, but I want to *see* farming and commerce and cities and villages. And that way maybe I can find a wife that I really love, who also knows about life in the wider world, who chose *me* when there were lots of men to choose from."

"I'm not sure war is the best way to learn about the world," said Umbo.

"Oh, come on," said Square. "I've learned enough history to know that war is the *main* way men have learned about the wider world through all of history. In every wallfold of Garden and back on Earth."

"And don't forget that you're dying to go through the Wall," said Umbo.

"Well, I *have* been asking about that since I was little," said Square. "I want to know all the languages, too."

"So you can swear in them all?"

"I'm already through with my bad-language phase," said Square.

"No, you're through with your trying-to-shock-me-and-Rigg-and-Loaf-with-bad-language phase."

"Close enough," said Square.

Umbo looked him up and down. He *was* strong — Loaf had worked him hard, putting solid muscle on his tall and sturdy frame. And he was smart. And wise. And . . . good.

That's what Umbo was afraid he would lose, if he went to war.

But it was goodness that was prompting him to go — the desire to spare Rigg the pain that was coming. Maybe that would immunize him against the love of killing. Umbo had seen men who got the love of violence into their hearts, and couldn't get it out again.

The man that he had called Father was such a one. Never a soldier, but he loved to hurt people, to see them submit to his will, weeping, frightened. He also had good sides to him, moments of kindness. But somehow his love of power over the weak had become the ruling force in his life. That would not happen to Square. He could not become such a man as that.

"I'll talk to them," said Umbo.

"Will you talk *for* my plan?" asked Square. "Or against it?"

"Don't you know me?" asked Umbo.

"You'll talk for it *and* against it," said Square. "So be it."

"You'll abide by our decision?"

"Until I get timeshaping powers of my own, do I have a choice?" asked Square.

"Remember this: If we decide to have you wait a few more years, that doesn't mean *we'll* wait a few more years. We may meet, and then immediately come back here at a time two years from now, to see if you still feel the same way."

"About what? Being Captain Toad in Rigg's place? Or exogamy?"

"Both," said Umbo. "Would you be all right by yourself for a couple of years?"

"I'm not by myself. I've got the children to look after."

"You know what I mean. By yourself without Loaf or Rigg or me."

"Will *you* be all right without *me*?" asked Square. "You know that I'm the only thing giving real purpose to your life."

"I'm King-in-the-Tent," said Umbo.

"Completely powerless, and you're not sure Queen Param loves you."

"What's not to love?" asked Umbo.

"I'm sure your list is longer than mine."

"Because I'm humble to a fault."

"Self-doubting, you mean."

"A problem you'll *never* have," said Umbo.

"I doubt myself all the time," said Square. "I just don't let it make me wonder whether I'm a good person or not."

"Because you're sure you are?"

"Because I am whatever I am, and whatever I say, and whatever I do, so I'm finding out what kind of man I am right along with everybody else."

Umbo chuckled. "I envy you."

"My astonishingly deep wisdom?" asked Square.

"Your facemask," said Umbo. "Because you know you can say outrageously stupid things and nobody can slap you because your reaction time is so fast."

CHAPTER 25

Preemptive

It wasn't hard to persuade the younger version of Professor Wheaton that time travel was real, and that the oldish man with them was Wheaton toward the end of his career. Wheaton had always been an open-minded guy, and a few minutes of disappearing into slicetime could be quite convincing. The one thing Wheaton doubted was that his future career was in anthropology. "I'm a philologist," he said.

"We had to catch him in his philologist phase," sighed Old Wheaton. "You'll get over it."

"I don't see why," said Young Wheaton.

"The need for employment," said Wheaton. "And the fact that whatever could be extracted from philology is already known. Besides, what does it matter that you've learned a half dozen languages? This boy can speak all of them."

Young Wheaton — Georgia — tested Noxon in several ancient languages, then shrugged. "Party trick."

In Gothic, Noxon said, "The only person who knows I got it right is you."

"Well, I'm not going to *lie*. You really are speaking the languages. Badly."

"My accent is identical to yours," said Noxon.

"Not it's not."

"It has to be. I'm a perfect mimic, and I learned the language from you."

"When? I never taught a class in Gothic."

"Just now," said Noxon. He turned to Ram Odin. "Georgia doesn't understand how I could have learned Gothic from him, after hearing him speak it for ten seconds."

"Not possible," said Georgia. "Not even for a savant."

"Not possible," echoed Noxon, "and yet you just saw it."

"For all I know, being a time traveler, you spent a year with a tribe that spoke Gothic with a particularly wretched accent."

"Georgia Wheaton is well known to be tone deaf," said Deborah. "No ear for accents."

"Not true," said Young Wheaton. "I speak like a native."

"Dead languages, so nobody could check," said Old Wheaton. "Perhaps another reason I abandoned philology. When I had a child to support."

With theatrical flamboyance, Young Wheaton buried his face in his hands. "He knows all my secrets. Why are you *here*?"

"To save the life of your brother Arnold and his wife," said Ram Odin. "And to save Deborah's eyesight."

Young Wheaton looked at Deborah. "You're the baby?"

"All grown up," she said. "You—*he*—raised me."

"Well, aren't I nice," said Young Wheaton. He looked at Old Wheaton with some admiration now, instead of annoyance.

"Tomorrow afternoon they will set out on a car trip," said Old Wheaton. "They'll get onto the freeway and die in a fiery crash. Deborah is dragged out of her rear carseat by a passerby, but her eyes were already burnt out."

"He's the only father I ever knew," said Deborah. "We'll continue to exist—without my eyes, without his philology—but *you* won't have to devote yourself to raising a baby, and my parents will get to raise a much prettier and better-functioning version of me."

"So you're going to this trouble for someone else," said Young Wheaton.

"It would always be someone else," said Deborah. "The undamaged baby. The only issue was whether to extinguish *me* or not."

"And we don't have any guarantee that they won't all get hit by a bus a week from now," said Noxon. "We're not going to keep coming back to fix things. People die and things go wrong. We have work to do."

"Heartless," said Young Wheaton.

"Don't judge," said Ram Odin. "Every change he makes undoes everything that happens in other people's futures. He tries to create minimal mess. But somebody won't get a job because Deborah's father isn't dead to create the opening. Somebody won't live in a certain house because Deborah's family will be living there. Lots of changes that we can't predict and won't understand. Maybe somebody else will now die, hit by the same incompetent driver."

"OK, I get all that," said Young Wheaton. "He *has* to be heartless, to a degree. I can see that."

"And now we need you to help us persuade your brother and sister-in-law to listen to us," said Ram Odin.

"I can't even persuade them to listen to *me*," said Young Wheaton.

"All we need is an introduction, with both parents and the baby in the same room. We can take it from there."

"Lanae is perfectly capable of refusing to believe the evidence of her own eyes," said Young Wheaton.

"But Arnold can bring her around," said Old Wheaton. "And she's superstitious, as I recall. Tell her it's bad luck to make the trip."

"Not my job," said Young Wheaton. "I'll get you into the house. You take it from there." He looked at Deborah. "I assume you have the same fingerprints as are on the birth certificate."

"A little bigger now," said Deborah.

"You'll do fine," said Young Wheaton.

"And then, after we've all saved their lives together," said Old Wheaton, "we'll go away and come back in about twenty years so we can live with you while we figure out how to prevent planetary genocide."

That led to another explanation, but in the end, everything went according to plan. It took a couple of hours to get Lanae Wheaton to stop yelling and demanding that they leave the house, then weeping over Deborah's missing eyes while murmuring, "My baby, my beautiful baby." Then Noxon had Old Wheaton, Ram Odin, and grown-up Deborah hold hands and he jumped them back into the future.

A different future now. One in which Young Wheaton lived in a different city, because he was a professor of ancient languages at a different university. "My vids of the Erectids!" cried Old Wheaton. "I left them in the house! They're gone forever!"

Deborah opened her purse and showed him the memory chips. "I thought of that and took them with us."

"You see why I couldn't part with her?" Wheaton said. "She's my brain."

"External storage," said Ram Odin.

"Nice to be needed," said Deborah.

They had a little money with them, but not enough for airfare. Wheaton's credit cards were for accounts that had never been opened, with numbers that belonged either to no one or to somebody he'd never heard of. Again, Deborah's purse was their salvation, but she only had about a thousand dollars. "I took it from your stash," she told Wheaton.

"My stash?" he asked.

"Remember I had you put a thousand dollars into a hiding place so we'd have emergency cash?"

"No."

"Well, I did, and you did, and this is it," she said. "Busfare, maybe?"

"A plane ticket for one, and the rest of us slice time?" asked Noxon.

"Better than two days on a bus," said Ram Odin.

"I've walked farther," said Noxon. "It's not as hard as you might think."

"We'd get arrested," said Wheaton. "It's very suspicious to be cross-country pedestrians wearing civilian clothes."

"And we can't live off the land," said Ram Odin. "All the land belongs to somebody, and there are still plenty of people who shoot trespassers."

"What an unfriendly country," said Noxon.

"Different time, different place," said Wheaton. "We think we're a very welcoming country. Generous and kind. Unless we don't like your language or the way you look."

Noxon knew he had the language right, so it had to be the facemask.

They reached Young Wheaton's apartment in Ithaca, New York, rather late at night. Not having cabfare, they had walked for more than an hour from the airport. At least they had no luggage. And they refused to let Noxon snare and cook food along the way. "Not legal here," said Ram Odin. "Not without a license."

"Well," said Deborah, "you can take *small* animals without a license."

"Possum," said Wheaton. "Coon. Squirrel."

"But we wouldn't eat those," said Deborah.

They talked for a while about why they would disdain perfectly good meat, until they got so tired from walking it stopped being fun to argue about nothing.

Philologist Wheaton was exactly Anthropologist Wheaton's

age now, of course, but they looked different. Philologist Wheaton was a little plumper. Softer. Paler. No outdoor life. Nobody looking after him. Noxon realized that Deborah really had made a difference in her adoptive father's life.

"You knew we were coming," complained Anthropologist Wheaton. "This is all the room you arranged for?"

"I have beds for everybody," said Philologist Wheaton patiently, "and I'll sleep on the couch."

"No," said Noxon. "I'll sleep on the floor. I prefer it."

"The couch is softer," said Ram Odin.

"Soft beds give me a backache," said Noxon.

"The old house was completely paid for," said Anthropologist Wheaton. "I grew up there."

"It was also in another state," said Philologist Wheaton. "The commute would have killed me."

"Do you have enough money to feed us all? We aren't sure how long we'll be here," said Ram Odin.

"I have plenty of money—I saved the amount I would have spent raising a blind daughter," said Philologist Wheaton dryly. "And if I start running low, you can skip into the future, avoid a few meals, right?"

"Not with any precision," said Noxon. "And we need time to assess the situation here in order to figure out how to prevent the destruction of my world."

"I wonder if I'm going to have trouble deciding whose side I'm on," said Philologist Wheaton. "I mean, maybe they have a good reason for attacking your world."

"Not *attacking*," said Noxon. "Garden has no defenses whatsoever. It's global destruction of an unresisting enemy."

"Except here you are, resisting."

"Right of self-defense," said Ram Odin.

"*You* aren't defending yourself," said Philologist Wheaton to Ram. "You're from *here*."

"But the planet Garden is full of my family," said Ram Odin. "Descended from my twin brothers."

"Defense of family," said Anthropologist Wheaton. "A basic principle of anthrope survival from the beginning."

"I'm against genocide in principle," said Philologist Wheaton. "I'm just saying, there might be two sides to the story."

"That's why we didn't send Earth a one-hundred-percent-fatal plague," said Noxon cheerfully. "That's why I came in person. To find out the other side."

"You have the toxins to wipe out life on Earth?" asked Philologist Wheaton.

"Not with me," said Noxon. "But I do know where to find a couple of dozen sentient mice who I'm sure know exactly how to re-engineer the virus."

"So you're the most dangerous person in the world," said Philologist Wheaton.

"I come to bring peace, not the sword," said Noxon. "I believe the reason for colonizing Garden was so the human race would be on two separate worlds. That way a single asteroid strike couldn't wipe out the species. But the first thing Earth does is wipe out the spare world. I certainly don't want to return the favor. I want to understand what it is about us humans that we can't stand to coexist. Especially when there are so many lightyears between us."

"Built into the anthrope genome," said Anthropologist Wheaton.

"Can you say anything that doesn't refer to your expertise in anthropology?" asked Philologist Wheaton.

"It always seems appropriate," said Anthropologist Wheaton. "It enlightens every moral discussion."

"I wish that saving young Deborah and her parents hadn't wiped out your entire career as an anthropologist," said Philologist Wheaton. "I doubt you'd think my many publications in linguistics and mythology are sufficient compensation."

"Nor would his publications in anthropology make up for the loss of yours," said Deborah, interrupting before her adoptive father could answer in what would certainly have been a non-conciliatory tone.

Anthropologist Wheaton smiled benignly. "I do have some vids you might like to see, completely vindicating some of my more speculative articles."

"I'd like to read the articles first," said Philologist Wheaton. "That way I'll understand better what I'm seeing."

"And I did love philology in my youth. Influenced by Tolkien, I'm afraid—didn't need more orcs and elves, just wanted more Old Mercian than we got from the Riders of Rohan."

Deborah explained to Noxon about Tolkien. "Some consider his *Lord of the Rings* to be the greatest work of fiction in the English language. I think there are a couple of worthier contenders, but *Lord of the Rings* is certainly the greatest work of fiction by a philologist."

Both her father and his twin laughed uproariously at that.

"For a blind girl you sure see clearly," said Anthropologist Wheaton.

"And for an anthropologist, you're sure insensitive to other people's feelings," said Deborah, just as cheerfully.

"Oh, I'm deeply sensitive to every nuance," said her father.

"You just don't care?" asked Noxon.

"I just want to get a reaction I can learn from," said Anthropologist Wheaton.

"I think Professor Wheaton here," as Noxon indicated their host, "has a good suggestion. Why don't we skip ahead to when the ship we call the Visitors departs from Earth, and then wait out the time till they return? If we can't learn what we need to at that time, we can always come back. And in the meantime, I can make some jaunts back in time and compile a decent fortune by buying a few shares of Xerox, Microsoft, Apple, a few others. Or even earlier, in the heyday of untaxed capitalism. We don't need a huge amount—just enough in a Swiss account that no matter what time period we need to visit, we'll have contemporary funds we can draw on."

"Deborah's been briefing you," said Anthropologist Wheaton.

"He's so ignorant," said Deborah. "It seemed the least I could do."

Philologist Wheaton took Deborah's shopping list to the grocery store, while Noxon, Ram, Deborah, and Anthropologist Wheaton busied themselves with glancing through the bookshelves and scanning their host's publications. "He writes very well," said Anthropologist Wheaton. "Clear prose, opinionated but with plenty of grounding in sources."

"Why does this sound like self-praise?" asked Ram.

"It's not," said Anthropologist Wheaton. "And if *I* had chosen to pursue philology, I can't help but hope I would have refrained from some of his stranger speculations."

"Because you never speculated in your anthropological work," said Deborah.

"Ah, but I can prove myself right, now. At least to my own satisfaction. Basketweaving Erectids! Ropes and twines! Deliberately planted and cultivated yams! Continuing communication between the alpha-centered forest group and the monogamous savannah group."

"Not monogamous," said Deborah. "We weren't there long enough to know that."

"Monogamy-ready, then," said her father.

"Don't you have a memory card with all your publications on it?" asked Ram.

"I do," said Anthropologist Wheaton.

"As do I," said Deborah. "I didn't think he'd be happy to leave all those behind."

"My darling girl," said her father.

"You *are* a darling," said Noxon, allowing no trace of irony to enter his tone. "I need a blind clerk with a good memory."

"And I need a facemask," said Deborah. "Maybe we can work out a trade."

"Let's see what the future brings," said Ram Odin.

After a few days, Noxon and Ram followed their host's suggestion, skipping ahead a few months at a time. Deborah and her father stayed behind, ostensibly to research worldwide public opinion and government actions, but mostly, Noxon believed, for the professors Wheaton to read each other's work and criticize it in a most friendly, collegial, and sarcastic manner.

Noxon and Ram lingered for a while after Ram's ship launched, and then again when the Visitors' ship took off. Ram was fascinated to study what scientists learned from his first passage through the fold. They had no idea of the split into nineteen forward ships and one backward one—though one mathematician did speculate that microdifferences among the onboard computers might cause a division of outcomes. To avoid any chance of that, the Visitors' ship was designed to use only one computer for navigation and guidance, and all other computers were switched off during the leap across the fold.

For a couple of months after the Visitors' ship was launched, Noxon and Ram skipped ahead only a few days at a time. Then Noxon stopped blind-jumping entirely. He only moved forward by very rapid time-slicing, so that they caught a glimpse of the intervening days.

Thus it was that they were time-slicing in the back bedroom of Wheaton's apartment when there was a blinding flash of light and searing heat. The floor disappeared beneath them; the whole house disappeared. They plunged downward, but Noxon kept on time-slicing, so the fires were out for days before they landed.

The building was gone.

In the midst of time-slicing, they couldn't converse about what just happened, but it was soon obvious that the event had flattened all the buildings in their vicinity. Forest fires had raged on the nearby hills, and here and there they were still smoldering, giving off a red glow at night.

Noxon increased the gaps in his time-slicing, so they raced forward, spending less time in any one minute or hour. The forest fires died out completely. Everything seemed calm. Noxon was about to bring them out of time-slicing mode when he saw several aircraft of strange, wingless design come hurtling by in the near distance, not very high above the ground. Only when they had passed by did he take Ram back to the regular flow of time.

"We've got to get out of here," said Ram immediately. "I think that was a nuclear blast and we're going to be eaten alive by radiation."

"Let's get to a place where there weren't any buildings or parked cars, so we can jump back safely." Noxon began scanning for paths so he could pick an appropriate moment to return unobserved. He tried to avoid noticing where all the paths ended abruptly with the blast.

"I didn't know anybody was on the brink of war," said Noxon as they walked.

"Nobody *was*," said Ram. "Nobody on Earth."

"What do you mean?"

"Those aircraft that just went by. They clearly don't operate by any technological system I've heard of. And I've heard of them all."

"Not of human origin? Or some country had a secret program?"

"Not made by *Homo sapiens*. And I'm betting they weren't Erectid ships."

It still took a moment for Noxon to be sure what Ram meant. Not anthropes. Not from Earth. "What do we do?"

"Get back into the past right now."

"This radiation exposure," said Noxon. "You know we took a lot of it while we were time-slicing, too. Only a small fraction of what it could have been, but it looks like we weren't all that far from the center of the blast."

"So we're probably dying already," said Ram.

"Any cures?" asked Noxon. "Any effective treatments?"

"Well, if your facemask can't cure it, I doubt anything *my* body can do will be of much help."

"So we need to go back and warn ourselves in person," said Noxon.

Ram understood at once. "Which will duplicate us."

"If you and I are going to die," said Noxon, "our copies need to go on. At the moment, I think we're more indispensable to the survival of the human race than ever."

"And if we don't die?" asked Ram.

"The more the merrier."

They could learn nothing. The next time they reached that point in time, at least they were out of town, well to the south. They had communications equipment, but there were no signals to pick up.

The third time, Ram and Noxon visited one of Ram's friends from the space program. They made their explanations and demonstrations and were given a connection so they could look in on the communications of the international space exploration authority. This time there was a little warning. A ship of some kind spotted just outside the orbit of Jupiter. And then a complete loss of control over all computers and communications for only a few minutes, and a near-simultaneous launch of all missiles from all nations.

Armed with this data, Ram and Noxon visited the same friend, played the recordings and showed the data from the near future. With a lot of "never mind how I got it," this data provoked some serious alerts and this time the spacecraft was tracked. It seemed to have come from a direction similar to the route taken by one of the exploratory drones sent out prior to Ram Odin's colonizing mission, when the space authority was searching for planets likely to be habitable. And this time, given some warning, some of the communications systems were uncoupled from the worldwide networks, so they remained under human control.

What Noxon and Ram took back with them this last time was a much clearer picture. The best guess was that the drone sent out more than two decades before had discovered, not just a habitable world, but an inhabited one. A world with space travel and a keen sense of umbrage, or paranoia about what a follow-up visit from humans might bring.

"Given what Ram Odin's expedition did to the planet Garden to get it ready for human habitation," said Noxon, "I can't say they were wrong to determine on a preemptive strike."

"We would never have attacked a planet with sentient life," said Ram Odin. "We would have moved on to the next prospective colony world."

"*You* would never have attacked," said Noxon. "But who knows what the expendables would have done while you were in stasis?"

Speculation was all they had to go on, when it came to causes and motives. Results were a different matter. The aliens had such advanced tech that, virtually unnoticed, they were able to infiltrate our computers and communications from a distance, read enough data to know our weapons capabilities and what targets to hit, and then activate the surviving nuclear arsenals of two dozen former nation-states. The killoff was nearly complete. Then the alien ship reached Earth orbit at incredible speed, and those aircraft sought out every source of radio signals and then every sign of body heat.

"There weren't going to be any survivors," said Ram Odin.

"So by the time the Visitors come back to Earth from their voyage to Garden," said Noxon, "they're going to find that they're the last human beings left in the solar system."

"Then why would they go back and destroy the surviving humans on Garden?" asked Deborah. Immediately she shook her head, answering her own question. "Right. It wasn't humans."

"They got inside our computer systems," said Ram Odin. "They knew all about my voyage and then the Visitors' trip, including all the data they collected. So it was the aliens who went to Garden and activated the built-in self-destruct system orbiting the planet. It was never humans from Earth at all. It didn't matter what the Visitors saw. Their ship's log would show the aliens that there was another clump of humans. They found us completely defenseless and wiped us out."

"I'm so glad we didn't let the mice come back and infect the human race," said Noxon. "But—no, the mice were going to sneak back *with* the Visitors. So they would have reached an uninhabited Earth no matter what."

"What now?" asked Anthropologist Wheaton. "You're the timeshapers."

"I think our mission just broadened," said Noxon. "Our job now is to save the whole human race. On both worlds."

"Even though this alien attack on us was not completely irrational?" asked Philologist Wheaton. "We have a history of wiping out other flora and fauna to make way for our own biota."

"This isn't about justice," said Ram Odin. "It isn't about right and wrong. It's about us and them. And I choose us."

"All in favor?" asked Deborah.

They all raised their hands.

"We can philosophize to our hearts' content after we've saved humanity," said Ram.

"Now all we need is a plan," said Noxon.

"I think I have another voyage ahead of me," said Ram Odin. "But with a different destination. How long do you think since these aliens first developed space flight?"

Meanwhile, the original Noxon and Ram Odin had both developed radiation poisoning. Noxon's facemask helped his body recover. Now there were two copies of him, though one was still in bed, sleeping almost constantly as his body's cells were rebuilt and cancers were eliminated.

There was only one Ram Odin, though. Only one person in their group who could pilot the starship they had stashed in Antarctic ice in the remote past. This time the mice would be given the freedom of the ship. This time, they would be turned loose on an alien world.

CHAPTER 26

Tidiness

Param stood in the Tent of Light, bending over the table, studying the maps with Olivenko, Umbo, Loaf, Rigg, Ramex, and Square. Ram Odin sat in the doorway of the tent, looking out over the meadow, either keeping watch or dozing—it was hard to tell which.

Param spoke little at these councils. Her natural disposition coincided exactly with good policy on this—for she had quickly learned that if she even hinted at a preference, Olivenko would start to bend all his ideas and argument to favor the course of action that he guessed she was favoring.

She had had to be careful even of her questions, until she finally said, rather testily, that she could not make any rational decisions unless she was sure she understood the situation, which meant she must ask questions. But how could she ask questions if people reacted by trying to guess what she *meant* by her question? "I mean—I *always* mean—that I believe I need to know the answer to my question. Nothing else. I don't *hint*. When I've come up with a tentative decision, I offer my conclusions for comment. It isn't subtle, is it? You all understand when I do that?"

They all did—but after that, Param was quite sure that they still tried to guess what her questions meant, which way she was leaning. They simply became more subtle about their responses.

It was annoying that, as Queen-in-the-Tent, at least for this corner of the realm, she had to be so scrupulous about even the slightest utterance. How constraining it was to have authority!

Yet she also remembered Mother's powerlessness in the pleasant prisons in which Param had grown up. Mother also had had to watch every word she said, but not because others would overobey her, trying to anticipate her decisions. Mother's constraints came from fear that the People's Revolutionary Council would suppose her to be trying to assert royal authority. So Mother, too, had to learn to speak far less than she thought.

It turned Mother into a monster of deception. What is it doing to me?

In private, she could ask Umbo. But she knew his answer: You're doing a perfect job of saying the very least that you can say. Yet when you do speak, it's always sensible and when you make decisions, everyone can see the justice, the wisdom in your words.

And then Param would wonder if Umbo said this because it was true, or at least he believed it was true; or did he say these things only to reassure her and make her happy? And if she ever made a decision that flatly contradicted the clear will of the council, would she be obeyed? She tried to rule by persuasion, by creating consensus, but that only worked when the decision had no urgency. As they prepared for the full-fledged all-out war, the clash of great armies, decisions would need to be made quickly, and she was quite aware that it was not just the Queen-in-the-Tent—herself—who had no idea what she was doing. Olivenko was well-read and clever, but no one knew what their army would do in real bloody combat, so he might be wrong about everything. So might Loaf. So might any of them.

"We can always go back and try again," said Umbo at such times. "Have I come to you in a vision and warned you not to decide in a certain way?"

"Well, not *yet*," said Param.

"Then your decisions obviously work out perfectly well."

"Or I haven't made any decisions with consequences that matter."

"That should ease your mind even more," said Umbo.

"Or whatever went wrong killed you and me and Rigg, and so there was no one to come back and prevent it all from going wrong."

"And if that happens," said Umbo, "then the Destroyers will come and wipe out all our mistakes."

"Unless Noxon succeeds in saving us," said Param.

"He hasn't yet," said Umbo.

"That we know of," said Param.

Then Umbo glowered and fell silent. It was obvious that even though Noxon was gone—millions of kilometers away on Earth, or else lost in the oblivion of some crack in spacetime—Umbo was still envious of the many weeks Noxon had spent in Param's company while they were teaching each other to use their time-shaping talents with more range and expertise.

Umbo's resentments were the worst thing about him. But in this case, Param had to admit that he was not so very wrong. It was irrational that even though Noxon was the very same person as Rigg, prior to the division between them, Param did not hold him responsible for all the annoyances Rigg had caused. Nor did she think of Noxon with the same sisterly affection she had for Rigg. There really were times that she wished Noxon were still here.

Though, to be fair, Umbo was a very kind and sweet husband, and he made no effort to interfere with her authority as Queen-in-the-Tent. If anyone spoke less at these war councils than Param, it was Umbo. He would not offer an opinion or even ask a question unless she commanded it, or so it seemed.

His diffidence was, of course, annoying, especially since it extended into the bedroom. Into all their time alone. He never even asked for intimacy. Never even waited around as if hoping. If she said—or implied—that she wanted him to share her bed, then there he was, always compliant, and in the moment quite enthusiastic yet also gentle. Always careful of every sound, every flinch, every cue she gave, whether it meant anything or not. This made him in some ways the perfect husband, the perfect lover—and in other ways, completely annoying. Wasn't there any moment in which he would step up and be her equal? Assert himself?

How could he? She had spent so many months openly disdaining him, before they married, and she was sure he remembered every slight, every offense. Umbrage was his normal state, and she had given him so much cause to doubt that she had or could ever have any respect for him that she could hardly expect him to behave otherwise. Loaf, Leaky, Olivenko, and Ramex had all explained to her, quite kindly, that any strangeness between Umbo and her was entirely the result of the way they had been reared.

"Actually, you're quite compatible," said Olivenko. "Now that you've stopped picking at him, he seems to be nearly perfect for you."

"Tiptoeing around me as if I were a sleeping lioness is not 'perfect,'" Param had replied.

"You *are* a lioness," said Olivenko, "and most definitely *not* asleep. I think he's doing very well, and for you to be impatient with him is not just unreasonable but destructive. He knows he's displeasing you but since the thing you're displeased at is how perfectly he avoids displeasing you, it's hard to imagine how he could act differently without, well, without displeasing you even more."

Thus they stood around the table, around the map, contemplating various potential battlegrounds. South of General Haddamander's main army was a place where the ground would favor Param's army—but, as both Loaf and Olivenko pointed out, victory would leave them no better off than before, since Haddamander would still be between their army and the capital. But if they simply took possession of the capital, it would be an easy matter for Haddamander to besiege them, leaving her to feed hundreds of thousands of citizens as well as her army.

"We could do it," said Rigg. "The way we feed our army now—by making purchases in the past."

"We're already buying up surpluses from five hundred years ago," said Ramex. "Not that there aren't plenty of other good years to buy from. But every purchase of grain improves the past economy, which changes history."

They didn't want to do that. Couldn't afford to find themselves facing a much more popular or powerful enemy than Haddamander as the general of Hagia's army. What if they changed history so the Sessamoto Empire was much better governed? So there had never been a People's Revolution? So that Haddamander was, not the scion of a persecuted noble family, but the pampered, celebrated son of a great house? Might he not have been married to Hagia in the first place, instead of Rigg's and Param's own father? Just how much could they meddle in the past without causing vast, confusing changes?

Yet they had to feed their army—and, if their army suddenly appeared in the streets of Aressa Sessamo, all the citizens of the city as well.

What they needed was a quick, decisive, irresistible victory. Param had expected Rigg to argue against something so violent, but he surprised her. "I know you think I'm a pacifist of some sort," said Rigg, "but that isn't so. What will save the most lives is to have a quick, brutal, thorough victory, so the war ends with the one battle."

"True," said Loaf. "No matter which side wins, a decisive battle would definitely shorten the war."

"I'd like us to win," said Olivenko.

"You know we'll win, eventually," said Square. "Because if we lose, Umbo will come back to this very meeting and give us the information that will let us make better decisions."

"Only if he has the brains to *stay* here during the fight," said Loaf, "so he doesn't have to travel back here, possibly pursued by enemies, after a devastating defeat."

Umbo merely shook his head.

"Umbo is right," said Param. "He can't stay here in the tent, far from any of the battle sites. How will he even *know* the outcome of the battle, or what went wrong, if he spends the whole battle here? If there's anyone who can easily evade pursuit and return here to give warning, it's Umbo."

Umbo said nothing. Merely continued looking at the map.

"And just as importantly," said Param, "Umbo is King-in-the-Tent. The soldiers need to see him with them. They love him and respect him, as a man, in ways they can't respect me, a woman."

Umbo glanced at her for a moment, then back down at the map. She could not read anything into his glance.

Silence around the table.

"It seems to me," Param finally said, "that every possible battle-ground has drawbacks and advantages. Every possible battle-ground has ways of turning into disaster or triumph. Is that true?"

Olivenko was quick—too quick?—to agree. But after only a few moments, Loaf, Ramex, Ram, Rigg, and Square concurred.

She almost said, Then we could cast clay and choose our battleground by chance alone. But she stopped herself, because another possibility came to mind.

"It seems to me," she said again, "that all our plans are essentially defensive in nature. Appear here, and fortify as we await their attack. Or appear there. Or there. Or in Aressa Sessamo. Or . . . is our army so bad that we can't use it to attack them where they are?"

"Our troops are well trained," said Loaf, "but training isn't battle."

"We don't know what they'll do, when men start to bleed," said Rigg. "Our army isn't composed of men who love battle. Only of men who hated Hagia's and Haddamander's rule, or who wanted to move their families out of danger. Not soldiers by choice or temperament."

"But we do have a force of extraordinary fighters," said Square.

"Are there enough of you to make a difference?" asked Ramex.

"You're the one with the magnificent electronic brain," said Square. "Work it out and advise us."

"It is not possible to predict the outcome of battles with certainty," said Ramex.

"So let's have the first battle and see how things work out," said Square. "And let's have Rigg or Umbo take all my Vadeshfolders back to meet ourselves, so we can double our strength. And then quadruple it."

"No more copying people," said Rigg. "It's a terrible thing and you shouldn't put anyone else through it."

"We won't do it anymore after we win," said Square. "You do what you must to win the war."

"And what if all your facemasks come through alive?" asked Rigg. "Which ones are married to their wives? Which are now single men, who remember having wives and children, but have them no longer?"

"Let's see how our first time through turns out," said Loaf, "before we go copying anybody."

"I think Queen Param's proposal is a —"

"It wasn't a proposal," said Param quickly. "It was merely a question about the defensive versus the offensive."

"I think Queen Param's question is one whose answer we've taken for granted," said Olivenko. "We should use our untrained troops on the defensive. But this may be a gross mistake. On the defensive, it is vital that the troops stand firm, give ground slowly, retreat in good order when necessary. Loaf and his sergeants have trained them wonderfully well, but when comrades fall beside you, war becomes a different thing — according to all the histories. And it's easier to get ignorant green troops to charge than to stand against a charge."

"There's no doubt that we could achieve tactical surprise," said Square.

"We can't bring the whole army through at once," said Rigg. "Not unless we have them all in one compact body, so they can all hold hands."

"Bring everybody through in as many groups as you need," said Square. "Just bring them all to the same moment."

"That means Umbo would have to do it all," said Rigg. "I can do that moving into the past, but only he has precision moving into the future."

Everyone looked at Umbo.

"I assume you meant to say King Umbo," said Param gently.

"He doesn't have to call me that," said Umbo softly.

"He must do it above all others," said Param, "because he is as much heir to the Tent of Light as I am, and there are those who would prefer his claim. He *must* speak of King Umbo by his title and with all authority, so no one has any doubt that Rigg supports his claim and mine."

Umbo shook his head. "Let's not get off the topic again."

"Olivenko," said Loaf, "are you advocating that we make a new plan, to appear in the midst of their camp and slaughter them in their sleep?"

"Not in their sleep!" cried Param.

"Queen Param," said Olivenko. "The goal is a victory so decisive the enemy can't recover from it. If we can kill one man in five before he even gets his weapon, the battle is nearly won."

"Except," said Loaf, "if we appear throughout their camp, then what happens to the organization of our army?"

"A mess," said Square. "Nobody knows which way to face. It becomes a melee, till the enemy forms a line somewhere."

"Haddamander entrenches and walls up wherever he camps," said Olivenko. "Attacking from the outside would be brutal."

"And attacking from the inside would reduce us to chaos immediately," said Loaf.

"And we're back to every plan having risks and benefits."

"Can't we make a plan to organize and avoid chaos?" asked Param.

"Every soldier would have to know the whole plan," said Loaf. "Never a good idea."

"Why isn't it a good idea?" said Umbo quietly.

Loaf shook his head. "The less the footsoldiers know of the plans of the commanders, the better."

"Isn't that so they can't betray our plans to the enemy?" asked Rigg. "But if we appear all at once, in the midst of their camp, with every soldier knowing exactly what's expected of him and where to form up as soon as his assignment is complete—there's no time for any of our soldiers to be taken and spill our plans."

Loaf nodded. "I can see that. I've had it ingrained in me that footsoldiers can never know more than their immediate assignment, but . . ."

"That's all we'll tell them anyway," said Square. "How to cause maximum terror and destruction for about five minutes, then form back into a coherent unit before going off in pursuit of fleeing enemies."

"You were actually paying attention when I lectured to you," said Loaf approvingly.

"Now and then," said Square, "when you're saying something sensible."

It was time, Param realized. "Now I will not ask a question. Now I'm making a decision. Let's take a few days, a week, whatever you think we need, to train the men to engage in a surprise attack, then form back into units for the pursuit and destruction of the enemy."

"And how to divide out small units to guard the prisoners. The ones who surrender." Rigg looked around, as if daring anyone to contradict him. "Many of them will throw down their weapons and our goal is not slaughter, it's destruction of the army. Capture is better than slaughter."

501

"Unless it takes too many of our men to guard them."

"I'll be there," said Rigg. "To take them into the past, without their weapons. King Umbo, too. We'll push them so far into the past there'll be no place for them to hide, no farmers or villagers to help them."

"No one can hide from a pathfinder anyway," said Square.

"I think it's a decent plan," said Olivenko. "Worth trying, to see what goes wrong."

"And there you'll be," said Loaf. "Rigg and Umbo, separated from each other and surrounded by enemies. Just one arrow or javelin away from stranding our army far from their wives and children, unable to come back and fix things if things go wrong."

"King Umbo can send them from a distance," said Rigg. "He doesn't have to be touching them."

"Then I'll do all the sending," said Umbo.

"The decision is made," said Param. "This is what we'll train for. How many days?"

"Till they know the drill," said Loaf. "It's not as if we have a deadline at *this* point in time. It's the arrival that has to be exact."

"I wish," said Rigg softly, "that there were some way for Noxon to send us a message when he completes his mission."

"There is," said Square. "The world isn't destroyed. Message received."

"Maybe I'll go forward in time while you're all preparing," said Rigg.

"Nothing's changed," said Umbo.

Silence again.

"I check every morning," said Umbo. "Nothing's changed yet."

Param thought of what that meant. Umbo leaping forward in time to see if the world was still destroyed on schedule, and returning because the destruction was inevitable.

Why bother doing all this, if relieving the people of the brutal regime of Hagia and Haddamander only bettered their lives for a couple of years, and then the world ended anyway?

As if he knew what she was thinking, Rigg said, "We have to fight and plan as if we had a future. In case we actually get one."

"Decided," said Param. "This command goes forth from the Tent of Light: So let it be done."

She hadn't learned the old rituals of command from her mother. She had found them in books. At first she thought it was ridiculous hocum. Now she understood that someone had to end the council by declaring specifically what had been decided and what must happen next. Without absolute clarity, people would go off and dither, especially if they had doubts about the decision.

Param knew what she had done. Upended all their plans, taken them from defense to attack, and because of her, enemy soldiers would be speared or javelined or sabered in their sleep, or in the moment when they staggered up from their beds, searching for weapons.

Unless Haddamander had anticipated exactly this strategy.

But he couldn't really know all their capabilities, because *his* soldiers had only faced Param's soldiers a couple of times, in minor skirmishes and in Captain Toad's last raid, which had seemed to Haddamander to be the first.

When Param spoke her decision, everyone left the Tent of Light. Except Umbo.

"There's always another choice," said Umbo.

"We're not assassinating them," said Param.

"They deserve no better, and it would save the lives of their men."

"It wouldn't," said Param. "Assassination would only invite new warlords to rise up and replace them. Their army must be whipped and *know* that it was whipped."

"Because that's what Olivenko—"

"That's what *history* says," Param answered.

He nodded, but looked a bit dejected.

"Umbo, murder isn't *in* you."

"It's in Rigg," said Umbo.

"It *was* in Rigg. *Once*. And it damaged him. Murder damages people."

"Or maybe it's that damaged people murder," said Umbo.

"Or both," said Param. "But we're not going to find out. We won't succeed at taking the Tent of Light only because I was willing to have my mother murdered for ambition's sake."

"You know they wouldn't hesitate to do it to us, if they thought they could," said Umbo.

"I know they already tried, before we first passed through the Wall," said Param. "I know we held hands and saved each other. But if we attempt to win by way of murder, then it no longer matters who wins this war—there'll be a murderer and oathbreaker in the Tent of Light either way."

"There's no moral equivalency," said Umbo.

"Rigg killed Ram Odin once in self-defense—and he couldn't live with it."

"That was Rigg," said Umbo.

"And you're a more ruthless killer?" asked Param.

"I might be," said Umbo.

"Let's see how this battle goes," said Param.

"You're right," said Umbo. "Maybe your mother and Haddamander will be the first to die in their tents on the battlefield."

Param shook her head. "You say all these things much too easily."

"I want to avoid the deaths of the obedient soldiers on both sides," said Umbo.

"I want to, too," said Param. "But it's not enough for us just to win. The enemy's army has to experience real, terrifying loss."

"I remember when Olivenko first said that exact phrase," said Umbo.

"He's a counselor," said Param. "A wise queen listens to wise counsel."

Umbo fell silent.

"The way I listened to you," said Param. "When you told us that the world still ends on schedule. Even though you had never told me you checked every day."

Umbo fell silent. In embarrassment?

"I listen to you more than anyone," said Param.

"Since nobody listens to me at all," said Umbo, smiling at her, "that's not hard to achieve."

"I meant that I listen to you more than I listen to anyone

else," said Param. "And not because you're my husband, and I love you. Though you are, and I do."

He showed no reaction.

"I listen to you because you speak rarely, but when you do, it always matters and you're always wise."

"Or if I'm not," said Umbo, "I can always go back and clean up the mess."

"Tidiness in a man is a worthy trait," said Param.

He kissed her. A brief kiss. More than brotherly, but far from passionate.

She kissed him in reply, with all the passion she wished he would bring to his kisses.

"Do you think this is the right time for that?" he asked softly, when they broke from the second kiss.

"Tell me when you start believing that I'm truly your wife," said Param.

"When that happens," said Umbo, "I won't have to tell you. You'll know."

CHAPTER 27

Retrieving the Mice

Because Noxon could see his and Ram's paths—and the paths of the mice inside the box—he was able to return only a few seconds after he and Ram had left them buried.

They had explained the mice to Deborah and Anthropologist Wheaton, including all the disobedience and attempted betrayals. "Why don't you just leave them there?" asked Wheaton.

"Because I promised I'd come back and let them out," said Noxon.

"It's one of his better traits," said Ram. "But it's also a serious weakness. And the mice really are dangerous and tricky."

"Are *we* in danger from them?" asked Wheaton. Noxon could see that it was Deborah he was worried about.

"Yes," said Noxon. "But only in the sense that the entire human race is in danger. Or that, if they were to kill me, the rest of you would be stranded in ancient Peru, thousands of years before any humans come to the Americas."

"I suppose that means no internet," said Deborah.

It took Noxon a moment even to remember what she was talking about. "Oh, yes, I forget how connected everyone is in your time," said Noxon.

"We never even carried mobiles," said Ram. "Didn't get into that mind-set."

"It's time to open the box, then close it and rebury it before Ram and I come back."

"You come back? Another time?" asked Deborah.

"We ran some errands," said Ram. "And left the starship where it would be buried in ice. Then we came back and talked about letting the mice out."

"But you didn't," said Deborah.

"And we didn't check to see if they were still in the box," said Noxon. "In case they weren't. Because that would mean we came back here and liberated them. As we're doing."

"And you didn't want to know?" asked Wheaton. "I can't imagine wanting *not* to know something."

"If we knew," said Noxon, "we'd make guesses about *why* we came back and that might change our behavior. Which might erase whatever future had previously ensued. Or might duplicate us."

"You have to be very careful," Deborah observed.

"Everything has unforeseen consequences," said Noxon. "And every attempt to make some things better is likely to make other things worse."

"Saving me?" asked Deborah.

"So far," said Noxon, "that's working out pretty well. But duplicating the professor, here? I'm not sure he's thrilled about the philologist version of himself."

Wheaton shrugged. "It's like finding out what I'd be like if I had never grown up."

"I liked him," said Deborah.

"How ironic," said Wheaton, "since it's clearly *you* that made *me* different from *him*."

"I have much to answer for," said Deborah.

"Should I open the box?" asked Ram.

"They can hear us already," said Noxon. "So here are the rules. The mice will all come out of the box and stay in a group, approaching nobody. Ram will close the box and rebury it."

"I have to do all the manual labor?"

"You're the trained pilot," said Noxon. "I have no skills."

Ram grinned.

"If the mice deviate from these instructions," said Noxon, "I'll kill them all."

Deborah looked skeptical. "Have you ever tried to catch mice?" she asked.

"In my previous life as a cat, yes," said Noxon.

"The facemask makes him very, very quick," said Ram.

"And I could go back and kill them in the past," said Noxon. "They understand that."

Ram opened the lid.

The mice swarmed out and formed a writhing heap on the bare dirt in front of the box.

"They look perfectly ordinary."

"Look again," said Noxon. "Their heads are quite large, for mice, and their bones and musculature are sturdier in order to bear the added brain weight. Also, they have tiny electrical connectors at the tip of each toe. Or finger. Or whatever. They can stick their paws into computer sockets and link up directly to their brains."

"So they're all computer peripherals?" asked Wheaton.

"No," said Noxon. "All computers are mouse peripherals."

"You came back," said a mouse.

"They're talking to me now," said Noxon. "You'll only hear my side of the conversation. I may switch languages."

"The mice talk," said Deborah.

"In very high voices," said Noxon. "And most of it is lying."

"So unfair," said a mouse.

"Judgmental," said another.

"Glad you're back," said a third.

"One of you at a time," said Noxon. "Who speaks for all?"

"For the moment," said one, "me." It was a female, and she moved toward him, away from the pack.

"No," said Noxon. "I know what you are. I want the alpha."

"You'll kill him," said the spokeswoman.

"That's quite possible," said Noxon. "But it's not my plan at the moment, because I need you, and I need to be able to assess your intentions and your capabilities."

"If you think you can possibly understand us . . ." said the spokesmouse.

"I understand you at least as well as you understand us," said Noxon. "The alpha, now."

Another mouse came forward.

"You hide your maleness well."

"Huge testes didn't suit our purposes," said the alpha. "We bred them out. What do you want with us?"

Noxon explained about the alien attackers.

"So you want us to prevent their computer infiltration," said the alpha.

"That might be interesting, but it wouldn't solve the problem," said Noxon.

"You're going to journey to their world before they evolved and destroy them," said the alpha.

"Now you're getting closer."

"Is there any way to assess their biology before we make that voyage?"

"No," said Noxon. "We never saw them come out of their airships and we're not interested in going back into the future to lure them out. We're going to leave from *now* and make the voyage."

"I understand your fear that they might overpower you," said the alpha. "It should give you some idea of how we feel about *you*."

"I know that you betrayed me regularly long before I gave you any reason to do so," said Noxon. "So now you see my dilemma."

"*I* don't," said Deborah.

The alpha rattled off his answer. "You need us to be free allies, but you can't trust us not to take over the ship during the voyage."

"I want to travel with you now as equals," said Noxon. "I want you to have full access to the ship's databanks. I don't see how you can be useful if you don't have your full range of information and power."

"All you have to do is explain why we need *you* now," said the alpha.

"Because I still have the power to decide whether to turn the alien world into a home for humans and mice of your kind, or simply another colony world for humans."

"So our alliance is based on your ability to kill us," said the alpha.

"Your physical powers are limited," said Noxon. "And your mental abilities depend on achieving a critical mass larger than the one you currently have."

The alpha said nothing.

"I know that every mouse except you is a pregnant female. But they are not actually gestating—the embryos are not developing."

"That thing doesn't give you X-ray vision," said the alpha.

"I know their hormones smell like pregnancy, but there are no fetal heartbeats and they haven't grown since the beginning of the voyage. My guess is that you've found a way to enclose a litter of fertilized ova into a sac and keep them from attaching to the uterine wall. So they can be pregnant the moment you decide."

"Close," said the alpha.

Noxon thought for a moment. "No, I'm exactly right. But instead of just one sac, each one contains several. And each sac of ova will produce a litter that's bred for different capabilities. So you can spawn—what, electronics whizzes? Spacetime displacers? Fast-maturing baby-breeders?"

"We're all fast-maturing baby-breeders," said the alpha. "But yes, you have the idea."

"When you were loose in the ship during the voyage here, before the expendable rounded you up, what did you do?"

"We were exploring the possibility of doing a displacement of the ship during the voyage."

"If you moved the inbound ship out of its one-to-one correspondence with the outbound version of the ship, it would have annihilated us."

"Unless we displaced the ship so that it didn't overlap with the original in any way."

"That would kill all living things aboard the ship," said Noxon.

"That's why we were going to try to move the outbound ship."

Noxon shook his head. "You aren't stupid," he said. "That might undo everything."

"We didn't actually do it," said the alpha.

"For smart mice, you're pretty stupid."

"Be fair," said the alpha. "We're only a couple of dozen. We don't get really smart until we have a few hundred."

"And that's another reason for you to want time to have a lot of babies."

"It would be nice if you didn't slice time the whole way to the alien world."

"I'm not going to let you have any babies until we've reached the alien world," said Noxon. "Until we see what we're facing."

"I think you need us to reach maximum intellectual capacity before then."

"Not until I know what I want you to do," said Noxon.

"Are you capable of such a decision without our advice?" asked the mouse.

Noxon immediately realized that they were manipulating him. Because the moment the mouse said it, Noxon was filled with anxiety that he knew would not go away until he agreed to let the mice reach the alien world in hundreds instead of two dozen. That anxiety was not rational. It was what the mouse wanted him to feel.

"Interesting," said Noxon. "You aren't behaving like a potential ally."

"Sorry, sorry, sorry," said the alpha.

The other mice were echoing him. "Sorry, sorry, sorry," they bleated.

"Why are they all squeaking?" asked Deborah. "What are they saying?"

"They're apologizing for their naked attempt at forcing me to obey them by influencing my emotions," said Noxon. "I'm pretty sure we can eliminate the alien threat without the help of the mice. The main reason I want to bring them is because I wanted them to exist on a second world, too. And that second world will *not* be Earth. Earth is the sanctuary for the pure, unmodified human species. The mice have two wallfolds on Garden. Apparently that's all they're ever going to get."

"Don't pretend you're trying to look out for our best interests," said the alpha.

"You know I'm not pretending," said Noxon. "But I place your best interests well behind the best interests of the whole human species—including your little subgroup. What good is it for me to save humanity from these aliens, only to have *you* destroy them instead?"

"We're not destructive," said the alpha. "We're makers and builders."

"You're human," said Noxon. "You make war and you eliminate anybody you think is a threat."

"You're a threat," said the alpha.

"And you've already thought of six ways to kill me," said Noxon.

"Only two with any real chance of succeeding," said the alpha.

"Let's not kill each other," said Noxon. "Let's travel to the alien world and work out a way to turn it into a haven for humans *and* mice."

Deborah gasped. Noxon turned to her.

"You're going to destroy the entire alien species?" she asked.

"That depends on how you define 'destroy,'" said Noxon. "For instance, if time travelers came back in time, when anthropes existed only as Erectids, and then prevented the development of Sapients, would you say they had destroyed the 'entire human species'?"

"What a fascinating prospect," said Wheaton. "If the experiment weren't so devastating . . ."

"Father," said Deborah. "That is *not* a fascinating prospect, it's genocidal."

"Genocide is what we saw them do to us," said Noxon. "Preventive diplomacy is what we plan to do to them. Unless it doesn't work. In which case, yes. Xenocide, the entire species wiped out, and without an apology or regret. Because when it's us or them, I choose us."

"Genetically speaking," said Wheaton, "it's the only rational choice."

"And if we fail," said Noxon, "and only they survive, then that's survival of the fittest, yes?"

Deborah looked away.

"They were the ones that determined not to leave us any option for survival," said Noxon. "I hope to be better than they are. But I don't see that leaving them any chance to destroy us makes us 'better.' It only makes us dead."

"Absolutely right," said Wheaton. "But you don't suppose we could kidnap a tribe of Erectids and bring them along?"

"Tempting as that prospect is," said Noxon, "what if we kidnapped the very tribe that was supposed to evolve into us? Or Neanderthals?"

"Well, these paths you see—surely you could *check*."

"I don't have enough lifetime to spend it tracing every path of every member of an Erectid bloodline across a million years."

"Oh," said Wheaton. "Oh, I see. Yes, that does bring mathematics into it."

"Besides, we already know what evolution does to Erectids. It lets them spread across the whole planet, developing into at least three human species that interbreed a little, until Sapiens emerge as they are today. They've had their evolution. So have these aliens."

"Are you so sure that we're better than the aliens?" asked Deborah.

"Maybe they create beautiful music," said Noxon. "Maybe their paintings are exquisite. But they didn't give us a chance to admire them. So even if we're not as good or decorative or accomplished or clever as these Destroyers, if I can whip their asses, their asses will be whipped."

"And that's how you see us," said the alpha mouse.

"You've proven your lack of interest in keeping your word and cooperating with me," said Noxon.

"What?" said Deborah.

"He's talking to the mice again," said Ram Odin. "You can tell by his tone of voice. When he sounds like he's talking to an ignorant child, then he's speaking to us."

Noxon ignored the gibe. "I can't make final decisions till we get to the alien world. We're going to approach them now, a hundred thousand years or so before they 'discover' us. Maybe their technology will already be irresistibly more advanced than ours. If it is, I hope I have enough time to jump our ship back in time until they aren't able to endanger us. I could use your help in monitoring the ship's computers to see if they're being interfered with. The expendable can't really help us with that because he's part of that computer system."

"We could do that," said the alpha mouse.

"But if I let you loose with the computers," said Noxon, "you could kill all our colonists. You could shut down life support."

"We would run out of oxygen and die before you even felt light-headed," said the mouse.

"Meaning that you've already thought of a plan to circumvent that problem," said Noxon.

"Well," said the alpha, "we're not sure any of those plans would work."

"Meaning that you're absolutely certain they would work," said Noxon. "So here's the bargain I'm offering. Once we get far enough back that we're technologically superior to them, then I'll decide—*I* will decide, not a committee—whether to establish a human colony there. That will depend partly on how compatible the existing plant proteins are with our bodies. And partly on whether we see any reason to hope that they might evolve a society that is capable of seeing us as a sentient species worthy of respect."

"I know *we* respect you," said the alpha mouse.

"You regard us as your toys, to be pulled apart and put back together at will," said Noxon. "I'm living proof of that."

"The facemask part of you wasn't our idea at all," said the alpha mouse.

"Your saying that makes me pretty sure that it was," said Noxon.

"Really," said the mouse. "All Vadesh. Well, him and Ram Odin. It's in the ship's log."

"Which you can rewrite at will," said Noxon.

"Only sometimes," said the alpha mouse. "And we don't do it, because we count on the log to tell us what happened in erased timestreams. You have to keep some things sacred."

"Here's the deal," said Noxon. "The survival of both our species is at stake. If we don't stop these aliens, they wipe out us *and* you. When we get to the alien world, I will do *whatever* it takes to prevent them from invading and destroying us. I will take *no* risk of their removing from me the ability to destroy them. Which means that I'm not going to try to negotiate with the very civilization that sent these invaders to wipe us out of existence. *That* civilization is already dead, period. I'm not going to leave even the slightest chance of its ever coming into being."

"Very wise choice," said the alpha mouse.

"You do understand that I can do the same thing with you," said Noxon. "I can go back to Garden, jump back in time, and prevent you from ever having been bred."

"The expendables will never let you," said the alpha mouse.

"I only have to show them the logs that record your absolute unreliability, and your ability to manipulate them, and they'll cooperate with me fully. You know it's true."

He let the mice think about that for a few seconds.

"There are several things we don't know and can't know till we get there. We don't know if our ship will jump the fold in twenty copies or not. If it does, we'll have twenty chances to establish viable colonies on their world, divided into wallfolds, just as on Garden."

"Nineteen," said Ram Odin. "I thought it was nineteen."

"Every ship will contain a Ram Odin and a Noxon," said Noxon. "And a couple of dozen mice. So if there's a backward-moving ship, it will have me there to turn it around, and it'll have the mice to see if they can detach it from the original outbound ship without the ship having to come all the way back to Earth."

"Makes sense," said Ram Odin.

"Only to the insane," said Wheaton.

"Maybe we can preserve the native biota to a greater degree

than it was preserved on Garden," said Noxon. "Maybe we can preserve the ancestors of these monster aliens, and help to shape their evolution so it doesn't get so dangerous. We *know* the ship's computers can be programmed to prevent the development of high technology because they did it on Garden."

"Or we can wipe out all the native life and make a new Earth," said the alpha mouse.

"Whether or not we have nineteen or twenty ships," said Noxon, "we can create as many wallfield generators as we want, and the expendables to tend them, right?"

"Yes," said the alpha mouse.

"Yes," said Ram Odin. "Very interesting. Wallfolds no matter what."

"So the deal I offer is this. All the wallfolds have the same technology cap as on Garden. Every wallfold has an expendable or two. But we create enough wallfolds that besides having enough for several—or twenty—human colonies, we also have one or two wallfolds which have only mice as their sentient occupants."

"How generous," said the alpha mouse.

"Irony is still a lie," said Noxon. "Hear me out. We also have a couple of human colonies that are *shared* with mice. Joint colonies. To see what happens. To see if we and you can grow and develop together, cooperatively or at least without slaughtering each other."

"Unlikely," said the alpha mouse.

"Why not?" said Ram Odin.

"I think it's very likely," said Noxon. "Especially because the ship's computers will be programmed to wipe out any wallfold where either the humans or the mice find a way to exterminate the other species."

"Maybe we can interbreed," said the alpha mouse.

"I hope not," said Noxon. "And we also have two or three wallfolds where the aliens are allowed to continue their evolutionary development—but with the same technology cap. At least one of *those* will also have mice."

"The aliens should *all* have mice," said the alpha mouse.

"They will have expendables. If possible, expendables redesigned to look like them. If not, then the same ones we have. They'll all be supervised."

"And that's the plan?" said the alpha mouse. "You thought of this all by yourself?"

"It's the obvious way to proceed," said Noxon. "Everybody gets a home."

"A reservation," said the alpha mouse.

"A place to develop independent of the others."

"But with a cap on what we can achieve," said the alpha mouse.

"Not really," said Noxon. "Because you'll still have the ability you have right now—to move objects and manipulate things as tiny as genes, in both space and time."

"They can do that?" asked Deborah.

"They're very talented," said Ram Odin.

"So everybody is completely at their mercy," said Wheaton.

"That's why we're making this deal now, while there are still only twenty of them," said Noxon.

"But they'll lie," said Ram Odin.

"I think they won't," said Noxon. "Because they can see that this is the best long-term protection for their descendants as well as ours."

"Why?" said Ram. "How? We can't develop our tech past a certain point, while theirs is invisible and already far beyond anything we can do."

"Because every human colony will start with a Ram Odin and a Noxon," said Noxon. "And that means that we'll have the power to go back in time and undo whatever the mice do wrong. Or even undo the original placement of the mice into the colonies. Because part of the deal is this: The mice go into stasis during the colony founding, and they don't get colonies of their own until at least three hundred years. And the release of the mice into each wallfold they're allowed to enter will take place in public, and under circumstances that will make it easy for future human timeshapers to come back and prevent it."

"That's not foolproof," said Wheaton. "I can think of—"

"So can the mice," said Noxon. "But whatever they think of, we can probably think of a way to get around them and undo it. *If* we choose to spend our futures in stupid competition with each other. But maybe we won't. Maybe the mice will see that keeping promises works out better for them than going to war with timeshaping humans."

"I see it already," said the alpha mouse. "And so will all my descendants."

"Come on," said Noxon. "The reason your testes aren't visible is because you've been castrated. You won't have any descendants."

"Not me *personally*," said the alpha mouse. "I think of all the babies in their uteruses to be my children, so to speak."

"Well, Father of Great Nations, answer me: Will you accept this plan and abide by whatever decision I make when we reach the alien world?"

"I accept the plan and I promise to abide by your decision," said the alpha mouse.

"How is that different from what you would say if you were already determined to break every promise and take over the world and the ship and everything?" asked Noxon.

"It isn't different," said the alpha mouse. "But I mean it. And you'll see that I mean it because I will no longer seize every opportunity to subvert you."

"So our alliance is set?" asked Noxon.

"We have only one condition," said the alpha mouse.

"Which is?" asked Noxon.

"You take at least one of us into the future with you and let her connect with your computer system when the aliens take it over. So we can make some assessment of what they're capable of."

"No," said Noxon.

"Seriously? Why not? Knowledge is essential."

"Knowledge is power," said Noxon. "You've been trying for thousands of generations to break into the programming of the ships that control Garden, in order to reprogram them to allow you through the Wall and to let you develop higher tech than they currently permit. And you've failed. But these aliens broke into our computer systems, took them over, and used them to destroy us. You want to see how it's done."

Silence for a few moments. Then: "That was truly *not* my plan," said the alpha mouse. "If it *had* been my plan, then that means I was already acting in bad faith and our alliance was already shattered. But I was acting in good faith. I really need to understand what their capabilities are. We will be much safer approaching their planet if I have some idea of how to resist them and keep them from taking over our ship remotely."

Noxon thought for a while. Finally he spoke to Ram Odin. "I think I'm going to take one of them forward in time to watch the alien invasion while hooked into the communications network."

"I thought your argument against that was excellent," said Ram Odin. "Flawless, in fact."

"It was," said Noxon.

"So what did they say to change your mind?" asked Ram.

"More promises," said Noxon, "which are exactly what they'd say if they're telling the truth *or* if they're lying."

"So you have no idea," said Ram Odin.

"You have to leap sometimes," said Noxon. "You have to trust."

"And if you're wrong to trust them?" asked Ram.

"It's in their self-interest to keep the alliance at least until we get to the alien world," said Noxon. "At least until we've eliminated that threat. After that—well, we'll see."

"That's it? We'll see?"

"All alliances between rivals take that form," said Noxon. "We work together as long as it makes sense to do so—and then see how the other side behaves when some of the incentives for cooperation are removed."

"Very wise," said Wheaton.

"It's time to get these mice out of here," said Noxon. "Come on, all of you climb up on me. The mice," he added quickly. "Talking only to the mice."

They scampered up into his clothing. The facemask remained aware of every one of them. "You won't regret this," said the alpha mouse.

"Good," said Noxon, already regretting it, yet sure there was no better way. "Now the rest of you, kindly take my hands. We're jumping back into the future one last time. I believe we have a car parked nearby waiting to take us back to civilization."

The decision about the mice had been entirely Noxon's to make. But since Deborah and Anthropologist Wheaton were not crucial now to any course of action, he could leave their future up to them.

"You don't have a place on Earth anymore," said Noxon. "There's a girl with eyes using your name and fingerprints, Deborah, and a charming philologist who has done rather a good job of keeping a dying discipline alive who needs no competing Dr. Wheaton."

"Especially since there's no record of my degrees or my publications," said Wheaton. "It rather blocks my ability to influence what passes for thinking among this sorry crop of anthropologists."

"I can offer you each your choice of improbable futures. You can voyage to the alien world and take part in the discussions, though not the decisions, about what we will do to prevent the destruction of Earth. Or you can voyage to Garden, my home, where I can promise you will have access to the full range of studies of—"

Deborah interrupted him. "For me, there's no choice but the world where I can get new eyes."

"You do understand," said Noxon, "that you might be unable to control the facemask. It's not a matter of what humans call 'strength of will.' Some of the strongest people I know have been unable to tame the mask. If you get eyes, but cease to be yourself, it would be a poor bargain."

"Then you'll go back in time and prevent it," said Deborah.

"But there you'll be in a world without replacement batteries, without charging stations."

"They're solar. We're not Neanderthals." She gave Wheaton an exaggerated wink, to prevent his objection to her pejorative use of "Neanderthal."

"They're solar, but not unbreakable," said Noxon. "Garden is not a very good place to be blind."

"I will bring spares," said Deborah.

"And the technology of our era *is* available," said Wheaton. "Each starship should have the ability to replicate her glasses."

"I didn't think of that," said Noxon.

Deborah raised a hand. "Something else must be said, however. Just because I will go to Garden or nowhere, that doesn't mean *you* must go with me, Father. The chance to study the evolution of two alien species—I think that not only will you *enjoy* that voyage more, you might actually be able to offer crucial insights as Noxon makes his decisions."

"What insights?" said Wheaton. "I know Erectids and other anthropes, and nothing more."

"You know how to see evolutionary patterns," said Deborah. "You know how natural selection works, how different societies promote the survival of some traits and not others. And there have been no human scientists on that road before you."

"Do I detect a desire to be rid of this old man?" asked Wheaton with a laugh.

"Do I detect a barely-concealed plea for validation?" asked Deborah. "You know I love you, and I'd like to think your work would not be possible without me to clerk for you. But that isn't true, and besides, you can have the ship pop out an extra expendable to take notes and look things up for you. Much more efficiently and accurately than I would."

"Very well, I suppose I can *work* without you," said Wheaton. But he looked grumpy, and that seemed to be a concealment of an underlying hurt.

"One world offers me eyes," said Deborah, "and the other offers you a chance to do seminal work. If Noxon and Ram succeed in changing the future of that world, you will be the *only* scientist to observe the alien society as it existed before human interference."

"We won't be doing much observation," said Noxon. "Particularly if we reach them at a time when they're already technologically ahead of us. We'll skedaddle instantly then."

"I've found that brave dead scientists don't contribute as much as prudent live ones," said Wheaton. "I'll study what there's time to study."

"It's where you want to go," said Deborah.

"All things being equal. But . . . nineteen wallfolds. A species of merpeople! Either world will do for me."

Deborah made no answer, even though both Noxon and Wheaton looked at her, waiting.

"You know I have a choice myself," said Noxon. "There are two of me now. One who went through the nuclear blast but managed to heal from it. One who didn't."

"Which are you?" asked Deborah.

"I'm the one who was warned and saved from the blast," said Noxon. "But my twin and I have worked it out. It's quite simple, really. There's some risk that he suffered damage to some or all of his gametes. The facemask heals damage it can detect, but it's possible for gametes to be motile and yet not viable, or viable but mutated."

"Ouch," said Deborah.

"Mine, however, were unharmed," said Noxon. "Not that there's *no* risk of mutation or deformation—any gamete can be damaged by the vicissitudes of chance. But . . ."

"So *you*, Mister Pristine Sperm, will go where you think your seed will be most needed," said Deborah.

"Not quite," said Noxon. "Chances are that both of us will be able to reproduce successfully. But we want to invest my superior odds in a particular way."

"I'm not sure why this is a matter for discussion with us," said Wheaton.

"Excuse me, sir, but I'm discussing the possibility of marriage to your daughter," said Noxon. "And explaining to you both why my twin and I have decided that where she goes, there go *I*. Not because we *expect* anything, or *require* anything. We're both quite smitten with your daughter. In fact, we're both very much in love with her. So on the chance that she might at some future point reciprocate . . ."

"Passage through the Wall apparently makes you awkward and stuffy in any language," said Wheaton.

"We want to offer her the best chance of creating a family with healthy, whole, unmutated children."

"Apart from that little genetic twist about being able to fiddle with time," said Wheaton.

"We're not sure whether that's a plus or not," said Noxon. "We do know that while pathfinding emerged at an early age, time manipulation came along much later. I don't think that she would find a nursing baby suddenly disappearing and then reappearing at another time."

"So you look at my breasts and think of attaching a baby to them?" asked Deborah.

Noxon looked at her steadily, trying to conceal his consternation. "I assure you that I'm a normal human male in most respects. But I'm an uxorious male, I believe the professor would say, and so I don't have the alpha male's assumption that all women are faunching to mate with me."

"Only to nurse your babies."

"Only to wish the babies they nurse to be healthy and not particularly weird."

"What if I like your twin better than you?" asked Deborah. "Pretty cheeky, to take the decision out of my hands."

"We're quite sure that you can't tell the difference between us at this point," said Noxon. "And also sure that our feelings toward you are identical, because we were in love with you long before we duplicated."

"When, exactly, did this overpowering passion first . . . overpower you?" asked Deborah.

"I first noticed it when you inconveniently got yourself killed by an Erectid stone."

"Clumsy of me," said Deborah.

"You didn't follow instructions," said Noxon. "And I knew, rationally, that I *should* consider the option of leaving that unfortunate event alone. But I did not consider it. I didn't actually give a rat's ass what *else* happened. Even if it would make saving Garden more difficult, I was not going to leave you dead."

"How gallant," said Deborah.

"I thought of going on without you and I found that unbearable," said Noxon.

"Yet because one of you is going to Garden and the other to the planet Hell, or whatever we're calling it, one of you *must* go on without me."

"Yes," said Noxon. "And so we decided, rationally, that we would offer you ourself at our best. My best. And the other would go about his tragic, meaningless existence without you."

"And now you're being ironic."

"I'm being quite sincere," said Noxon. "My twin is quite broken up about it. But he was the one who insisted that we make the decision on this basis—this *rational* basis—rather than drawing straws. Or making *you* choose, which would have been arbitrary and cruel to you."

"Which of you farts in his sleep the most?" asked Deborah.

"We've never measured," said Noxon. "But if you prefer that as a basis for the decision . . ."

"I believe you'd do it," said Deborah.

"You're the one who brought relative nocturnal flatulence into the discussion," said Noxon.

"I had a condition once," said Wheaton. "I tried eating an Erectid diet, back when we still had some unfortunate and inaccurate ideas about what they ate. Deborah may have an exaggerated idea of the importance of avoiding flatus in her pursuit of happiness. It only lasted a few weeks, but—"

"It lasted nearly a year, despite my begging," said Deborah. "Noxon, I'm touched, you must understand, but . . ."

"Deborah Wheaton," said Noxon, "I'm not really proposing marriage to you. Not yet. I know you can't possibly give an answer now. I'm just saying that our decision rests upon your decision. Unless you are sure, right now, that no man with a mask like this can . . ."

"As I was saying, before you interrupted—and please don't go back in time and stop yourself from interrupting me, because that might create yet a third Noxon, and I'd have to choose between the rude interrupter and the even ruder correcter of interrupters—"

"As you were saying," Wheaton prompted her.

"I'm still sorting out whether I'm in love with you or the amazing things you can do. Human females are attracted to power. That's simply a fact. And so my feelings of attachment to you are suspect, because they began immediately upon my learning of your ability to vanish and reappear, and then to go back in time."

"Did my saving your life help or hurt?" asked Noxon.

"It complicated matters, of course," said Deborah. "Now I have to sort out how much of being in love with you stems from gratitude, and how much from girlish awe at a champion alpha male, and how much comes from my enjoyment of your quirky personality and the prospect of having you as the father of my children."

"Please wrestle with this quandary as long as you like," said Noxon. "I'll be content with whichever source of love you decide to go with."

"Oh, just tell him yes and get it over with," said Wheaton. "It's been obvious from the start that you two were made for each other."

"I'm used to keeping company with a genius," said Deborah. "An irascible one, but . . ."

"I'm not irascible," said Noxon. "In fact, I'm downright rascible."

"That's a false etymology," said Wheaton. "The 'ir' in 'irascible' is not a negator, like the 'ir' in 'irresponsible' or 'irrespective.' The root of 'irascible' is the Latin 'ira,' meaning 'wrath,' and—"

Deborah stopped her father with a kiss on his cheek. "I'm sure he was making a joke, not asserting an etymology, Father."

"Why are you kissing *me*?" Wheaton retorted. "*He's* the one most in need of kissing, I think."

"Now he'll think I'm kissing him out of obedience to you,

instead of as the result of my own uncontrollable ardor," said Deborah.

Whereupon Noxon sprang from his chair, took her in his arms, and kissed her without regard for her immediate motive. She responded with as much enthusiasm as was appropriate with her father present. Which was to say that, upon repetition, in private, the whole business seemed to work much better.

CHAPTER 28

Face to Face

Param insisted on visiting the battlefield immediately after victory was assured. "They have to see me there," she told Olivenko. "I'm in no danger, but the soldiers need to see me there with the dead, with the wounded."

She was relieved that before Olivenko could answer, both Rigg and Loaf came in on her side. "She's the one they fought for," said Rigg. "They'll love her for it," said Loaf. And Olivenko could only smile and say, "I salute the Queen-in-the-Tent for her courage and generosity of spirit. I would never advise her to go against her own noble instincts."

"Olivenko, you are so full of poo," said Param.

"I meant every word," said Olivenko, smiling even more broadly.

Now, the sights and smells made her wish she had not been

so noble, or that someone had argued against this. Every corpse told a story to her soul: This was someone's son. This man had hopes and dreams. Even if his only joy was to drink and carouse, those days are over.

"I can see that the smell bothers you," said Loaf quietly. "But I assure you, today the bodies are still fresh and the rot has not set in. Tomorrow I would urge you strongly not to come. You would vomit, and that is *not* something your people need to see."

Param had been trying *not* to think of vomit, since, as with yawning, the very thought made it more likely she would do it. But she understood his point, and stopped allowing herself to imagine these as living men. She cast her eyes toward them, but did not allow the sights to register. She was not here to learn about all the positions a broken body can collapse into when death comes by sudden violence. She was here to be seen caring about the fallen. So she fixed the proper expression of sympathy and barely-contained grief on her face, and allowed herself to be led where there were the most spectators to see how the Queen-in-the-Tent loved her soldiers.

And when a particularly pungent spot made her gorge rise, she allowed herself to burst into tears so she could be led away from the malodorous spot. Thus she prevented herself from throwing up and disgracing herself. Vomiting was not sympathy. Nausea and nobility were not compatible. But weeping went well with both sympathy and nobility, especially because she was a woman. She noticed that Umbo matched her step for step, but did not weep. She didn't know if this was because he had seen worse, or smelled worse, or cared less, or was simply stronger than she was. Probably all of those were true.

This is why she was on the battlefield when the emissary arrived from Mother's army. Param did not recognize the man, but that did not surprise her. In Flacommo's house she had seen only sycophants, and mostly those who were in favor with the People's Revolutionary Council. None of those would be in General Haddamander's army.

"Hagia Sessaminiak sees no reason for this war to continue," said the emissary. "She is ready to recognize her daughter, Param Sessamin, as Queen-in-the-Tent-of-Light, and her husband as Umbo Sissamik."

The names were right: "Sissamik" as the male consort of a reigning queen; "Sessaminiak" as a former queen, now rightfully deposed. Deposed, *not* abdicating voluntarily; that would have been Sessaminissa, and it was a decision that could be rescinded. Mother was saying that she was prepared to recognize that she had been thrown down, and could not rise again.

"I am sure that Mother has terms and conditions to propose," said Param to the emissary.

She noticed that none of her own people showed the slightest sign that they were worried she would say the wrong thing or agree to too many concessions—or, even worse, needlessly prolong the war out of some point of pride.

"Hagia Sessaminiak wishes to meet with her daughter and her son face to face to make the formal surrender," she said. "Whether her consort, Haddamander Citizen, should be with her is a point on which she will gladly bend to your will."

"Such a meeting will not be pleasant for anyone, but it is wise for there to be a public ritual of surrender, and for Mother to do it personally," said Param. "I commend her courage and generosity to our people. Let the time and place be worked out with General Olivenko or someone he designates. I will attend, as will my brother. Now you must excuse me. I am visiting wounded soldiers, and must not be delayed any further."

With that, Param swept away, leaving Olivenko to deal with the logistics of the meeting.

That evening, in the meeting of the council of war, it was Param who broached the obvious problem. "Of course it's a trap," she said. "I'm assuming it's an assassination attempt, though they must know it's impossible to kill us."

"It is far from impossible," said Olivenko, "and you can be sure they've been wracking their brains for a long time, devising a foolproof plan."

"And they are not fools," said Param, "so it may work. Therefore, before Rigg and I go, we will publicly invest Umbo as Sissaminkesh, heir to the Tent of Light if both Rigg and I die."

Umbo gave a bark of laughter. "If you die," he said, "I might as well call myself Ring-in-the-Sky for all the attention anyone will pay to me as king."

"They aren't going to die," said Square. "My Masks and I will never allow it."

"You and the Masks will not be there," said Param. "It will be only Rigg and myself, along with a few witnesses. There will be no fighting."

"But if it's an assassination attempt!" Square cried.

"It *is* an assassination attempt," said Param.

"Or a kidnapping," said Rigg.

"But between us, Rigg and I can get ourselves out of anything. All that anyone else would be is a distraction, someone for them to hold hostage in order to get us not to resist them."

"No one can stand against facemask soldiers," said Square.

"So far, you're right," said Loaf. "But imagine that you fought, and were victorious. Then everyone would say it was Captain Toad and his Masks who broke the truce and slaughtered Hagia's men."

"There will be witnesses!"

"Their witnesses will say whatever they've been told to say," said Loaf. "And their supporters will believe any lie."

"There has been enough killing," said Param. "They will try to kill us, and they will fail."

"Or they'll succeed," said Rigg. "Either way, they'll be the ones who betray their word, not us."

"You speak blithely of dying," said Loaf, "because you've never done it."

"Neither have you," said Rigg.

"But I've seen it more often," said Loaf, "and I've never seen any of my friends who was happy to do it. Or any of my enemies, for that matter—they seemed to be quite reluctant to begin, and it took a good deal of exertion to get them to change their minds."

"We won't die," said Param.

"Everyone dies," said Loaf. "But it's also true that there's no escort we could give you that would improve your chances. What we *will* do is station Umbo in a location that you know about, but they do not—right, Umbo? You'll go there in the past and then jump forward?"

"Will I be able to see what happens?" asked Umbo.

"If you're close enough to see," said Loaf, "I imagine you'll be close enough to be seen. What matters is that *they'll* know where you are. So if things go badly wrong, but one of them survives, they can go to where you are and put a message into your hands, warning you to warn *them* about the danger. Then either they don't go after all, or they go in prepared."

"Good plan," said Umbo. "But I also want to be able to see."

"We'll look for a hiding place that can do that," said Rigg. "Once we have some idea of where it will be."

It turned out to be a place that was far from any of Haddamander's army camps, far from any major cities. As they approached along a road in deep woods, Rigg looked at the tangle of paths up ahead. "I think they've prepared this place especially for us, to block our escape."

Param was not surprised. "How can they block an escape into the past?" she asked.

"They dug a deep, wide pit," said Rigg. "I can see the paths of the men who dug it out. If I jump us back into the past, it'll either be underground, killing us instantly, or it'll be in the midst of the men digging—who were warned, I'm sure, to watch for us to appear suddenly among them."

"Interesting," said Param. "And we can be sure they'll have barriers made of stone or metal to keep me contained."

"They promised," said Olivenko, "to have no one carrying

any kind of metal or stone larger than a single coin within a walk from the place."

"It'll be interesting to see what they've devised," said Param. "They made their plans based on what they knew of our abilities. But those have changed. Noxon and I worked on my slicing. I can go backward, for one thing. And I can slice forward at such a pace that they could pass iron bars through me for hours without my heating up more than a degree or two."

"And if they find some way to defeat that," said Rigg, "remember that I have a facemask and I'm trained as a fighter now. Not just the boy they knew in Aressa Sessamo."

"Armed only with a knife," said Loaf.

"A knife in the hands of a masker is like a hundred arrows," said Rigg.

"Is that a quotation from something?" asked Olivenko.

"From me," said Rigg. "It's a thing I said while approaching the trap laid by my mother and General Citizen."

"I'll write it down," said Olivenko, "so other people can say it again, quoting you."

"That's assuming anybody ever reads anything you write," said Param. "I'm sorry, Olivenko, but scholars are rarely read by anyone but other scholars."

"But I'm a victorious general," said Olivenko. "And Rigg is a great timeshaper. Even if they don't read *my* works, they'll want to remember him and his."

"Enough," said Loaf. "I think when we crest this rise, they'll be visible to us and us to them."

"Time for you to all drop back into the past," said Param.

"Not yet," said Loaf. "Not until we've seen the place. So Umbo can come back and hide and watch."

They reached the crest and looked down into a narrow valley, with a deep pit in the middle. The pit was nearly filled by a large one-story house with a sturdy-looking roof.

"First time it rains," said Rigg, "that pit's going to fill with water."

"Maybe they're hoping it'll do that, and we'll drown while slicing," said Param.

"Don't point, Umbo. Just tell them where you'll be."

"The trees on the north end of the pit," said Umbo. "I'll pop in there just about two minutes from now."

"We'll notice the spot as we go down to the house," said Param. "Thank you, Umbo. Thanks to all of you. Either we'll come out of this with a treaty of surrender—*their* surrender—or we'll have Umbo popping up in front of us to tell us not to do this."

But Umbo was already gone. As were the others. Param and Rigg walked down the hill without anyone close at hand. A few witnesses had been sent ahead and were seated with a few unarmed men from Haddamander's army on a platform overlooking the pit.

"There's no one at all inside the house," said Rigg. "No one in hiding places, not even in the roof."

"I'd say Mother and Haddamander missed some opportunities there."

"Or they've had good reports on Captain Toad's ability to see where everyone is hiding."

"You've never been Captain Toad, as far as they know," said

541

Param. "Square did the job, the only time *they* remember."

"Ah, but he has a facemask, and nobody can hide from a face-mask. Not if they're breathing or their heart is beating."

A voice came from the platform of observers. "Hagia Sessaminiak is approaching from the other side! Please wait to enter the house until she is there!"

Param and Rigg waited outside the open door. They could see right through the large room to the door on the other side as it opened and light streamed in. There stood Mother, looking as she always had, and a step or two behind her, General Haddamander Citizen, a bit more posh than in his old People's Army uniform.

Mother and Haddamander stepped into the room. "Please come in," Mother said.

Param stepped forward, holding tightly to Rigg's hand. If she had to slice time, she didn't want to have to search for his hand before disappearing.

Mother and Haddamander walked to the center of the room. Mother held up a paper. "Here is our instrument of surrender. For all of us to sign."

"Perhaps if we had a table, Mother," said Param.

Haddamander turned and shouted toward the other door. "Bring in the table!"

"We wanted the room empty when you arrived," said Mother. "So you'd see there was no trap."

"Which means," murmured Param, "that there's a trap." She spoke so softly that she couldn't hear her own voice—but she knew that Rigg's facemask would let him hear.

He squeezed her hand in reply.

A servant came into the room, carrying a very small table with only a single leg. He fitted it into a prepared notch in the floor.

Param wasn't a genius of mechanical reasoning, but even she could see that the table would easily serve as a lever now, if there was some sort of control embedded in the floor. But could they really expect she and Rigg would fall for such an obvious device?

Well, yes, they could, because they *were* falling for it, not in ignorance, but with eyes wide open.

"What a clever little table," said Param. "Mother, you planned for everything."

"Come and sign, my dears. When the war is over, I hope we can sit and have a wonderful conversation."

"That would be very nice, Mother," said Rigg.

Param and Rigg now stood right up against the table.

Haddamander, reached across the small table, gripped the side nearest Rigg and Param, and pulled the whole thing toward himself.

There were sounds of shifting metal from the walls, the ceiling, the floor.

"Good-bye, Mother," said Rigg.

Param took that as her cue, and began slicing time, not the way she used to, but so deeply that Mother and Haddamander were barely a blur as they threaded their way out of the room.

No one else came in. No one had to.

For the shifting metal had been a series of counterweights and controls. Thick slabs of metal rose up out of the floor and down from the ceilings. None were right where the table was — nothing would have struck their bodies immediately. But if Param were

543

still slicing time the way she used to, she would have recoiled from this metal, because the pain of trying to pass through it would have been excruciating.

It was possible to thread their way out the way Mother and Haddamander had gone, but Param was quite sure there were archers ready to shoot them if they appeared through that door.

To go through any other door, however, would have forced them to pass through metal.

Even at this level of slicing, there was some heat from passing through the metal bars. But it was trivial—rather as passing through plaster walls had been, back in Flacommo's house.

The only problem with slicing time at this pace was that their movement across the floor was maddeningly slow. Especially considering that only moments after Mother and Haddamander had left, the house caught fire.

The wood of the house must have been soaked in something highly inflammable. The fire seemed to start everywhere at once.

Param sliced time even more sharply.

The fire was out in only a few moments, though they felt the searing heat of it, like one blast of hot air from standing too close to a furnace.

The ceiling collapsed onto them—with all its metal bars and the heavy framework holding it together from the top. But slicing time this drastically, even the frame caused them little pain.

Days and nights passed by in flashes of light and dark. It rained and then stopped raining, but only a little water got to them. It occurred to Param that she ought to be thirsty. But no. She had only been slicing time for a few minutes. The world around her might have gone through half a year by now, but . . .

Snow fell around them and lingered for a few minutes. Then again, deeper, and staying longer. When winter ended, they were only halfway through the forest of metal bars and burnt wood.

How had this looked to Umbo? They went into the house. A few moments later, it burst into flame . . . and they never came out. Umbo would know, of course, what they were capable of doing, and that her time-slicing could easily take all this in stride. Still, there was a limit to how long he would wait.

Had he gone back to join the others and decide what to do? Or had he already decided to warn them not to go in? Fire and an elaborate metal framework — not worth the effort? Perhaps Param and Rigg had already been warned, had *not* come into the house this time through. But *this* iteration of Param and Rigg had not been warned, and so they would continue in this futile evasion of a danger that their alternate selves would never face.

I was once murdered in the Odinfolders' library, by the mice, Param remembered. She remembered it as information she had been told, for Rigg had shown up to rescue her before the mice could bring in the metal bar to kill her. But there had been a version of her that died. Rigg had seen the body. Her corpse. Nobody in *this* timestream had ever had to deal with burying that body, because *this* was the timestream in which she did not die in the library. Instead, this was the timestream in which she would die here in this burnt-out, metal-lined pit. For there were archers stationed around the edges of the pit, and torches burned every night to make sure they did not escape under cover of darkness. Mother was not giving up. She and Haddamander had learned their lesson back at the Wall, when they had waited for days and yet Param and Umbo had never come to the ground where they jumped from the rock. Mother was going to have her assassins wait till the end of the world, if that's what it took.

The end of the world.

Winter again, as they reached the edge of the burnt-out building and passed beyond the metal frame.

And still the archers waited, watching. Still there were men with heavy metal swords waiting just beyond them.

They were into their third summer of slicetime as they faced the spot where once a wooden stairway had carried them down into the pit. The stairway was gone, taken away as the observation platform had been. The walls of the pit were cut sheer, unclimbable—especially unclimbable as they were, clasping hands. If they let go of each other to climb, they would become visible to the archers. If Rigg jumped them back in time, they'd either be buried over their heads in undisturbed earth, or surrounded by the workmen digging the pit or building the house.

Rigg turned to face her, and winter came again as they changed hands and stood facing the other way, toward the south now, their faces into the sun as it rose, fell, rose, fell, sliding across the sky like butter across a hot pan.

She could see that Rigg was shaking his head and tightening his grip. She did not understand why. Until there was a sudden bright flash and a wave of heat washed over them. Far more intense and longer-lasting than the heat of the burning house.

The world was ending. They were slicing time right through the coming of the Destroyers.

Rigg had kept count of time. He had been expecting them. He had shaken his head to tell her not to stop slicing.

The forest all around them had been knocked down by the distant blast, but the wall of the pit had sheltered them. The heat had been so intense that the fallen trees burnt up like paper, and even the metal inside the pit had grown soft, had bent and collapsed toward the ground like sugar candy melting in the rain.

But they had only endured a few microseconds of the heat before it passed away, and so they were not consumed like paper or melted like sugar.

This is the end of the world. And we, the unwarned ones, must continue to exist like this, surviving what killed most others.

But not *all.* For the people who had written the Future Books to the Odinfolders had hidden somewhere to write of what happened and then send the books into the past to give warning. So . . . how did they die, those who managed to survive the first blast? What would happen now, to end their lives?

Rigg pulled on her gently and they walked away from the edge of the pit, whose lee had protected them. They did not walk back into the ruins of the house. Param wondered why they did not simply return to regular time. Why keep slicing? There were no archers at the edges of the pit *now.* They had been blown away by the first shock wave of the blast, and no doubt quickly burned when the heat arrived.

Out of the lee of the pit wall, they had a good view of sky in all directions, and Param joined Rigg in scanning the sky for . . . for something. Had he somehow used the knife or the jewels to summon a flyer from the buried starship? No, impossible. The Destroyers would have found the buried ships right away and eliminated them. The Visitors from Earth might have been surprised by the nineteen wallfolds, each with an exact copy of what had left Earth as a single starship. But the Destroyers came already knowing. The ships were gone; the expendables and flyers and orbiters were gone.

But there were people in caves who might still live. People in pits. Were the Destroyers so thorough that they would now come to search for the survivors and kill them, too? Were they so angry or fearful of the inhabitants of Garden that they could not bear the thought of even one staying alive? Even this brother and sister who survived one assassination attempt already?

There was something moving across the sky. Far too fast to be a bird. Yet it looked nothing like the flyers from the starships. It was smaller—that became clear as it came closer.

Rigg resumed walking. That made sense—even slicing time at this pace, if they held still they would be visible.

But the aircraft came directly toward them. It was drawn by something else. Not sight, because they were invisible. Or were they? Could this machine "see" what was only in existence for one nanosecond per second? Or was it sensing the heat their bodies gave off? It must be faint, with such brief existence. Yet it might be detectable.

The aircraft came to the pit and hovered over it. It was much smaller than the flyers. It began to settle toward the ground.

Rigg was tugging on her hand, signaling her. Winding his hand around so she'd know he wanted her to keep walking. Well, of course she would!

Then he let go of her hand.

In that instant he became visible to whatever or whoever was in that aircraft. She did not stop, though. Her slicing continued and so did her walking. Whatever he was doing, he did not want to have to worry about her becoming visible. He was the one with the facemask, the ability to jump back and forth in time; and he was body enough to explain their heat signature, or whatever else had drawn the aircraft.

Now that he was not attached to her, he moved around in a blur as other people had done.

The aircraft dropped to the ground like a stone. But no, it must have settled gently; its descent only seemed like plummeting because Param was slicing time.

The side of the aircraft opened up and . . .

Param had expected a man to come out.

Instead, it was something low and sleek, many-limbed. Like a roach, like a centipede, a fast-moving thick-bodied short-legged spider. It charged straight at Rigg.

Only Rigg wasn't there. Someone beside Rigg pushed him out of the way. And the someone was . . . Rigg.

He had jumped back in time and pushed his former self out of the way faster than his reflexes, even enhanced by the facemask, could have done. Now there were two Riggs, each armed only with a jeweled knife.

And now there were four Riggs. Eight. To Param they seemed

to appear rapidly, but of course it must have been at least minutes between appearances; maybe an hour. The fight was a blur to her. She wanted to slow down her slicing in order to watch, and she did so, but not so much that she was in any danger of being seen.

At least two dozen Riggs were fighting the thing. It was firing some kind of weapon—she could see beams of light—but whenever they shot at a Rigg he was no longer there. And after a while, two of the Riggs, acting together, cut off an arm holding the weapon. Then two of the Riggs turned the weapon on the creature and killed it.

They stood still, all two dozen Riggs. Then they began to carve the thing open, using the jeweled knives, until it was open and eviscerated on the ground.

It was not a machine, as she had at first supposed. It was not a creature from any wallfold on Garden. Or from Earth.

The Visitors had been human. But the Destroyers were not.

Several of the Riggs turned toward her—for of course they could all see her path—and held up a hand, signaling her to stop her time-slicing.

She did.

The air stank worse than the battlefield had, a few days ago. A few years ago.

"Not human," said one of the Riggs.

"There are so many of you," she said.

"Maybe," said Rigg. "Or maybe none of us exist. Depends on what Umbo did. Or didn't do."

"What is it?"

"I don't know," said Rigg. "But in case we *can* get back in time and give warning, I'm going to leave the jewels. Or one of these knives. So let's get inside that aircraft and let the logs record as much as possible."

"Won't there be more? Won't they come to kill us?"

"Probably," said Rigg. "So let's not be here. But first, this machine." He turned to his other selves. "Only one knife, the one we're going to take back and leave with Umbo."

"He's already got one," said a Rigg, then laughed.

"I've got such a sense of humor," said the Rigg who was speaking to Param. "I really enjoy my own company." But he said it wryly, as if it were not quite true.

"I don't know quite what this knife can do," said a Rigg inside the aircraft. He was pushing the blade point into various things that might or might not have had something to do with computers on the ship. "If there are radio communications, maybe it's catching them. Maybe it's interfacing with the computer. Maybe this is all wasted time."

Another Rigg called from outside. "They're coming."

The Rigg holding the knife that had recorded the inside of the aircraft came and took Param's hand, as she looked to the sky and saw at least ten of the same kind of aircraft racing toward them. Not as fast as it had seemed when she was time-slicing—but it must be going *much* faster than the first one had come, to seem so fast to her even in realtime.

"Should I slice again?" she asked.

"It tracked us even when we were slicing," said the Rigg who was holding her hand. "So we're just going to go."

"But the archers, the—"

"I'm not going back *that* far," said Rigg. "Give me some credit." And with that, he jumped them back and the alien aircraft disappeared. He pointed toward where they had waited for the firestorm to end. "It's about a week ago. We're still there."

"What are we going to do?"

"Climb out of here," said Rigg. Almost at once he had bent over and made his hands into a stirrup for her foot. She stepped and he boosted her up to where her hands could reach the edge of the pit. Then he raised her foot higher, then gripped her thigh, her shin, to push her higher, higher.

"Just clutch at the grass, dig, whatever it takes. Get over the edge. Get up onto it."

She obeyed, feeling even more urgency than his voice suggested.

Then she stood atop the pit, looking down at him. "Now what?" she said.

"Now lie down and reach one hand over. Get a good grip with your toes and the other hand. Don't try to pull me up. Just stay in place and I'll try to climb your arm till I can get a good grip."

It took him several tries, but he ran at the wall and scrambled up it until he gripped her hand. He was heavy, and it felt as if he were going to pull her arm out of its socket, but then, a moment later, he was pulling himself over the edge. It was almost easy-looking, to see him do it. But then, he was trained as a soldier. He was a boy. A man. He had climbed a lot more things in his life than Param ever had.

"Let's get away from the pit and into the woods, so we can go back in time before the Destroyers. Preferably before they built the pit."

"And find Umbo?"

"Find him," said Rigg, "but not talk to him. Not *appear* to him. We'll see where he hides, and then we'll go back earlier and leave him a message."

It took very little time then, to make several jumps. Rigg knew right where Umbo had hidden, because he could see his path. Then he jumped back to about an hour before Umbo would arrive, and left him a note wrapped around the knife.

The note said: "Stop us from going in. Get this knife to the ship. Saw the Destroyers. Not human. Not from Earth. Maybe Earth was destroyed first. Very hard to kill them. You'll see. Hope Noxon succeeds in stopping them before they get here."

"You didn't sign it," said Param.

Rigg looked at her in consternation. "Umbo knows my handwriting."

"It was a joke," said Param. "What now?"

"We leave here before he arrives."

"And go where?"

"Our place is in the future."

"Why there?"

"Because in the future we won't inadvertently change the past any more than we already have by leaving that note and the knife."

"But now you don't have a knife," she said.

"If we're lucky, we'll cease to exist as soon as he finds the knife."

For the moment, though, he jumped them back in time to an innocuous era, an empty stretch of forest with no recent paths in it. It might be centuries ago, for all she knew.

"Why can't we stay *here*?" she asked. "If no one visits here."

"Because we didn't."

"But if we don't change anything . . ."

"Even sophisticated know-it-alls like us need more human company than each other to survive. As leftovers, as extras, we need to go to a time where we can live without changing history."

"Rigg, I don't want to die."

"The human dilemma. None of us wants to die, but all of us have to do it."

"What about another wallfold?" she asked.

"All occupied."

"Vadeshfold?"

"Square is going to put a colony there. It belongs to them."

"You have a facemask. I'll get one, too."

"No," said Rigg. "And you know why."

Param couldn't help it. She started to cry.

"Param, we always knew that what mattered was the survival of the human race on Garden. Not our individual lives."

"Well, we've either saved the human race or failed again, but what about us? Our mission's over, and here we still are."

"Once we get past the Destruction," said Rigg, "the Destroyers will hunt us down and then our troubles are over."

"And those other Riggs?"

"I think they put up a good fight but the ten aliens who were converging on them killed them all."

"Couldn't they have kept duplicating till they outnumbered them all?"

"Could have," said Rigg, "but to what end?"

"To stay alive!"

"I was staying alive long enough to get information about what that creature was. Its biology. How it could be killed. How its weapons worked. What was inside that aircraft. And to keep it from killing you. And to live long enough to pass all of that on to Umbo and stop *us*, the real us, the earlier us, from getting trapped in that pit."

"What will *they* do? The earlier us, when they get the warning?"

"Well, you're the Queen-in-the-Tent," said Rigg. "What would you order?"

"I'd ask for advice."

"Nobody has any," said Rigg.

Param thought for a moment. "Just get away?"

"Not a bad plan," said Rigg. "But that leaves Mother and Haddamander to proclaim that we refused their surrender."

"Bring an army and trap them in their own firepit," said Param.

"More satisfying, but then we're the ones who betrayed and assassinated *them*."

"What, then!" Param demanded.

"As I said, I have no idea. No advice. So . . . aren't you glad that you and I don't have any such decision to make?"

"Because we're just going to go into the future and die!"

"The simplest thing would be to let the Destroyers strike

while we're right out in the open. Let the blast take us the way it did the archers."

"Was it painless for them?" asked Param.

"I doubt it, but I bet it was quick."

"Why don't we just disappear?"

"Should we go back and leave another note saying that when a timestream is changed, we don't disappear, we're still around trying to figure out how to stay out of the way?"

Param sighed. "What would that accomplish?"

"We don't even know if it's true," said Rigg. "Maybe Umbo hasn't found the note and the knife yet. Or hasn't given warning to our earlier selves."

"What does 'yet' even mean?" said Param. "When *are* we? In the past or the future from that moment?"

Rigg laughed. "I wish I'd thought to bring a book to read."

"That's how we're going to face the end of the world? Reading a book?"

"What's your plan? To quarrel right up to the last moment?"

"Yes," said Param. "That's what I command."

"Let's go for it, then," said Rigg. He took her hand and they jumped into the future.

The woods around them had changed. The path that had been near them was overgrown now.

"So how long till the fire?" asked Param.

"I'm not Umbo. I can't jump into the future with any kind of precision."

"Well, I certainly picked the wrong person to die with, didn't I."

"Sorry," said Rigg. "If it's any consolation, the you that survives will have Umbo to console her."

"I *hate* her," said Param. "The selfish, privileged, ungrateful idiot."

"Well, I love her," said Rigg. "I admire her. I think she did amazingly well with everything life dealt her. And I'm reasonably sure she'll go on making good decisions, even when they don't work out as hoped."

"If they don't work out, they weren't good."

"Yes they were," said Rigg. "Always good, because you're good." He touched a finger to her forehead. "In here." Then he kissed her forehead and hugged her. "Slice time, by Silbom's left elbow! Slice us up to the moment of the flash and then we can face it like . . ."

"Men?"

"Like extra copies of good men and women," said Rigg. "Like expendables."

CHAPTER 29

Visiting

With perfect mathematical predictability, Ram Odin's starship passed through the fold nineteen times, arriving 11,191 years earlier, the ships just far enough apart to give them maneuvering room. Collision-avoidance systems automatically made the ships drift apart in different directions.

In the cockpit of each ship, Noxon said, "Nobody kills anybody, please. That includes the expendables."

"We can't be killed," said the expendable.

"You know the history I'm trying not to repeat," said Noxon.

"I wasn't going to give that order," said Ram Odin.

"Since history repeated itself in so many other ways," said Noxon, "I was merely urging that we not follow the same script."

"Agreed," said Wheaton.

"I detect no attempt by the aliens to communicate or interfere with our computer systems," said the expendable.

"Did we arrive before they achieved high technology?" asked Wheaton.

"Radio waves, broadcast not focused," said the expendable. "Use of electric power. Illumination on the nightside."

"So," said Wheaton. "Not a minute too early."

"Not if they follow the trajectory we followed on Earth," said Ram. "Only a few decades between widespread electricity with radio and the development of space flight."

"It may be even narrower because they have such a strong incentive to get into space," said the expendable.

"What incentive is that?" asked Ram.

"Their binary," said the expendable. "It is also inhabited." The expendable seemed about to say more, but it froze for a moment. "A twentieth ship has appeared."

"He did it," said Noxon.

"Who did what?" asked Wheaton.

"Well, *I* did it," said Noxon. "I was watching carefully during the jump through the fold. If we divided, I was going to try to snag the backward-moving ship and bring it back into the forward timeflow."

"The ship reports that you failed," said the expendable. "The backward-moving ship in fact moved backward, not making the jump through the fold. But the mice on that ship were able to reprogram the computers to avoid the twenty-fold duplication and then jumped the fold going backward, in order to separate the backward-moving ship from the outbound ship that was us just before our jump."

"My head hurts," said Wheaton.

"It does not," said the expendable. "But your lie is apparently intended to express humorously exaggerated confusion which you do not, in fact, feel."

"Exactly," said Wheaton. "It's nice to have someone get my jokes, even though you have to explain them aloud."

"I wanted to confirm that I had understood," said the expendable.

"If they jumped the fold backward," said Ram, "how are they here?"

"Noxon was able to reverse timeflow and rejoin our space-time," said the expendable. "Very good work."

"Thanks," said Noxon. "But it wasn't me."

"It was you-ish," said the expendable. "It's within your capabilities."

"And then what?" asked Noxon. "He jumped forward to our time?"

"The backward-moving ship had not made the 11,191-year pastward leap that these nineteen ships made. So it arrived in this space in the future, relative to our current timeplace."

"What did they see there?" asked Ram.

"Not very much," said the expendable. "The aliens immediately attempted to seize control of the ship's computers, remotely. The mice were able to resist their reprogramming, which was feeble and unsophisticated compared to the one they will use near Earth several hundred thousand years from now. Then the Noxon of that ship attached to *our* paths and jumped back to our time, when the aliens are not able to project their computing prowess this far into space."

"Narrow escape," said Wheaton.

"It was a very good thing that we had the mice with us," said Noxon.

"Thank you," said the alpha mouse. "We're glad to reward you for refraining from crushing my head."

"I never *wanted* to do it," said Noxon to the mouse.

"Talking to the mice?" asked Wheaton.

"I wonder," said Ram, "if our presence here, now, accelerated the aliens' development of the ability to make remote assaults on human computing systems. Having seen us enter their space . . ."

Wheaton agreed. "Why, it might be that our presence is what led them to attack Earth!"

"No," said Noxon. "They attacked long before we ever showed up here."

"We're here *now*, and that's hundreds of millennia before the attack," said Wheaton.

"Prepare for your head to hurt again," said the expendable.

"Let me guess," said Wheaton. "'Before' doesn't always mean 'before.'"

"The calendar and the clock keep a single line of time," said Noxon. "But with us, causality jumps all over the place. We're here *before* the invasion, by the calendar, but we're here *after* the invasion, by the causal chain. Their invasion is what *caused* us to come, so by cause-and-effect, the invasion was first."

"I can't even make my little joke," said Wheaton, "because the expendable already said it."

"I anticipated your humor?" asked the expendable.

"You stepped on my joke," said Wheaton. "Clever, but not polite."

"You'd already said the joke," said Ram, "so it wasn't going to be funny this time. Whereas the expendable stepping on it, *that* was funny."

"Amusing, anyway," said the alpha mouse.

"The mice don't think any of this is all that funny," Noxon reported.

"Oh, the women are laughing uproariously," said the alpha. "I'm the one who isn't hysterical about it."

Noxon could see that the female mice were busy at various tasks throughout the ship, and not one of them showed any sign of paying much attention to what they were doing.

"What are you doing to the ship?" asked Noxon.

Noxon could see Ram stiffen a little—he must know Noxon was talking to the mice, and so he feared that the mice might be doing something dangerous and irrevocable.

"We're making the same alterations to this ship that our counterparts made to the backward-moving ship," said the alpha. "So we can jump the fold without making nineteen forward copies and one backward one."

"Are we planning to jump again?" asked Noxon.

"I believe that when the expendable finishes explaining about the civilization on the binary planet, you'll decide that ten of these twenty ships should jump to a spot much nearer the binary."

"Will they still skip eleven millennia back in time?" asked Noxon.

"No. Curing the replications also cures the time skip."

"Are you ready for me to explain about the binary planet?" asked the expendable.

"*I* am," said Ram. "Unless the mice now command the ship."

"They've fixed it so we don't split into nineteen pieces every time we jump," said Noxon.

"You asked them if we're planning to jump again," said Ram. "Why would we do that?"

"Let's hear the expendable and find out," said Noxon. "The mice apparently already know what he's going to tell us."

The expendable took a breath before proceeding. Such theatricality from a machine that doesn't need to breathe, thought Noxon. "Earth's Moon was important to the evolution of life, by causing tides and controlling other cycles," said the expendable. "But this world is really two planets, nearly equal, as close as they can be without tearing each other apart with tidal forces."

"So both have atmospheres," said Ram.

"Both have life?" asked Noxon.

"Both have widespread electricity and radio communications," said the expendable. "They each monitor the other's radio broadcasts, and I believe the ability to interfere with and eventually control remote computer systems was developed by the nearer planet in order to use it against the farther one."

"They have a million kilometers between them," said Ram, "and they're *attacking* each other?"

"That suggests reciprocality," said the expendable. "The nearer planet is attacking the farther one. The farther one seems to be working only to protect their own systems against attack."

"Let me guess," said Ram. "The one that attacked us is this aggressive one."

"I don't know," said the expendable. "Whichever world emerges victorious, it will be convinced that the only way to deal with aliens is to destroy them utterly."

"So even if it's the nice guys on the far planet," said Noxon, "they might still be the enemy that attacks Earth."

The alpha mouse spoke to Noxon. "We don't know which one is our enemy. Both must be brought under control."

"It seems wrong to punish one world for what the other world did," said Noxon.

"We're not *punishing* anyone," said Ram. "We're saving the human race against a threat, and we don't know which of these worlds poses that threat."

"We know that both of them pose a threat," said the alpha.

"It's *possible* that both pose a threat," said Noxon. "But to take preemptive action against both seems unfair. Stifling a civilization, a *species* that might be completely innocent—"

"Hold on," said Wheaton. "Garden has already tried dozens of ways to forestall the destruction of humanity, so there are lots of timestreams in which *one* of these species wipes out all rivals and rules this bit of the galaxy. The other one was probably destroyed before the victor ever came near us, so *we're* not the ones who snuffed them out. All *we're* doing now is creating one slim timestream in which the human race survives. It is not so very much to take for ourselves, compared with what *they've* taken already."

"So you're arguing in favor of xenocide?" asked Ram.

"Not at all," said Wheaton, looking horrified. "Nothing of the kind! Garden has endured for eleven millennia with tight restrictions on their ability to develop high technology, right?"

"Yes," said Noxon.

"And that was a lid placed on the planet by other humans, right?"

"By computers," said the expendable, "but obeying human orders."

"So if we go into the past and put such a lid on both these species," said Wheaton, "we're doing to them nothing that we haven't already done to ourselves."

"To one *portion* of our species," said Noxon. "Earth didn't put any such lid on themselves."

"We don't *have* to destroy their whole biota in order to set up colonies here, do we?" asked Wheaton.

"It depends on what proteins they produce, and whether we can digest enough of them," said Ram.

"I don't suppose *now* would be a good era in which to make our investigations," said Wheaton.

"You want to go into the past and see them early in their evolution," said Noxon.

"I am what I am," said Wheaton. "But I'm also right."

"Put us back a few hundred thousand years ago," said the alpha mouse, "and *we'll* be their lid."

"The mice have already suggested," said Noxon, "that ten of our ships go to the other world, and ten stay here."

"I wonder if versions of you are saying exactly the same thing on all nineteen of the other ships," said Ram.

The expendable answered. "The exact wording is quite different, but yes, on every ship you have reached approximately the same point in your discussion."

"What have the others decided?" asked Ram.

"They're all asking their expendables what the others decided."

"We haven't decided anything," said Wheaton. "But the only sensible thing is to go back in time, split the fleet in half, and explore both worlds to see what damage we might have to do in order to use them."

"But we don't even know what the sentient species *look* like on either world," said Noxon. "How will we know which life forms in the past are going to evolve into them?"

"We have images of both species," said the expendable. "Both worlds are regularly broadcasting visuals using primitive raster scans." Holograms appeared in the middle of the cockpit. One species was low to the ground, with many limbs, all of them capable of grasping, and many of them with sharp claws or blades at their fingertips. The other species was tripedal, tall, and gracile, with a head crowned with vicious-looking horns. All three feet were prehensile, and one of them had two thumblike projections.

"Let me guess," said Ram. "The low, scuttling one is the aggressive species that's trying to take over the other side's computers."

"Wrong," said the expendable.

"You wanted the roachlike one to be evil," said Wheaton, delighted. "Easier to hate them!"

"Oh, I could easily hate them both," said Ram. "For all we

know, they teamed up to attack us. We never saw who was piloting those aircraft."

"It's too dangerous to go into the future to see what happens," said the alpha mouse. "Our counterparts on the twentieth ship are still searching to make sure they've cleaned out all the intrusions."

"The mice don't want to go into the future to learn any more," said Noxon. "If *they're* scared of the aliens' capabilities, we'd be crazy to make the attempt."

"So we just go blindly backward," said Ram.

"To find out if we can leave the flora and fauna on either world intact," said Wheaton.

"We *can*," said Noxon. "We can always decide not to establish colonies on either world."

"That's not an option," said Ram. "We're here to neutralize the threat. We have no way of monitoring whether we've succeeded without establishing a permanent, technologically powerful presence."

"That's not really true," said Noxon. "For instance, we could drop off the mice a million years ago and then pop back to *this* time to see where we stand."

Ram laughed. "We'd find that the mice were completely prepared to destroy us, take over our ship, fly back to Earth, and take over everything."

"We would never," said the alpha mouse.

"I was just pointing out that if we establish human colonies, it's because we *want* to, not because there's no other way," said Noxon.

"Well," said Ram, "whatever we do, I don't propose to leave it all up to the mice."

"The other ships have all decided to go back and test the proteins on both worlds," said the expendable.

"How do we divide the fleet?" asked Ram.

"The computers have already divided the ships randomly into two groups of ten. We're in the group that stays at this near world, while the others jump the fold to the far one."

"The one with the tripods," said Wheaton. "That's a shame — I was most interested in studying *them.*"

"That's how all the Wheatons felt," said the expendable. "But then they all decided that both species need to be studied, so half the Wheatons have to take the second choice."

Wheaton sighed. "I suppose for every Professor Wheaton who lost, there's a Professor Wheaton that won."

"Depending on how you define 'won' and 'lost,'" said the expendable. "You could say that they all win, with an entirely new sentient species to study."

"I feel much happier already," said Wheaton.

"Ironic or sincere?" asked the expendable.

"Pissed off but compliant," answered Wheaton.

Noxon sliced them through the time it took for the ship to fly into stationary orbit around the near planet. At Noxon's insistence, the mice stayed on the ship with him and Ram, as Wheaton and the expendable flew down to the surface. "The scientist and the robot can do the job perfectly," said Noxon. "The time traveler and the pilot have to stay here, in case we have to undo something horrible the mice have done."

"So untrusting," said the alpha mouse.

Noxon regarded this comment as not worth answering.

Wheaton and the expendable made frequent reports during their days of data collection. Ancestors of the scuttling aliens were easy enough to spot—they were already as close to sentience as, say, *Homo habilis*. Using tools, but not yet making fire. "It is difficult for Professor Wheaton to stay focused on the project at hand," said the voice of the ship. "He keeps wanting to go backward and forward and the expendable has to keep reminding him that only Noxon can do that."

During one of the lulls between reports, while Ram was exercising, Noxon said, more to himself than to Ram, "I miss Deborah."

Ram didn't answer, but the alpha mouse did. "Why didn't you simply copy her and bring her along? There'd be twenty of her now. Plenty to go around."

"She wanted eyes," said Noxon. "The twenty who came with *us* would be disappointed for the rest of their lives."

"What?" asked Ram. *Now* he heard.

"Just talking with the mice," said Noxon.

"Whatever you say to them, they're going to use against you later," said Ram.

"Unless we use it *for* you," said the alpha mouse.

"He can't hear you," murmured Noxon.

"I wasn't talking to *him*," said the alpha.

"I'll eventually find someone among the colonists," said Noxon. "I'm not worried."

"You're really strange-looking," said the alpha. "Most of the colonists will be completely repulsed by you."

"Is that why all the females were pregnant five times over before they came on this voyage?" asked Noxon. "So they wouldn't have to do something as repulsive as mate with a small-testicled male like you? Or was I right that you were castrated?"

"I don't have body-image issues the way humans do," said the alpha.

"No, you don't have any kind of shame at all," said Noxon.

"Someday you'll understand us," said the alpha.

After three days, thousands of samples had been brought aboard and stored in the gene banks. The conclusion was clear. Most of the proteins that humans needed could be found readily among the native flora and fauna on both worlds. And a simple array of fast-spreading, highly edible plants would make up the deficiencies. "We can release any Earth fauna we choose," said Wheaton, "and thus we'll have meat to eat and enough plants for a varied and pleasing diet."

"That's what they've found on the other world," said the expendable, "except that they need to spread a different array of Earth plants."

"So, no destruction?" asked Noxon.

"Are you disappointed?" asked Ram.

"I still think that walls are a good idea," said Noxon.

"Because you grew up in a wallfold," said Ram.

"We can give the mice one wallfold," said Noxon. "And reserve one on each world for the aliens alone."

"And give us one to combine with them," said the alpha mouse.

"If we give one wallfold to aliens and mice together, we have to make sure there's a tight lid on their technology," said Noxon. "I'm afraid of what their combined abilities might lead to."

"Happiness and peace for all sentient species everywhere," said the alpha mouse.

"No doubt," said Noxon.

"Same discussion on most of the other ships," said the expendable.

"Most?" asked Ram. "So we've diverged?"

"Two ships on the far world and one here have to deal with a Wheaton with a broken hip," said the expendable. "It slowed down the decision making."

"I thought you'd protect me," said Wheaton accusingly.

"I can't always anticipate the stupid choices of human beings," said the expendable.

"Stop bickering," said Ram. "Dividing up the world is the obvious choice. We have to decide what to do with the extra humans who won't be needed to found a colony in three of the wallfolds."

"We can establish more wallfolds than we have ships," said Noxon. "Let's make thirteen colonies on each world, ten for humans, one each for aliens and mice, and one for both."

"Must there also be a colony that includes both mice and humans?"

"I hope not," said Wheaton.

"Of course," said Noxon.

"At least don't let *ours* be that colony!" said Wheaton.

"You'll get used to them," said Noxon.

"That means you already agreed to have ours be the human colony that has mice," said Wheaton.

"Unless you plan to mate and settle down, Professor," said Ram, "I think all the copies of you should regularly visit all the colonies. Sleep in stasis in between inspections. See how the alien species are developing, now that they have humans and mice interfering."

"Assisting," corrected the alpha mouse. "At least that's what *we'll* be doing."

"I think that's an excellent plan," said Wheaton. "I only wish I could publish my findings."

"You should write down everything you see and conjecture," said Ram, "and we'll eventually share it with every world."

"One more need," said the expendable. "A name for each of these worlds."

"'Garden' is already taken," said Noxon.

"I don't think the worlds should be named for any of *us*," said Wheaton.

"Never crossed my mind," said Ram.

"Said the man with two wallfolds named for him," said Noxon.

"*I* didn't name them," said Ram. "*I've* never been there."

"How about Roach and Tripod?" asked Noxon.

"'Roach' is hardly expressive of a desire to get along with them," said Wheaton.

"All that 'Roach' will mean in a generation or two will be the name of a world," said Noxon.

"The human settlers will know from the start," said Ram. "They may never let go of the associations. We need them to speak of the natives with respect, at least inside the shared wallfold."

"Melody and Harmony," said the alpha mouse.

"Just as I was thinking 'Noise' and 'Nasty,'" said Noxon, "the mice suggested 'Melody' and 'Harmony.'"

"As long as *this* is the world that's called Melody," said Ram. "We came here first."

"And we have such lovely voices," said Wheaton.

Other suggestions were made on other ships, but in the end the idea of Melody, though attractive to most, was superceded: One world was named Treble, since the Tripods had high and piping voices, while the other was named Bass, because the Scuttles made sounds that were so low that many of them could not be heard by humans. Neither species had anything that could be called a language yet.

Thirteen wallfolds on each world, with the native species each confined to the area where, in the original timestream, they had achieved full sentience. The mice were satisfied, and the natives didn't get a vote, so everything proceeded peacefully.

Inside every wallfold that included a Noxon, he and the expendable made a jaunt into the far future, not just to see how their own colony had fared, but to check the wallfolds that contained either mice or natives, or both. The orbiters provided firm calendar dates based on stellar positioning, so that the Noxons could observe both the year when their ships arrived and the year when Earth had been invaded in the old timestream.

There were no spaceships in any of the futures, nor technologies that allowed communication between wallfolds, except by way of the expendables. The natives had evolved sentience in all four native wallfolds, though whether they were the same as they would have been without human interference, it was impossible to say. In each wallfold shared with mice, the natives and the mice were at peace, and the Scuttles and their mice had evolved a system of shared cities, with some dominated by the Scuttles and some by the mice. The Tripods were less cooperative—with the mice and with each other. They were torn by warfare, but so were most of the human wallfolds, so that was hardly a reason to make any changes.

The visiting Noxons all reached the conclusion that their original mission—to keep these aliens from destroying the human race—had been achieved, and it had been done without depriving the proto-sentients of a chance to achieve their evolutionary potential.

Then the Noxons of each world met with each other in one of the grounded spaceships and conferred about the only important decision remaining to them.

"There's a lid on development of technology," said the first speaker in each conference, "but we represent something far more dangerous than any weapon or tech. The ability to go into the past and wipe out whole timestreams. We had to use that ability when the future of humanity was at stake. But now, will Treble and Bass be better off if these timeshaping genes are part of the mix, or if we allow our abilities to be extinguished by not reproducing?"

And in both conferences, another Noxon pointed out the obvious. "There are timeshapers on Garden, no matter what *we* do here. And Ram Odin has already married and had children in every human wallfold. He was the source of these genes in the first place."

And another said, "The mice knew how to send objects through time and space when they got here. They knew how to manipulate human genes to create the original Rigg and Param and Umbo. We'd be fools to think they've forgotten that knowledge. For all we know, they all have the ability to manipulate time. Should we let the mice have such power, while we give up our only possible remedy?"

"So we keep the ability in the gene pool? So that we aren't at the mercy of the mice? Or the humans from Garden, if they ever come here?"

"This ability exists in the universe. We'd be fools to throw it away, when we might need it someday. It saved us once."

"But only because people of extraordinary decency and wisdom wielded it." And while they all laughed at such ironic self-deprecation, they also knew that it was true.

"Sentience always carries with it the power of destruction. We must work to make sure that decency and wisdom are part of the heritage of every wallfold, and then trust our descendants to use this power responsibly, if they have it at all."

This became the consensus of both conferences. Using the ships' computers, they communicated their decisions across the space between Bass and Treble.

Then the Noxons were carried back by flyers to each of their wallfolds, where they married the women they already loved. There would be no stasis for them, no attempts to live across the ages and keep track of what the future brought. Nor did the Ram Odins attempt to keep watch over the future. That was for the Wheatons to do, as they carried on their evolutionary studies.

And since they were already getting old when the colonies began, after a few centuries or millennia they either allowed themselves to retire and die, or their wakings became so far apart that they could not be said to live in any of the wallfolds anymore.

But the children of the Rams and Noxons grew, and became whatever they would become, and in the course of the generations, their genes became mixed with the rest of the population, and their stories and ideas became part of the lore of every culture that arose. Among the mice as well, the memory of Father Starpilot and Father Timeshaper were preserved. And it was hard to guess which would have more influence in shaping the future, the stories or the genes.

CHAPTER 30

Dispositions

Rigg sat with Ram Odin in the control room of the Vadeshfold starship, along with several hundred mice, and confessed his own ambivalence. "I've watched the log of dozens of myself fighting with these inhuman Destroyers, and I want them to come again, and this time find all the computers of Garden closed shut against them. Let them come to ground here and find every wallfold armed and ready to fight. They *can* be beaten."

"By a timeshaper with a facemask, who can duplicate himself until he vastly outnumbers a single Destroyer," said Ram Odin. "What wallfold can match that?"

"At least, if they can't turn the weapons in the orbiters against us, we have a chance."

"Yes," said Ram Odin. "What that lost version of you and Param discovered has tipped a balance. Perhaps it even tipped it enough. Perhaps the solution of our problem was in our own hands after all. And I'm relieved to know that our enemy is not the humans of Earth."

"But what can we think, except that the Destroyers massacred the humans of our ancient homeland before they ever came here?" said Rigg. "That's why I have to hope that Noxon will succeed in stopping them there, saving humanity on Earth. But then they'll never come here at all, and we will never find out whether this reprogramming of the computers did the job. Whether we were able to defend against them."

"I can live with not knowing that," said Ram Odin. "If it means the Destroyers never come. So many lives will be saved that way. So if I had a choice, I would choose Noxon's success over having a chance to see whether our brilliant musine friends have done the job here well enough."

Rigg heard the mice as Ram Odin could not. "Of course we did the job."

"They're bragging," said Rigg. "But I'm afraid that they've done a great deal more than build a wall that the Destroyers can't penetrate."

"What could we possibly do?" asked a mouse. "Why are you so suspicious?"

"For instance," said Rigg, "what if they are the ones in command of all the starships now, instead of you or me?"

Ram Odin shrugged. "Then maybe the world bows to a hybrid conqueror, half man, half mouse."

"We have no such ambition," said a mouse. The others echoed the assurance.

"They're all innocent of plots and schemes," said Rigg.

"The innocent and the guilty all say the same thing, with equal fervor," said Ram Odin. "Can your facemask tell the difference?"

"Not really," said Rigg. "They're always lying, always concealing something. But since everything they say is deceptive, it's impossible to tell whether the exact words they're saying right now are a direct lie, or a truth that conceals a deeper lie."

"Very subtle," said Ram Odin.

"I can't very well feel morally superior to them," said Rigg. "If they weren't listening to all our conversations, we'd lie to them, too, or at least hold back our plans. They may have human genes and, collectively, intelligence to match our own—"

"Surpass it, you mean," said a mouse.

"By about ten thousand times," said another.

"They're quite vain," said Rigg, "and they grossly overestimate their own mental prowess, but that only proves how much they resemble humankind. What they *won't* do, even if they take over the computers somehow, is use that power to destroy all life on Garden. If we have to choose between a tyranny of rodents and the utter destruction of our species, I'll hold my nose and take the rodents."

"You smell worse than we do," said a mouse.

"I bet they're telling you how much worse *we* smell," said Ram Odin.

"See?" said Rigg. "They're not as subtle as they think."

"How will we know if Noxon succeeds?" asked Ram Odin.

"In all our planning, we never got that far," said Rigg. "It was hard enough to think of a way to get him to Earth and after that, he had to figure out how to stop the humans there from destroying us. We had no idea that he'd have to stop an alien invasion. If he succeeds, he may have to do it in some way that prevents him from *ever* coming back here. He may be stuck on the aliens' home world."

"What if Noxon comes in exactly the way that the Destroyers have always come?" asked Ram Odin. "What if our new defenses kill him before he can tell us of his success?"

"Our defenses don't kill anybody," said a mouse.

"We're blocking out their computer commands, not blowing up their ships," said another.

"Though we could work on that."

"Don't," said Rigg. "Please. Let's wait and see if what you've already done is enough."

"If Noxon *can* come back," said Ram Odin, "he's bound to be as smart as you. He'll think of the danger. He won't return at the time the Destroyers always came."

"He might have the use of a starship. The backward copy of the original. If he can turn it forward, he might make another voyage, another jump through the fold."

Ram sighed. "And that means he might return eleven thousand years ago, with nineteen copies. Maybe we should be checking the past to see if he's succeeded, instead of looking toward the future."

"If he returns in the past, he can slice his way forward. Or jump. Who knows how precise he's learned to be? He and Param accomplished a lot together before he left."

Ram Odin rubbed his eyes with his fingertips. "I'm tired. Since Noxon could return at any time in the existence of Garden, I don't think it will hurt anything if I nap now."

"We should actually leave some open time here on the bridge," said Rigg, "so that if we have to come back and tell the mice that they need to do more, there'll be an open space for us to return to."

"Yes, Rigg, you can have a nap, too, if you want," said Ram Odin. "You don't have to come up with theories in order to justify your need for sleep."

"Good, they're leaving," said a mouse. "We can take over the world now."

"The mice are trying to see how gullible we are," said Rigg.

"We're as gullible as they need us to be," said Ram Odin. "Once they take over the ships, they control all our information. How can we possibly check them? So let's go to sleep and then decide whether to bounce into the future to see if we've succeeded."

The door opened as Ram Odin approached it. Vadeshex was standing on the other side. "Oh, you've already heard?" asked Vadeshex.

"Heard what?" asked Ram Odin.

The mice swarmed through the door. "Stop that!" said Rigg. "When you do that we end up stepping on some of you."

"We don't mind," said a mouse.

"Much," said another.

"Well *we* mind," said Rigg. "It's sickening to feel your little bodies crunch under our shoes. Especially since the one we step on might have been conversing with us a moment before."

The mice swerved to the edges of the doorway, and many of them clambered up onto Rigg's and Ram Odin's clothing to ride them out of the room.

"What's happening?" Ram Odin asked Vadeshex.

"Noxon is back," said Vadeshex.

"Successful or not?" asked Ram Odin.

"When did he arrive?" asked Rigg.

"He arrived with the Visitors," said Vadeshex. "He brought a blind girl with him, and they immediately came back to a time when the two of you were here in my starship. The flyer is bringing them."

"Did they stop the Destroyers?" Ram Odin insisted.

"Of course," said Vadeshex. "He wouldn't have come back with *that* job undone."

"Did the Visitors *know* they were bringing him?" asked Rigg.

"I don't think so," said Vadeshex. "But I wasn't there when they arrived. Or rather, I'm sure I *will* be there, but I at this moment have no idea of anything except that they called for the flyer, and yes, they stopped the Destroyers."

"Have you notified everybody else?" asked Rigg.

"The other expendables are spreading the word among those who care. The Odinfolders are celebrating. All the mice in Larfold are celebrating on the beach with the Larfolders as they come out of the water."

"And Loaf and Leaky? Param and Umbo?"

"Ramex is heading for them right now, in his flyer," said Vadeshex. "Give me credit for knowing my job."

"All the expendables and all the ships' computers were notified at once," said Rigg. "You had nothing to do with it, right?"

"Well, true," said Vadeshex. "But I think it's significant that Noxon and the girl are coming straight to *me*."

"To us," said Ram Odin.

"To me," said Vadeshex. "The girl is blind. Her eyes were burned out and she wants to try a facemask to see if it will restore her eyes."

"She's from *Earth*?" asked Rigg.

"Where else would he come up with a human girl?" asked Ram Odin.

"Will the facemasks work with people who aren't part of Garden's gene pool?" asked Rigg.

"She's a cousin of Ram Odin's," said Vadeshex. He turned to Ram. "Apparently you had cousins named Wheaton. Arnold and Lanae's daughter, Deborah."

"Of course," said Ram Odin. "They died in an accident. Wasn't her uncle taking care of her? He had an odd nickname."

"Georgia," said Vadeshex.

"How do you know all this?" asked Rigg. "How long did you wait to come tell us?"

"As you ask me questions," said Vadeshex, "the flyer is passing along the questions and then I'm getting their answers. Why do you always see some kind of conspiracy or wrongdoing in everything I do?"

"Because he thinks you're even more deceptive and evil than we are," said a mouse perched on Rigg's shoulder. "And that's saying something."

"I'd roll my eyes," said Vadeshex, "except that Rigg gets testy when I do such human gestures."

"I'm still going to go take that nap till they get here," said Ram Odin. "And maybe I'll sleep a little better knowing that the world has been saved."

"Saved," said Rigg, "but the computers have still been reprogrammed by the mice."

"If we have to," said Ram Odin, "somebody can go back and tell us not to have them do it."

"Oh, that's right," said Rigg.

"See?" said the mouse on Rigg's shoulder. "We are helpless before your superior powers."

"Poor babies," said Rigg. "You gave us those powers, so don't blame us if we use them."

"You mean you believed that story about how we altered you genetically?" said the mouse on his shoulder.

Rigg stopped cold.

"What did he say?" asked Ram Odin.

"Something that I halfway hope is true," said Rigg. "But if it is, I'm not sure I want to know it. I'm sure *Umbo* doesn't want to know it."

"I'm lying," said the mouse on his shoulder. "But it certainly startled you."

"Were you lying then?" asked Rigg. "Or are you lying now, because you saw how it startled me?"

"What did he say?" asked Ram Odin.

Vadeshex answered. "He told Rigg that the mice didn't really do any genetic alterations to promote his and Param's abilities."

"Well," said Ram Odin, "is that true?"

"I have no way of knowing," said Vadeshex. "We can't monitor changes on a genetic level, not from a distance."

"What about Umbo?" asked Rigg. "Was that brutal cobbler his father or not?"

"Bring me a genetic sample from Tegay and Enene, and one from Umbo, and I'll test for paternity," said Vadeshex. "Till you do that, I can only say that Umbo does not look like Tegay."

"I could really come to hate these mice," said Rigg. "If you didn't really alter us genetically, why did you tell us that you did?"

"We did alter you," said the mouse. "I was joking, and it's getting funnier by the second."

"I'm going to take a nap, too," said Rigg.

"But now you won't sleep half so well," said the mouse.

"Get off my shoulder before I pick you off and crush your head," said Rigg.

"Violence is such a *human* trait," said the mouse.

"So is merciless goading and perpetual lying," said Rigg. "When Mouse-Breeder made you, I wish he hadn't added in those traits."

"I'm going to get down," said the mouse, "if you promise not to kill me."

"I thought it didn't matter if we stepped on a few of you now and then," said Rigg.

"Well, in my case, it matters to *me*," said the mouse.

"I won't kill you as long as you don't scurry under my boots."

The mouse made a flying leap and landed on Vadeshex,

whose hand flashed out, catching the mouse between his fingers. Vadeshex crushed its head and popped the mouse's corpse into his mouth.

Rigg almost puked on the spot.

"I can process any animal or vegetable matter," said Vadeshex, "and I didn't want the corpse cluttering up the corridor."

"Why did you kill it?" asked Rigg.

"Because he was causing problems with his lies," said Vadeshex.

"Or else he was causing problems by telling me a truth I wasn't supposed to know," said Rigg.

"One of those," said Vadeshex.

"Wake me when they get here," said Ram Odin. "And don't eat any more mice in front of Rigg. He's more squeamish than you think."

"I was raised by one of these machines," said Rigg. "I still think of them as people, even though I know better."

"Poor Rigg," said Vadeshex. "Try to sleep."

Rigg held back any kind of retort, mostly because he couldn't decide on which of them he should use. He went into his cabin and stripped off his clothes, shaking out the mice. "All of you get out of this room and don't come back in without an invitation."

The mice scurried out the door. The facemask assured him that they were all gone. Rigg lay down on the cot. "I want to sleep," he said aloud to the facemask.

The facemask always understood, whether Rigg framed the request in words or not. Moments after Rigg lay down, the facemask dropped him into unconsciousness.

• • •

It was the ship's voice that woke him, not Vadeshex, which was fine with Rigg. The facemask had him alert in a moment, with no residual grogginess. Rigg pulled on his clothes and went down the now-empty corridors to the open area where everyone was gathering. Param, Ram Odin, Umbo, Loaf, Leaky, Square, Olivenko, Vadeshex, Ramex, and a few hundred mice.

"Are we waiting for anyone else?" asked Ram Odin.

"Just Noxon and Deborah Wheaton," said Vadeshex. "And here they are."

Noxon came into the room, accompanied by a girl who wore a thick band across her eyes. It was obvious by the way she moved that she wasn't blind at all.

"Hi," said Noxon. "We did it. Or, well, another copy of me did it, along with Ram Odin and her father, Professor Wheaton."

"How?" asked Param. "What did they do?"

"Deborah and I saw them off in the starship. They left a couple of hundred thousand years before the aliens came, and when we hopped back to that time, the aliens didn't come after all, so I assume they succeeded. I have no idea how."

"She's not really blind," said Loaf.

"She has no eyes," said Noxon.

Deborah tapped the band over her eyes. "It's a machine," she said. "Not as advanced as *their* visual units." She indicated Vadeshex and Ramex.

"We waited until the Visitors came back from Garden," said Rigg. "In the original version of history, the Destroyers had already wiped out human life on Earth before they got home. We sliced our way a few dozen years, just to be sure the Destroyers never came."

"The expedition you call 'the Visitors' gave a very favorable report," said Deborah. "They recommended that this world be left completely alone to go on developing without interference."

"And the government made that official policy," said Noxon. "Doesn't mean it'll *stay* the policy, but it's a good sign. They stuck with it for a dozen years or so. Then we popped back, got on the Visitors' outbound ship, and sliced our way through their whole voyage."

"They never knew you were on the ship?" asked Umbo.

Noxon gave him a withering look. "Give me credit," he said.

Umbo grinned. "We may call you Noxon, but you're still Rigg."

"I'm not sure how to take that," said Rigg.

"It's pure flattery to both of us," said Noxon. "You should all know that I didn't plan on coming back here. If I hadn't accidently duplicated myself, I would have ended up with the backward Ram Odin out at the alien world. Presumably they're colonizing the place now. But as long as this copy of me existed, I thought I might as well come home."

"With a friend," said Param.

"You can never have too many friends," said Noxon.

But the way Deborah threaded an arm around his waist made it clear enough that this wasn't an ordinary friendship.

"My job is over," said Noxon, "but I realize you're still caught up in the war against Haddamander and Hagia. I don't want to distract you."

"We no longer have such a tight deadline to work with," said Olivenko. "Since the world isn't ending a couple of years from now."

"The ship told me that you already knew the Destroyers were aliens," said Noxon. "Rigg and Param got bounced past the Destruction and had some kind of fight, yes? I've never actually seen one of them. Do you have it recorded?"

"Rigg makes us watch it twice a day," said Ram Odin.

Rigg shook his head a little.

Noxon grinned. "Well, I want to see you whip them."

"I only fought one, and it took more than twenty of me to bring him down," said Rigg. "And it wasn't actually me. The ones who did the fighting left the knife and the ship's logs with Umbo, and he stopped us from getting into the fight. So all I know of it is what the ship's log recorded."

"Nice to know you had it in you though, isn't it?" asked Noxon. "You're the one who saved the world."

"Well, as I said, that wasn't *me*, either. You and I are just copies of the heroes."

"Good enough for me," said Umbo.

"Only now both of us are back here," said Noxon. "So we still have to try to keep out of each other's way."

Rigg shook his head. "Square taught me how to get the face-mask to give me a new face. Turns out we have a lot more control over our appearance than we knew."

"That's right," said Noxon. "You look like *me* now. I mean, the way we were. Originally. I didn't even realize it because that's how I'm supposed to look. Can you get my mask to do that?"

"Why?" asked Rigg. "With you butt ugly like that, people can tell us apart really easily."

"And who is Square?" asked Noxon.

Leaky sighed a little.

"All will be explained in due time," said Ram Odin. "But I think it's clear now that you've saved the world, we have a war to fight, and your—friend? Wife?—wants a facemask."

"I want it even more now," said Deborah. "I won't have to be as ugly as Noxon after all."

"You can be whatever you want," said Square.

"*If* you can control the facemask," said Param. "Not everybody can."

Ram Odin once again tried to take control. "Please. We've all seen each other, we know pretty much what happened, and we can get the details in the days and weeks to come. Let's let Noxon and Deborah do what they came here to do, and the rest of us should get back to our responsibilities."

"How did it work out with the mice and the computers?" asked Umbo.

"As far as we know," said Rigg, "the mice now rule the world."

"I'm so relieved," said Umbo. "You and Ram Odin were doing kind of a lousy job of it."

"Well, now you get to be king," said Rigg.

"Just a figurehead," said Umbo.

Param took his hand. "He keeps saying that, but when I try to give him responsibilities he refuses."

"I don't want to be in charge of anything," said Umbo. "I just want to be able to complain about it."

"He works hard," said Param, "and he does a good job."

"But Square and his maskers do all the heavy fighting," said

Umbo. "We're still trying to figure out how to end the war, now that it's obvious their armies can't stand against us and the people want to be rid of them."

"You'll think of something," said Noxon.

"This is what power looks like?" said Deborah. "The people in charge of a war. You're the Queen-in-the-Tent?"

Param smiled. "Pretty hard to believe, isn't it?"

"No, you're very royal," said Deborah. "But you also look younger than me."

"They're children," said Loaf. "Brats with way too much power. Now that the world isn't going to end, we're going to have to put up with a lot of nonsense till they grow up."

"Come on," said Noxon. "If we don't go now and get your facemask, they'll keep you here for hours with their blathering."

Deborah grinned at them all and let Noxon lead her out of the room. Vadeshex followed immediately. The rest of them stood there looking at each other.

"I was in the middle of a nice nap," said Rigg.

"Mine wasn't all that nice," said Ram Odin. "I kept seeing Vadeshex popping a bleeding mouse corpse into his mouth."

"Thanks for putting that image in my mind," said Param.

"Anything for the Queen-in-the-Tent," said Ram Odin. He left the room.

"Want me to take you all back to Ramfold?" asked Ramex. "Or somewhere else?"

"The enclave will do," said Loaf. "Leaky has to serve dinner and I've got trainees to supervise."

"I thought they were all trained," said Umbo.

"He means *my* people," said Square. "We've got some new recruits who just got control of their masks."

"What are we going to do?" asked Umbo. "Are we going to go ahead and just get rid of Hagia and Haddamander now?"

"We aren't going to assassinate —" Param began.

"Wrong words," said Umbo. "I mean, why don't we just kidnap them and stash them back a few hundred years ago? In another wallfold where they aren't royal and don't have anybody who'll obey them?"

Rigg laughed. "I can think of a few wallfolds they'd really enjoy."

"I don't want to torture them or even punish them," said Param. "But yes, Umbo, that's a good idea. Just put them in a place where they can't do much harm and maybe they can make a life for each other."

"And then we'll find out whether we're any more fit to rule than they were," said Umbo.

"Well, if you're not," said Rigg, "we can always bring back the People's Revolutionary Council."

The meeting broke up then, and they all made their way to the Ramfold flyer. Rigg ended up bringing up the rear, and as he reached the bridge leading from the ship to the tunnels beyond, he found Umbo waiting for him.

"Hi," said Umbo.

"I think everything's worked out pretty well," said Rigg.

"I told Ramex to tell Vadeshex to tell Noxon that I saved Kyokay's life. He'll want to know, right?"

"Too bad you won't tell him yourself," said Rigg. "It's a pretty amazing story. You're the only real hero among us now."

"Except Square. And when I watch you fighting the Destroyer—"

"Wasn't me," said Rigg.

"Was too," said Umbo. "But that's not what I wanted to talk about. I just—seeing Noxon with the girl. With Deborah."

"It would have to be a blind girl to fall in love with that ugly face of his," said Rigg.

"I've got Param, and you know that I've been in love with her all along. And Noxon looks really happy with her—she really seems to care about him."

"Looks like," said Rigg. "But look, Umbo, if you're worried about me, don't. I've seen a lot of wallfolds. I'm thinking of going back to one of them, maybe. I met some people. Some places where I might want to live."

"Really?" said Umbo. "Because I was kind of hoping you'd find some nice girl and hang around with me and Param. We've made a pretty good team, when you think about it."

"Had our ups and downs."

"I don't want to get sickening about this, but I was hoping you'd stay. You're my best friend, Rigg, even though I was a real pain in the butt for a while."

"But I'll still be here even if I go," said Rigg. "I mean, Noxon's me, right?"

Umbo shook his head. "Yes. I know. You've seen most of Garden, he's been to Earth, and I'm just—"

"You're just King-in-the-Tent, and married to my sister," said Rigg. "You know that wherever I go to live, I'll come back and visit whenever I want. I'll be married and have kids and I'll get up from dinner and say, 'I'm going to take a walk,' and then I'll get in the flyer, come visit you for a week, and then get back home a few minutes after I left."

"Sounds like a decent plan," said Umbo. "I hope that's all we ever have to do with our timeshaping, once the war is over. No more saving the world. No more changes to make."

"That's the best plan," said Rigg. "It worries me, that these powers are loose in the world. We were clumsy enough, and dumb enough, but it all worked out pretty well. What if some of our descendants are, I don't know, kind of awful. What if there's somebody like Haddamander. Or Hagia. Or—or Tegay. You know what I mean."

"Param and I have talked about that. We even debated about whether or not we should even *have* children. But here's what we came up with. The mice brought us together, at the peak of our abilities, to save Garden and then, it turns out, to save Earth and everybody. But now our kids will marry people who aren't timeshapers, and their kids will dilute the genes even more. Maybe when the human race doesn't need saving, this ability will fade out, weaken, or become like our abilities were, before we put them together. You seeing paths. Me slowing people down, or speeding them up, or whatever. Just little things. Interesting but not scary. Not world-changing. That's what we think."

Rigg thought about that for a few moments. "I really like that idea," he said. "I hope it's true."

"We can also try to raise our kids to be really decent people."

"That's a good idea, too, though children become whatever they want to be," said Rigg.

"I know it's crazy, Param and I both thought it was insane when I first suggested it, but now we think it might be true. I mean, I think it *is* true. That the human race was really determined not to be destroyed. And so it first got the Odinfolders to think up a machine that could send back the Future Books. And each time through history, humanity kept gathering its strength, and finally, between the Odinfolders and the mice and whatever genes were floating around in Ramfold, plus Ramex raising you and training me and Param—the human race needed us, and so it made us. And now it's all worked out. So . . . it doesn't need anybody to have our abilities anymore."

"I'll have to think about that for a while," said Rigg. "It sounds too good to be true. But then, sometimes good things *are* true."

"So Param and I aren't going to worry about the future. I mean, yes, we'll try to govern well and plan things so that there's a good chance of Ramfold having peace and freedom and prosperity and all that. But when we die, it won't be our job anymore. We don't have to deal with all of history. We're going to allow ourselves to make mistakes without always going back to fix them. We'll do what regular people do—we'll fix them *after* the fact. No more miracles. Just . . . life. Just doing our best, and living with the consequences."

Rigg heard this with relief. He hadn't realized that these were exactly the questions that had tied him up in knots for a long time. "You know, Umbo, that's the smartest idea I've heard in a long time."

"Kind of surprising, I know," said Umbo. "I mean, hearing it from me."

"Not surprising at all," said Rigg. "I'm going to try to think of it that way. Because your plan, it's the only path that leads to something like a normal life. Toward, you know, being happy."

"Or being really miserable," said Umbo. "And that's going to be the hardest thing. What if one of our kids has an accident?"

"Then go back in time and save him," said Rigg. "Don't be stupid. We won't use it to mess with other people's lives, but if you've got a power like this, you don't let really bad things happen to the people you love most. The way you saved Square. That was right."

Umbo shook his head ruefully. "There are other opinions on that."

"He's alive, and he's got a real purpose, and when the war's over, he's got a family and a colony and you know what? Nobody can say you were wrong. Not even Leaky."

Ahead of them, Leaky hesitated, as if she had heard her name and considered turning around. But then she walked on, and Rigg and Umbo lowered their voices.

"I'm glad I decided to follow you when you left Fall Ford," said Umbo.

"I'm glad you did, too," said Rigg. "And I'm glad you forgave me for Kyokay."

"You didn't do anything to him."

"I'm glad you believed me," said Rigg. "You didn't have to."

"And you didn't have to forgive me for blaming you falsely."

Umbo grinned. "We're just a couple of remarkably generous people."

"In the long run," said Rigg. "Ignoring a few really big blunders along the way—from both of us."

"It all worked out."

"It's still working out for *us*, but yes, for the world as a whole, it all worked out. Good job, us!"

Umbo laughed at that, and they clapped each other on the back and shoulders and then they were at the transport that would carry them back out to the flyer. They crowded onto it with the others, and then it took off and swept them down the tunnel, out of the belly of the mountain, to the empty city where Vadeshex had managed to let his humans destroy each other. Only now even *that* mistake was undone, because Square was going to bring his people back, and eventually this city would be full of humans again. Humans with facemasks, so they were partly from Earth and partly from Garden. Still alive, part of each other now. That was the greatest triumph in all of this, Rigg thought. Undoing the bad stuff, that was big, that was vital. But the *good* thing was giving the life that evolved on Garden a chance to express itself again, to be part of a civilization. To be part of *us*.

Maybe Rigg would come to Vadeshex, in the end. Maybe he'd pick some time a few hundred years from now, when Noxon and Deborah had already lived their lives and had their children and grandchildren. Then Rigg could come along, three or four or ten generations later, and see if there was somebody for him, and together they'd make a few facemask-wearing babies.

Watch them grow. See who they became. That's what it was all about, wasn't it? Those were the paths Rigg liked best.

No matter how twisted his own path might have been, weaving in and out of time, that was what he had always hoped for. Maybe his path could end up that way after all. Time would tell.